BLUR

Vijay S. Shertukde

Disclaimer

This book is entirely a work of fiction. All characters, names of characters, locations, events, political events, cultures, procedures of law, technical and medical procedures, or religious practices/descriptions that appear or are portrayed in this book are purely fictitious and bear no resemblance to any community or person, living or deceased. Although real persons, both deceased and alive, are mentioned in the book, the extent that those persons are depicted as being involved in the events related in this work should not be considered factual. Any superficial resemblance to any names, to any real-life characters or history of any person is coincidental. Any resemblance whatsoever is unintentional.

BLUR/VijayS.Shertukde

Library of Congress Control Number: 2014901462

ISBN-13: 978-0-9913926-1-2

To my late father Advocate Sitaram G. Shertukde
First President of the Bar Association of Mumbai for three
consecutive terms after Independence

And

To my late father-in-law, Dr. Mukund S. Agaskar
Head of the History Department
Leader of Jansangh Party (Present BJP) North Mumbai

Mother (Ai) you instill the inoculations (Sanskar)
When I was a child
You left us early
I miss you very much
I offer my obeisance to you

The orange sun (Arun) emerged at horizon
Emitting the tender rays (Kiran)
Praying (Aradhana) to Supreme Conscious
With the vibrating sound of OM
With humility (Vinita)
To proclaim the new beginning

To my wife Vinita

Memories make what we are
Dreams make what we will be
(Chinese proverb)

Author's Note:

I am indebted to soldiers, spies, and war-zone reporters from many countries. These unknown courageous heroes are the real protagonists. They risk their lives to try to make things better for us in the respective parts of the earth that we call ours - *Dharti Ma* (Mother Earth). This novel is an expression about clash of neocolonialism and terrorism on the backdrop of secularity with philosophy of non-tolerance.

I also salute to lonely soldiers who are relentlessly fighting the war against corrupt administration in a political arena. These individuals symbolically support the famous quote from Bhagvat Geeta "Whenever there is a problem, God will arise to protect people."

In the past, I read various books including religious scriptures and books on comparative religion. I am also a passionate reader of spy and mystery stories and came across books on terrorism and war in the Middle East and I began writing a non-fiction book. Then I heard the news about the blast in Mumbai, which was my hometown, and other terrorist attacks in the divided Secular Indian subcontinent. That inspired the idea of putting the concept of the non-fiction book into a spy-fiction form. As a result, I began writing this novel by putting together my technical knowledge and combining that with my understanding and feelings about the political and the social environment.

The plot and the war described in these pages are all too real but this book is a work of fiction intermixed with denotation of a few political scenarios and events as necessary to strongly emphasize inner feelings. They should not be considered as factual. In the novel, I have named many organizations such as the spy agency ISHWAR, the test laboratory GEETA, and the Clan of Wolf Head associated with the characters and events that are purely imaginary

The world today is complex. Political upheaval at one end may cause the market to crash at the other end. Weapons manufactured in China or the US could end up in the Middle East or Africa, and poppy fields of Afghanistan could increase the drug usage in America. I put many of these ingredients together to make a synergistic novel that will intrigue readers. The criticism of traditions and culture is more like pointing out the idiosyncrasies of our present system and thought processes.

In this novel I used the Sanskrut (Sanskrit) words and names from the Hindu mythology as they are spelled e.g. Yog, Karm, Sanyas, Dharm, Adhyay, Prakruti, Kshatriy, Vaishy, Kshudra, Mahabharat, Ramayan, Krushn, Shiv etc., not as they are pronounced e.g. Yoga, Karma, Sanyaasa, Dharma, Adhyaaya, Prakriti, Kshatriya, Vaishya, Mahaabhaarata, Raamaayan, Krishna, Shiva etc. This is intentional to make it easier for readers to read. The pronounciation is simple.

— Vijay S.Shertukde

Nomenclature

ISHWAR™ - The Institute of Scientific and Human Warfare Analysis and Research

GEETA™ - Gayatri Energy Enterprise and Testing Agency

RAW (RIAW) - Research, Investigation, and Analysis Wing

AWD - Advanced Weapon Development

TIW - Technical Intelligence Wing

EIW - Electronic Intelligence Wing

SSIW - Signal and Satellite Intelligence Wing

ASIIW - Analysis, Synthesis, and Imagery Intelligence Wing

INTERPOL - International Criminal Police Organization

GCHQ - Government Communications Headquarters of UK

IBP – Intelligence bureau of Pakistan

DIO - Department of Intelligence Oversight

BAT Company - Biochemical and Arsenal Testing Company

TNSA - Tehrik-e-Nafaz-e-Shariat-e- Ahamadi

TNSS - Tehreek-e-Nafaz-e-Shariat-e-Salafi

SIMI - Students Islamic Movement of India

RSI - The receiving surveillance instrument

ICRC - International Committee of the Red Cross

ISI - Inter-Services Intelligence

EAB - Ehtesab Arsenal Bureau

Defence Minister (India) – Defense Minister (US)

Intel - Information acquired through intelligence by analyzing data

7

Contents

Prologue

Brutality culminated in the Medieval Ages
The invasion continued from the late antiquity
They wore the mask of the wolf
To masquerade the identity
They silently carried out operations
Executed, murdered, and robbed the weak without mercy
To accumulate wealth for themselves
No one knew who they were
They formed a secret society
They saw the power of domination
Hidden under the disguise
From the world, that was heaven
They brought the chaos
They call themselves a Clan of Wolf Head

Screams shattered the stillness of the night. The shrill reached all the way to the slave quarters. Narayan, a 14-year-old slave, heard and ran toward the palatial mansion. He recognized Kunjali's voice. The door was not locked. When he opened the door, he saw Kunjali lying on the floor. The blood from her head dripped on the floor and stained the carpet. Her hand was over her stomach, the head of the *katyar* (a small knife like dagger from India) was visible from her palm, the blood spilling over it. Her dark eyes were stark open with fear. She writhed in agony as Narayan ran toward her. She twitched when she saw Narayan coming and turned her neck slightly. Her finger lifted up. Her soul left the body through her eyes. Hand fell to the floor; there was no sign of life left anymore.

Narayan looked up from Kunjali and saw a 60-year-old ferocious-looking man standing, holding the railing, and glaring down indignantly to the floor. The man's choleric face gasped through his mouth. Enraged, Narayan charged toward him, clutching his fists, and climbing the stairs by skipping the steps. The old man drew his gun and shot. Narayan stumbled, rolled down the stairs, and landed next to Kunjali. The boy slumped to his death.

The old man shouted, the slaves ran in and stumbled upon two corpses. They picked them up, removed the *katyar*, wiped it, and cleaned the floor, but bloodstains were still visible. They left with the bodies. A mile down the road there was a swamp. They stopped, hurled the bodies in the murky water, and listened to the flutter of feeding alligators.

The swamp stuttered

Stillness returned

The darkness of the night cloaked

The disgrace of humanity reproached

* * * * *

Major John Hamilton was a Major in the British service in India. He spent most of his time in the Northwest part of India and had a major role in the Durand Line Agreement of 1893 that put an imaginary division between Afghanistan and the Continent of India. He retired in January of 1899.

Leon Chevalier was a very influential landowner. He belonged to an extremely rich family in America. He owned many cotton fields and sugar plantations in Louisiana. He studied with John Hamilton and James Andrew Broun-Ramsay. James was a distant cousin of Leon in England. Both the Chevalier and Broun-Ramsay families were extremely influential and enjoyed the confidence of the British

Monarchy. James was the Earl of Dalhousie. Later, they went their separate ways. James went to India as Lord Dalhousie with the East India Company, John joined the army and went to India with a post of Major, and Leon returned to America.

Over the years, Leon and John kept in touch. When the Major retired, Leon invited him to Louisiana. Leon wanted to know about the development in the other hemisphere. John was also thinking of settling in America. During his tenure as Major in the British Army, he had looted substantial wealth from Indian Monarchs and Nawabs, either as bribes, or by force. He never declared that wealth and paid taxes to the East India Company or to the British Monarchy. It would have been a problem for him to take that undeclared wealth to Britain.

The invitation turned out to be a golden opportunity for the Major. He accepted the invitation and moved to America with his wife and two sons. Mrs. Hamilton and their sons stayed in Chicago with her uncle and aunt. On his way to Chicago via Portugal, John bought two slaves. The boy, Narayan, and the girl, Kunjali, both kidnapped from India and transported with other slaves for auction in Portugal. These slaves were a gift to his old mate in America.

The Major awoke early in the morning. He went down the stairs of the antebellum home and decided to take a short walk in the garden. He went around the house, saw the wooden slave quarters behind the house, and turned back.

The slaves arranged the breakfast on the coffee table and were standing in the corner with their faces down. Leon came down and the Major joined him for breakfast.

Leon casually remarked about the slaves, "Did you bring them from India?"

John answered, "I bought them in Portugal for you."

"They are dead now; they were very arrogant, not disciplined."

"That is the problem with these Indians," the Major added.

"I tried to get the girl down under me, and she screamed," Leon said. "When I turned my back, she picked up the *Katyar* you sent a couple of years back from India during Christmas, thrust it into her stomach, and jumped from the railing."

He looked at John; John did not say anything.

The boy charged, I shot down the bastard," Leon commented.

John said, "We have lots of problems with these Indians. They are not easy prey. The women will commit *Johar* rather than be touched by strangers in India."

"What is *Johar*?" Leon enquired.

"It's a kind of suicide, where a woman jumps into fire when her husband dies in a war because of the fear of molestation by enemies."

"You are joking!" Leon said.

"No, I am not."

John Continued, "Many Indians are educated. Most of them went to England, earned a law or science degree, returned back, and demanded independence."

"What are you saying?" Leon blurted.

"We came to America and Canada and got rid off most of the Natives. We did the same thing in Australia and New Zealand to wipe out the indigenous population. How come you failed in India?" Leon exclaimed.

"Well, there is more communication now," John wiped his forehead. "British Lawyers like Peter Foreman and Hopkins are demanding justice. The educated Indians have joined hands with them. Revolution may take place soon," John added.

"Is that so? We didn't have to worry about that here," Leon said.

"Things were different before. We wielded our soldiers to fight and kill. We made them believe these natives were enemies and they were barbarians. There was not much communication. They trusted us," John laughed. He continued, "We fooled the crown, fortunately some of the knights were with us. We, Clan of the Wolf Head, under the name of the East India Company, manipulated the events, and orchestrated the orders. Our soldiers did not think too much. They only followed orders."

The Major stopped to gather his thoughts. "That is not the case now. Because of the increased communications, any atrocities are disclosed back to Britain and there is an outcry. Britain learned its lesson because of the American Revolution and became wiser. The common British or French soldiers who once followed orders blindly do not take this nonsense anymore. They realized that these are innocent people just like them with different shades of color. Coupled with the outcry from common British and Europeans, it became more and more difficult," John was gasping.

"Hmm…" Leon said. "How did you manage the Durand Line Treaty?"

"Well, Afghanistan was infested with internal civil wars and ethnic conflicts. Most of the Central Asian land was under Russian control."

"Don't forget the Caspian connection," interjected Leon.

"I wished we had someone like our Arab friends in Russia. Since it was a no-win situation, our Arab friend was instrumental in creating Afghanistan as a buffer state," added John, "and while doing that, he helped us to divide ancient Pashtun tribal areas."

"How did that help?" Leon asked.

"It presented the potential to create problems in the future. We do not look solely at the present. That is our way. We do not know the answers yet, but we cannot achieve our goal unless there is a conflict," added John. Leon had a queer smile.

Leon arranged an excursion to the swamps this morning for Major Hamilton. "Have you ever seen the egrets, herons, and pelicans? You may even see an alligator, interested in hunting alligator?" Leon chuckled. John listened. He had never seen alligator, but he knew that there were alligators down south in India. He never had a chance to go there.

"Do you know these swamps were considered forbidden lands by Native Red Indians?" Leon smiled. John was more interested in an alligator hunt.

They left immediately after breakfast, but never returned from the alligator hunt. Leon tried to help John from falling and both fell into the swamp. There was a flutter.

Water turned red

Hunters were hunted

Alligators feasted

Justice was served.

Chapter 1

Blur

I t was hot and crowded near India Gate in Delhi around three in the afternoon on August 21. The India Gate monument attracted tourists and citizens alike. This 140-feet-high monument stands at the center of New Delhi and resembles the Arc de Triomphe archway. Similar to its French counterpart, the India Gate monument commemorates the Indian soldiers who lost their lives fighting for their country.

Another memorial, the Amar Jawan Jyoti, was added later. The eternal flame burns under the monument arch to remind the nation of the soldiers who laid down their lives in the Indo-Pakistan War of December 1971.

The cars, scooters, bicycles, and motorcycles lined Rajpath Boulevard up to the monument and although it was warm, the place was crowded. Some were seated on the lawn while children played. Others wandered around and families snacked on fruit *chaat* spread with hot and spicy dressing, *bhelpuri* with hot, sweet, and sour chutney, spicy *chana jor garam* made from chickpeas, fried lentil *dal* fritters, potato chips, ice cream, candy floss, cola and lemonade.

It happened at 3 p.m. sharp. No one knew exactly what happened; a slight blur in the air, an indistinct agitation, and everyone in a fifty-foot radius of the India Gate died on the spot. The people standing a distance away from the gate were stunned. Tourists filming the India Gate caught the event on their cameras or camcorders; some even forgot to stop the video. For a few seconds, they all froze like statues. As soon as the realization struck, chaos ensued.

The cowards started running away; the braves ran toward the monument to see if they could help. The police arrived immediately; the wailing sirens of the police cars filled the air. No one could explain what had happened. There was no blast, no destruction or fall of the monument, no screams and no blood ... just corpses. It was just a blur in the air and death on the ground of 60 or more. The dead included humans, dogs, cats, and birds near the India Gate Monument.

The Police Inspector was the first to arrive at the site. He called his superior and within ten minutes, the Assistant Commissioner of Police, and other police officials joined them. The noise of the ambulance sirens added to the cacophony of chaos.

Paramedics jumped out of the ambulances and began collecting the bodies. The police started searching the belongings of the dead to identify them. The Inspector talked to his superior and asked permission to call the Research, Investigation, and Analysis Wing (RIAW or simply RAW) the secret service agency of India since the incident looked like a terrorist plot.

Ramanuj from RAW arrived with Suhasini Gupta of the Electronic Intelligence Wing and Pranav Chaturvedi from the Technical Intelligence Wing. Their quick arrival surprised the Inspector and he realized that whatever it was, it must be much bigger and more complex than he thought. Ramanuj immediately contacted the Central Bureau of Investigation (CBI), the premier investigative agency of India.

The Police Inspector acted diligently. He realized that the photos and films taken by the people would provide useful information for the investigation. With the help of the police lab and the cyber division of the RAW, he started downloading the pictures and videos from cameras and camcorders.

At first people were not willing to come forward and share information from their expensive units, or lend those to the police department with the fear that the police may not return their expensive units or the units may be damaged due to mishandling. However, when they saw police were downloading the photos and videos on the spot and returning the units immediately, a few others from the crowd came forward and shared their photos and videos. What they had seen was so catastrophic that no one grumbled.

The police interviewed several witnesses and gathered available electronic media footage for the investigation. The Inspector noticed a camera mounted 12 feet high on the monument itself. He pointed out the camera to Ramanuj and they removed the camera and downloaded the footage.

By evening, the police had gathered information. The ambulances and coroner vans had lifted bodies and cleared the area. The gathered data revealed the same puzzling account that at 3 pm, anything and anyone within 50 feet of the monument instantly fell dead and there was no obvious weapon. They provided the information to the press. There were many speculations from the media and panic spread throughout Delhi and the Nation.

* * * * *

Cloudy weather covered London on August 21. There was no rain, but it was muggy and warm. Nestled in the heart of London, Trafalgar Square is one of the city's most vibrant open spaces. The largest square in London was busy during the afternoon at three. The roads around the square form part of the A4 highway. Nelson's Column is at the center of the square flanked by fountains and guarded by four monumental sculpted bronze lions. It is a tourist attraction and both Londoners and tourists enjoy the square.

It again happened in Trafalgar Square at 3 p.m. sharp, London time. An indistinct blur washed over the area, a slight turbulence, and all close to the Nelson Monument died on the spot. There were more than 50 people. Scotland Yard arrived immediately with the Crime Scene Investigation (CSI) Team. Ambulances followed them. The police started identifying the dead with the driver's licenses found on the bodies. The ambulances took bodies to the morgue.

Scotland Yard was aware of the incident that took place in Delhi a few hours earlier. They went through the similar exercise of downloading the available pictures and the videos taken by the bystanders, tourists, and street surveillance cameras. In one of the videos, they spotted someone throwing an item through a cylinder-like structure.

A hood covered his face, but a picture taken from a tourist camera gave the police a closer look at him. They contacted the Government Communications Headquarters (GCHQ) for further information. It operates from several locations in the UK and overseas. However, there was no recent chatter or communications between the known terrorist groups. The simultaneously occurring event stirred fear. Cautionary warnings sent all over the Western Hemisphere. Security became tight at all tourist spots throughout the Western countries.

* * * * *

During the middle of the summer in Washington, D.C., the Crystal City Shops were crowded with tourists. Just off the Jefferson Davis Highway in Arlington, Virginia, the shopping center is nestled only 10 minutes from the downtown Washington, D.C. area. The shops in Crystal City are an interesting mix of highly acclaimed restaurants and offered over a hundred stores and variety of services – even a Cinemax theater. It was August 21. Like Delhi and London, the blur happened at exactly 3 o'clock in the afternoon, the blur in the air, an indistinct turbulence. The people in front of the shopping mall were all dead. Several onlookers took photos with iPhones. The police arrived immediately with an array of ambulances and coroner vans. More than 50 people died in the blur. The police began processing the scene.

Miss Kiran Hopkins arrived at 2 p.m. at Reagan National Airport. About 45 minutes later, she got out of the airport. The agency car was waiting outside the airport to pick her up. They were near the Jefferson Davis Highway. The car slowed down due to heavy traffic when Kiran heard the breaking news on the car radio. According to the announcer, a blur attack had happened in D.C. near the Crystal City Shops next to Reagan National Airport. She just heard the news on BBC at the air- port about the blur attack in London and the one in India.

She saw someone wearing a hood running, getting into a car, and heading toward the Jefferson Davis Highway. She became suspicious. An impulse took over. Kiran told the driver to follow the car and as the agency car approached the other car; she took her semi automatic out.

The driver of the other car saw that. He accelerated as the agency car chased him. Traffic was heavy. The man stopped the car at the highway curb and got out with a mechanism in his hand. He had clear instructions to bring the mechanism back. He knew he would be killed if he failed. He ran.

Kiran got out of her agency car and sprinted after him. She saw the mechanism in his hand and was aware of the danger. She was apprehensive... wondering what he held might be the key to so many people dying mysteriously. She knew she had to catch him. She saw the hooded man crossing the highway and jumping onto the truck driving on the road below the highway going in the opposite direction. She saw another truck coming up behind. She crossed the highway, jumped on the road below, smelled the exhaust, felt the heat of the exhaust on her face, sweat running down her cheek and back from the heat. Kiran ran faster and jumped onto the other truck just in time. She saw an overhead bridge and the hooded man ducking to miss the bridge. Kiran also hunched to miss the bridge. Kiran took her semi automatic out and shot. She missed.

The trucks were in the slow lane. Because of the heavy traffic, both trucks slowed down. She saw the hooded man jumping and barely catching the ladder of the van from the fast lane. Kiran saw a motorcycle slowing down in the fast lane. She jumped from the truck, flashed her CIA badge, and requested his help. The rider was aware of the news and realized the gravity of the situation. He immediately obliged and gave her key to the motorcycle.

Kiran continued her chase on the motorcycle. The motorcycle approached the van. She saw the man firing a shot at her. Anxiety took over for a split second seeing the barrel pointed at her. Her heart missed a bit, she quickly regained her composure and moved sideways in time to miss the bullet. Her heart was pounding with fear. The bullet went through the window of the car in the other lane. She saw the driver in the other lane swerving and slamming the brake. The squeal of the tires made a screeching sound. The car behind rear-ended the car in front. There was a small pile-up on the highway.

Kiran aimed and fired a shot. The bullet hit the terrorist in the leg and he felled from the van. Kiran stopped the motorcycle, checked the terrorist for weapons, and restrained him. She picked up the mechanism and checked his wallet and pockets. There was no identity. A police car siren wailed; an ambulance followed behind. It was a chaotic mess.

Chapter 2

Beauty and Brains

The heavily armed Islamist militants stormed and burned the mosque and several buildings around in Tripoli, Libya. This attack was among several recent assaults on the shrines and graves associated with mystical Sufi practices that most Salafis considered un-Islamic. The Salafi militants had been blamed for a bomb attack against the US Consulate in Benghazi, and a string of bomb and rocket attacks over the summer against Libya offices of the International Committee of the Red Cross (ICRC).

The reluctance of Libyan authorities hampered American investigation into the attacks. They did not want to act against the Islamist extremist suspects who belonged to powerful militias. The United States had only a handful of CIA operators in Libya. Intel of the arms' shipments during the tumult of the rebellion provided by them was not enough for further planning.

Veronica Ivanovo chose Kiran Hopkins and Anthony Hurtz for the Libya operation. Anthony Hurtz resembled to an Arabic origin with his goatee. Kiran Hopkins, with her mixed heritage, could also pass as a Muslim woman. They both were good field agents, both knew the Arabic language, and were highly skilled in analyzing the data.

Veronica explained their assignment, "You will fly to London on a business visa from Reagan National Airport as private citizens with US passports under the names Ayesha Basheer and Emran Khalid. You will have a day stopover in London before flying to Tripoli. Make your own arrangements in London, in separate hotels. The next day you will fly to Tripoli. Upon exiting the airport, look for two Libyan taxi drivers carrying the boards with names Ayesha and Emran. They will take you to your hotels."

"Now listen carefully," Veronica's voice was serious.

"In your room you will find two envelopes with coded welcoming messages in Arabic. The hotel staff always opens every envelope, and from the coded message inside, they will get the impression that you belong to a terrorist organization. The delivery time is on the front side of the envelope. Those two envelopes will carry separate delivery times. You will open the safe in the hotel room with that delivery time code. There will be a small iPad in the safe. Your thumbprint and passwords will activate the iPad."

Veronica looked at both of them. They both nodded affirming their comprehension. "Open it, read the messages, memorize, and take the iPad to the bathroom. Press the *Menu* button then find the *Applications* button and press it. The self-destruct mechanism will burn the device to ashes in 60 seconds. Clean the sink. Both iPads have the same information; in the event one of you is detained at the airport for some unforeseen reason, the other can download the instructions from other iPad. The iPads also include instructions about what to do, if one of you is detained. Your main task is to gather information, decode and analyze the data, and generate leads to identify terrorist cells receiving illegal weapons."

"What happens if we both get detained?" Anthony asked.

"The self destruct mechanism in both devices will automatically start 12 hours after your arrival and burn them to ashes," Veronica replied. "If that happens you will either come back with the return flight or be sent to jail." Veronica's face became stern, "My advice is to swallow the cyanide pill. You won't sustain the torture, and you are dead anyway."

Chill went through their spine, neither Anthony nor Kiran wanted to die so young, but they knew the risks when they took the oath.

"Let me caution you, the US government authorities are equally worried about the consequences of their covert hand in helping to arm Libyan militants. This is a delicate assignment because of the illegal involvement of US-based companies; you may come across secret and conflicting information. Do not share that information with anyone and communicate with me directly through a priority channel," Veronica warned.

Kiran and her partner, Anthony Hurtz, were on their way to Libya. It was more than a seven-hour journey to London. Kiran was thinking about her days with the CIA; how she started her career, completed her MBA... and she fell asleep.

Kiran completed her degree in computer science at Berkley. Because of Ruben's influence, she also took a course in journalism. She wanted to learn Hindi or Bengali language but the school only offered courses in Urdu and Arabic languages. She learned those languages. As a student, she became very much interested in system analysis. She also looked at the   curricula for a Master's in Business Management (MBA) at Berkley.

She started reading the description of the course. The students in the MBA course analyze, model, and design business systems and process requirements using common tools and methodologies and apply concepts from class to a real-life systems project of their choice. They are introduced to the principles and techniques of systems analysis and design methods with particular emphasis on information systems..." It took her almost an hour to digest the information. The curriculum for MBA was interesting. It became clear to her that in today's dynamic environment, the big companies were striving to improve their operational efficiency. They depended on technology to improve efficiency. However, these systems and enterprise projects required managers to understand the system development processes and successfully deliver the complex systems from a business process perspective.

One evening she spoke with one of the senior colleagues, Lisa Hargrove. Lisa was staying in Arlington, Virginia. Kiran kept in touch with her since her early school days, when she had worked as an intern in Washington, D.C. Lisa liked her and acted as an unofficial mentor to Kiran. Kiran told Lisa about her plans, expressed her interest in system analysis, and explained her reasons to go for MBA. Lisa listened intently. She was impressed with her insight and informed, "We are looking for summer interns to work in the System Analysis Division of our company, Simon Morgan International (SMI) Company, a multi-national company (MNC), in Arlington, Virginia. Would you like to apply?" Lisa did not tell her that the MNC was a front for the company that deals with various projects for the White House and Pentagon.

"Oh yes, I would love to apply," Kiran blurted.

Lisa gave Kiran the website for an application form, "if you are interested, you could e-mail the application to me and fax it to the number provided on the application form as soon as possible."

Lisa cautioned her, "Remember, the deadline is approaching fast."

Kiran thanked her for the information and went to the website, completed the form, got the necessary recommendation letters from professors, and sent the application.

Ruben had already started working for the Tribune. He visited Kiran every weekend for dinner in their favorite restaurant near the campus. Kiran gave him the tentative information about her intention to go to Virginia if they offered temporary internship.

"That's great, Kiran! I'll surely miss you, but I promise I'll certainly visit you on Independence Day weekend."

"Really?" Kiran was thrilled. Then she told Ruben of her plans for starting MBA at Berkley. At that time she had no idea what future awaited her at the Capital. Just before exam, she received an interview call from the Arlington facility and they accepted her for the internship. She was to join the facility immediately after the examination.

After the finals, Kiran flew to Washington D.C. Lisa came to the airport to pick her up. She offered Kiran to share her apartment during Kiran's stay in Virginia. Kiran accepted the offer. The next day Kiran reported for duty. The receptionist took her to the Personnel Department to complete the necessary paperwork and hiring formalities.

After completion, Kiran was assigned to the White House as an analyst where she met Veronica Ivanovo. Veronica headed the NSA (National Security Agency) Analyst branch affiliated with CIA. She worked with one of Veronica's assistants who explained principles and techniques of the system analysis, design methods, and her job assignment. Kiran showed exceptional inclination toward the systems modeling, design, and implementation of the information systems. She had a particular knack for information systems and data model processing information received from agents abroad. Veronica and

Lisa both were impressed with Kiran's dexterity to handle such intricate systems.

About two months later, Veronica called Kiran to her office. "Hello Kiran, sit down, please. Would you like to have some coffee?" Kiran accepted the coffee.

"Is there anything I can do for you?" Kiran asked politely. She was not sure about the purpose of the meeting.

"Relax," Veronica said. "How do you like the work here?" Veronica casually inquired.

"I love it," Kiran responded. "It has given me a great opportunity and insight. I appreciate it. Thank you."

Veronica looked at her. Her sharp eyes were trying to penetrate her thoughts, "Well, I have a proposition for you. How would you like to work with us at CIA?"

Kiran was perplexed; she did not expect this. However, she realized the new opportunities on the horizon, "Yes... but..."

Veronica interrupted her, "We can offer you a job; you can also do your MBA at the Georgetown University. With your credentials, you will have no problem being admitted to the program. I also know the Assistant Dean of Admission. I can certainly put in a good word for you."

Kiran wondered how could she do both, the job with the CIA that she never dreamed she would get, and the demands of the post-graduate work? Veronica read her thoughts, "You'll start part time while you are studying. You'll report to Lisa Hargrove for day-to-day assignments as a System Analyst. She is your immediate supervisor. You are smart and I can see from your resume that you are the athletic type. Eventually, the job may lead to a field assignment because we could use your talent in foreign countries. So, think of the career goal as System Analyst cum Field Agent." Veronica also explained the salary structure, benefits, medical insurance, and other job logistics.

Kiran was excited and thrilled at the proposition, but she kept her composure and her face did not reveal the excitement.

Veronica continued, "Take your time, think about it, and let me know in a couple of weeks. However, there is a condition," Veronica paused and looked at Kiran. "It is a Top Secret position and your identity as a CIA agent must remain confidential. No one should know that you are working for CIA, not your boyfriend, and not even your family. All they have to know is that you are working for SMI Multi-national Company as a System Analyst with offices in the US, Dubai, and India and you are studying for MBA at Georgetown University. If you decide to accept the job, I'll provide you with the further details. Can you deal with this secrecy?" Veronica asked.

Kiran nodded her head and said, "Thank you, I appreciate your trust. I am very much interested. I'll start processing the application for Georgetown University. I'll talk to you Monday." Kiran could not believe her luck. She liked the job and the people. To work with them was a plus and the opportunity to get her MBA at Georgetown University was her dream.

"Wake up, Ma'am. We are descending to Heathrow," the flight attendant woke her up. Kiran opened her eyes. It was early morning in London. Kiran and Anthony completed the customs and took separate taxis to different hotels. It was a cloudy day in London; luckily, there was no rain, an uneventful sightseeing day.

The Next day, they traveled to Tripoli and reached their destination in the late afternoon. They both saw the taxi drivers with their nametags waiting for them at the gate. The taxi drivers drove them to the hotels. It was a subtropical hot climate; Kiran did not see any clouds. Tripoli was the main hub of Libya's economy. The heavy evening traffic flooded the road. Most of the cars were big. The people were crossing the road between cars. On both sides, there were concrete buildings, with stores below covered with aluminum shutters. There were many open places where one could buy kebabs and other Lebanese food specialties. Pungent aromas filled the atmosphere, and to her surprise, they made her hungry. On the walls, there were torn posters of Gaddafi. She saw many dilapidated buildings and refugees wandering on the streets. Sporadic gunfire could be heard throughout the city and there were an abandonment of trucks and burned cars on the roads. A few transport helicopters flew above the city. The country remained in the grip of violence and chaos. The bittersweet feeling of emancipation from dictatorship mixed with apprehension was obvious. Kiran felt that the country was coping with the continuing violence.

The taxi drivers left them at their hotel. They registered at the front desk, got their room keys, and went to their rooms. They found their envelopes and followed the instructions. Then they freshened up and got some rest. In the evening, she went down to the restaurant in the hotel wearing Muslim attire. The host summoned the headwaiter.

"Right this way, *Mohtarma* (Ma'am)," the headwaiter guided her to a table and left the menu on her table.

Anthony came down few minutes later. The dinner was delectable with kebabs, a piece of steak over white rice, salad, vegetables served with Lebanese sauce, and a sweet dish "*Kaak Bi Haleeb*" a Lebanese milk cake. The belly dancing show was in progress in the dining room. Kiran left immediately after the dinner, but Anthony enjoyed the dinner and the show.

The next day Anthony came down first. Thirty minutes later Kiran also came down and checked out of the hotel. There was a Lebanese man waiting in the hotel lobby for her. The Lebanese man beckoned her and they went out together to the shop. Anthony was already there. Once they both were inside, the Lebanese man left and Anthony asked the shopkeeper, "I am looking for *Kebab-E-Masti*, is the place here or around the corner?"

The shopkeeper answered, "*Kebab-E-Masti* is down the road, wait here, I'll get someone." He looked around, waited for two customers to leave, and then closed the door and ushered Kiran and Anthony inside another small room that opened to a big room. The room was equipped with all the modern electronic gadgets, laptops, communication facilities, etc.

Kiran and Anthony both were surprised; this was one of the US covert facilities. They both went through the stacks of papers, various encrypted messages, and data received. They deciphered the encryption, arranged the data, reviewed the papers, put all the information into the laptop, and analyzed it. It was a cumbersome task to separate fake in- formation, unnecessary data, and deliberately directed information to the wrong places. It took them two days of hard work to identify seven possible targets from hundreds of addresses and places. It was necessary to check each one of them thoroughly in order to identify which one was the terrorist cell.

The tunnel below the facility led to an apartment building. The two furnished rooms in the apartment building with food and other amenities was their haven in Tripoli.

On the third day, after completion of the analysis, they reported to Veronica and informed her that they came across many US companies, including some US government contractors involved in an illegal operation. They also told her about seven places that they identified as possible targets and requested her permission to visit those places to determine the exact locations of the terrorist hide out. Veronica was very pleased with their work.

The next day, they both wore Islamic garb and started visiting each place one by one. They visited four places on the first day but had no luck. The next day, they took a taxi and went to the other side of the town near the Tripoli Zoo. The place was south of the city center. There was a small bakery next to a grocery shop. They both went inside the bakery. One of the men from the hotel was there. He had opened those envelopes and assumed them as the terrorist. He called them inside. They were welcomed. Their leader sat on a big chair and told them about their activities. He requested a large supply of weapons and ammunition for their next operation. He also told them to go to a bank in Martyrs' Square where they would arrange for a transfer of funds. In fact, that was the next stop on their list. The square was a normal place of business.

They came back, contacted Veronica, and gave her the addresses of those two places. Their task was over and they were on their way to the airport with the American passports.

A few miles down the road, the car exploded; the police discovered two burned bodies, a male, and female. The police found their passports in the aluminum brief case indicating their names as Ayesha Basheer and Emran Khalid, both from the United States. The Libyan police formally reported their deaths to the American Consulate and gave the half-burned passports to the American Embassy in Tripoli. In the middle of the night, two Black Hawk helicopters wiped out the bakery near the Tripoli Zoo and the bank in Martyrs' Square. That night Kiran and Anthony were about to take a flight back to the United States using their real passports when Lisa called them and told them to proceed to Islamabad.

Chapter 3

Ishwar and Geeta

T he essence of the war is a violent clash between the wills of the political leaders and/or military leaders. The purpose can differ in each case. The most obvious purpose is domination – establishing superiority and grabbing the land.

However, this clash of civilization can go much deeper due to the religious beliefs and introduce another element of religious conversion. The friction caused by the war, the uncertainty of the outcome, fluidity of movement of the military, the added element of terrorism, array of disorders due to the massacre of the masses, and losses to essential services like water, electricity, sewage system, and hospitals, and complexity combined with the human dimensions make war an unpredictable activity. To succeed in war, the Army, Navy, and Air Force must operate effectively in this uncertain, chaotic, complex, and fluid environment. This is only possible with intelligence.

The primary focus of intelligence operations is to generate strategic intelligence. The intelligence supports planning to conduct tactical maneuvering. Guarding sensitive information from an enemy and feeding false information to enemies to prevent subversion and sabotage are also crucial methods that make intelligence a valuable commodity for security. The deep penetrations (double agents or sleepers) in the enemy territory are important to gain information or feed false information. Intelligence has two aims – the first is to reduce uncertainty by providing accurate and the timely information of the relevant knowledge about the threat and the second is to provide counter intelligence (CI) to protect assets. This information is data.

The data is a body of knowledge. There is a clear and significant distinction between the raw data, information, and intelligence. The intelligence is not a mass of unfocused data or even a collection of related facts. In fact, giving a commander every piece of data without providing reason, purpose, and necessary information for him to act or formulate a plan of action can increase uncertainty by overloading the commander with incomplete, contradictory, or irrelevant information. The data becomes intelligence when it is in context and provides an accurate and meaningful image of the hostile situation. Intelligence developed by analyzing and synthesizing collected raw data provides information about political systems, social setups, and military configurations.

The raw data collected is the spurious data of related and non-related information. Eliminating unrelated information is crucial. Various methods used to eliminate unrelated information are random data sampling, weighted data sampling, or mathematical series of data sampling. After eliminating the non-related information, processing the collected data to gather facts turns the data into information, which is then translated and correlated to provide mental awareness of the knowledge. This awareness further helps to discard irrelevant data or to go back to the spurious data to arrive at the relevant information or knowledge. The related knowledge is evaluated and analyzed to turn the knowledge into useful information to convey the intelligence. The data has to correlate in the context of the situation to provide an accurate and meaningful image. The situation inferred must be hostile. Segregating or integrating and combining separate elements, to form a complete logical output is intelligence.

This collected and processed logical output is then converted into intelligence through the application of experience and judgment. The analyzed information is the relevant information. The relevant information synthesized to build a coherent picture to determine its significance. This picture helps predict possible outcomes of environmental conditions and the enemy actions. Humans understand situations best as images and use them to form mental pictures. The intelligence is produced and disseminated in a graphic form whenever possible. The results are in the form of intelligence product. The process is complete when the knowledge provided is applied to influence decision making. This formatted intelligence is conveyed to the RAW agency to act and investigate. From RAW, it goes to various divisions of the Army, Navy, and Air Force for necessary action. The Indian military needs this intelligence to protect its border from external threats and to deal with the internal threats created due to the basic mistake of secularity defeating the whole and soul purpose of democracy. This is the purpose for establishing the National Security Division of India (NSDI).

The head of the NSDI, Commander Sitaram Bhosle, occupied room 11 on the 9th floor, called Room 911; the most feared and admired room of the main tower of the complex of the Institute of Scientific and Human Warfare Analysis and Research (ISHWAR), the spy agency of India. The Institute had the responsibility for monitoring the affairs of intelligence and executing the necessary action to relieve the threat to the security of the country.

The inside walls of room 911 was covered with lead casing to prevent electronic snooping and coated with acoustic barriers to make it soundproof. The bulletproof glass covered the window opening to the garden side. The air conditioning vents were wired with a specially designed magnetic field to prevent penetration of the room by any digital device. This floor and the floor below contained the most sophisticated gadgetry and equipment, including the main computer control.

After becoming the head of NSDI, Commander Bhosle separated the field officers from the technological wings. The field officers' wing is the Research, Investigation, and Action Wing (RIAW). The pronunciation of the short form RIAW later became RAW for ease of convenience. All field officers had Commando training, especially skilled in the art of combat and use of weapons and machineries of various makes and models. They investigate and act on the Intel received and complete the mission that may include follow up, surveillance, pursuit, quick destructive raids against enemy-held areas, the rescue of hostages held in enemy territory, and the performance of similar logistics operations as necessary. They train double agents to penetrate enemy territories deeply. They deal with the affairs of the foreign countries and cooperate with Central

Bureau of Investigation (CBI). The CBI is the premier investigative agency of India. It is responsible for a wide variety of criminal and national-security matters. It investigates various crimes that might threaten India's national security and handle internal affairs of the country. It is India's official Interpol Division headed by the Union Minister of Internal Affairs. He reports directly to the Prime Minister. The CBI headquarters is in New Delhi under the guidance of another director.

The technological wings are broadly divided into four different categories. The four categories are Technical Intelligence Wing (TIW), Electronic Intelligence Wing (EIW), Signal and Satellite Intelligence Wing (SSIW), and Analysis, Synthesis, and Imagery Intelligence Wing (ASIIW). Nevertheless, their tasks are intermingled. Their main task is collecting, processing, analyzing, and synthesizing the data to form intelligence. The Intel is given to field officers of RAW for further action. After completion of the necessary action by RAW agents the outcome of the results are provided to the Army, Navy, and Air Force as necessary.

The functions of the four wings are:

Technical Intelligence Wing (TIW) is responsible for:
• Counter-intelligence and counter-terrorism tasks
• Intelligence collection in the border area
• Data gathering
• Obtaining information about foreign governments, corporations, and persons

Electronic Intelligence Wing (EIW) is responsible for:
• Cyber security
• Internet monitoring
• Electronic intercepts
• Monitoring of sound waves
• Cryptology systems
• Cryptanalysis
• Encryption of sensitive data processing

Signal and Satellite Intelligence Wing (SSIW) deals with:
* High tech surveillance
* Satellite monitoring
* Monitoring military links of other countries
* Terrestrial monitoring
* Hardware and software for strategic monitoring

Analysis, Synthesis, and Imagery Intelligence Wing (ASIIW).
The objective of the department is Information Analysis and Synthesis:
* Collect political and military information from other divisions
* Analyze Data to place in a meaningful context
* Perform processing and sampling of data
* Synthesize the relevant information
* Format intelligence
* Provide accurate, timely, and relevant knowledge about the threat
* Imagery and communications intelligence
* Keep sensitive information from the enemy and feed false information to prevent subversion and sabotage

Even senior field officers of the RAW were required to get clearance from the Commander's office for accessing the super-secret holy ghosts of the NSDI consisting of these four divisions, strictly on a need-to-know basis. There was a reason behind this. The field officers traveled globally sometimes as undercover agents. They were super spies, but the enemy could capture them and under extreme torture, could compromise their integrity. The Technological Wings are the super network of information. Commander Bhosle wanted to protect this holy grail of secrets under adverse condition.

Commander Bhosle was from the Maratha community of Maharashtra born in Kolhapur, Maharashtra. His family ties closely associated to the Dynasty of Chhatrapati Shiwaji Maharaj, a crowned king of 16th century. During the war with Pakistan, he played a key role to tear down a Pakistani secret post high up in the mountain. For his gallantry, Indian Military awarded Vir Chakra, an army medal of honor in the Indian (Bharatiya) Army. He quickly climbed the ladder and became Lieutenant General in the Indian Army. Soon after, the Intelligence Bureau of India offered him a job in Delhi.

A dedicated professional, Commander Bhosle worked his way up the ranks very quickly. This was an extremely difficult task, especially when the envious colleagues, and Delhi bureaucrats, who could slander and condemn anybody's reputation without any reason or rhyme, surround you. However, the previous Commander Badrinarayan Dwivedi took him under his wing. Commander Bhosle played a vital role in subverting the attack on the Prime minister's life during Sikh revolt. So, when Dwivedi retired, he suggested Commander Bhosle for the position. The Prime Minister had no problem accepting the recommendation.

Commander Bhosle learned many tricks while working under Badrinarayan Dwivedi. The experience gathered during years of working as an agent taught him three things: the absolute power of information, the fallibility of human nature, and the manipulative tendencies of religious faith. Commander Bhosle had two qualities that served him well. He had keen perception to find his way through the thoughts of leading politicians as well as his opponents, and avoid the politicians who were either corrupt or under duress. The capital's bureaucrats and his opponents maintained a fearful proximity from Commander Bhosle for his capability of staging a coup at the most unexpected moment. They nicknamed him Chanakya, the spymaster from the fourth century BC.

The ISHWAR complex, the spread-out structure of the cluster of buildings around the main building, housed India's super-secret warfare paraphernalia. The complex is located in the city of Indrapuram (meaning abode of the King of God Indra) a fast-developing modern metropolis. It is a self-contained mini-city. The excellent infrastructure provides a place for commercial complexes, developed industrial estates, and state of the art high-rise structure for residential complexes with all the amenities and facilities for high quality living including quality educational institutes, medical centers, and slew of shopping centers and malls. The entire structure of the ISHWAR complex with the contemporary architecture was befitting to the background of Indrapuram. The short form ISHWAR means almighty, and although unintentional, it carried significance of a high standard and might.

The satellite communication network tapped the major Foreign Communication protocols and enveloped the designated areas of the Chinese and the Pakistani communications. The arrays of bunkers below the building housed the Crisis Management Center (CMC) and the Command Head Quarters (CHQ). In the event of a nuclear war, these two designated secret facilities would activate to become functional. The NSDI exchange capabilities were also wired to another underground complex, located somewhere in Ghaziabad, Delhi that accommodated the Supreme Command Operation Center (SCO), the emergency functional head quarters for the President, the Prime Minister, and his Cabinet, as well as the Chiefs of the Armed Forces.

The Test Facility - Gayatri Energy Enterprise and Testing Agency (GEETA) and the ISHWAR Division were affiliated. GEETA is located in NOIDA, a short form for New Okhla Industrial Development Authority. The local government established the city as part of an urbanization program during the controversial emergency period in India around 1975. NOIDA is a fast-growing region and one of the largest industrial and educational centers in India. It is a prime hub for many multinational firms and a center for the meetings, conferences, exhibitions, and similar activities because of its 10-mile proximity to Delhi.

Chapter 4

Deep Penetration

The Partition left India's Defense Administration in a precarious situation. It was dangerously lacking in security or stability. The Defense Organization of divided secular India was in an unfamiliar territory. They wanted to protect the country from unknown conditions or disguised enemies from both fronts. The secularity was a curse. They were neither able to discriminate against Muslims because of secularity, nor trust them fully because of the fear of treachery or possible allegiance to the enemy on the other side of the border. There were forces within Islamic communities of secular India who hated Hindus. The hatred was not because of personal enmity but because of Islamic preaching to convert everybody to Islam or to kill who does not wish to convert.

Unfortunately, for India, the father of the nation never understood this thought process ingrained in the Muslim cranium. Behind the pretense and slogans of secularism, the corrupt hierarchy of leaders and their followers uplifted the minority Muslim community as the needed vote bank to topple the balance every five years or incite communal riots when needed to benefit them.

The Bureau of Intelligence Department of India was in a quandary after the transfer of power in post-partition India. The new ruling administration with the mythic of non-violence echoed the slogan of secularism while the boiling cauldron of communal hatred besought the haunted souls of both Hindu and Muslims. Trust was a very thin line. The Bureau Chief of Intelligence was faced with a Herculean task–he had to sieve through the clump to recruit credible aspirants who can be trusted with the secrets of the nation. It was difficult to penetrate as a double agent to Pakistan for a non-circumcised Hindu agent not familiar with Muslim mannerisms.

The Pakistan Bureau of Intelligence, on the other hand, enjoyed built-in advantages over India. They could infiltrate Indian Territory anytime as Indian Muslims and exploit the vulnerability of Muslim minds wavering between Islamic teachings and loyalty to the newly formed national mettle. They could recruit the Muslim talents within India as double agents by fiddling ingenuously with their Islamic faith when necessary or easily contaminate the minds of Muslim population of India by infusing the thought that India is rightfully theirs. They could easily instill in the Muslim minds that Hindus are parasites and create a desire within to either convert or kill Hindus – which became the basis of terrorism.

Impeccably dressed in military paraphernalia, Commander Badrinarayan Dwivedi was the bureau chief. He received his training at the Dehradun Academy. After graduation, he joined the Indian Army and soon became part of the commando force. During the 1971 Indo-Pakistani War, he played a significant role in India's involvement to liberate Bangladesh. Commander Badrinarayan Dwivedi had two goals - first, to infiltrate the bordered nation to get the Intel detrimental to India's security and second, to penetrate the Indian Muslim community to insure the internal security. Hindu agents did not have access or the capability to do these tasks. He decided to continue to train his own agents and provide them the Muslim identity, so they could infiltrate both the bordered nation and the internal Muslim communal territory to gather the intelligence. The previous chief, Ashutosh Mukharjee, started this project and the infrastructure was in place.

Manubhai Singhania was a sergeant in the Indian Army. His grandparents were from Lahore. He heard the story of the massacre many times from his father. In the middle of August of 1947, the train from Lahore was bringing his family along with many others to Delhi. Muslims attacked the train and hacked all passengers to death. His father survived because he hid under a dead body and remembered seeing his mother and father being hacked by a Muslim with a sword before he lost consciousness.

Manubhai still carries that sheer contempt that he heard and experienced in his father's voice. After finishing school, he traveled with his parents to Jammu to see his *Mausi* (Aunt - Mother's sister). His father and mother went out to get some sweets. Manubhai was at his aunt's home talking with his cousins. In the bazaar, his father thought he saw his childhood friend from Lahore and approached him. No one knew what really happened. Police found two bodies on the streets of Jammu covered with blood. One of the bystanders recognized the woman's body and led the police to her sister's address.

The 17-year-old Manu became an orphan. The news of his parent's murder struck him like lightning. The police accounted the murder to Pakistani infiltrators based on the information gathered from the witnesses. The grief-stricken Manu was left alone in the world. His aunts and cousin tried to console him and tried to persuade him to stay with them in Jammu, but he came back to Delhi. School was over, but the revenge was burning within him for Muslims. One of his teachers advised him to join the Indian Army where he can serve the nation.

Pakistan started the operation "Azad Kashmir" to infiltrate Pakistani Forces into Kashmir. They wanted to incite Muslim villagers to rebel against the rule by the Indian government. During the war, Manubhai patrolled the border. One night while on patrol, he noticed some movement. With his night binoculars, he saw two Pakistani soldiers. He gathered that these soldiers were on a reconnaissance mission. They were beckoning the Pakistani Squad about 500 yards behind to advance. There was no time to waste.

Manubhai stealthily went inside the small camouflaged tent, woke up the six soldiers, and informed them about the approaching attack. As he came out, the two advancing soldiers came close. He swiftly attacked them and slit their throats. The Pakistani soldiers moving forward, unaware of the impending danger, were met by a volley of machine-gun fire.

The agent accompanying the Indian soldiers saw Manubhai's swiftness and daring. During a discussion with Manubhai, that agent sensed the contempt he carried for Pakistanis.

The agent talked to Commander Dwivedi about him. "Do you believe this Manubhai has tenacity, endurance, patience, and strength to act as a double agent?" Commander Dwivedi inquired as he was looking for a double agent.

"I believe so. Manubhai is a hefty personality with a muscular body. He is strong and quick. His family is from Lahore and he hates Paks, there is no harm asking," the agent replied.

Commander Dwivedi interviewed Manubhai and found him suitable. Manubhai accepted the position and Commander Dwivedi assigned him to Ajit Deshpande, who worked under the alias Akabar Khan to make him a perfect Muslim – the term usually used is *Pucca* (perfect) Muslim, although he was not sure whether Manubhai wanted to become a double agent in Pakistan; that assignment in- volved a circumcision procedure.

Ajit Deshpande blindfolded Manubhai and brought him to a dairy farm called Arzoo. The farm was equipped with electronic surveillance and the fence energized with electric current during the night to deter intrusion from all sides. During the first 15 days, he could not go out of the fenced hutment area. His training began on the second day. The first two weeks were spent in exercising and learning the secrets of the tradecraft necessary for survival. Manubhai demonstrated excellent progress. After 10 days in confinement with Ajit Deshpande and Kewal Ahluwalia, Ajit talked to Manu openly and explained the purpose of his training.

"It may take you about six months. You will learn everything about Islam and its customs. However, you will have to undergo a minor surgery for circumcision."

"What!" Manubhai exploded.

"You heard it correctly," Ajit alias Akbar told him.

"Think about it for a couple of days. I'll explain all the details later after you have accepted the assignment. After completion of training and formalities of circumcision, you'll be sent to Lahore or some such place with cover identity. Let Kewal Ahluwalia tell you his story."

Kewal shared his experience, "I was in Lahore working for a supply company supplying goods to Defense Supply Division of the Pakistan army. I had a good rapport with traders and the people working in the Division along with senior army officers. They devised another plan, Mission Kashmir before Operation Gibraltar, to infiltrate villages near Jammu in Kashmir area. I sent back the information and the Indian army successfully destroyed their bases making it impossible to carry out the plan.

Unfortunately, one night I went to a Chandani *Maykhana* (Chandani Bar) for a covert mission. I had few drinks and then I slept with the girl from the bar. She noticed that I was not circumcised. The next day, she told the story to another girl. The story reached the pimps in the red-light colony and it spread fast. I discovered that my cover was blown. Before they could arrest, I took the plane to Istanbul and never returned. I went to the Indian Embassy in Istanbul and from there I came to Delhi."

"What will be my future if I accept the assignment?" Manubhai asked.

"Same as any other double agent ...," Kewal hesitated, then continued his story, "I am going to tell you another story without telling you the exact names of the places, so if you decide not to accept, there is not much lost. We have another agent in Karachi. He is mar- ried to a girl from Spain and has a villa in Spain. He is making lots of money as a successful trader and agent. He has his own business in Pakistan; no one has yet suspected him.

Let me caution you, there are no guarantees. Few like him became extremely wealthy; the Agency does not mind that, you can keep the money. If you are caught, the Agency won't protect you, but if your cover is blown then get out of Pakistan as fast as possible, as I did. If not, take a pill. I'll explain that later."

It took Manubhai almost eight months. He learned Urdu, mastered the *Quran*, *Hadis*, all the intricate details of *Namaj Qalma*, and personal law. Akabar Khan alias Ajit Deshpande explained to him the meaning and helped him practice.

"Recite after me, *Bismillah-ur-Rehman-e Rahim* (In the name of Allah, the Beneficent, the Merciful), *La Ilaha Illa llah Mumammad-ur-RasuluWah* (There's no God but Allah, and Muhammad is his

Prophet). This is the *Qalema-e-Tayeb*, the essence of all praises of the Almighty Allah and his Prophet, Muhammad, son of Abdul Muttalib, of the tribe of Qureysh."

Ajit alias Akbar also presented a copy of the *Quran and Hadis* to Manubhai Singhania.

"Keep these Holy books with you. These Holy books are the foundations of Islam. Read them, recite them, and don't forget the *Namaz*, five times daily," he had taught Manubhai all the nuances of *Fejr* prayer, *Dhuhr, Asr, Maghrib, Isha, and Jumma Namaj* rituals with meticulous stress on the rituals of *Ruqu* (bending properly) and *Sizda* (obeisance in a prostrated position), and the ritual of *Roja* (Ramadan fasting).

"These practices are essential for your survival. Remember that Muslims, like Jews and Christians, are people of the books, *Ahl-e-Hadis*, unlike Hindus."

Manubhai became familiar with all the Muslim mannerisms and underwent the process of circumcision. He was ready.

"Manu, henceforth, I'll call you Jahangir. You are no longer Manubhai. You have to forget that identity and start living your new cover. Jahangir Singhania, a Muslim from Sindh Province, will soon emerge in Lahore. You'll start working as a laborer and work your way up, get a job at the Lahore Station as a coolie. You will carry enough funds with you to start your business of small parts. Soon enough, funds will start coming to you to expand your business, don't ask how. Become friendly with the people in the supply business supplying parts and other mundane items to Pakistani Defense Ordnance Division. You are a Muslim from this day forward. Your life should resemble that of a devout Muslim, there should not be any inconsistency or error," he spoke without any modulation in his voice.

For the next two weeks, Jahangir Singhania lived at 24/12 *Gali Shahi Alam*, near the slums of Delhi. He was living the life of a Muslim in the surroundings that had not changed in centuries. It was frozen in time; life stood still behind the walls of the great ramparts of the old dilapidated mosque. Kewal Ahluwalia helped him in finding the place. He moved around the smaller lanes and market places, communicated with people, and tested his interaction like a Muslim.

He sensed the different ambience of the civilization captured in the frozen city of the capital of Emperor with decrepit glory. They lived in the past; the British invaders have not changed them much. He found the same frozen trends in the lanes and markets of old Karachi and Lahore. A unique rhythm runs through the veins of the people in these traditional settlements, living on either side of the border. Jahangir began his new life in the slums of the same city of Lahor where his ancestors lived for generations.

Chapter 5

Family

The birthday party celebration was in the full swing. Logan was holding a birthday knife with the Mickey Mouse handle. Ruben was standing next to him. Logan's mother, Sophia, was standing behind him holding his hand. Ross Martini, the proud grandfather, was standing next to Sophia, behind Logan, with his wife, Cynthia. Logan was ready to cut a beautiful Victorian-style ice cream cake made with layers of chocolate, vanilla, and pistachio ice cream, about 14" in diameter. Logan's name was on top with a birthday greeting and a number three-shaped candle in the center. The birthday party décor was Mickey Mouse, with the plastic table cover, the banner hanging from all sides, the children wearing party hats and holding blowouts, the red and black curling ribbon circled the table with an assortment of the streamers, and the Mickey Mouse balloons clinging the ceiling of the den. The children were standing around with watery mouths, wishing Logan would hurry up and cut the cake, so they could devour it. The professional cameraman was ready to shoot the photo with the relatives standing in a semi-circle with the children.

The glass door on the right side led to the dining hall. The Rosewood Mahogany Calais dining set with the two captain chairs and six side chairs was in the middle. The cloth table cover with the Mickey Mouse face knitted in the middle covered the gorgeous large table, just for the birthday party. The snacks and soft drinks with the Mickey Mouse lunch plates, napkins, and paper cups decorated the table. The door on the left leading to a study and sitting room was lined with mahogany shelves and cupboards and the thick plush neutral-color carpet on the floor.

The mahogany table was on one side with the executive dark-brown leather chair in the middle. The chair was facing the semi-circular sectional whole-grain, same-color leather sofa. A three-piece, coffee-brown color fabric set with two circular side tables and a round wooden table in the middle added a sleek semi-contemporary nuance with the oil paintings hanging on the wall opposite the window on the other side. The three tall arch windows facing the west added a dramatic tone to the room. The windows were covered with a white sash curtain and a light-brown color, pleated, and draws draperies complete with tiebacks and a swagged window treatment added an air of elegance.

The ornamental garden covered the outside of the house with the lush lawn. The double door entrance opened to the den. The oil paintings by distinguished artists hung on both sides of the wall opposite each other. The high ceilings with the large windows covered with the jalousie-type blinds, the white sash curtains, and the pleated draw draperies complete with tiebacks and valances added the touch of elegance. The cherry bronze solid hardwood floor accentuated a cozy warm atmosphere of the whole room and the party. It was a six-bedroom house with all the bedrooms on the second floor accessed via a staircase on one side.

Ross Mancini, a short, portly, Sicilian-born man was a small-time hood. He came to the United States with his parents when he was 10 years old. His parent opened a small bakery shop in the Italian neighborhood. For a while, he worked in the bakery and then found a helper's job in a nearby garage. He had an aptitude for auto repair. He could have made a decent career for himself, however, that was not his fate. Soon he got involved in the stolen car business. He married a local Italian girl, Cynthia, and she gave him a son named Noah.

Cynthia was not happy with Ross's success as a Don. She wanted him to lead a normal life. She had a high school diploma. She made sure that her son Noah got a decent education. Noah was not so bright, but he completed high school and went to college, finished his degree in economics, took the certification test, became a certified accountant, and started working as an accountant in a local firm in Chicago. The local school board needed a treasurer, one who was also a certified accountant. Cynthia volunteered her son for the position to her friend who was an elected member on the school board. Noah's company supported such social activities. He became a volunteer treasurer on the school board and began taking an interest in the church activities. At one of the school board Christmas parties, he met the love of his life, Sophia, a beautiful widow. She was working as an administrative clerk at the school.

Mario was Sophia's first husband. He was in the Army. Sophia was young when she had fallen in love with Mario. After the completion of her school graduation, she married Mario. She had no inclination to attend college like her friend, Olivia. Instead, she started working as a clerk in the school. Her parents died in a car accident one year after her marriage. They left their house to her. Soon after her parent's death, Mario was called to Vietnam. He never returned.

One afternoon, she received the dreadful news and soon after that, Mario arrived in a body bag. The town and the Army personnel gave him an Army funeral. Sophia was devastated. After the death of Sophia's parents and husband, Olivia's parents, Matthew and Ava Esposito, comforted her and watched over her. Olivia also slept in Sophia's house many nights to keep her company. That was a solace for Sophia. She started keeping herself busy in her work.

It started as a casual friendship with Noah. At first, she was reluctant because of the Mafia connection of Noah's family. She talked with Olivia and Olivia's parents – they all agreed that Noah was a good boy, his active participation in the Church and the school made a considerable impression. They had a big wedding in a local church. Sophia was quickly and closely involved with her new family. A few years after the marriage, she gave birth to Logan. By that time, Noah had started many small businesses with his father's money.

Logan Mancini and Ruben Joshi had known each other since they were babies. Ruben's real name is Ravindra Joshi. It became a chore for kindergarten children to pronounce Ravindra, and in a couple of weeks, Ruben became a short and easy form from Ravindra. From then on, throughout his school and college days, everyone called him

Ruben. Ruben's mother, Olivia, and Logan's mother, Sophia, were neighbors when they were young. They went to the same school, attended the same church, sang together in the Church choir, and shared the secrets of the childhood fantasies about boys; their friendship continued, as they grew older. In college, Olivia fell in love. Sophia was the first to know about this love affair.

Chapter 6

From India with Love

Pralhad Joshi came on a scholarship from the Indian Institute of Technology (IIT) in Mumbai. After the first semester, he got a teaching assistantship. Olivia was in her third-year economics class. One afternoon, Olivia was searching some information in the university library's computer. In the middle of the search, the computer froze. Pralhad was sitting behind her working on a project. He noticed the uncomfortable look on her beautiful face. He got up from his seat, walked to her table, and saw the locked screen on the computer.

Olivia had seen Pralhad a few times before, usually working with computers, and heard that he was a computer geek; a foreign student from India getting his PhD in Computer Sciences. He resolved the glitch and helped her find what she was searching. Later, they left the library together. During a conversation, they found that they both shared a love for drama.

"In Mumbai there is an Intercollegiate Drama Competition each year. Almost all colleges from Mumbai participate in the competition," Pralhad shared his college experience in India. He continued, "Although I am a science student, I loved drama and participated in the drama competition every year."

Olivia told him that she was a member of the drama club and invited Pralhad to join. He joined the club and was surprised to learn that Olivia was the president of the club. Because of his different accent, he was an odd fit in the club and became the subject of mild ridicule.

A cosmopolitan city like Mumbai is a melting pot for different dialects from the various states of India. At IIT Mumbai, Pralhad met students from Tamilnadu, Kannada, Andhra, Gujarat, UP, Bihar, and Punjab, each with different dialects and carried the distinctly different nuances of English pronunciation when they conversed. The local students always made fun of the pronunciations of students from the Northern or Southern parts of India. Pralhad was familiar with mild ridicule. He had teased the students from other parts of India. So he knew this teasing was just in fun and no one meant any harm. It did not bother Pralhad. However, he never imagined that this accent would land him the love of his life.

Olivia was looking for a character with an accent, for a role in a drama that she was staging at the local theatre. It was a humorous role but extremely significant. In the acting role, the character ridiculed local traditions with mild jokes in a funny accent. The role needed maturity and understanding. Olivia thought Pralhad would be perfect for the role.

The drama was a success. Everyone praised Pralhad's acting – the way he took on his character and ridiculed the local traditions made observers realize their misconceptions... and made them laugh, too. The drama brought Olivia and Pralhad closer to each other. It was not long before they realized they were falling in love with one another.

It was Thanksgiving weekend. Olivia asked Pralhad about his plans for the holidays. "Well, I have so much work, and the library is open on Friday, so I guess I'll take advantage."

"Would you like to come to our home for Thanksgiving dinner?" Olivia invited him.

"Are you sure your parents won't mind?"

"They'll love to have your company. My dad likes to talk. He'll probably bore you to death," she said smilingly. Pralhad was happy and accepted the invitation. He liked Sophia.

Her parents were congenial to him. He immensely enjoyed the traditional baked turkey with dressing and home-cooked Italian dinner. He expressed his appreciation and gratitude to her parents. After the dinner, Olivia's father discussed various subjects with him. He noticed Pralhad's manners, his way of presentation, his depth of knowledge, and maturity. He was impressed with this young man.

The next week, Pralhad abruptly stopped Olivia in the college lobby and asked, "Would you like to go on a date with me?"

He wasn't sure what her response would be. She was happy that Pralhad took the lead. One date led to another and their relationship deepened and grew serious. Olivia always shared her secrets with Sophia. She told her about Pralhad. Sophia was newly married to Noah Mancini. She was happy to hear about Olivia's love affair and supported her whole-heartedly.

One day Olivia asked, "Pralhad, do you have a girlfriend in India?" Pralhad laughed and responded, "Fortunately, I didn't fall in love with anyone back home, and my parents had not yet fixed an arranged marriage. I am so glad I met you."

Olivia was puzzled. "What's an arranged marriage?"

Pralhad thought for a moment then explained, "It means that groom and bride families arrange a meeting between a boy and a girl. Both parties can reject each other if they don't like the other for any reason or feel there is a mismatch. However, if they both like each other and agree to the marriage, then the marriage takes place soon."

Olivia was shocked. She could not believe that anyone would get married like this. Then she laughed, "You are kidding me, right?"

Pralhad said, "My parents saw each other for 15 minutes, and then within two months they were married. They are still together and in love with each other."

Olivia was confused and sad, too. She realized that his upbringing was much different living in the Indian culture. His parents might have dreams about him. Her intrusion could create agitation. It was a dilemma.

She did not say much.

The next day, Pralhad called his parents in India and sent them the photo of Olivia. At first, Pralhad's parents were not happy. His mother was dreaming of traditional Hindu Marriage. They both were not ready for this. However, when they received Olivia's photo, both adored her at first sight.

Soon, Pralhad proposed to Olivia. At first, she was not sure. She decided to talk to his parents in India over the phone. Although she could not see them, the conversation emitted a warm feeling and she was very pleased. That evening, she talked to her parents. They liked

Pralhad and had no problem with this marriage. Olivia was elated. She called Sophia and conveyed her news. A month later, the two were engaged.

In April, before Pralhad finished his Ph.D. degree, his mentor asked him whether he wanted to continue for another two years teaching in the same university beginning in September. Pralhad accepted the offer. The university registrar's office processed the two-year extension of Pralhad's work visa. Pralhad shared the news with Olivia and asked her to marry him that summer. Olivia was thrilled and told her parents the news.

Olivia, her parents, and her aunt and uncle went to India for the wedding. It was a colorful event. For Olivia and her family, it was surreal, an untainted enchanting experience of the primal nature from an exotic land on the other side of the world. It was like a dream. His parents and relatives were affectionate, hospitable, and courteous. A month later, when the couple was returning to America, Olivia saw the tears in the eyes of her mother-in-law and was touched by the intensity. Olivia always remembered her words before leaving, "Now I am giving my child to you, please take care of him; he is yours now."

No expectations, no demands, just the touch of sacrifice, Olivia was moved, speechless. She embraced her, and then bowed before her and her father-in-law, and touched their feet to receive blessings. Although it was warm and rainy in Mumbai in June and July, the whole one and half month was like a walk on the seventh cloud of a rainbow for her.

Chapter 7

Business

Both Sophia and Olivia were pregnant around the same time. Olivia gave birth to Ruben, and after a couple of weeks, Logan was born. The boys went to the same school in Chicago and their friendship continued, not because they had anything in common, but because of their mothers' friendship. Their nature, thinking, and habits were two poles apart. Logan was aggressive and had a streak of cruelty; not so obvious, but perceptible enough to notice. Ruben was a strong and athletic type but calm and quiet; he would help others, and many times, he would be a go between Logan and other school-children. He was a bright student, first in the class. Logan always copied Ruben's homework.

When Logan was 6 years old, Noah's father Ross, was tortured and murdered by one of the local Mafia families of the south side because of a territorial dispute. The murder of his father changed Noah's life. At first, he was mad and angry, but slowly he seemed to be calmed down, although, the volcano of anger was fueling under the veneer of placidity. He became vicious and cruel. Later, he erupted and killed the entire Mafia family who killed his father. No one could prove anything. Soon he became a hired killer and started gaining a reputation as a murder specialist.

His name spread fear as the top torturer among mob families and he developed a fearsome reputation. People were afraid of Noah. No one outside the Mafia circle knew anything about specific pursuit in which he partook. He became one of the strongest and richest hoods in the outfit and overlord of the lush north side. He was the murder suspect on several occasions, but the judicial system could not prove any of those allegations. He kept a low profile, continued his church work, and his political and social activities. He was also a member of the school board.

As a front, he carried out a few 'honest' businesses like dairies and restaurant franchises. He had started these businesses on a small scale. Now he expanded them. People gossiped behind his back. They said that many of the dairy farms and franchises he acquired presumably by making offers to the owners they could not refuse. He made these offers after his hoods wrecked their businesses.

By profession, he was an accountant. He knew the loopholes. As time passed, he started expanding his empire by owning motels, nightclubs, and office buildings. He had extensive holdings in the shipping companies and the Las Vegas casinos. He got interested in the shipping industry owing to the addition of the illegal weapons business.

His reputation soon reached to the business communities. On many occasions, he persuaded plaintiffs to drop millions of dollars of lawsuits against leading Chicago politicians. He was one of the top power brokers within the Chicago outfit and considered as the Chicago Syndicate Leader. He was an expert in political fixings and in corrupting the police officers. He started lending money to the Chicago police captain. This captain was the head of the department intelligence unit.

Sophia found out about his reputation, and tried hard to persuade him. However, he was a changed person. She could not talk about this to her friend, Olivia, or to Pralhad. It affected her health. She was devastated within. She suffered deeply for a woman of such a young age. First, she lost her parents; next death took her first love Mario away. A few years after Logan's birth, she lost Cynthia, who actually adopted her like a mother. After that, her father-in-law Ross was tortured to death, and that took Noah away from her toward wickedness. Blow after blow, the suffering slowly began eating at her mind bite by bite.

Olivia visited her often but was not aware of the real cause behind Sophia's illness. Sophia did not say a word to her. Her health was failing. The headaches took over. Everyone was worried about her health. Later examination revealed the cancer in her brain. It was spreading fast and she died when Logan was 14 years old. In spite of all his wickedness and viciousness, Noah truly loved Sophia. He never re-married after her death. Logan missed his mother a lot.

During his mother's last days, Logan came close to Ruben and Olivia. That closeness lasted for a year. Slowly, he drifted away; his nature succumbed to innate wickedness. His instincts occupied his mind and the brain. He began avoiding Ruben and started visiting Olivia less and less. Olivia thought it was natural; the boys were growing.

Both Ruben and Logan finished their final that was the last year of the school. Ruben was accepted to the University of California and Logan joined the University of Chicago, but was not sure what he should do. His mother was no longer there to guide him. He did not have a brain like Ruben to study further or the people skills like his father to continue in local politics. He decided to continue, like his grandfather, helping the family in various shady businesses.

During those days, Noah Mancini came across Boss Jr. Meijer. He was one of the partners in the law firm of Meijer Rosenthal and Associates. The head office was in Boston. The Boss Jr. Meijer was handling his business from Chicago. He handled Noah's business. The law firm was just a front for Boss Jr. Meijer. He was a "plant" for the Mafia's major long-term investments; the main asset of these plants is their anonymity. The "plant" is similar to a "deep agent or sleeper" for Intelligence Agencies. He led a normal life and no one would suspect that he had any connections with the Mafia.

This was particularly helpful for Fredrik Gustav, an American with Yugoslavian heritage. During 1980s, Fredrik was a weapon-dealer who supplied arms to Africa and the Middle East. He had many connections in Russia and Chechnya. During those days, he encountered the secret organization – Clan of the Wolf Head. Fredrik did not know the real name of the organization or names of any members. He called them the Colonist. It was a powerful organization led by a few anonymous people around the globe. The telephone was the only contact between him and the organization.

The organization was affiliated with many government and industrial complexes in various countries. The US head of the organization realized Fredrik's potential in facilitating the deals of arms and weapons illegally. He picked him up and put him as the assistant manager of the Biochemical and Arsenal Testing (BAT) Company. However, if there were any problems, the organization could resolve them swiftly.

Fredrik did not know where the guy lived or his real name or what he did, but he sensed the power and the strength behind the entity. That was all he needed to know. Fredrik carried out many successful operations for the BAT Company and was later selected for a position on the Board of Directors of the BAT Company.

The BAT Company was a front for the illegal transfer of arms and weapons dealing operations. The company did a lot of testing for the chemical companies in the state and out of US. The testing operations aided in the easy transportation of the arms and weapons out of the country. The BAT Company was in Chicago. Fredrik was searching for a strong right-hand-man who could manage the dealings of the illicit arms and weapons trade.

Noah Mancini had a fearsome reputation. His holdings in the shipping companies, the Las Vegas casinos, and his obscure association with the "Plant," the law firm of Meijer Rosenthal and Associates from Boston, Massachusetts, was known in mob circles. Gustav realized the potential Noah's outfit could offer to help build the business of illicit drugs and transfer of arms and weapons. Therefore, Fredrik extended his hand to Noah and offered him the partnership.

Chapter 8

Face of the Devil

Ruben heard the scream, inched forward, and saw the body lying in a pool of blood. Ruben saw that Logan had a bloodied knife in his hand and he stood over the body. Liam Mancini, Noah's nephew, was next to him. Noah Mancini was behind Logan. Three others were standing next to him. Ruben had seen Mendoza Bartoli, known as Super Fixer, and Carlos Garcia, known as Point Blank, but he had never seen the third guy before. They called him Robert Lange. It was a scary scene. Ruben never saw this side of the Mancini family. He froze.

Ruben had come to say goodbye to Logan before leaving for vacation to India. It was late in the evening. The cloud-covered sky made it even darker, although the weather channel forecasted no rain. He decided to walk to Logan's house. When Sophia, Logan's mom, died, he visited often to comfort him. Over the years, his visits waned. Ruben and Logan knew each other since childhood but they never became close-knit friends. He liked to be seen with Ruben because he was the captain of the school football team and girls were passionately mad for him. Ruben was friendly but only dated a couple of them. Behind his back, Logan used his friendship with Ruben to get a few girls into bed.

Olivia visited India many times during summer vacation with Pralhad and Ruben, becoming familiar with Hindu upbringing. She liked it so much that she continued as much as possible to bring Ruben up with similar *Sanskar* (inculcation).

Ruben enjoyed his summer vacations in India, chats with cousins Arvind, Sushama, Nirmala and others, discussions with grandparents and aunts and uncles, all left a distinct imprint that was different from many of the boys here. Ruben also heard the love story of his parents from Aunty Sophia many times.

He was only 12 years old at the time of his thread ceremony. He would never forget the chanting from the priest. His uncle translated the chanting to him during the ceremony. He remembered the words, "You will follow celibacy until you complete your studies." These incidences left a positive impression.

Sophia teased Olivia about Hindu upbringing. Olivia always argued with her, "It is not much different from the upbringing in any sensible moderate to conservative family in America."

"What about dating?" Sophia interjected.

"Well, Sophia, it is not that they don't fall in love. In India, they just want to finish their schooling first. They prefer to wait until they are older and mature."

"And get wise!" Sophia giggled.

"I think that is good, see how many problems we have here because of teenage pregnancy?" Olivia said.

Sophia worked in a school before, so she was aware of the problems of teenage pregnancy.

Ruben and his parents were leaving for India the next day. The registration for classes at the University of California would not start until late August. Ruben wanted to spend his last summer vacation before leaving the house for college with his parents in India. He also had another motive. Pralhad and Olivia got married in India 20 years ago in the first week of July. Ruben called his aunts and uncles in India to arrange a celebration for their wedding anniversary with all of their relatives. He wanted it to be a surprise for them, so he requested his relatives not say anything to spoil it.

Logan knew that they were leaving for India. He saw an exquisite-looking Indian dress in a magazine that he wanted Aunty Olivia to buy so he asked if he could stop by that afternoon to show her the picture. Olivia was home, but Logan never turned up. She thought that Logan might just want to bid them goodbye, so she told Ruben to go to his house.

Noah Mancini was discussing a lost crater with his nephew, Liam Mancini, in the study room while Logan and Robert Lange sat on the sofa. Mendoza Bartoli and Carlos Garcia stood quietly behind. There were no expressions on their faces. Both were known killers and problem-fixers for the Mancini family. Carlos Garcia was an excellent shooter, which was how he got the name Point Blank. Mendoza Bartoli was a strong, hefty man whose specialty was inflicting bodily injuries like broken legs or jaws; this was how he became known as Super Fixer.

The crates containing illegal arms and weapons were sent to Karachi, but instead, the shipment ended up in Afghanistan. Someone in the Indian Intelligence Network noticed it and informed CIA agents in Afghanistan. American soldiers captured the shipment.

"Thank God there were no marks on the craters and no bill of lading; otherwise they would have traced it back to BAT Company and Fredrik Gustav. Gustav would have had my skin," Noah said.

Liam's father, Elijah, died last year. Since then, Liam had been handling illegal weapon shipments to the Middle East.

"Any thoughts on this Liam?" Noah asked.

"Logan gave me the instructions to load them on the tanker. I collected the craters from the warehouse of BAT Company and loaded them on the tanker," Liam said.

He looked at Logan then continued, "The tanker was going to Karachi via Greece."

There was a knock at the front door. Liam was expecting Suleiman Quasim to come and shed some light on this mix-up. He got up and went to open the door. He brought Suleiman in to the study and told him that they had been discussing the lost craters.

"What happened to the craters? How could the American soldiers get their hands on them, Suleiman?" Noah asked in hostile tone.

Suleiman was dumbstruck. There was a silence.

"Suleiman, how did shit loads of craters ended up in Afghanistan?" Mendoza Bartoli retorted, the viciousness audible through his tone of voice.

Suleiman first looked at Noah and then at Logan. He sensed the tension and hostility. He responded, "The tanker was going to Karachi. The instructions were not to collect any cargo from anywhere but go straight to Karachi after refueling in Greece. Of course, that is not what happened." He hesitated, looked at them, and then continued. "When the tanker stopped in Greece for refueling, the crew changed hands. They collected more cargo – that was not supposed to happen. But the Captain got greedy. During that process, the unmarked craters were unloaded. I guess they ended up in Afghanistan. The new crew did not know anything about it." He stopped.

The door was open, so Ruben entered the house. He heard a commotion as he walked toward the study. No one saw him as he stood behind the door and listened to the argument about the misplaced craters. He heard the words like craters, arms, weapons, and Karachi, all in a foreign accent. He concentrated as they talked about illegal supply of arms and weapons to Pakistan. He was shocked and could not believe his ears.

"*Gustakhi Maff* (sorry), this should not have happened," Suleiman said in his *Muslim* accent. "But, you know, it was not my fault," he added.

"Whose fault is it then?

How has that shit load ended up in Afghanistan?"

Noah shouted. His pitch was rising and there was menace in his voice. "We lost $1 million in this deal," he shouted at the top his lungs. "Do you know bull head what happened?

You... you... bastard?

Who the hell told those soldiers about the shipment?"

Suleiman did not respond.

"A million dollars is a lot of money, you asshole! We lost it because of your stupidity!" Logan roared.

The remark aggravated Suleiman. He tried to control himself as he responded, "*Ji sarkar* (yes, sir), I understand, but I gave clear instructions. I told Logan to have your man on the tanker to accompany the craters all the way to Karachi. See this note." He took the note from his pocket to show them. Logan got up and stood in front of Suleiman.

"What note?" Logan roared at Suleiman.

That remark provoked Suleiman. Suleiman was now agitated. He looked at him indignantly and said rudely, "*Chup baith jahil* (shut up you fool), you spoiled brat!"

Logan took his knife out and swiftly advanced. Before Suleiman could react, Logan thrust the knife into his gut. Noah tried to stop him, but it was too late. Suleiman screamed and fell down. He was gasping for air as he lay in a pool of blood. Logan, with a bloodied knife in his hand, was standing over the body.

Suleiman was writhing in pain. Logan stabbed him again. Ruben was perplexed and stunned. He had never seen this side of Logan before. He did not know whether to intervene or call the police. He was sweating profusely and terrified. He left quietly.

The next day, Logan came to say goodbye to Uncle Pralhad, Aunty Olivia, and Ruben. Olivia just left for the last minute shopping. Her niece Nirmala had finished her degree in computer science so she went to buy perfume and lipstick for her as a graduation gift. Logan gave his size to Uncle Pralhad and showed him the picture. It was a *Sherwani*, Indian long coat, embroidered with gold threads, fastened with gold-threaded buttons, and with tight-fitting *churidars* (pants) loose around the hips and thighs, but tight around the ankle. Ruben did not see any expression on Logan's face. He now knew the face of the Devil.

Chapter 9

Body

Girls with bikinis were serving the drinks to the customers. The cacophony intensified with a striptease accompanied by loud music from the band and the roar of excited customers. The nightclub was swinging with beer, wine, liquor, and dance. At the age of 17, Anastasia Petrov, a tall blonde, who barely completed 10th grade, had left the school and started serving drinks in a nightclub owned by a local Don. She was from a suburb of Chicago. She had a beautiful face, a slim body, and voluptuous breasts. She quickly became a dancer and had a short fling with a pit boss who introduced her to drugs and then to prostitution. It was a short ride from a high-roller hooking companion to a $50 quickie in a seedy hotel room.

James Montenegro saw Anastasia performing striptease many times. He became friendly with her, but his motives were different. The Mafia family owned the nightclub. Over the years, James trained her to be his informant inside the club. She never gave him the big bust he had hoped for, but he remained her friend so that she could be his ears in the nightclub. James completed his diploma in criminology and started his career in the crime branch of the Bureau of Alcohol, Tobacco, Firearms, and Explosives (ATF) going after weapons and drug. He ran the Organized Crime Agency Strike Force in Chicago and was involved in finding the terrorist cells. He had an excellent record.

Suleiman was into drugs and weapons. He ran many illegal deals of drugs, weapons, and arms transfers between US manufacturers via local mafias and terrorist organizations in the Middle East and

Africa. On the side, he also dabbled in human trafficking to satisfy the lust of those Khans and Khojas of Dubai and Saudi Arabia. This *Muslim* American noticed Anastasia and took an extra interest in luring her with big tips. She danced on his table many times when he came to the nightclub. The two became friends; Suleiman took her out a couple of times for dinner. Anastasia developed a thing for this rich *Muslim*, probably because of the big tips.

Few years back, James Montenegro arrested a crime boss, Jacob Ricci, who was running an illegal drug business on school and college campuses. The case became front-page news because it dealt with local students. The case was tight with proof and testimonials. Jacob was a cousin of Noah's mother, Cynthia. The Mancini family tried their best to suppress the testimonies, but the media and community pressure was so high that, though there was a rumor the judge was biased, the Defense Attorney could not overturn the decision. The Don Jacob Ricci got a maximum prison sentence.

Recently, James was chasing after a terrorist group. Tips from Anastasia gave him information about the local house. ATF agents surrounded the house, and in exchange of fire, all the terrorists died except one, but he would not give any information. He received one bullet below the chest and one in the shoulder, and on the way to the hospital, he died in the ambulance. The papers found in the house revealed the terrorist plot to blow up a downtown mall and the location of a terrorist cell in Afghanistan. The ATF forwarded information of the terrorist cell to the CIA and the American Army Division.

That evening, James Montenegro got the tip to be at the entrance of the nightclub around 1 a.m. Anastasia worked in the same nightclub. He visited that club often. The confidential informant (CI) did not give much information. James and his partner were outside the club at a quarter to one. There was a truck parked near the curb a little bit away from the club. At 1 a.m., he saw Suleiman and his Romanian friend coming out of the club with Anastasia and a couple of other girls. Anastasia was leaning on Suleiman and it was clear that she was either drunk or drugged. They opened the back door of the truck and lifted Anastasia and the girls inside the truck.

Suleiman and the Romanian went back to the nightclub. The truck driver immediately started the truck. There was not much traffic on the road. James sensed that something was wrong; it had the smell of human trafficking. James started his pursuit; he followed the truck as it headed east toward the highway.

He called the ATF branch, asked for backup, and gave them the direction in which they were heading. There was not much traffic on the highway at that time of the night. The local police put out roadblocks, but the truck drove through them. The helicopter hovered above and followed the truck from the sky. It quickly escalated to a high-speed chase. The truck was speeding and they could not shoot at the driver because that could cause a serious accident and may fatally injure the girls inside. They did not know how many girls were inside–it was possible there might be more captives.

They were very close. James made a brave attempt and jumped at the passenger side of the truck. The driver was concentrating on the road. He did not expect intrusion. James broke the window with his .45 magnum and opened the door. One of the pieces of glass hit the driver. The driver slowed down to get the control of the truck, and tried to push James out. James pointed the magnum at the driver and ordered him to stop the truck. When they opened the truck, they rescued five more girls.

The girls were shivering with fear; some were wounded. Police took them to the local hospital for treatment. Nurse Tania from ER took them in. The doctors from ER treated the girls and later released them in police custody for debriefing. Before leaving the hospital, James made a lunch date with Tania.

The driver did not know much. His job was to deliver the girls to the address in New York. The ATF boss called the New York office. They raided the place. Later that night, James visited the police station where the police were taking their statements. They issued an arrest warrant for Suleiman, but he disappeared. They found out that he left the country. James received a medal from the Mayor of Chicago for his bravery. Anastasia was the only witness against Suleiman. Police and James watched her for few days. Since they did not notice any activity, they stopped watching over her. She remained performing her striptease show in the same nightclub regularly.

James went to the nightclub after a few days looking for her to get some information. She was not there. He went to the club again the next day, late at night, and asked Anastasia's friend about her. The girl said she had not heard from her in the last two days. Thinking that she might be sick and needed more help, James requested her friend to take him to her apartment. The girl knew James as Anastasia's male friend so she agreed to take him to her place.

The door was open. The girl pushed the door, went inside, and her scream shattered the stillness of the night. The smell of the rotting flesh suffused the apartment. Anastasia was lying on the sofa, half-naked, her legs spread apart, and her throat slit. The floor was covered with her dried blood.

After the kidnapping incident, James saw Tania a couple of times and took her on a dinner date. Love between the two began to blossom. He also found out that she had a daughter who had finished high school and would be going away to college. Her daughter left Sunday morning to go to the University dorms and Tania was depressed. To brighten her mood, James took her to an elegant restaurant for dinner. He ordered a bottle of champagne to toast the success of her daughter. The food was delicious. Her mood lifted after a couple of glasses of champagne and the sumptuous food. James took her to her apartment after a late night dinner.

Tania opened the empty apartment. She turned around; his hand lightly caressed her shoulder. She looked at him and her wooing look invited him in. His lips brushed hers; she embraced him. Feeling exciting allure for more, she moved against him – her body wanting his caress. His tongue tasted the sweetness of her mouth and ignited flares of desire throughout her body. An exultant sensation wafted, and a moan of passion escaped her lips; a mutual shudder ran along their length. They settled back silently, held each other gently, and drifted off to sleep. Tania liked him. They became close after that night, but sometimes his profession scared her. Her husband was in the army and lost his life in the war in Afghanistan. The memory of his loss still haunted her.

* * * * *

Noah Mancini was upset with Logan. Suleiman was lying in his own blood on the carpet, eyes open, life already gone. Suleiman was still clutching the note, which Noah carefully untangled from Suleiman's hand. The note had instructions in Urdu with poor English translation indicating that the person should accompany the shipment of craters and stay with it until it reaches Karachi Port. Noah looked at Logan; his eyes reflected disappointment. Logan walked out. Noah called Fredrik Gustav and told him the whole story, including the killing of Suleiman by his son, Logan.

Fredrik was furious. Suleiman was a link between Pakistan and the US. He was a successful smuggler of illegal arms and weapons to many countries in the Middle East. However, he was more worried about Suleiman's close association with the terrorist group. It would have been difficult to justify his death. He had to make up some story about his death. Terrorists would want revenge. They would not let the murder of one of their brothers go unpunished. He told Noah not to get rid of the body and to wait for further instructions. Fredric called an emergency telephone number and relayed the incident. Point Blank and Super Fixer wrapped the body in a plastic wrapper, cleaned the area as much as they could, and told Noah they would get the carpet changed.

Recently, James Montenegro followed a case of an illegal transfer of arms and weapons to the Middle East. Because of his previous dealing with the CIA, he also got a lot of cooperation and leads from the CIA in the Middle East. In one of the photos they sent, he noticed Suleiman who was still a suspect for the human trafficking case in the US. He followed the lead and found out that Suleiman was back in the US. James made some enquiries in the nightclub. Super Fixer found out and informed his boss. James was becoming a pain in the ass for Mancini family, Fredrik, and his BAT Company. After dialing the secret number, Fredrik called his contact at the nightclub and secured some old photos taken at the club. Then he called the plant, Boss Jr. Meijer, and arranged to open an account in one of the banks in the Cayman Islands.

Later Fredrik called Noah and told him to throw the body near the dumpster close to the nightclub. The next day, police found the stabbed body of Suleiman Quasim, and found his address in his pocket. The police went to the address and searched. They found some photos of Suleiman with Anastasia and James, and the offshore account number. The police checked the account information and discovered that it was under James Montenegro's name, and there was a recent deposit of $200,000. James had no knowledge of this offshore account. The police could not prove any connection between him and Suleiman or between James and his offshore account. His boss realized it was a frame up, but his hands were tied. The pressure was high.

One day, his boss called him, asked him to resign with half pension, and promised that his retirement fund would remain intact. James Montenegro's life was ruined. He knew the Mancini Family was behind it. He was angry. He promised to himself that one day he would find the connection between the Mancini Family and illegal weapons and drugs and would expose the family. That night he went to see Tania. He was almost drunk. He told Tania what happened and left.

Chapter 10

Vacation

P ralhad, Olivia, and Ruben left that afternoon. It was a direct flight
from Chicago to Mumbai and took about 18 hours of flying time.
Throughout the flight, the face of the devil and the body lying in
the pool of blood haunted Ruben. He wanted to talk to mom, but with
the involvement of Uncle Noah, Logan, and her relation with Sophia
Aunty, Ruben did not know how she would react. He did not want to
spoil their vacation and wedding anniversary. He kept quiet.

It took them almost a week to overcome the jet lag. Afterwards,
they went to see all of the relatives in Mumbai, took a short trip to
Pune and Nasik to meet more relatives, and visited Goa to see their
family Deity's temple. Santosh, Pralhad's brother, rented a Toyota
Innova A/C van with a driver and Ruben's cousin Nirmala joined
them. It was a fun trip, which made Ruben forget the grotesque
memories of that fateful day of murder for the time being.

On their anniversary, Santosh drove Pralhad and Olivia to a hall.
The two were surprised to find all their relatives gathered to celebrate
their wedding anniversary with *Puja* (prayers) *and Arti* (prayers done
during *Puja* with lighted lamp). Nirmala took the honor to wave *Arti*
in front of Pralhad and Olivia for them to accept the blessing from
God; a traditional Indian custom. Both Pralhad and Olivia would
remember the day for a long time to come.

A week later, when Ruben returned after meeting other cousins,
he found Nirmala avoiding him. He saw tears in her eyes. He asked
her, but she would not talk. After persistence, she broke, "I am in love

with Satish Patil, a student from my college. He completed his degree two years back. He works for the Multi National Company (MNC) and was given the opportunity to go to the US for two years."

"That's good news, why are you crying?" Ruben asked.

"Well, he wants to marry me before he leaves and take me with him," Nirmala answered.

"So, what's the problem? I believe you are willing to marry him, am I correct?" Ruben asked.

"Yes, I want to, but my parents won't allow that. Satish is from the different caste, and we are Brahmins."

"What?" Ruben exploded.

Nirmala told him about her parent's effort to arrange her marriage in their caste. Ruben was aware of the Caste system in India, but he never liked the implication of the practice in day-to-day life. In fact, last summer he went to Hindu Mandir conference with his dad and made a presentation on the Caste system, as one of the speakers from the youth group. Many attendees from India were also there, and they congratulated him on his clear and candid presentation. Ruben talked with Olivia about Nirmala. She cautioned him that the arranged marriage was a family matter and an extremely touchy and sensitive issue. She gave him an idea and told him to present his last year's speech tonight.

In the evening after the meal, they sat in the living room, chatting leisurely. It was Saturday. Pralhad's other sister and brother with their spouses and children came to visit them. It was a small gathering of all family members. Olivia announced that Ruben wanted to present his speech that he gave last year at the Hindu Conference. Everyone was excited and gathered around him.

Ruben took the center seat; he cleared his throat.

"Uncles, aunties, cousins, and my parents, last summer I presented this topic at a conference. I wanted to share with you the short form of what I said. The subject was India's *Varn* (class) and Caste system."

He continued, "French Missionary Dubois wrote in his book that the institution of *Varn* and Caste among the Hindus was the happiest effort of their legislation. He was convinced that the people of India never sunk into a state of barbarism because of the Caste system. He continues that India kept up her head, preserved, and extended the sciences, the arts, and civilization because of these classifications."

He paused, looked at everyone, and continued, "The author Charles F. Andrews put to Gandhiji the purely hypothetical question about marriage between two lovers; would he oppose the marriage on the ground of difference of *Varn* and Caste or creed?

Mahatma Gandhi answered in vague terms that he would never give his consent to such a marriage. It would be contrary to his ideas of religion thus to transgress the boundaries wherein the society was born. He would not personally agree to a marriage out of caste. Then he went on talking about untouchables, the controversy by itself. After his previous response, the discussion about untouchables did not make much sense, but to a layman, it indicated hypocrisy. Probably, Mahatma Gandhiji might not have had that intention."

Ruben saw a kind of appreciation on Uncle Santosh's face. He continued, "This system of classification kept the people together and promoted the feeling of obligation toward one another. This classification of class and caste system assigned to an individual his own profession. The system provided the people with goals, objectives, and functionality. It offered protection and security, provided the atmosphere for growth and development. This practice helped for refining the knowledge gathered during the dawn of civilization. The rigid regulations, the strict code of morality, and the ethics put a control over the societies from abandoning themselves to their natural barbaric inclination. Without the prudence of those who devised the institution of the class and caste system, they could not have preserved the scriptures of Ved (Veda), Upanishad, Ayurved, and other sciences and skills perfected over millennia. One can deduce that, due to the class and caste system the religious development, and civilization as a whole did not lapse into a state of barbarism. The development in the arts, science, religion, literature, and philosophy would have been lost in oblivion if not for the existence of the class and caste systems. Some did take advantage of the system and brought injustices and misery by promoting discrimination and hate. However, it is also true that the class and caste system kept the society within the limits of duty and obedience."

Niramala was very confused. She was expecting sympathetic reciprocation from her cousin from the other side of the globe. Ruben smiled and continued.

"The question for us today is… was this class and caste system based on birth, or was it based on abilities? We should look into it. The injunction that *kshudra* should not study Ved was put when the classification under *Varnashram* (Class System) was not based on birth, but purely based on *gun* (capability), and that is because a person of low intelligence regardless of whose progeny he or she is would not understand the deeper meaning of Vedas and memorize them. They could very well misinterpret it. As a result, we can conclude that this system of classification was never based on birth, but was determined by *gunas* (capabilities).

Now with the modern techniques of communication and writing, there is no need to hand down professions and skills. We can document and preserve progress and advances. The schools and universities are available to train the young minds according to their aptitudes and skills. This is the dawn of the progressive civilization. In fact, we can compare the class and caste system of Hindu society to the present system and subsystem of professionals. Instead of *Brahmin* (intellectuals), *Kshatriy* (Warriors), *Vaishy* (people in business, craft, trades, etc.), and *Kshudra* (people who do menial jobs), we have doctors, professors, lawyers, engineers, accountants, entertainers, garbage collectors, handymen, and various other professions similar to a class and caste system."

Ruben saw a hint of a smile on Nirmala and his mother Olivia's face. He also saw that Uncle Santosh was puzzled.

He added, "Take some of the examples from our Mythology, in *Ramayan* the story of *Shabari and Nishadaraj*, both belonged to ig-noble classes of *Kshudra* are revered in the lore. The monkey *Shree* (respectable) *Hanumanji*, the tribesman from the forest dwelling tribes of the South revered as one of the Hindu deities. *Satyavati* was a fisher woman from *Vaishy Varn* in the Mahabharat and her husband was a *kshatriy*, but her son *Ved Vyas* was a venerable Brahmin who wrote the epic of Mahabharat. Shiv, the God, appeared as *Kirat* from low class *Bhill* community. Mahabharat revered him. *Ghatotkach,* the son of *Bhim* who was from *kshatriy* class and *Hidimba* a likely tribe's woman of *Kshudra* caste from Himalay, was the revered warrior. They are all revered by us."

"Don't you agree Kusum Aunty?" He addressed the question to Nirmala's mother.

She was startled, "Y...es..." she fumbled.

"The caste system still exists in India. Although it is not that rigid anymore, unfortunately it exists with the weight of superiority and inferiority complexes attached to it. Interclass and intercaste marriages are not popular, but they take place often. The intellectuals are trying hard to change the system. However, now the system does not preclude the progress of an individual based on his birth. A son of a carpenter can become a lawyer or a doctor, a tea seller can become a minister, and it is possible that a progeny of a chief minister can be an entertainer.

The concept that Rama, Govinda, Somya – Tom, Dick, and Harry are sons of so and so aristocracy, therefore, they are also blue-blooded is no longer acceptable. The significance of the class and caste system by birth should be diminished if we want to have a happier life. I just added the last sentence." Ruben said smiling and he stopped. All his cousins clapped.

Ruben said, "Uncle Santosh, you are my dad's elder brother and oldest in the family. We all respect you. Although I am brought up in an alien environment, I still understand our values and morals. Nirmala is my cousin. I want to see her happy."

Santosh, first looked at his wife, saw the question in her eyes, looked at his daughter, the pleading eyes begging him. He looked at Pralhad and Olivia; he loved and was proud of his younger brother. His nephew's clarity of thoughts, the knack of presentation and persuasion impressed him and he looked within for the answers. All were looking at him.

It started as a presentation, but its purpose was lucent now. A Brahmin girl, Nirmala's love affair with Satish Patil, a boy from Maratha community, was on everybody's mind. Uncle Santosh was traditional. It was not easy for him to accept. He struggled within.

He looked at Nirmala and said, "Invite Satish tomorrow."

There was a sigh of relief from the entire family. Nirmala was profoundly grateful to Ruben; she embraced him as tears of joy rolled down her cheeks.

Everyone wanted the marriage to take place before Pralhad, Olivia, and Ruben's departure to the US. Satish was to leave in a few months. They called the priest. He went through the Indian calendar and found out the *Shubh Muhurta* (Auspicious day) for performing the marriage ceremony. It was the last Saturday in July. With not much time to waste, the entire family, including the Patil family, got together. The invitations were sent, the new jewelry purchased, and dresses for the bride and groom bought. A hall for the wedding ceremony and *Sangeet* was reserved, the lunch and dinner menus selected and the orders placed with a caterer.

For Olivia, it was a re-creation of memories from 25 years back. For Ruben, it was an experience; he enjoyed the whole ceremony of his elder cousin's marriage. He also twitched the groom's ear, which was an honor and one of the marriage traditions. When the marriage ceremony was over, before leaving, Nirmala and Satish bowed before all elders and received their blessings. Nirmala's mother, Kusum, hugged her, tears rolling down her face; Nirmala walked down to Ruben, hugged him, and burst into tears. No words could express the mixed emotions of joy, gratitude, and trust.

"Hey, sis, don't think you can get rid of me so easily. You are coming to the US, and once you are there, I will come and haunt you." Everybody laughed.

A couple of days later, on the evening news, Ruben heard about Mumbai Bandh. He asked Kusum Aunty about the meaning of Mumbai Bandh. Kusum Aunty explained that Mumbai Bandh meant Mumbai close... all shops, taxis, buses and other means of transportation would not be open for business. Due to the lack of transportation, many offices, including government offices, would remain closed.

"Why are they doing this?" Ruben asked.

"It's a protest against Government corruption. Sometimes they use this form of protest to show their dissatisfaction toward the political system and secularism; it's complex and mixed. There are many issues."

"Please tell me," Ruben insisted.

Aunty Kusum said, "My views are biased. They are more sensitive, inclusive, and narrow; you should ask your father. I doubt that his views are any different compared to my views, but he may have a much broader perspective since he has seen the world."

"I will ask him, but I want to know your views," said Ruben. He added, "Your views might be biased, but they would be realistic from your point of view. You know Dad. He talks in much broader perspective but then loses the personal touch, the ambience, the emotions, the sentiments, the sensitivity... I want to know all that from you."

Kusum thought that he was a bright kid; in her thoughts, she praised Pralhad and Olivia for his upbringing, and said, "Tomorrow is for political leaders' corruption, money lying in Swiss banks, bribery in the Government offices, and unequal treatment, which includes minority issues, Muslim issues, disparity in law, etc."

"Wow, that's a big menu, please explain step by step," Ruben requested.

"Let me think...," said Aunty Kusum. "Many of our political leaders are corrupt. They have looted the people. People are hassled by the greed. These leaders, along with some business entrepreneurs, amassed a fortune, some say more than trillions of dollars. They have neither declared these monies, nor paid taxes on them. They have hidden this black money in Swiss banks and in some Island banks. Thus, they are of no use to India's economy. The bribery in government offices is skyrocketing. The day-to-day affairs for resolving administrative problems through municipality and other government and non-government offices like utilities, electricity, and the Public Works Department (PWD) are a nuisance. These are the main issues behind tomorrow's Mumbai Bandh."

"I heard about that from Dad," Ruben added. "But what about this disparity of law, Muslim issues, and minority issues that you spoke of?"

"They are added to it," Aunty Kusum responded. "The other day, you talked about the class and caste system. The government has added a quota system that gives preferential treatment to low caste minorities... to provide jobs in government, admission in to colleges without any credence to the qualification, ability, or requirements. That creates a lot of problems."

"We have some similar issues in the US. They are serious but do not go to this extent," Ruben said.

"But here in India, the Government took the minority issue to the extreme for vote bank. On top of that, the Government has different laws for Muslims. For example, they can have four wives, paid time-off on Friday afternoons, paid pilgrimage-visits to Hajj; there are many issues like that...," Kusum stopped. She saw her husband, Ruben's Uncle Santosh, entering the room. He heard some of the conversation and invited himself in the discussion.

He continued the discussion further, "Our Government, under the name of secularity, is notorious for its hatemongering proclivity; it plays a disastrous role to drive a wedge in Hindu society and weaken it. I agree, many of these Government officials are Hindus; however, they are corrupt, they have sold their souls for black money, and they have no shame. This is our misfortune, and it leaves India more or less ruled either by the Muslims or by Christians.

The situation for Hindus in India, in short, is abysmally apocalyptic. Many of the middle and upper-middle class Hindus are busy in their daily chores like earning a living, making money, pursuing intellectual path to provide glory to India, celebrating festivals, building temples, and living their lives. Our adversaries have made their entry into Indian politics with the help of Hindu traitors by using vote banks and minorities. They hatched sinister plans to obliterate Hindu *Dharm* politically from the Indian soil.

What these traitors do not realize is that by their own doing, eventually they will be enslaved, too. By the time, they understand the truth it will be too late. The minority is just a spectacle, a show to deceive the masses. The Hindus are under multi-pronged seize.

The Muslim population in the world is about 2.3 billion. They populate more than 54 countries. It is a paradox that with approximately one billion adherents in the world, Hindus do not have even one country, where they could live without any fear of being terrorized.

We should learn from history. In the past, during the medieval period, Afghans and Moguls took advantage of our internal squabbles and used us. We fought their battles, and finally, they subjugated us. The British followed using much of the same tactics later. The disunity is created in the name of class and caste system, minority and religion basis, myopic vision, and selfish, corrupt, greedy, and egocentric attitude. The Muslims, Christians, and Communists take advantage of this internal schism, just as the British did, and they vie to control Hindus politically using each other." Santosh looked at Ruben and continued.

"We did not learn from our past. We could not fathom this dichotomy. We Hindus are becoming second-class citizens in our own backyard. Our Hindu traitors have entrenched themselves in the corridors of power and reduced our perspective of reality. We have to shed these excessive scruples and make a Machiavellian move to end this sordid chapter of servitude and vulnerability."

To Ruben, it was a dose of Indian politics.

Chapter 11

Clout

The most influential man in politics, not only in Illinois, but also in Washington, D.C., was Senator Frank Fitzroy. He was in politics for more than 25 years. He came from elite family with money to back him up and the brains to know how to use it, two extremely vital things in American politics. With a penetrating look and serious face, he emitted the aura of authority and power. He started his career in politics early after graduating from the University of Notre Dame.

He married Catherine Newberry, his high school sweetheart from Champaign, Illinois, the only daughter of Richard Newberry, an extremely wealthy man who was on the board of directors for several corporations. Originally, from Scotland, Newberry's family immigrated to the United States in the eighteenth century. They had connections with British Royalty.

The couple settled in Champaign, Illinois. Catherine gave birth to Elena two years after their marriage and she died when Elena was 10 years old. The Senator never thought of remarrying and focused on taking care of Elena.

After completing high school, Elena went to the University of Chicago. She took courses in Black American History and African studies. She had a generous heart like her mother. Eventually, Elena completed her Ph.D. and she joined as a lecturer at the University of Illinois in Urbana- Champaign for a few years. When she grew weary of the University life, she went to Africa as a volunteer. The Senator didn't like the idea, but he could not refuse Elena. She was his weak point.

Frank Fitzroy traveled between Champaign, Chicago, and Washington, D.C., for business, as well as for fulfilling his political duties. The Senator owned many tobacco plantations in Mississippi and Louisiana, coalmines in Illinois and Oklahoma, and oil fields in Alaska. He also owned casinos in Las Vegas and Reno and was a sleeping partner in a couple of nightclubs in Chicago. He was serving his seventh term in the Senate. He had a reputation as a man behind the curtain; he prided himself on picking up winners in politics.

Early on, Senator Fitzroy marked Henry Giarrusso as an ambitious, promising star. He had known Henry since he was a boy. Henry's father was a Senator from Illinois. Senator Giarrusso and Senator Fitzroy were good friends and both represented the Republican Party of Illinois. The Giarrusso family emigrated from Hungary to the US during World War II. Henry's father was born in Chicago just before the end of the WWII. Senator Giarrusso was a heavy drinker and known as an amorous adventurer in the inner circles of the elite group, but no one talked about it openly. Because of his bad habits, he died prematurely of heart failure. Henry's mother followed him. She died from brain cancer. After his father's death, Senator Fitzroy consoled Henry and they met regularly for lunch or on the golf course.

Henry handled legal issues for Frank. Henry also handled his real estate deals and casino matters. His skill in handling cases and his attention to details impressed Frank. Henry was quick, handsome, and articulate. His naïve charm drew people to him. Frank noticed that. Henry had no idea how closely Senator was watching him. A few years after evaluating Henry, Frank met with Robert Lange in Chicago.

"I think we've found our next candidate."

Robert Lange was a man with a controversial past. He came from a middle-class family. His father owned a bakery on the north side of Chicago in the Mancini family neighborhood. His mother and father both worked hard to make a living. Robert went to school and later attended university pursuing a major in political science.

Robert married an Italian girl from an affluent family in the neighborhood who never asked questions. They had two children. At the age of 56, his father had a heart attack and died. His mother followed him the couple of years later. That was an inopportune time for young Robert. He lost his job because the firm he worked for downsized. His mother-in-law suggested that he should call Noah Mancini. Out of loyalty to the Old Italian family connection, Noah helped him. In return, Robert started doing collections, negotiations, and similar odd jobs for Noah.

Robert was skilled in his job. In a couple of casino negotiations, he met Senator Fitzroy. Senator realized his potential in handling people and negotiating skillfully with clients to produce results. He talked with Robert about his background and discovered that he had a degree in political science. Recently, one political issue was bothering the Senator. It was all over the news and media. Robert was aware of it. The Senator discussed the issue with Robert. His insight and professionalism about the problems, and his suggestions about ways to bring about a reasonable solution, impressed the Senator. Soon, Robert became a right-hand man to him.

With his family and two children, Robert kept a decent front; people liked him. He understood the dynamics of politics better than anyone Frank had ever met. Robert knew where the votes were and how to get them. He had a keen sense of what the public wanted to hear and when they wanted to hear it. He also understood what the public did not want to hear or had become tired of hearing. Robert's integrity to the Senator was unequivocal. Because of his connection with the Mancini family, he was useful to the Senator to carry out the tasks that needed serious attention and that no one wanted to know about. Robert Lange knew how to get the job done.

"The man I have in mind to run for the Governor's seat is Henry Giarrusso."

"Isn't he the attorney from your hometown?"

"Yes, he is. He would be an acceptable choice; he would listen to us. I think if we get behind him, he can win the election."

"He has no experience."

"Don't forget his father served the State of Illinois for 12 years. People know his family and they know his name. He is not a complete stranger," Frank answered.

"It's an interesting situation, Senator."

"We will have to plan the campaign, the advertisements, TV and talk shows, and town hall meetings. What do you say, Robert?"

"Have you talked with him? Does he know?" Robert asked.

"Not yet, I thought of discussing this with you first."

"He looks a tad bit young for the job, Senator."

"I am sure we can work out the details, Robert."

Two days later, Senator Fitzroy invited Henry Giarrusso to his house for a dinner. Robert also came to Champaign to meet him; actually, the Senator told Robert to rate him for the job. Before dinner, Robert had a long chat with him over the glass of whiskey. Robert recognized the predatory characteristics of the young man. Both hunger and greed, though not obvious, were ingrained within Henry. He nodded affirmatively to the Senator. After dinner, Frank, Robert, and Henry sat down in the study, each with a glass of liquor.

"I want to make a proposition," the senator said to Henry. "How would you like to go for a gubernatorial candidacy, Henry?"

Henry was taken aback. He never expected the proposal coming from such an influential man in politics. Soon, the shock wore off.

"What!" He exclaimed.

"Would you like to be the Governor of Illinois?"

Henry looked at him in surprise.

"I... I haven't thought about it. I guess... I would love the opportunity."

"Well, Robert and I are thinking about it. It would be an excellent opportunity. What do you say, Robert?"

"Next year is an election year. The applicants are just starting to line up," Robert stated.

"That gives us plenty of time to build you up. People will know about you, what you stand for," added Senator.

"That's true. You already have a solid reputation as a successful attorney. We will get them to know you," said Robert.

"We are behind you. You can't lose," the Senator assured him.

Henry knew what a powerful man the Senator was, and with the back up of his well-setup political organization and the massive financial resources, he could turn the myth into reality, "I... I don't know what to say, Senator."

"Think about it. I am going to Washington tomorrow for the congressional meeting, when I get back, we'll discuss the plan. Remember, we need total commitment," the Senator warned.

"Yes...I...I assure you."

The Senator looked at him with the piercing eyes, "I want you to be aggressive. This is just a start. Look at the big picture. The sky is the limit. Serve a couple of terms as Governor, do a decent job, make an impression on voters, then think about the next step.

"Next step..." Henry muttered.

"The White House," blurted the Senator.

"You mean the presidential election!"

"That will be our next campaign," said the Senator.

Henry gulped. He must be joking, he thought.

The Senator looked at him, studied the expression on his face, read his thoughts.

"I don't joke about this. This is the age of mass communication. With Twitter, Facebook, and e-mail, your name can go all over. Every TV station will advertise your campaign."

"Do... do you mean that... I can make such an impact?" Henry said.

"You have a charismatic smile; you attract people. They genuinely like you. It's the same quality Reagan and Clinton had."

Upon his return from Washington, the Senator called Robert and Henry into his office. They discussed the plan for the campaign for the gubernatorial office. A few weeks later, work began. Henry Giarrusso's name with his alluring smile appeared on all available billboards throughout the state of Illinois. Television advertisements with his smiling face and one-line message in bold letters broadcasted throughout the day on all TV channels. He appeared on various talk shows. Robert arranged seminars through universities and churches; organized political rallies in every town and city. With massive advertisement, his popularity started increasing week by week. He was slowly getting ahead in the race, gaining points against the competitors.

In the living room of the mansion, Robert and the Senator were watching TV over a glass of Chivas Regal.

Robert expressed to the Senator, "Sir, I think in another few weeks, he should be ahead in the polls."

Frank nodded. "I am sure Robert."

He looked at the screen and thought to himself, Henry Giarrusso is going to win the election. There is no doubt about it.

Chapter 12

Race for Governor

The talk show host was ready to receive Henry Giarrusso for his TV interview. With his brilliant legal career, he was one of the strongest contenders for the race. He was interviewed on various talk shows on the leading television stations – WGN, WLS, WBBM, WMAQ, WTTW, WCIA, WICD, and on the popular radio stations, WTMX, WGN (AM/FM), WGCI, WBGL, and WLRW.

Very handsome with curly, blackish-brunette hair, striking blue eyes with a grayish tinge, slim build, and that wide smile radiating warmth – he was a ladies' man and the most eligible bachelor at the age of 33. Women in Champaign, Illinois pined for this young dashing man. He had the reputation of having slept with most of the women in Champaign.

"Everyone had heard of Henry Giarrusso, a candidate for Governor of Illinois. There is no need for introduction," the host of the talk show started the interview. "Let's start from the beginning," he continued. "Why are you running for governor?"

"It's simple. Illinois is a wonderful state. We live and enjoy our life here. It is a microcosm of the entire country, with Chicago in the northeast, and many small industrial cities and agricultural production in central and northern Illinois. We should start making full use of our natural resources like coal, timber, and petroleum in the South and make our state energy efficient. We have a broad economic base in our state. Illinois gave the country three presidents." The interview went on like this for 15 minutes.

* * * * *

Elena was with the peacekeeping force in the Eastern Kivu Province of Congo. She was excited when she got the job. However, a few months after reaching the Congo-Kinshasa Campsite, she learned about the difficult situation that surrounded the area. The central government and the rebel splinter group M23 signed a peace agreement to establish peace in the region. However, the stability was getting worse. She completed a year in Africa. She worked on a research study with the Institute of Development Studies.

In regions like Congo, Ivory Coast, Sierra Leone, and Somalia, the efforts to prolong conflict were deliberate. The research focused on meeting the challenges of peacekeeping initiatives in these regions. Her school work on Black American History and African studies came handy during her time in Africa. She wanted to continue longer, but during last six months, her father, Senator Frank Fitzroy, was worried for his daughter's safety, although she was not in any imminent danger.

It was one of the largest peacekeeping forces in the world. However, the UN and West did not resolve the complicated local conflicts. The situation threatened to reignite a civil war. The UN pushed for the deployment of surveillance drones in the area. Some volunteers from her research team were also packing up to return to their homelands. The Senator was fully aware of the instability of the situation and pressured her to return home.

She flew back midweek during the middle of the campaign. The Senator greeted her warmly. He was happy to see her. The next day, Senator told her that he would be throwing a small dinner party to celebrate her return from Africa, and requested her to stay home Sunday. Elena knew the affection of her father and his extravagant attitude. The party gave her an opportunity to call few of her friends. The Senator invited a few close colleagues who had political clout, along with Robert and Henry for dinner. Robert arrived at 6 p.m. sharp. Henry arrived few minutes later. Robert ushered him in and theatrically announced his arrival as the future Governor of Illinois.

Elena knew Henry from her college days. She greeted and congratulated him. They chatted for a few minutes about the old days. The Senator was not aware that Elena and Henry had known each other since college. Elena had a crush on him. She dated him a few times, but never got close to him because of his amoral nature. He still looked as charmingly handsome as before, and had the same alluring wide smile that attracted Elena to him years ago.

Elena and Henry were touched to meet again after so many years, but she held back. His amorous past stood between them like a wall. She knew that her father was backing his campaign for the governorship. The newspaper review predicted his success.

"Maybe he has changed from his amorous past. He is more mature. I should not hold his womanizing college days against him, should I?" She was going back and forth in her mind.

Henry asked her a question. She looked at him. It was the same alluring eyes and haunting look that attracted her before.

"Yes? What?" She roused from her thoughts.

"How was Africa?" Henry asked about her volunteer work in Africa.

She was not sure how to react to this question. She left her research project halfway completed in Africa. Their group did not complete the development of the new approach to resolve the con- flict and challenges of peacekeeping initiatives in the regions. She and her team had so many ideas… she was all bottled up inside. The unexpected question popped the cork.

"We were so close to the completion of our research. It would have provided an amicable resolution. The presence of the Hutu Army, the Rwandan militia, and the local militias plundering the country created instability in the region. Our team had to leave. They could not complete the work," she responded.

"It makes me mad. To resolve the differences in Congo, they use a concept of top-down approach. They focused the attention on the reconstruction of the national government." She paused and looked at Henry; he was intently listening to her.

"In countries like Africa, it is two-tier arrangement. First, you need to establish trust between citizens and the associated community governments. Second, you need to have an amicable understanding between local administration and the national government. We examined the data. It revealed that a weakness of administration leads to national conflicts. Conversely, our work also showed that when local government performed effectively, it lessens violence even if the central government fails. One cannot achieve the peace by circumventing these channels."

Henry looked at her and added, "Isn't that what the International peacekeeping forces are trying to achieve? Aren't they trying to achieve peace in the region?"

"We must realize that International peacekeeping will be effective only if it stays there long enough to understand the situation. The UN should give them an opportunity and not rotate them every six months or so. The UN should realize the complications of these conflicts. These conflicts could restart a civil war due to the twisted priorities. The continuity will provide enough opportunity for peacekeeping forces to understand the situation. Their job is to intervene to bring the settlement between the contentious participants. In countries like Africa, amicable compromise is an essential element between locals. International sponsors should support them."

Neither Henry nor Elena realized that the guests were gathering around them. Elena continued, "To give you an example, when M23 organization took over Goma the population had to face many problems; rape, and assaults on women, recruitment of child soldiers, looting, killings, food shortages, loss of electricity, lack of water and sanitation. These scarcities provoked the outbreak of illnesses and created tension."

Suddenly, she stopped noticing the gathering around her. She felt awkward and shy.

The Senator smilingly came forward, clapped, embraced her, and said to Henry, "I didn't realize my daughter is so smart." His eyes were shining with pride.

Henry looked at Elena. She was looking down. He came close and whispered in her ear; "can we discuss this over a lunch tomorrow at Phoenix café, around 1 p.m.?"

She nodded.

The next day, Elena and Henry met for lunch at Phoenix café. Elena complimented Henry for his achievement.

"It's your father who is helping me, you know that Elena?"

Elena nodded. "He likes you very much."

They both ordered the same dishes that they used to take for lunch when they were dating.

She looked at him, "you remember…"

"I never forgot," Henry responded.

He reassuringly put his palm over her hand on the table. She did not move, her piercing look penetrated the blue of his eyes, the pleading face, and the same alluring smile that haunted her before.

"I want to see you again Elena," Henry implored.

She consented. They decided to see each other again.

Elena was contemplating. Her work in the Congo woke her up from the lullaby of her rich and cozy upbringing. She opened up to Henry. Sometimes she talked about her incomplete project, other times about the condition of women in Africa, the poverty, and the cruelty that she saw. Henry was a good listener. These luncheon meetings became therapy sessions for her. Elena was sensitive to these issues. With her stay with the Peace Corps, she also came to know about the heinous game of politicians that played a key role in many countries.

With Henry's attentive attitude, she became relaxed and opened herself to him. She knew that Henry would be Governor soon. Her stories would give him some insight and human angle that would help him govern the state. She did not recognize the wolf behind the mask.

Her roommate during her stay in Africa with the Peace Corps was a young woman, Mohini, from India. They became close-knit friends during their stay. While parting from the Congo, they both decided to keep in touch. It was Friday night. After dinner with her father, she casually called her friend Mohini in India.

It was Saturday morning in India. They had a long chat. Mohini told her the story of the gang rape that happened recently. After finishing the call, Elena went to get the full story on the Internet. Henry called when she was reading the story. He wanted to ask her to join him for a picnic the next afternoon, just the two of them.

The next day, Saturday afternoon, Henry picked her up at her home and they went to a well-guarded secluded park. She brought a sandwich for both of them. It was a semi-cloudy day in early September. The leaves were turning to a pale-orange color. The story of the gang rape clouded her mind. She wanted to forget the story and enjoy her time with Henry. They sat down on a wooden park bench. Henry was carrying a newspaper. She took the middle page out from paper to spread on the table. The page was carrying the same story. She saw the headlines.

"Did you read this story Henry?"

Henry watched the TV news last night that mentioned the rape incident in India.

"It's nasty business, isn't it," said Henry.

Elena told him the conversation she had with her friend Mohini from the Peace Corps the night before.

"The gang rape was heinously shocking. The victim died few days later. The political attitude was even more shameful. One of the rapists was a juvenile kid who happened to be the most vicious devil. Not only did he rape the woman twice, but also he ripped out her intestines with his bare hands. How could he do that? Some of the politicians are defending his rights as a juvenile on TV. It's downright disgusting. Don't you agree?"

Henry would have preferred a more romantic afternoon, but he went along with her.

She continued, "The more disgusting is the brutality of the police against the demonstrators who were demonstrating for a speedy trial, equal punishment for all perpetrators, and to bring radical reforms to the legal system to ensure justice and to make women's lives safer and more secure. I thought India was a peaceful nation that boasts non-violence of Gandhi. Is this the non-violence they boast?"

Henry coughed and nodded. He did not comment.

Elena's outburst was clear. "They say that decision to shift the rape victim to another country for further treatment was more political than consideration for her health. It was already clear that she would not survive for long."

Elena abruptly stopped for a moment. She was trying to recollect her conversation with her friend. Mohini was extremely enraged at some people like a spiritual Guru and anti-Hindu Parliament Member who made some rubbish statement blaming the victim.

"Do you know what Mohini said? The spiritual Guru made a statement that the victim could have stopped the attack if she chanted

God's name and fell at the feet of the attackers, non-violence preaching of Gandhian philosophy. Isn't this idiotic? The Anti-Hindu Parliament Member blamed the rape incidence as the result of Indian women adapting to Western lifestyles. It makes me mad...

On top of that, the lawyer is blaming the couple for being on the street late at night, using public transportation. Are we seriously talking about a reformed India or medieval India? Kusum was saying that the political machinery is very slow to carry out appropriate course of action." She looked into oblivion, "It's a cruel joke to civilization."

She picked up the sandwich and offered it to Henry. "I am sorry. I wasn't going to bring up the subject and spoil your mood, but this headline from the newspaper brought on the outburst," she apologized.

Henry smiled. "You are too sensitive and kind. I liked that."

They ate the sandwich, and for the next couple of hours, they talked about his gubernatorial campaign, upcoming appearance at the local church, his ambitions, what he wants to do for the state, the TV interviews, and so on. As the evening approached, the clouds grew darker and soon the drizzle started. They picked up the lunch boxes and ran toward the car.

"Would you like to come to my house? It's not far from here," Henry asked.

With long discussions, awkwardness started melting. Elena saw through his ambitious and aggressive nature and she liked it. She felt comfortable with him. His house was only a 10-minute drive from the park.

A verdant lush lawn with a garden in the front yard was planted with flowers like camellias, azaleas; a couple of rose bushes and green vines surrounded the residence. It was a recently built three-bedroom cottage house. The gables faced the front. The outside style was from the earlier years of settlement.

The house itself was impressive with high ceilings, large windows, and wooden floors. The décor of the living room was contemporary with the modern furniture and the landscape painting in the middle between two windows. The small family portrait of his parents was hanging on opposite walls with a corner fireplace. The living room opened to the kitchen.

Henry went in to the kitchen, took out a couple of flanks of steaks, marinated them with soy sauce, garlic, and herbs, and put them on a grill. He took a couple of potatoes and put them in the microwave for baking, took California-style frozen vegetables from the freezer and boiled them on the stove. There was salad in the refrigerator. It took him less than twenty minutes to prepare dinner. Elena was hungry and she admired his dexterity for preparing an impeccable dinner in such a short amount of time. He served it with red wine. They both ate dinner and sat on the sofa.

There was a little chill in the air. The lull of red wine and steak made Elena less tense. He took her in his arms. Elena enjoyed the warmth of his body and the smell of the cologne. She felt the love in the air. She had read romantic stories before, but nothing had prepared her for the feeling she was experiencing. Because of the atrocities she saw in the Congo, she thought that amorous lyrics were the wistful dreams of unfulfilled souls. She did not feel that now. She felt more beautiful, the world livelier... the magic was in the air.

She took a deep breath. Henry looked into her eyes for a long time. She met his gaze. He held her tight, kissed her passionately, her breast pressing against his chest. She felt the longing for the flesh with a slight hollow feeling in her chest. She kissed him hard. She was in his arms. Eyes partly closed, she embraced him. It was an out-of-this-world feeling Elena had never experienced as they reached climax in synchronism. She was in a different world.

* * * * *

In the evening, Robert and the Senator were discussing the campaign strategies and polling results. They were favorable.

"You should know, Henry and Elena are getting very close. Elena likes him," Robert told the Senator.

The fact that Henry Giarrusso might marry his daughter was an unexpected plus.

"Robert, their marriage should happen soon. I want Elena and Henry to enter Governor's Mansion together." The Senator was happy.

Chapter 13

Healing

It was a hot summer in Chicago. Ruben returned from India with his family. The next day he went to Logan's house to deliver the *Sherwani* and other gifts from India. Logan was not home. Ruben felt relieved. He didn't want to meet the devil. The image of the murder was ingrained in his mind. The vacation in India helped in healing the scar, but sometimes memories would haunt him in the middle of the night. Robert Lange was there with Uncle Noah. He gave the gifts to Uncle Noah and asked him to convey his goodbyes to Logan. A week later, Ruben left to continue his undergraduate work in Journalism at the University of Berkeley.

His parents accompanied him to the campus. The next day was orientation and student registration. After completing all the formalities, he headed to his dorm. He found out that his roommate, Nikhil Choudhary, a Bengali from Kolkata, India, was a postgraduate engineering student. Normally, the dorms for undergraduate and postgraduates were different, but Nikhil had to wait to get his scholarship approved, which took time. By the time Nikhil could register, all accommodations in the postgraduate section were full, and the rector of the dorm placed him with Ruben. Ruben had no problem; on the contrary, he was excited to share a room with a student from India. Pralhad and Olivia left the next day.

Nikhil Chowdhary came to Berkeley for his Ph.D. in optics and photonics technologies – the study of electromagnetic energy. The basic unit is the photon, but the study required comprehensive knowledge of optics, laser technology, electrical engineering, material science, and information storage and processing. Throughout his academic career, Nikhil always stood first in the class. In his final year, in the Institute of Technology of Banaras Hindu University, Banaras, Nikhil got an opportunity to study under a visiting Professor from Berkeley, Professor Thomas Jordan.

Professor Jordan noticed the brilliance of Nikhil and his grasp of physics, especially in the electromagnetic energy field. In one of his papers, Nikhil wrote about the build up of high intensities using electromagnetic radiation with laser using optics. He showed a preference for conducting further research in the effects of microwave radiation on photons.

The Professor was involved in similar research. He was impressed with Nikhil's insight into the subject. He asked Nikhil if he wanted to continue the research in the field in the US after he completed his master's degree at the Institute. Nikhil was excited. He accepted the offer. Professor Jordan arranged for Nikhil to go to Berkeley on a full scholarship.

Nikhil was born in one of the villages of Assam near the border of Bangladesh. The infiltrator from Bangladesh frequently attacked border villages. One night, the infiltrator attacked his village; gang raped his mother in front of his father, then hacked both his mother and father and torched them to death. Nikhil was only 8 years old; he was hiding inside the hut, clutching a photo of his parents.

The next day, the rescue squad listened to the account from villagers who were still alive. They found Nikhil hiding and took him to one of the orphanages in Kolkata, which was managed by Hindu *Seva* (Aid) *Samiti* (Society) under Swami Vivekananda Kendra (Institution).

Ms. Sumitra Dutta, a volunteer of the Swami Vivekananda Kendra, was the matron. She was a widow of the soldier who lost his life during the war with Pakistan. She noticed the brilliance of this young orphan and took a personal interest in his studies. He started calling her *Mai*. Ms. Dutta loved to hear this word from his mouth.

Sometimes during the middle of the night, Nikhil would wake up screaming and sweating from nightmares of the grotesque images of that horrible night. It took few years for Ms. Dutta to soothe his tormented mind. She realized that Nikhil would never forget the visions of the night of his parents' murder. The only solace he had was their photo and his childhood memories of his village in Assam.

Nikhil stood first in the whole district in his final year of the school board examination and got a full scholarship to the Institute of Technology of Banaras Hindu University, Banaras. Nikhil joined the University with physics as his major.

Within a couple of weeks, Ruben and Nikhil settled in to their new environment. They became friends and talked about the life in India, Ruben's childhood, and his parents although Ruben never mentioned the murder incident that he witnessed a couple of months back. One day, Ruben asked Nikhil about his childhood. Nikhil broke down and narrated the incidence of his parents' murder. The gruesome story shocked Ruben; he did not know what words he could say to comfort Nikhil. He was quiet. The memory of the murder still haunted him; he could only imagine the agony that was tormenting Nikhil.

Two tormented minds were living a strange coincidence under the same roof. That is nature's way of healing. The college football forum selected Ruben for the football team. With football practice, homework, debate society, and his college schedule, Ruben had no time left for thinking about the devil. Nikhil got the teaching apprenticeship after the first semester.

In the second semester, Ruben got a telephone call from his cousin, Nirmala. She came to the US with her husband, Satish. Their two-bedroom family quarter arranged by Satish's company was not far from Ruben's dorm. Ruben went to visit them with Nikhil. Nikhil enjoyed the get together, especially the home-cooked meal. It reminded him of Datta *Mai's* home-cooked meals.

The following weekend, Ruben called Nirmala and asked her about going to the *Mandir* (temple) in San Francisco on Sunday morning. Nirmala loved the idea. They were surprised to see the elaborate structure, the deities, and the arrangement. However, the modus operandi of the *Puja* (prayer) ceremony followed by cacophony of *Bhajans* disappointed them. On the way back home, Nirmala and Satish both criticized the singing of *Bhajan* part. Ruben had heard the similar comments from his other Indian friends before.

The younger generation enjoyed the discussions in the yearly conferences arranged by Hindu organizations like Hindu *Mandir* Society and others. These conferences were particularly instructive, provided constructive ideas, and gave a chance to the younger generation to express their vision freely. Unfortunately, these occasions came only once a year and no one ever did the follow up on implementation of suggestions.

"You know, Ruben," Nirmala continued, "Our *RRushis* (sages) in the past created four Vedas. One of them was *Samved*, a complete science on how to pronounce and sing in harmony. The *Samved* deals with the prosodic structures of the songs for chanting at various ceremonies. To teach the melody is the precise purpose of this *Samved*. The *Samved* contains directions for correct modulations, intonations that include a change of syllable, repetitions, the breaking up of words, the insertion of pause, syllable, or interjection, etc. It is the notion that, when the hymns chanted to the melody of the *Samved*, the chant has mystical interpretation and serves an esoteric purpose. I don't know whether it is true or not, but I know for sure that it provides peace of mind and calms the nerves."

"Does that mean that the people who cannot sing should not pray?" Nikhil asked.

"Not at all, one can pray at home or sing in soliloquy. One can learn music. I know a person whose voice quality was bad. She studied music and *Ragas* (musical melodies), and when I heard her singing, it was marvelous. *Mantras and Bhajans* are supposed to emit positive vibrations, provide peace of mind, and calm the nerves. Instead, this kind of public show-off, not only create unhealthy vibes but also, adds negativity by the un-uttered remarks and comments by other dissatisfied growlers," Nirmala paused.

"That negates the whole purpose," Satish added.

"You know, Nirmala, when we go to Saturday Indian parties with our parents, it is the same situation. We go to other rooms and start watching football or baseball game. It is so sad because, I hear India has a glorious heritage, but our elders never tried to pass that on to us, Saturday night get-togethers would have been an excellent opportunity, but they had missed it, and in turn, we, the second generation Indians had lost it." Nirmala and Satish both understood the anguish of Ruben.

Ruben and Nikhil were happy that Nirmala and Satish were in the US. Every alternate weekend, they visited Nirmala and Satish and had a home-cooked dinner. Ruben called his mother, Olivia, and told her everything. Olivia and Pralhad were both worried about Ruben going all the way to California. That anxiety disappeared after Nirmala's arrival in the US.

The first year of college was over for Ruben. During that summer, Ruben got a job on the college campus. Ruben and Nikhil both took a week off and went to Chicago to Ruben's home. Nirmala joined them too, but Satish couldn't come because of his job. It was a fun filled seven days for Nirmala and Nikhil. Pralhad took them around to nearby places.

They all took a two-day visit to Niagara Falls. Ruben had been there a few times, but watching it with Nikhil and Nirmala with their awe inspired wide eyes was even more fun. Nirmala and Olivia became very close during this visit. Ruben had no time to visit the Mancini family. The nightmares for Ruben and Nikhil would never go away but had gone quiet for a while. The seven days were soon over and they all returned to the campus.

That was the first day of the second year. Ruben was reading some notices on the board. He looked at a girl standing next to him and immediately recognized her. She was the girl from D.C.

He exclaimed, "Kiran... Kiran Hopkins."

Kiran looked at him, "Ruben... I didn't know you joined Berkeley. How neat to see you here. How are you doing?"

The summer before his final year of school, Ruben Joshi got an internship in the Student Program with the US Department in Washington, D.C. There, he met Kiran Hopkins, the student from Cleveland, Ohio. She was working there as a student intern, the cutest girl among the interns. Kiran was tall, slim, and had the complexion of a Greek goddess – a combination of white American and fair-skinned Bengali with ebony black hair. Kiran was the object of every intern on the D.C. political campus. Both Kiran and Ruben were working on the same project. Kiran was one year junior to Ruben. They became good friends and kept in touch for a while.

Kiran's father, Professor Hopkins, taught political science at the University. Her mother, Priyanka, was an analyst with a major bank in Cleveland. Priyanka Chakraborty was from Kolkata, West Bengal, and came to Harvard for postgraduate studies 25 years back. She met Lawrence Hopkins, fell in love, and married him.

At first, her family was opposed, more out of the concern for her well-being. However, during her pregnancy, Priyanka's mother came to help. She saw how kind and friendly Lawrence was and all of her doubts disappeared. She was thrilled after the birth of her first granddaughter, Kiran. Priyanka named her daughter after her close friend Kiran to whom she met in Pune, Maharashtra during her master's degree in Business Management.

Both Lawrence and Priyanka took Kiran to visit Kolkata a few times. Priyanka had a large family in Kolkata and during every visit; all of her relatives gave so much love and affection to Kiran that she was like a spoiled princess. Kiran loved her visits to India, enjoyed being the center of attention, and learned many Hindu customs and traditions. Her relatives from her mother's family gave her the glimpses of Hindu heritage.

The sudden reunion brought more thrills and fun. Ruben showed her the campus and introduced her to his roommate Nikhil. Nikhil had been given the option to take a room at the postgraduate dorm, but they both decided to share the room again. The next weekend, Ruben invited Kiran to go with them to Nirmala's house. She welcomed the invitation and enjoyed the company of Nirmala and Satish. Nirmala urged Kiran to visit again.

On one of their visits to Nirmala's apartment after lunch, Satish talked about the news from northeast India about infiltration and the changing demography. Ruben looked at Nikhil. The anger was clearly visible upon his face. While Satish analyzed the news, tears were forming around Nikhil's eyes and he blurted his thoughts about the inefficient and irresponsible behavior of the Indian politicians for that region. He narrated his own story before talking about Assam. Satish and Nirmala, as well as Kiran, were speechless and felt his grief.

In spite of being a physics student, he was knowledgeable about Assam and northeast politics. He continued, "It's a beautiful place with fertile soil and abundant natural wealth, including oil and forests. Bangladesh has its eyes on it. These areas are becoming victims of Pakistani politics of infiltrations and religion. They crushed law and order. They murdered my parents. Developments in Assam and the northeast region are classic examples of how societies, civilizations, and nations provoke their own ruin and destroy themselves," he paused.

Ruben was trying to say few soothing words.

Satish added, "The Muslim population is growing by leaps and bounds due to massive infiltration."

"And massive conversion of poor Hindu Bengalis," added Nikhil. He continued, "Not only have these infiltrators with new-found political muscle become more brazen in their demands, but they continue to move forward, taking the land and daring the locals and state government to dislocate them. Gang rape is on the rise, as they hear almost every other day that young Bengali Hindu girls as young as 10 or 11 years old are gang raped and murdered brutally or left to commit suicide with shame. Instead of being grateful to the country that gave them security and protection, they indulge in crime and anti-national activities. Our corrupt Hindu politicians support them for their vote banks. When I was in Banaras, we joined hands with students from Kolkata and protested about it, but it was all in vain."

"I read somewhere that Kuldip Kaul, our Prime Minister, who represents Assam in the Rajya Sabha, doesn't give a damn, excuse my language," said Satish.

"No one knows what goes on behind the face. You won't see any expression, no grief, no smile, nothing, just a statue. Another upcoming youthful savior Bahubal Khoja is clueless about the problems in Assam, his senses are impaired with drugs," added Nirmala.

"He doesn't care about India, and neither does his mother Suvarna Khoja," Nikhil blurted.

"Our police commissioner from Kolkata gave orders to the police to go tough on the Hindu agitators," added Satish.

Nirmala pondered, as she was reminiscent, "The biggest failure has been the ideological divergence that happened a few decades before our birth. The partition left after the cessation of the Muslim component became the secular state. The secularist establishment using the garb of Ahimsa (non-violence) has spent the last six decades telling

Hindus that this country does not belong to them. The consequences of such behavior are becoming starkly visible. Can such leaders, administrators, and media represent the country?" Nirmala's tone was melancholy.

Kiran felt awkward. She visited Kolkata a few times and was aware of many of the issues. Ruben was also getting restless with the discussion. The problems, the concerns described by Ruben's cousin, her husband, and his best friend were real to them. They were emotionally involved in it, part of it. He knew his father also felt the same. They were dear to him; he loved them. However, they both felt alien. Nirmala looked at them, at their uneasy faces. She said, "Ruben, Kiran, I understand, don't feel left out. Remaining neutral may be more beneficial to resolve these issues than our emotional involvement. You and your generation of Hindu-Americans may eventually succeed in areas where we failed. You can find answers and implement solutions using your upbringing instilled with the sense of freedom. Sometimes destiny plays strange games. Who knows? You could be instrumental in bringing changes for the Independent Hindu Rashtra."

It was getting late. All three of them had a busy week ahead. Ruben was the editor for the university newspaper, *Orbit*, a biweekly publication. He wanted to check the final version before sending it to print. He was also going to participate in a debate on the gun-control issue. Kiran was going to write an essay on teenage pregnancy. Nikhil was going to set up a lab project for the second-year student. Nirmala prepared a sumptuous dinner. The dinner was ready and they all dined together. Nirmala told Kiran not to help her clean the table or wash dishes so they could leave early and return to the campus on time.

Kiran started on her essay that same evening. She wanted to submit it by Tuesday. She covered issues like the psychological and socioeconomic impact of pregnancy on teenagers. She wrote about the lack of collective and community support, difficulty for completing further education, social humiliations and limitations, inexperienced parenthood, and sub-standard upbringing of these babies.

She emphasized how this one-sided responsibility was borne by these juvenile female teenagers. The central theme focused on drug and alcohol abuse by these teenage girls brought on by the stress and tension of teenage pregnancy, ruined their lives as well as the lives of the newborn babies. She cited many examples and references to support her argument. When she finished the essay Monday evening, she was satisfied. Her professor complimented her and recommended the article for publication in the university journal.

On Thursday afternoon, Ruben hurried to the debate hall. He was going to talk about gun control and the right to bear arms. The hall was full because of the topic. The opinions divided equally between for and against gun control. Ruben looked at the crowd, and after a few introductory words, he began his address:

"The time was late seventeenth century. We just won independence. The settlers in America were busy exploring the Wild West. Weapons were necessary for self-defense and for the protection of land and households. It also helped organize a militia system to enforce the law and order and to deter the tyrannical intruders. The Pennsylvania Constitution of 1776 asserted that the people have a right to bear arms for the defense of themselves and the state. During the pre-revolutionary period, the colonial militia was composed of colonists. Some of them were loyal to British imperial rule. There was distrust and opposition to these Loyalists in the militia. Later, the Patriots favored independence from Crown's rule.

The right to bear arms originated with English law. The text of the English Bill of Rights of 1689 included language protecting the right of Protestants against disarmament by the Crown. The US Supreme Court had acknowledged this historical link between the English Bill of Rights and the Second Amendment.

Now the times have changed. The settlers were no longer exploring and America is no longer under Crown rule. There is no need for a militia. We have sufficient police forces and an effective judicial system in place. The Pennsylvania Constitution of 1776 asserted that the right to bear arms for defense was necessary during that period. It was the need of the time. Therefore, they introduced the amendment in 1791. However, times have changed. We should also change, given that times are different today.

Some people argue that they want to have weapons, so they can fight the intruders. Do you think ordinary citizens with no formal training in handling weapons or guns can protect themselves and their families against armed barbarians attacking their house for plundering? First, they will come to rob you around midnight. You are fast asleep. Even if you tried to get to your gun, it is possible that these robbers could take it away from you and shoot you with your own gun instead of using their gun because the bullet from the gun could give away their identity.

Sometimes I heard the argument that women leaving the office late in the evening needed the gun to protect themselves from the muggers. Honestly… the spray mace would be more effective to deter such attacks than retrieving the gun from your purse, cocking it, and firing. In addition, firing the gun needs courage and determination that most women and even men lack. It's not that easy to kill someone regardless of the reason. Mental preparedness is absent. Using mace is faster.

There are many pros and cons on the issue. I am not denying that, but there is no perfect ordinance that we can implement. I have also heard arguments like cars and planes kill people so should we stop driving them or flying by planes? However, we forget cars and planes help us travel in a shorter time; in case of emergencies, these means of transportation are the lifesavers. We can go back and forth, but that will not resolve the issue.

The next statement may hurt some of you and I apologize in advance, but let us be pragmatic. The people like us wrote the Constitution. They did so based on the needs of the time. The right to bear arms came from Britain, and although it was evil, it was unavoidable at that time, so our ancestors incorporated it as an amendment. It is no longer 1791. We are in the twenty-first century. Is there a need to carry this evil anymore? This also brings about another issue – everyone carried arms in those days. It was a way of life. So why did our ancestors think to bring this issue up and incorporate it in to our Constitution as an amendment? Does anyone know the answer?" Ruben paused, looked at the audience, and continued.

"I can think of one reason; the colonial power was gaining strength all over the world, in Australia, New Zealand, Canada, and here in the US. These so-called colonists were killing the indigenous people in these places and replacing them with the immigrant population from European countries under their rule. These power mongers established laws prohibiting natives from carrying arms and weapons to continue their dominance. The common masses that migrated here in search of a new life had no such intention. They fought to get out from under the rule of this Colonial power and achieved freedom. Some of them even fought for the rights of the indigenous populations. Probably, our ancestors, in their far-reaching wisdom, thought to make the right to bear arms part of the constitution so the common immigrants would have arms and weapons to fight any future aggression and prevent cruelty from these power mongers. It's just a thought; if you find this ludicrous, so be it. I am not going to argue."

There were some commotions in the audience. This was altogether a new argument. No one had ever heard this before, and no one knew how to react.

Ruben continued. "Consider what happened in Sandy Hook Elementary School. It was not just an isolated incident; it is happening all over in schools and in houses. The children are dying accidentally. The death of youngsters by bullets on street corners is also on the rise. You all have heard the case of Representative Gabrielle Giffords of Arizona. An assailant opened fire during a meeting with constituents and shot her in the head. The bullet went straight through the side of her skull. There are countless incidents like this. I could go on all afternoon. The question of the hour is how long Americans are going to continue the evil that came from the house of Britain. We got rid of them in 1776. It may be high time for us to end this crisis. The days of the Wild West were over a long time back. Isn't it time to get rid of this legacy?"

Ruben continued like this for another ten minutes. When he finished, there was a pin-drop silence for a few seconds. It took some time to digest the catchy term "legacy of the British." Then both sides clapped and gave a standing ovation to Ruben. The student who was talking against him made a mistake and justified the British legacy, which was not that effective.

Chapter 14

Investigative Reporting

Ruben finished his master's degree in journalism and started working for the San Francisco Tribune. He had worked at the Tribune previously during the last two summer vacations as intern. His roommate Nikhil Chowdhary had finished his Ph.D. thesis two years back and had joined Ballistic Projectile Dynamics, Inc., a research facility in Seattle, Washington. Nikhil and Ruben both kept in touch with each other, and a couple of times, Nikhil flew to San Francisco to see Ruben. Satish was in the US on a temporary assignment for three years. After the completion of his assignment, he and Nirmala both left for India. Kiran stayed in Washington, D.C. and remained busy with her MBA.

The San Francisco Tribune was a decent place to work. Ruben already knew many reporters, so it was not an alien surrounding for him. He helped other reporters put stories together, review the writ- ten versions, check references, and worked as a gopher as needed. Six months passed and he still did not have his own story. He went to see Mr. Craig Thomson, the managing editor.

"I really think I'm ready for my own assignment," Ruben said earnestly. "If you give me a chance…"

"You are doing a good job. I got a very positive feedback; continue with what you are doing now." He looked up at the scanner, "Well, we just picked up the message from the police scanner printout on the wire, there is a major accident in Claremont. I was thinking of sending Mr. Edward, but he had a dentist's appointment. If you want to cover it, go…"

Ruben read the wire printout, collected all the details, and rushed to the site. It was a major accident. It involved a big truck driven by a sleepy elderly truck driver, a grey Chevy Camaro driven by a drunken migrant worker working on a nearby construction site, and an SUV driven by a woman with two school-aged girls.

Ruben reached the spot in time. He got the opportunity to talk to the woman. The woman driving the SUV and the two girls sitting in the back seat were not badly hurt. He had gotten the story from two girls before police intervened. The police took the woman and two girls to the hospital for a further checkup. The truck driver was not hurt, but he was incoherent. Ruben tried to talk to the driver, but police arrested him and took him to the hospital for a drug test. The worker died on the way to the hospital.

Ruben interviewed some of the passerby to get a more realistic perspective. He also visited the construction site to find other workers who might have been in a drunken condition. He did find a couple of workers who were intoxicated. As a result, his article criticized the construction management.

Ruben later went to the hospital. He talked to the woman about the accident. She was in a better state of mind to give a more precise account of the incident.

At the intersection, the light had just turned yellow when the truck crossed it and hit the Camaro that was coming fast through the red light. The truck hit the Camaro on the driver's side. The SUV was at the crossing. With the impact from the truck, the Camaro hit the SUV sitting still at the crossing. Ruben covered the story from all angles – from the sleepy driver who had driven the whole night to the innocent victims at the crossing. Ruben wrote the complete story with human angle and pragmatic perspective. The readers liked the story.

"That wasn't a bad job," Craig told him. "Not bad at all…"

"Thank you," Ruben responded. He knew Craig well, he never commented on the news story of any reporter. Even a brief remark like that coming out of his mouth meant a lot to Ruben.

It was Friday evening; most of the staff had already gone. The scattered weekend staff for the evening was just entering the office building. Ruben was walking through the tele-printer room and heard the printout coming over the wires. He walked over and read the lines: In Belmont, California, there was an attempted rape of a 14-year-old girl. The girl was walking home from school...

Ruben read all the details. Craig had already left, so he decided to go and get a complete story. When he reached the police station, he found out that the girl was a black belt karate champion. The middle-aged culprit who attacked her got a surprise. He did not know what hit him. Now he was in the police custody, and the police were taking the girl's statement. Her parents were also there.

Saturday morning, the tribune had the caption on the front page with the complete story:

FOURTEEN-YEAR-OLD KARATE CHAMP
SURPRISED THE RAPIST

Monday morning Craig called and complimented him. He was seriously thinking about this young man.

A few days later, Ruben got a chance to cover another story. It's so happened that Craig was coming toward Mr. Edward's desk. Mr. John Edward was a successful middle-aged reporter who had covered many stories for the Tribune before.

"Did you get the interview, John?" Craig asked.

"Sorry, there is no way I could pass the front lobby. I went to the medical center and they said there's no one by name Diana Robert registered as patient in the hospital."

"You mean Senator Robert's wife isn't a patient there," Craig said loudly, "I know damn well she is there. They're covering something up, damn! I want to know why she is in the hospital."

"Hmm... did you try the regular tricks like a box of chocolates, a get-well card, a flower delivery?" Craig asked. "I tried every routine trick. Nothing worked. The hospital staff is refusing to admit that she is there as a patient. I don't see any way to get to her, Craig," John blurted.

Ruben stood there watching Craig walk away. On an impulse, he decided to take a chance. He walked to Mr. Edward's desk.

"I have a friend working in that hospital. Is it all right with you if I go there and try to get any information?"

Ruben was a junior reporter with the Tribune. He had helped Mr. Edward before to prepare few reports. Mr. Edward liked this young man.

"Hey, Ruben… go ahead man, try your luck. If you get a story, give it to Craig, and get him off my back," he said smiling.

Ruben went to a local shop that rented the dresses to the theatres, and rented a coverall with a fake logo of the Governor's office and a chauffeur's cap. One hour later during visiting hours, Ruben was entering the medical center. He did not know anyone in the hospital. He only said that to John to get his permission.

He read somewhere that the Senator's wife liked to carry her teddy bear as a good luck charm since she was a child. He went to the gift shop. The gift shop was overflowing with a wide array of greeting cards, cheap toys, balloons, get-well banners, junk-food racks, and gaudy items of baby clothing and blankets with pink and blue ribbons.

"May I help you?" The store clerk asked.

"Yes. I'd like," he paused for a moment, "give me this box of chocolates," he pointed to the big box, "and a teddy bear over there." He bought both items, purchased a greeting card, and scribbled something on the inside. Then he went to the flower shop to buy a bouquet of flowers.

He arranged everything properly, straightened his cap, and walked to the information desk in the hospital lobby. "I have flowers here for Mrs. Diana Roberts."

The receptionist shook her head. "There's no Mrs. Diana Roberts registered here." Ruben looked straight in her eyes, "Well! That's too bad. Governor told me to deliver them here." He showed the card to the receptionist. The inscription read, "We are praying for you, get well soon." It was signed, "Robert Trenton."

The receptionist looked at him uncertainly.

"I'll take them back," he turned his back.

"Just a moment," the receptionist stopped him.

"You can leave them here; I'll get it delivered to her."

"I wish I could do that, but sorry," Ruben interjected. "Governor asked that they be delivered personally." He looked at the receptionist's badge. "You are...Wendy Hunt...

Governor's assistant may ask why the flowers were not delivered."

She was agitated, "I don't want any problems. Go to the room 1021 and deliver."

Diana Roberts was in her middle 40s. She was an attractive woman. She was just waking up, still drowsy; she looked at Ruben. Ruben stared. It was obvious that she was under the heavy influence of prescribed drugs. She saw the flowers and the teddy bear.

"Who sent them ...?" The words barely came out of her mouth.

Ruben kept the flowers on the table and handed the teddy bear and the box of chocolate to her.

"The card and gifts are from a well-wisher," he said.

Mrs. Roberts was reaching for a glass. Ruben poured some water and gave it to her.

"Can I do anything else for you?" Ruben asked.

"Sure," she said, looking suspiciously at him. "You can get me out of this stinking place. The hospital staff won't let me have visitors. My husband had an affair with one of his staff, and I'm here with a nervous breakdown. I am sick of seeing all these doctors and nurses pampering me."

Twenty minutes later Ruben walked out of there with a complete story about Senator Roberts and his affairs causing a nervous breakdown of his wife Diana Roberts lying drugged in the hospital bed. The story made the front page. Both Mr. Edward and Craig Thompson were surprised and pleased with the dashing performance of this young reporter.

Craig asked Ruben to come into his office.

"How would you like to have a regular beat?" he asked Ruben.

Ruben was thrilled, "Great! I would love to," he said. It was difficult for him to suppress his pleasure.

"There is an assignment, I believe you will like it," Craig said.

"Sure," Ruben said.

"Did you watch the PBS documentary – The Story of India?" Craig asked.

"I watched it. Michael Wood did a good job but there were too many omissions. I wasn't much impressed."

Ruben added, "I met Michael Wood in one of the conferences arranged by our university."

"Well, I heard similar remarks from a few of my business acquaintances from Silicon Valley. They were also talking about the Aryan Migration Theory of Lord Macaulay."

"Yes, I read about it."

"I got interested when I heard. These are all intellectual bunches. They all cannot be wrong. Do you think you can write an article?"

"Sure, I would love to," Ruben was excited.

"Good, how would you like to do some research and prepare an article for our Sunday section two weeks from now?"

"Well …" Ruben hesitated, "Do you think people will like it? There are many controversies. I know Indians would love it, but what about others? They may not like the Tribune criticizing the PBS documentary or Michael Wood."

"Well, half of the people here and in Silicon Valley are Indians. Most of them are in IT, a treasure of information. Write your article. It will bring criticism, but that should be all right, more sell for the newspaper. Bring some different perspective about this migration or invasion theory as they call it. You should have no problem preparing the article," Craig said.

Ruben had a difficult time hiding his excitement. He was familiar with the subject matter. He had many discussions with his father, as well as Nirmala, Satish, and Nikhil. He had only one concern - many Americans, not only in California, but also all over the state, read the Sunday Tribune. They liked the PBS documentary. The producer, Michael Wood, was not an adversary but an ally of India.

"Yes, I would love to do it," he started thinking. He had some ideas that he knew would not hurt anybody's feelings.

Chapter 15

Story of India

C raig liked Ruben. The quality of his work and the investigative aptitude were impressive. He wanted to make sure that Ruben could handle independent research.

Ruben went to the library and checked out the tapes of the PBS documentary show on "The Story of India." He interviewed a few people to get their reaction, talked to his father, and called his uncle and cousin, Nirmala. Nirmala was excited when Ruben told her about his project. During those interviews and the discussions with the family, he got other clues—the books written by Lokmanya Tilak, a study by Bradshaw Foundation in collaboration with Stephen Oppenheimer, and another angle about the Aryan Invasion Theory (AIT) or Aryan Migration Theory (AMT) depicted by Lord Macaulay in the eighteenth century. It gave him a much different perspective. He began writing:

VEDIC CIVILIZATION AND ARYAN INVASION THEORY

The Story of India is about the history, the religion, and the culture of India. India has thousands of years of history interwoven with diverse religious thought processes and varied cultures. It is a story of the journey of humankind. One has to go way back in time to study the evolution of the Vedic Civilization and to understand the Aryan Invasion Theory (AIT) or Aryan Migration Theory (AMT). The AIT and AMT are discredited today.

The journey began with the evolution of humanity. There were no written records or documented evidence. This article discusses the truth and controversies in appropriate perspective without criticism of any other religion, faith, or culture. The AIT or AMT is the hypothetical scenario about the migration of the herdsmen and hunters according to the colonial scholars. They supposedly migrated from central Europe to northwest India around 1500 BC., captured the indigenous people of India, and imposed the so-called Aryan Culture upon them. European and British colonialists promoted this hypothesis to ensure their supremacy in India. There is also a similar argument provided to the Anglo European origin of Sanskrut (Sanskrit). The colonial scholars found some parallelism between Latin and other European languages with Sanskrut. As a result, the European colonialism jumped to the conclusion that the language of the conqueror was the origin of the language of the conquered.

The Bradshaw Foundation had done a study in collaboration with Stephen Oppenheimer called "The Journey of Man." The Indian scholar and the political leader, Lokmanya Bal Gangadhar Tilak, wrote books "The Arctic Home in the Vedas and Orion or Research into the Antiquity of the Vedas" around 1893 AD. This Bradshaw Foundation study along with the materials in Ved (Veda) and the books written by Lokmany Bal Gangadhar Tilak provide a clue about the origin of the Vedic civilization. This review also shades light at the origin of Sanskrut, the language of the Vedas.

For more than 160,000 years, humans had lived in Africa. They were what we call today, the modern humans or Homo sapiens. In East Africa, scientists found the earliest known archaeological evidence of our mitochondrial DNA and Y-chromosome of our ancestors. The humans traveled across the Sahara Desert up the Nile River Valley. Most of them died due to global freezing. The survivors traveled through the Arabian Peninsula toward the Continent of India and China, and continued further south to Indonesia. Most of the population was wiped out by the nuclear ice age, which occurred because of the super eruption of Mt. Toba around 75,000 BC in Sumatra, Western Indonesia.

Later, around 50,000 BC, a dramatic warming of the climate in the Northern Region happened. The warming of the climate allowed re-population and migration in a northerly direction toward the Arctic region. The broad division indicates that there were three different races of humans – Caucasian, Negroid, and Mongoloid. However, the mitochondrial DNA showed that all living humans descended from the same source. The mutation clocks of mitochondrial DNA and the Y-chromosome tick at different speeds.

We have no evidence about the culture of that generation. The study does indicate the warming of the climate in Arctic regions and an ice age in the lower regions. Combining this study with references from Ved and Lokmany Tilak's books establish adequate inference that there was a population growth in the Arctic region. Due to the migratory nature of humans, some of them moved to the North and South America via Siberia and Alaska. Around these times, humans from the Arctic region experimented with fire, domestication, and farming. The Sanskrut language in its crude form might have been used to communicate during that era. This was the dawn of civilization. It was the beginning of the thought process and the seed of cultural progression. We can infer that the progress of humankind began in this era.

Around 12,000 BC to 10,000 BC, when the glacier retreated, the population started shifting down the globe. These people migrated in various directions, some traveled toward the continent of India, the Middle East region, and the European Peninsula. Some migrated to America via Siberia and Alaska, the same link that was abruptly broken during the earlier ice age.

Over time, some groups wandered off and settled in various places in different parts of the world. Each group adapted to their environment that allowed them to deal with the conditions in which they lived. The people who stayed in Africa retained their high levels of melanin to protect them from the UV radiation of the sun. Groups that later became Caucasian lost most of their melanin due to the sun not beating down on them. In the Siberian region, a group evolved resembling the typical Mongoloid race around 14,000 B.C.

Their ancestry is traced to China, Tibet, and America. Modern DNA testing has shown that, genetically, we are the same through 100,000 plus years of migration. Even a blue-eyed, blonde-haired Scandinavian may variously have been African, Middle Eastern, and Eastern European throughout his ancestral history.

In the beginning, this culture spread all over the globe. It was a slow process. The climate change might have taken more than a few millenniums. Humans were looking for favorable climatic conditions. The ice was shifting toward the Arctic region and the climate in a lower region was becoming habitable. The humans traveled all the way to the continent of India searching for habitable climates and eventually settled in that region. Then, the evolution of a thought process began. The seed of the thought process that germinated in the Arctic region now flourished into a tree of knowledge in the area around India. It may have taken a few millennia for this evolution.

The evolution progressively took its present shape, with the sophisticated scriptures and philosophy, in the continent of India. This progression eventually became the Vedic or *Sanatan* culture, known today as the Hindu culture or colloquially known as Hinduism. Those who migrated to other parts of the world carried a similar imprint but later consumed with other thought processes. However, some similarities do exist even now.

There is no proof that the Sanskrut language and books of Ved developed in the Arctic region. However, the basic imprint of the culture that spread all over the globe was the beginning of *Sanatan* culture. We can make this statement with the certainty because the culture still exists in the continent of India in a much evolved and sophisticated form. There is a famous line from the Ved, "*Vasudhaiv Kutumbakam*," which means the entire earth is a family. The possibility that this line originated because of the migration of people and their cultural thought process that emerged in the Arctic region and later spread all over the world is very plausible. The whole earth in this context is all the people of the world who carried with them the imprint of this thought process of *Sanatan* culture that evolved during the dawn of civilization.

In the epic of Mahabharat, there are references to the North Solstice and South Solstice during the death of the Warrior General *Pitamah* (Great Grandfather) *Bhishma*. These references to the North and South Solstice are particularly significant. How is that reference emerged in the epic of Mahabharat? The existence of Mahabharat is from the time unknown. It goes back a few thousand years in the BC period with the story referring to the places in India that also exist today. How did they know about North and South Solstice? North and South Solstice are only in the Arctic region, not in the continent of India.

The only conclusion is, although humans originally migrated from the African continent, the human civilization began in the Arctic region and then spread all over the world. The same thought process traveled to the continent of India and later shaped into the form of sophisticated philosophy. That was the beginning of the Vedic civilization in the continent of India.

The Sanskrut language in the crude form might have started in the Arctic region. That is why we see some similarities between Sanskrut and other European languages. The Sanskrut, the Ved, the Upanishads, and other Vedic scriptures developed later in the continent of India.

The human wanderers from Africa trod across the globe but the human civilization had its roots in the Arctic region. The final evolution of this civilization took place in the continent of India. The Hindu civilization and the philosophy of Hinduism began a few millennia back on the banks of the rivers *Sindhu, Saraswati,* and *Ganges (Ganga)*. This philosophy continued to flourish in the second and third millennium until now. The Vedic literature, the philosophy of Hinduism, Aryans, and Hindus, comes from the continent of India. The civilization and the religious faith became known as Vedic civilization and *Sanatan Dharm* commonly known as the Hindu civilization and Hinduism. This is the background information needed to understand AIT theory discussed here.

In such a vast span of time, there were records of sporadic civilizations in various parts of the world. However, there was no record of any archaeological excavations to indicate a developed and sophisticated civilization in any other part of the world except in the northern part of the continent of India. The discovery of the archaeological sites of Indus-*Sarswati* goes back to many millennia that reveal development of civilization in northern part of the continent of India.

The archaeological excavations around Mohenjo-daro and Harappa indicate that around 8000 BC timeframe, there was a developed civilization that existed in these regions. Later, this civilization continued as Indus-*Sarswati* civilization up until 2000 BC. Around that time, there were major tectonic shifts, possibly accompanied by volcanic eruptions, which drastically altered the flow of the river and eventually dried up the riverbed of *Saraswati*. Ved referenced the *Saraswati* River. The civilization shifted toward and flourished around the river Ganges (*Ganga*) because of the drying of the *Sarswati* River. These references in Ved, Puran, and the mythological epics depict the life in those eras. These stories of the Mahabharat and Ramayan could be true stories based on the findings of the city of Dwaraka - the city found under the sea near Gujarat, India described in the epic of Mahabharat, and *Ram-setu*, the bridge under the sea from the Rameshwar Ocean front to Lanka described in the epic of Ramayan. This bridge is still visible from a helicopter or air- plane (present secular government administration wants to destroy this underwater link). The archaeological findings include the existence of horses and chariots around 4000 BC. There is also evidence of iron in India. The artifacts of deities found among the archaeological excavation are in line with the religious practices of India that still exist today.

The Ved and other sacred scriptures written in Sanskrut are a so-phisticated poetry depicting advanced cultural and philosophical thought processes of the Hindu philosophy or the *Sanatan* philos-ophy. The philosophy dates back prior to 2000 BC and beyond. The literature is available on the Internet. The sophisticated philosophy as depicted in the Hindu scriptures and the evolution of the Sanskrut are dated back prior to 3100 BC. There is no reason to doubt that the imprint of similarity between Sanskrut and other European languages is due to the migration of the population that had started around 12000 BC to 10000 BC from the Arctic region when the crude form of Sanskrut started as a way of communication.

The continent of India was a much bigger area compared to the present-day divided secular India. The mention of the Battle of the Ten Kings in the seventh chapter of *Rugved* references many dynasties such as Bharat monarchy, Purus (refer to a later day Persia), Bhalanas (refer to the people from Bolan Pass), and the Paktha mon- archy. These tribes are the contemporary day Pathan or Pasthun or Pakhtun in Afghanistan, Panis (refer to the Scythian monarchy), Druhyus, and so on. In fact, the reference to the Battle of Ten Kings indicates the local indigenous king Sudas of Bharat monarchy defeated his enemies – the other Hindu monarchies. These monarchies are - Purus, Bhalanas, Paktha, Panis, Druhyus, and others. The king Sudas of Bharat monarchy drove them to Iran, Afghanistan, Persia, and beyond revealing that it was not Aryan invasion to India but the other way around. It was the migration of the defeated Hindu dynasties to countries outside India, to Afghanistan, Scythia (Panis Monarchy, Iran, Ukraine and steppe of Eurasia), Parthia (region of northeastern Iran political and cultural base of the Arsacid dynasty, rulers of the Parthian Empire), Persia (*Purus* Dynasty), Pashtun (*Pakhta* Monarchy) and so on.

Afghan means *Upgan*. The word Afghan comes from the Sanskrut word "*Upgan.*" The word '*gan*' means a group of people, and the word '*up*' means nearness. Hence, in modern nomenclature, the word *Upgan* means nearness of groups or allied communities, which are the monarchies that lost the battle and fled to northwestern direction. *Stan* is the Hindi-Persian word for the Sanskrut word "*Sthan*," it means "the place of" or "the land of." Therefore, the land of *Upgans* is *Upganisthan* or modern-day Afghanistan. This is the land of allied Hindu monarchies. The various Hindu monarchies lost the Battle of Ten Kings and fled, and eventually settled in places like Iran, Ukraine, Persia, Afghanistan, in the northwest direction of the continent of

India. It was not Aryan invasion to India but the migration of the defeated Hindu dynasties to countries outside India.

The author Edmund Leach wrote a paper on "Aryan Invasions over Four Millennia." I am quoting a paragraph from his paper below:

"I think the puzzles have sensible anthropological solutions, but this is not the place to put them forward. The essence of the matter is that we must recognize that the standard Max Muller – derived story is wholly implausible. Instead, we should pay special attention to the likely state of affairs around 500 BC. We should then recognize that the versions of Buddhism, Jainism, and Brahmanical Hinduism that were current at that time are best understood as contemporaneous structural transformations of a single system of ideas and ritual practices. Vedic texts may have a bearing on this system of ideas, but they are not primary in either a chronological sense or a theological sense. The Aryan invasions never happened at all. Of course, no one is going to believe that."

All archaeologists familiar with the archaeology of the Indian subcontinent agree there is no sign whatsoever of any invasion at any time between 2000 and 1200 BC as manipulated and claimed by British colonists.

The new secular administration in India started by the great souls of Indians trained under the educational system of Imperial Colonialism, and their followers, drenched in corruption and sycophancy may finally succeed in destroying the veneer of this thought process of Hinduism. The politically motivated corrupt Hindu politicians support them to appease the secularist administration or biased ignorance under the influence of the Macaulay's system of education – the British colonial gift to India in eighteenth century – or both. As a result, the Hindu civilization may follow the same path as other civilizations that perished in the sinkhole of the time.

The article provided quotes from a few archaeologists about AIT, recounted the brief history of India, and the culture of India of last 2000 years. It quoted following examples:

- Mathematical treatise by Lilawati – a female mathematician from 600 AD,
- Chhatrapati Shiwaji Maharaj, the king of Maratha and the founder of the Maratha Empire that ruled India 200 years from 16th century through 18th century, expanded to North, Central, and Midwest part of India, and restrained the expansion of the Moghul Empire
- Bravery of Rani Lakshmibai
- Subhash Chandra Bose
- Veer Savarkar and Other freedom fighters

At the end, the article concluded as follows:
Combining the information from:

- Timeline
- Bradshaw Foundation Research
- Lokamany Tilak's books
- Ved
- References of North and South solstice from Mahabharat
- The findings of the archaeological excavations
- The similarity with the religious practices of the present-day India

It is clear that this evolution of the advanced philosophy and the sophistication as depicted in Hindu scriptures is the Vedic civilization and *Sanatan Dharm* (religion) commonly known as Hindu civilization and Hinduism. The theory of AIT or AMT is nothing more than a colonial myth. It is not an invasion as suggested by AIT or migration of the herdsmen and hunters as described in AMT, but the migration of the defeated Hindu dynasties to countries outside India. The Aryans also known as Hindus developed the thought process and philosophy in the continent of India.

Do not mix Aryan and the symbol of *Swastik* with the interpretation of Hitler. In fact, the Hindu auspicious symbol of *Swastik* and the symbol of Swastika that Hitler chose are different. The Nazi used the right facing form (in some cases left facing form) and tilted the symbol at an angle of 45 degrees with the corners pointing upward. Hindu *Swastik* is in the right direction and not tilted. Consider it as a divine intervention that the auspicious symbol did not want to associate with cruelties and atrocities.

Our journey began from the continent of Africa. We do not know any other civilization that still exists from the time unknown from the continent of Africa. Most of the civilizations were destroyed during various calamities. The only civilization that still exists since the first spark of civilization emerged is the Hindu civilization also called as *Sanatan Dharm* civilization.

Mr. Craig Thompson read the article and made a few editorial changes. He was taken aback with some of the thought processes and eye opening references. At first, he was in a dilemma. Then he made some research on his own and found out that Ruben's logic made sense. There was no way to authenticate that period with a definite conclusion. However, based on the references provided, he felt comfortable enough to back him.

It was a controversial article with a very different perspective. The West does not like such controversy. The terminology that is more accurate is something Westerners prefer to ignore. As a result, the article incited floods of comments, the praise as well as criticism, and... hate mail. Some were angry that the Tribune would publish such an article. Thompson received a letter from the leader of a local church group, which he published in the next week's Sunday edition of the Tribune. He thought that would appease the people. However, to his surprise after reading the letter from the leader of the church group, some of the prudent American scholars and professors from universities criticized the head of the church as a narrow-minded individual. The attack turned toward the opposing group.

Most of the references were available on the Internet. The student body did a detailed research and dug out more evidence in support of the article. The demand for the paper was so high that the Tribune had to print another edition that Sunday. The demand continued to grow with publishing comments and criticisms through the following Sundays. The sale of the Sunday Tribune increased. The article received nationwide publicity that was beneficial for the business.

Craig's friends from the Silicon Valley were so impressed with this young writer that they not only promised their advertisements to the newspaper, but also arranged a function to honor this young journalist. The Tribune received an official notification expressing dissatisfaction and interfering with the internal Indian politics from the Indian General Consulate's office of San Francisco. That was the climax. Upon advice from attorneys, the Tribune decided not to publish that letter.

Chapter 16

Foreign Correspondent

Thanksgiving is one of the busiest travel holidays in the US. The San Francisco airport was extremely busy with passengers trying to catch flights to reach their destination in time to eat Thanksgiving dinner with their families. The weather was cold and foggy with sporadic ice patches on the ground. Due to inclement weather, a few flights cancelled and frenzied passengers lined up in front of reservation counters to get seats on whatever flights were available to reach their destination.

The airport ambience was flooded with a chaotic melody of crying toddlers and babies, people arguing loudly with the reservation clerks at the counters, students playing radios loudly, and cancellation or boarding of flight announcements coming out of the speakers. In spite of the discordant sound, the aura of the holiday season was obvious.

Three weeks earlier, Kiran called Ruben and complained about not getting vacation to go home during the Thanksgiving holiday. "Ruben, I am just back from India about three weeks ago and again next week they are sending me to Dubai to train some new employees."

Neither Ruben nor Kiran's family knew that she was just back from Libya demolishing few terrorist cells. Kiran was looking forward to spending the holidays with her family. However, immediately after Thanksgiving she would have to fly back to Afghanistan or Pakistan, she was not sure where and her manager would not commit or sanction four days of vacation. That was the nature of the job.

Ruben called his parents in Chicago and told them that if they would not mind, he would like to go to Washington and spend Thanksgiving with Kiran so she will not feel lonely during the holiday season. Ruben called the airline and got through at just one minute past midnight. Cancellations had come through and he was lucky to book his ticket in such short notice during the holiday season when most of the flights were already fully booked.

Wednesday morning, Ruben went to the San Francisco airport and found out that his flight to Washington Reagan airport was cancelled. He was at the reservation counter and the reservation clerk was helpful. Since he needed only one seat, she could find an alternate flight on Delta that did not go to Reagan airport directly, but flew to D.C. via Atlanta with a four-hour layover at Hartsfield airport in Atlanta. The problem was that the only seat available from San Francisco to Atlanta was a business class. The flight was leaving immediately, and the seat would have gone vacant. Since Ruben had no baggage to check in, she talked to the supervisor, and got Ruben a seat on the plane in business class at no extra cost. Ruben thanked her and rushed to the boarding terminal.

He settled in his seat comfortably next to an older woman and looked around. The flight attendants were serving alcoholic drinks and appetizers free of charge, an uncommon scene in tourist class where you pay for everything except tea, coffee, water, and soda. Of course, travelers also get a packet of peanuts, pretzel, or biscuits at no cost. He ordered thinly sliced chicken served with goat cheese, pecans and beets, a medley of fruits containing sliced apples, strawberries, banana, peaches, and pears topped with caramel and whipped cream with a glass of wine.

"Hungry this morning...," the woman seated next to him made a jest at conversation.

"Yes, I came early to catch a flight that I found was cancelled due to inclement weather and had to wait almost two hours to get this alternate flight. I couldn't even leave my place in line to go and get something to eat. By the way, my name is Ruben Joshi," Ruben introduced himself to her.

"Ruben Joshi … a dashing young journalist from the San Francisco Tribune, isn't it?" the woman exclaimed.

"Glad to meet you, my name is Mrs. Penelope of ICNN. I read your article – Vedic Civilization and Aryan Invasion Theory – well written," complemented Mrs. Penelope and added, "You made quite a stir with the article, young man, if I remember correctly."

"ICNN…Independent Cable News Network, wow…," Ruben blurted, "I have heard the name. Your headquarters are in New York, a huge place."

"Have you seen our office?" She asked.

"Only from outside when I was vacationing in New York with my parents a few years back." Ruben answered. "After graduation, I applied to your organization for a job, but there were no vacancies at that time," Ruben took a sip of wine.

He noticed that Mrs. Penelope had not ordered anything but coffee. He looked at her… she understood, smiled and said, "I just had a big breakfast in the Airport Hilton. The hotel airport shuttle brought us here in 10 minutes. I am full for now." She continued the conversation, "Well young man, do you like working at the Tribune?"

"Yes," Ruben said eagerly, "It's a great organization, a good place to work. Although, it is a local job and I am still young. I would want to go to other countries, explore other places," Ruben expressed his wish.

"Really… That is interesting," she looked at him keenly, and then paused for a moment… she had good vibes from this young man. She added, "I am an Assistant Editor for the Foreign Affairs Division at ICNN. We have an opening that had just become available in our Foreign Branch. I haven't yet advertised," She hesitated for a moment. "A foreign correspondent is a dangerous assignment in the war-torn Middle East," she uttered the word of caution.

"I would love to apply for the job," Ruben jumped in eagerly.

"This is my card, with my company address, my cell phone number, and e-mail address. When are you going back to San Francisco?" She asked.

"I'll be back by Monday morning," Ruben responded.

"Send an official copy of your resume with a cover letter to the personnel office to my attention by overnight express. Be sure it reaches our office by Wednesday and e-mail the copy of your resume to my address. I'll be on vacation until Tuesday and will return to the office on Wednesday. Call me Wednesday morning on my cell."

Ruben was happy to hear those words of encouragement from Mrs. Penelope and expressed his gratitude several times over his meal and while watching the in-flight movie.

Meeting Kiran during Thanksgiving was the pinnacle of his mini-vacation. Kiran was still sharing the apartment with Lisa Hargrove. Ruben visited them a couple of times before so Lisa knew him well. Each visit he stayed with them, he occupied the living room sofa.

Kiran ordered a fried turkey for Thanksgiving dinner and prepared fried spicy fish fritters, a Bengali specialty that she learned from her mother. Ruben told her about the possible new job opportunity as foreign correspondent and his discussion with Mrs. Penelope, his co-passenger on the flight from San Francisco to Atlanta.

Kiran was thrilled. She thought that if he becomes a foreign correspondent then the CIA wouldn't mind if she revealed her identity as a CIA agent to Ruben. She already started dreaming about meeting Ruben somewhere in the Middle East.

Three days went by fast. Although it was a sad goodbye, they both were happy that they spent time together during the Thanksgiving holiday. Lisa also enjoyed Ruben's company, especially in the holiday season.

* * * * *

Manhattan Island was the financial center of the world and Ruben felt the contagious excitement of the surroundings. He checked in to the Pennsylvania Hotel on 7th Avenue. ICNN had already made the reservation for him. The next morning, he went for his interview. It was a large building, but he never imagined the scale of its size. There were a few shops on the first level, and above that, a real estate agency occupied two floors. Next was a banking office and above that a law firm that occupied a few floors. ICNN occupied the top 30 floors. He signed in at the receptionist's desk with his letter for an interview.

Mrs. Penelope was in a meeting, but she left instructions at the receptionist's desk to give him a guided tour of the facility. Next to the receptionist's desk was a door for the mini-theatre. The mini-theatre occupied almost four floors and accommodated an audience for TV shows and interviews. Above that was a newsroom with the modern sea of electronic gadgetry to broadcast news around the world. The newsroom took an entire floor. The tour guide explained that the stories and newsbreaks come here from all over the world, and they synthesized the news for broadcast.

The endless rows of cubicles populated the rest of the floors occupied by hundreds of people. He stood there speechless at the scale of what he saw. Each floor had signs indicating the functions and departments like Personnel, City Desk, Editorial, Metro News, Art, Sports, Video Editing, Information Technology (IT), Foreign Desk, and so on. The Foreign Desk was a large section with signs of each nation's flag and the name of the capital city of that nation below the flag. The whole ambience was an extravaganza of variegated colors of neon signs, screaming, showing a power, and superiority of the entity.

It was an informal interview. Mrs. Elizabeth Penelope had all the information about Ruben and his aggressive attitude to go after and compile the news. She already made up her mind to hire Ruben for the job. She knew he was the right person for the job – young, ambitious, and enthusiastic. His complexion, a mix of Indian and Italian blood, made close resemblance to an Arab. It was the right choice to send him as a foreign correspondent to the Middle East, where he could easily mix with the locals and gather the news without being shot.

She made him a formal job offer. Ruben had already decided to take the job. In spite of the danger, which excited his young blood even more, he was never going to let go an opportunity like this. She discussed salary and other details with him.

"Remember, you will be going to the Middle East after six weeks of training. It's a war zone, an extremely dangerous situation. If you still want the job, it is yours. Before leaving, you will be given a crash course of the Arabic language." Mrs. Penelope intently looked at him.

"I would love the job, and I accept the offer. I would have to give three weeks notice to the San Francisco Tribune after I get the offer in my hand, and then I will join you."

Mrs. Penelope smiled and congratulated him. Then she told her secretary to take him to the Personnel Section to complete the formalities.

A week before their departure, Elizabeth Penelope called him in her cabin and briefed him on his assignment.

"You'll have a truck in Kabul or in Pakistan. You will need the satellite to transmit your stories. We don't own one, but we normally buy satellite time from a US, Indian, or Yugoslav company that owns the satellite depending upon availability. Whenever possible, cover the stories live, but don't endanger your life or the lives of the associates accompanying you. Your team will tape most of the stories. Adolph Newton will provide the details of what he wants. The local studio will do the sound tracking. Adolph is one of the best producers in the business, and the Arab cameraman knows his job well. I don't anticipate any hornet's nest. Any questions?"

Ruben didn't know what to ask, so he shook his head in a negative gesture.

"Adolph wants to have few words with you. Wednesday morning, go to his cabin on the 27th floor. I believe 2719 is the room number." Penelope wished him a bon voyage.

Ruben looked at his producer Adolf Newton, who was a very talented and enthusiastic personality, bald with a gray beard, and about 45 years old. Ruben found out that he had produced many highly rated war news shows on television, and is an esteemed personality in the TV industry – especially in a Foreign News Division. Ruben considered himself lucky to have such a person accompanying him on his first mission. Ruben was a bit apprehensive, although he was eagerly looking forward to his new mission.

Adolph was brief but emphatic, "You're going into an active war zone. There will be shooting all around you. There's no guarantee you can protect yourself. Bullets don't give a damn to whom they kill. In the middle of action, the tension starts to grip your brain. You are caught between apprehension and vehemence. It makes you reckless, the excitement of covering live action can induce you to do stupid things that you wouldn't normally do. You have to control that adrenaline. Play it safe all the time. No news is worth your life. I will be with you, so will the cameraman. I'll tell you what to cover and when to duck. Always be attentive…"

The lecture continued for another 10 minutes. Adolph covered most of the issues that seemed pertinent, "I am off for the next two days. I'll see you at the airport on Monday bright and early. Oh, excuse me, on Sunday night. It's a midnight flight, so be there at least two hours before the scheduled flight time."

Ruben was listening to every word intently. Before leaving the news desk, the news editor told him that the destination could change abruptly and to be ready for such changes. They would land in Frankfurt then go to Kabul. In Kabul, they would meet with their Arab cameraman, Asif Basher, who would be their guide and translator. He knew many Arabic dialects and could help them communicate with locals in the area.

"Fasten your seatbelts, please," the flight attendant announced.

"Here, I come… Afghanistan."

In Kabul, Asif Basher was waiting for them with the news, "We have to fly to Aleppo International Airport. I have reserved seats for us on the Syrian Arab Airlines. The flight is at 7 o'clock tonight. We have seven more hours to go. In the meantime, you can take a rest in the hotel I have reserved for you here."

They all sat in a Land Rover. Asif drove them to the hotel. On the way to the hotel, he briefed them about the situation in Syria, "I have reserved three rooms for us at the Springhill Suites run by Marriott. We do not own a truck or satellite so I have also rented a truck and we can always buy time from an Indian or Yugoslavian satellite as available. I will know more about the arrangements when we get there."

"Is there any news out of Syria?" Adolph asked.

"The situation in Syria is getting worse. We already have a photographer who ICNN borrows from time to time. We'll know more when we get there," Asif responded.

They reached Aleppo in the late evening. The airport terminal was modern. The structure was Islamic architecture. The utilities like banking, health care, postal services along with duty-free shop, and other amenities were available. They wanted to use the toilets. The washroom facility was on the basement floor next to the stores. Some stores were still open. The prayer hall occupied the other side. Ruben was surprised to see a prayer hall at the airport. He had seen interfaith chapels and synagogues at the US airports and heard about the scene of Ocean Churning (from Hindu Mythology) at Suvarnabhumi International Airport of Bangkok. However, one would never see a Hindu Temple or statue of Hindu Deity at the Indian Airports in secular India, Ruben thought. They left the airport and went to the rental office to rent a truck. Asif received a call and they all rushed to the bombing site.

"This is Ruben Joshi of ICNN reporting live from Aleppo, Syria," Ruben began his first televised war correspondence in the midst of the aftermath of a suicide bomb blast at a mosque in Aleppo.

"The explosion tore through a mosque during evening prayer hours. A suicide bomber killed the senior Sunni preacher and longtime supporter of the President along with at least 41 others attending the prayer. The media blames the bombings on Islamic extremists who are fighting with the rebels in Syria's two-year-old civil war. Nevertheless, yesterday's explosion marked the first time a bomber had detonated a bomb inside a mosque…," Ruben continued for another two minutes.

In the background, the footage showed the aftermath of a suicide bomb blast, including scenes of strewn limbs and body parts, scattered blood, dead bodies carried by soldiers, and the sound of wailing prayers in Arabic.

The story and footage covered by Ruben of ICNN was received well internationally. The fact that Ruben and his crew happened to be there immediately after the blast was just a stroke of luck. The site of dismembered limbs, scattered blood, dead bodies, and the wailing of the injured was too much for Ruben to swallow. The images haunted Ruben throughout the night. A couple of times he woke up from the dream sweating all over.

The next day, they went to the other parts of Damascus, where Ruben saw tens of thousands of displaced people.

He reported, "This is Ruben Joshi of ICNN reporting from Damascus. There is an enormous need of humanitarian efforts required for the tens of thousands of displaced people to survive. Several roads, hospitals, schools, and other public facilities have been damaged; essential public services such as the distribution of power and the supply of clean drinking water have been disrupted because of the heavy fighting that has plagued the area over the past few months. The Syrian Arab Red Crescent is delivering food and household essentials, with International Committee of the Red Cross (ICRC) support. In addition, the ICRC is ensuring that potable water is available to people…"

The background showed the fallen buildings and structures and the people walking on the damaged roads due to the explosions. The cameraman, Asif, was quite good; he picked up the appropriate sites to go with the reporting that made the dramatic impact on audiences worldwide. Ruben also reported the announcement by UN Secretary-General to launch an investigation into the use of chemical weapons in Syria and the news they received on Syrian arms trafficking.

"This is Ruben Joshi of ICNN reporting from Karachi, Pakistan. The police from India successfully rescued the band of girls being transported from Indian Territory to Pakistan and other Middle East countries. In a shootout, police killed the four gang members, including a woman who was transporting these girls from villages of India via Rajasthan route in a truck. Two gang members ran away and crossed the border into Pakistan. The government of India requested the cooperation from the Pakistan government to catch the gang members. The girls were between the ages of 13 and 16. They gave the names of the local gang members. Police are still searching for these gangsters. One of the informants told us that this flesh trade business has been going on for a long time, and the police are trying their best to catch the culprits. However, due to the lack of government support, there has not been enough progress."

Today, Ruben was reporting from Libya, "Tripoli's interior ministry stated that the government would not risk a fight with Salafi Muslims.

Yesterday's attack raises the stakes for the fledgling post-Qaddafi state. In the coming weeks they will name the new government. The new government will be hard-pressed to get a grip on security to reassure both Libyans and foreigners. The roots of Libya's security woes go back to when revolt erupted in Benghazi against Muammar Qaddafi. The war brought down the dictatorship and delivered much of the arsenal into the hands of local militias. Many are still unwilling to give up their weapons. A drive through Libya remains a tour of checkpoints, with armed young men stationed at the outskirts of many cities and towns. Interim authorities outgunned by militias had to work with them to keep the peace. Those in larger cities are often cooperative, but smaller groups can prove difficult..."

They had to cut short his reporting because the local militia's troops were approaching fast. As the news truck sped away, there was a sharp jerk. One of the truck tires was punctured. They saw two Humvees with US flags passing. They stepped out of the truck and the Humvee doors opened. It happened so fast, he did not even have the time to think. Ruben felt the pull on his hand and he was inside the Humvee. He saw his cameraman and producer were pulled in by another Humvee. He looked up and was shocked.

"Kiran ... what on earth are you doing here! Aren't you supposed to be in Dubai training new employees?" Ruben couldn't believe his eyes; he didn't even realize he shot the question. Later, Kiran explained to him her actual job function. He did not know what to say. It was obvious that her parents were also unaware about her real job.

All three of them, Ruben, his producer, Adolf, and the cameraman thanked the American soldiers and got out of the Humvees at the next UN Post. He did not say anything about Kiran to Adolph or Asif. At the UN campsite, they managed to get satellite time and reported their escape from the rebellion troops. That was quite sensational news. However, Ruben's parents were worried.

James Montenegro tried not to miss his broadcasts. He had the utmost regard for this young energetic reporter reporting from the dangerous zones. This became the daily routine – today in Damascus, tomorrow in Libya, or somewhere in Middle East, then to Afghanistan or Pakistan. His dramatic reporting style and young charismatic face soon became a common household name in the US.

Chapter 17

Flesh Trade

The crowd assembled on a playground in a town of Arnakulam, a small town in the state of Andhra Pradesh, India. The people praised Mahamantri (Member of the Parliament) Balu Naidu, Minister of External Affairs, for his generous donation to schools and orphanages in the nearby area. The ambiance resounded with slogans of praise for Mahamantri Naidu-ji. For them, he was the savior of the poor, protector of women's rights, and liberator of untouchables. On the platform, Mahamantri Naidu-ji addressed the crowd in resonant voice about various government subsidiaries and programs for helping needy women and children, promoting education among boys and girls from poor as well as schedule caste families, and the orphanage centers. His volunteers distributed clothing, food, and books provided through government funding for such activities. His assistants made sure that only 20 percent was distributed, and the remaining 80 percent went into Naidu's safe.

It was almost midnight. Kalia Mutku loudly called the police chief (Thanedarji) of Arnakulam from the entrance of the Police Station.

"Thanedar Sahebji, Bada Sahib (Big boss) sent two Angrezi Sharab (English wine or whisky as in this case) for you and Sipahis (Police)."

"What can I do for you, sir?" The police chief asked politely.

Kalia Mutku, a loyal servant of Balu Naidu the Bada Saheb, was not a stranger to the police chief. Kalia, a six-foot-tall man with dark mahogany skin and muscular body, was a harbinger of death. It was clear from his tone that he was afraid of Kalia. Kalia gave him the bottles wrapped in papers. There was 10,000 Rupees inside the wrapping.

"Drink this *Angrezi Sharab* with your police, and if you get any calls tonight, don't answer them."

"*Ji, Hoozur* (yes sir), *Ap chahe vaisa hi hoga* (your wish is my command)."

Kalia, with his heavily armed gangs with guns and batons, went to the nearby area of cobblers, scavengers, and sweepers around 2 a.m. They covered their faces and fired a few shots in the air. The occupants from the cluster of huts came out and gathered into a small square outside after hearing the noise. They were confused. They saw the armed gangsters. They thought that it was a dacoit attack to plunder the village. These raids were common occurrences.

The gang members pointed the guns at the crowd and surrounded them. They separated the young girls from the crowd at gunpoint. The barely clothed girls shivered with fear. Few from the crowd tried to resist. They fired shots. The bullets penetrated their bodies… they dropped dead. They secured the screaming young girls with ropes, and herded them through the crowd toward the bus parked nearby.

One skinny girl got her hand out of the roped knot and ran toward her parents. Kalia fired a shot… she died on the spot. The truck left immediately after loading the girls. Kalia ordered the baton charge on the remaining crowd. The hoods left in the Jeep after warning the villagers not to inform the police if they would want to live.

The bus transported girls to the Kandukur oceanfront. A small cargo vessel was waiting for them. There was a woman onboard. She provided the girls with blankets and clothing. She wanted to make sure that each one was in healthy condition so they could fetch a good price. Her stern voice warned them not to make a noise. There were about 30 girls. They could sell each girl for 50,000 Rupees. That was cool 1.5 million rupees (Indian currency). After paying all expenses, Naidu would pocket 1 million Rupees (approx. 10 Lak rupees).

In the silence of the night, they all were transported to a large cargo ship and reached waters of Karachi via Lanka, two days later. They all succumbed to their fate. There was no use resisting. They saw the fate of the young girl who tried to resist – Kalia shot her on the spot and left her body behind in the village.

The Sunayana Moodguli with light olive skin was in the kidnapped crowd. She was about to finish her schooling and start college. All her dreams shattered. The woman noticed her beauty, separated her from the herd, and comforted her. Upon arrival, they took her to Islamabad, converted her to Islam with a name Surayya Kaif, and sold her to an elite courtesan house, *Mohabbat-E-Masti*, in Islamabad at a high price. The woman pocketed the difference.

The madam of the courtesan household, Malika Husaini Shafi, was a kind woman. She saw the scared frail figure driven out of her wits with fear. Surayya alias Sunanyana was sobbing, sporadically mumbling words of prayers to protect her from evil. She wanted to go home. Malika Husaini sat next to her and tried to comfort her. After a while, she stopped sobbing.

It was Saturday afternoon. The finale of the dancing competition was on TV. Surayya started watching TV to forget the agony of her misfortune, occasionally humming the tune, involuntarily her hands and feet tapped to the rhythm. Malika brought some food and milk for her. Surayya looked at her with a plaintive face. She had many questions but was afraid to ask her.

"Did you watch this competition before?" Malika asked her.

Surayya hesitated…, "We had a communal TV provided by *Tahsildar* (government officer in the village). It was in the big hut in the center of the village. Saturday afternoon, all adults were busy working, so children from the village watched the programs."

Malika watched her face, "Do you like singing?" She discerned a twinkle.

"Yes, I learned songs and dance steps by mimicking the programs on TV." Surayya responded and added, "All children and grown ups over there watch these programs and learn to dance and sing."

It was the blessings of TV programs like this. They distracted the minds of the helpless population and prevented them from focusing on the real issues. The attentions of the younger generations were diverted to activities like dancing and singing, and worshiping actors and actresses. Instead of food, take a dance pill, *Jay Ho* (be victorious) on an empty stomach.

Malika was a shrewd businesswoman. She saw the future profit. Instead of using the girl for prostituting for a few rupees, she decided to train her in dance and music. A sophisticated and trained dame can earn a fortune. Malika realized her potential. It would take some time, but she could use her for affluent clientele.

Surayya eventually accepted her fate. As time passed, she grew accustomed to this new lifestyle. She was the bedmate of many high officials of the Pakistani armed forces. At night after too many drinks, they babbled a lot of secret information. During her school days a few years back, she read spy thrillers. These stories gave her an idea – maybe her chance to take revenge. She did not know how, but she decided to make a mental note of the secrets she heard.

Chapter 18

Persuasion

Mahamantri (Minister) Balu Naidu, the Minister of External Affairs and Deputy Chief of United Front of India (UFI), was on his way to London. It was not an official visit. A company in the UK was negotiating a deal with government officials in India to open a manufacturing plant in Andhra Pradesh. The as-associate of the company was going to meet with Mr. Naidu to make an underhanded deal. It was a common practice for foreign companies to bribe the local government officials in India to facilitate services such as land permits, utility permits, and expedition of the approval processes by using their political influence. His personal assistant managed to buy the business-class ticket with government funds, a practice used by politicians all over the world.

The flight was from Mumbai to Heathrow via Dubai. The Shiwaji Chhatrapati Terminus in Mumbai was busy with passengers, many Westerners, beautiful white women, and handsome men, in colorful Punjabi dress of Kurta and Pyjama embroidered with silver and gold border were roaming around. Some wore heavy perfume, which permeated the air and masked the odor coming from the restrooms.

Indians were fully clothed in suits and ties, garlands of flowers around their necks and *kunkum tilak* (red dots, in this context an auspicious symbol) on their foreheads. There were wives going first time abroad who were clinging to their newly wed husbands, clad with gold and diamond ornaments, draped with expensive silver, and gold-embroidered saris and *kunkum tilak* on the forehead. Mr. Naidu had a wheeled carryon suitcase only. He was just in time so he went through the security check and proceeded directly to the boarding gate of the Arab Airlines flight to board the plane.

Mia (Mr.) Zafar Ansari boarded the plane in Dubai and took the seat next to Mr. Balu Naidu. The beautiful flight attendant served free alcoholic beverages and a sumptuous dinner to all business-class passengers. Mr. Ansari picked up his glass, looked at his neighbor, and said, "Cheers."

Mr. Naidu also picked up the glass. "Cheers," he returned the compliment. Their conversation began over the dinner served by the attractive flight attendant. Mr. Naidu found out that Mr. Ansari was staying in the same hotel in London where he had reserved his room.

"It's an elegant hotel. The last time I was in London, there was a club in Soho near the hotel with many beautiful women. I had a wonderful time over there."

Mr. Naidu was listening. Mr. Ansari noticed the lust in his eyes. He continued, "Maybe I'll go there tomorrow. We can go together if you are available; you can join as my guest, my treat."

"Oh, yes. I am free tomorrow evening. I will certainly join," Mr. Naidu pounced on the invitation and relished the idea of a free dinner invitation.

The courtesans flirted with the clients, the ambience of sensuality wafted. Women who wore bikinis with their tops off served the drinks and food. The circular sitting arrangement, two round bars on the middle of a stage with a couple of women artistically exhibiting various body parts, heightened the sensuality. The semi-loud music and the aroma of expensive alcoholic drinks permeated the air.

The club atmosphere was extravagant and lavishly decorated. Mr. Naidu could not take his eyes off the stage or his hands off the thigh of the young girl sitting next to him. He was happy. The afternoon meeting with his client was eventful. In the evening, he met Mr. Ansari as planned.

Mr. Ansari was an excellent host. An appetizer of fried chicken and mushrooms followed by beef stroganoff, vegetables, and baked potato were served with exquisite red wine after half a dozen shots of Chivas Regal, which lulled Mr. Naidu into a kind of stupor. He would have never eaten this food in Hyderabad and would have staged a rally to protest against cow slaughter. However, that was for an Indian cow. He had no qualms savoring the British cow.

Alcohol and delicious food with wine made Mr. Naidu's spirits high and lusty for the warm and young flesh sitting next to him. Mr. Ansari signaled the girl and they both helped Mr. Naidu to a taxicab and took him back to his hotel room.

The next morning, Mr. Naidu and Mr. Ansari met in the lounge of the hotel for breakfast. Mr. Naidu was happy to see Mr. Ansari and invited him to visit India. He boasted about his political power and his position.

"I would certainly love to visit India. In fact, I have a business proposal for you that might benefit both of us if you are interested," Mr. Ansari suggested with a smile.

"I am all ears," blurted Mr. Naidu.

"I work for a weapons testing facility in the US as a troubleshooter and facilitator of problems. It is an undercover position. Because of this delicate situation, I am not on their employee list, although I am on their payroll. Do you follow?"

Mr. Naidu nodded his head. He was wondering what this had to do with him.

Mr. Ansari noticed the expression of confusion on Mr. Naidu's face. "Let me get to the point. You will do a little favor and I will pay you 100,000 dollars upfront in any account you want," he looked at him. Mr. Naidu was salivating with the mention of 100,000 dollars and he was ready to sell his mother for that price.

"Yesterday you told me that you are the Minister of External Affairs in India and Deputy Chief of United Front of India (UFI). All you have to do is to use your position to find out the projects that Gayatri Energy Enterprise and Testing Agency (GEETA) of Delhi are working on. You see, this is a competitive world, and it is vital for our company to know the secrets of our competitor. It should be an easy task for you."

"Sir, what do you take me for? This is not an easy task. It's treason. I could jeopardize my position," Mr. Naidu showed false anger. But he didn't want to blow up the deal. He was thinking how he could extort more money out of this.

"Well, is quarter million dollars enough?" Mr. Ansari asked.

"Mr. Ansari, this is a risky operation, consider increasing to at least two million dollars. What do you say?" Mr. Naidu spoke cautiously.

"Take a look at this envelope," Mr. Ansari handed him an envelope.

Mr. Naidu took the envelope and opened it. There were a few pictures of him with the girl from the bar in compromising positions. The nakedness was vivid. "This is blackmail," shouted Mr. Naidu.

"Calm down, there is no need to get excited. It will remain a secret; just do this for us. You know what will happen if these pictures get published in the news."

"Sir, I have no technological background, and what you are asking is highly technical. I have not even finished my high school graduation, I had only finished ninth standard with barely passing grades... forget about reading technical diagrams. I have difficulty understanding reports written in English and Hindi prepared by our Indian Administrative Services (IAS) officers. I just sign them. How do you expect me to do this?" Mr. Naidu whined.

He was wondering... quarter million dollars was a large sum. He did not want to let it go, but how could he pull this off?

"You need not worry about that. I have a fellow in Hyderabad who is a professor of physics at the University. His name is Dr. Bhujang Iftekhar."

Naidu listened.

"Use your position and influence to get him a job at the GEETA facility. Use excuses like minority, secularity... whatever you can think of. Bribe the authorities. It shouldn't be too difficult for you, should it?" Mr. Ansari paused, looked at Naidu's face to make sure he comprehended and continued. "Once Professor Bhujang joins GEETA, he will do the rest and keep you posted. You can call me then. I will give you a special number to call so no one will be suspicious. Okay?"

Mr. Zafar Ansari was not part of any weapon testing facility in the US. He was the Deputy Chief of the Intelligence Bureau of Pakistan (IBP). He knew beforehand about Mr. Naidu's trip to the UK. He had completed a thorough check on Mr. Naidu. His investigation revealed Mr. Naidu's corrupt and lusty nature. He knew that with right buttons, he could persuade Mr. Naidu to place Professor Bhujang inside GEETA. The whole operation was pre-planned.

Bhujang was an Indian Muslim. He was born in Hyderabad, India. His grandfather was one of the leaders of the Muslim League in Hyderabad before India's independence and continued the same social status after independence. Bhujang's father continued to work in the Muslim League as an administrative officer in the local government department. Bhujang's mother was a converted Muslim from a poor Hindu family. She was a beautiful woman. Bhujang's father kidnapped her. His grandfather intervened, converted her to Muslim, and she became a third begum (wife) of Bhujang's father, *Mia* (Mr.) Salman Iftekhar.

It was strange that, in a secular India, Muslims can still have four wives by law. A Muslim leader can kidnap and convert a girl from a poor Hindu family without any fear or consequences. Bhujang's mother named Bhujang after his Hindu grandfather. Bhujang was a bright child and had an inclination for physics when he went to college. He also got interested in the Muslim cause and joined the Students Islamic Movement of India (SIMI). He earned his Ph.D. in physics and started working as a professor in college before joining the GEETA laboratory.

Chapter 19

Hindu Kush

Mia (Mr.) Zafar Ansari of Pakistan IBP was on his way from Islamabad Airport via the Islamabad Highway linking the *Shah Rah-e-Azam* known as Grand Trunk Road to the Defense Supply Corporation office. His brother, Brigadier Habib, was the head of the Defense Supply Corporation. Both brothers were shrewd politicians and business minded. They took complete advantage of their positions, one as deputy chief of IBP, and the other as head of the Defense Supply Corporation of Pakistan, they knew how to exploit and maneuver windfall in their direction.

The Pakistani generals' hatred for *Kafir* India gave them a convenient opportunity and the US provided unlimited funding for procurement of weapons and logistics. They manipulated the funding and accumulated millions of dollars in the name of Allah. They deposited the money safely in their Swiss accounts. Allah was the greatest nectar that sanctified the manipulation and exploitation and blessed their account in the Swiss bank. The funds in the Swiss bank multiplied with American funds in the name of Allah. Keeping unrest in secular India, eclipsed by corrupt politicians, provided another opportunity to accumulate more money by illegal transfer of weapons to rebellious Muslims in Kashmir and other parts of India.

Habib was a conduit to Karachi, Islamabad, and Mumbai-based dons who smuggled opium, heroin, and young girls – known as the flesh trade between India, Pakistan, Afghanistan, and the Frontier Provinces. It was easy to cross a territory between India and Pakistan for malefactor dons on either side of the border. This was useful to the drug cartels controlled by the powerful Corps Commanders. Ansari brothers diverted the profit to their Swiss account.

Passing over the curve of the cloverleaf on the Zero Point Interchange of highway reminded Zafar Ansari of the curves and the warm body of Surayya Kaif, known as The Queen of Hearts. After finishing his business with his brother Habib Ansari, he was going to spend the night with her.

He remembered the incident a year ago when the Indian Minister Naidu accompanied a UN delegation to a conference on security issues that addressed weapon, drug, and flesh trafficking issues between India, Pakistan, Afghanistan, the US, and Western countries. He applauded the UN mission to bring under control the sins of men and requested US to give more funding to the project. Pakistani media hailed him as a true friend of Muslims and a leader of the society for a crusade against weapon, drug, and flesh trafficking. This mockery got a front page in both Pakistan and Indian media.

During the conferences, Begum Surayya warmed his bed at night in the hotel room. On the final day of the conference, he was leaving from the hotel when he received a call from India. He talked with the caller in *Telgu* and gave further instructions for transportation of heroin coming from Karachi port. He wanted Kalia to go to Karachi Port to pickup the merchandise. He took the name of Kalia during the conversation. Surayya heard the conversation and realized that Naidu was the cause of her downfall. She wanted to kill him on the spot. However, before she could react violently, *Mia* Zafar and Habib Ansari entered the room to bid adieu, followed by a hotel porter. Habib introduced his brother Zafar as Deputy Chief of Intelligence Bureau of Pakistan (IBP). Minister Naidu was surprised; he thought that Zafar worked for an American Company.

For Habib, that was a successful mission because he pocketed many contacts during the conference. He did not care for the issues because those issues were his bread and butter. As a true Muslim, he never touched drugs. *Sharab* (wine) was his occasional weakness, but he knew that by spreading a *chaddar* (a fabric sheet) in a mosque, he would wipe out his sins, like Catholics giving confession to a priest in the church to absolve their ill doings, or the sinister Hindu bathing in river Ganges to liberate himself from sins.

The officers like him lived inside an invisible dome and were not susceptible to daily sufferings of the common human beings. They never smelled in their invisible dome the stinking body of a dead soldier rotting in the ditch after protecting his country. He was like a high priest in front of a sacrificial fire, offering human flesh and sufferings, and screams of virgins to the altar of ardent patriotism, rotting in the vat of abomination and religious intolerance. Redemption of the soul lies in Jihad done by others for the cause of people like him.

Mia Zafar Ansari and *Mia* Habib discussed the UK endeavor. This industrial espionage could become a profitable endeavor, depending on what information they could get from Bhujang, the physicist planted in GEETA facility.

"Maybe it's a good idea to visit our Al Qaeda partners, just in case," *Mia Zafar* thought aloud.

"According to my information, the test laboratory GEETA is involved in developing advanced weaponry projects. I don't think India is developing any chemical warfare weapons, but you never know. They have excellent scientists working at the facility." *Mia* Zafar was thinking about his discussion with Mr. Gustav of the BAT Company during his visit to the US.

"This could be big," Mia Zafar spoke loudly, his inner thoughts blurted out involuntarily.

"I think, Habib, it is a time to bring both of the directorates of Inter-Services Intelligence (ISI) and Ehtesab Arsenal Bureau (EAB) into the picture. I know Babar Ali Khan, Assistant to the Deputy Chief of ISI. He could be a useful contact and ally to have on our side."

"But, why EAB?" Habib was curious about his brother's thinking.

"Well, this Accountability Bureau, the EAB, is in command of the nuclear arsenal. *Mia* Hashim Kazi is in charge. Their office is in the Hindu Kush region where Pakistan has kept their arsenal in the underground bunkers. No one knows exactly where. It is a secret. Few handfuls have the knowledge. However, if we come across some information from the GEETA laboratory, they want to know. We can always get our cut, even a hefty one, if we keep them in the loop," Zafar paused.

Mia Habib was pragmatic. *Mia* Zafar was a combination of emotionalism mixed with pragmatism. As a Deputy Chief of IBP of Pakistan, *Mia* Zafar traveled to the Hindu Kush region many times. Chitral is the pinnacle of Hindu Kush region. He remembered the highest peaks and their beauty, as well as countless passes and massive glaciers. The word *"Koh" or "Kuh"* means mountain. Therefore, Hindu Kush means Hindu Mountains. The Hindu Kush is probably a corruption of *Hindi-Kash* or *Hindi-Kesh*, the boundary of Hindustan. However, the Hindu Kush mountain range deliberately named by the Muslim conquerors as Hindu Killer, because many of the conquered Hindu slaves died due to the extreme cold in the region.

Mia Zafar did not care much about the history, but as a young boy, he read all this information when he was doing a school project on Hindu Kush. All he remembered was a winding chain of mountains with some lofty peaks located in Nooristan resembling to the Karakoram Range that extended westward from Tibet into Pakistan. These were the most difficult terrain and ideal for hiding the nuclear arsenal.

"I know a guy *Mia* Zia Akram. He works under *Mia* Hashim Kazi." "So, what do you have in mind?" Habib interjected. He was confused. Having many players meant sharing the profit. However, Zafar's concern was safety. He didn't want this to turn into an act of treason. Keeping them informed will keep them in the clear. He explained that to Habib.

"This also gives me a chance to meet our allies in Al Qaeda camps near Hindu Kush." *Mia* Zafar was the brain. He wanted to make sure all avenues were open. The discussion with Mr. Gustav was looming over his mind. *Mia* Habib was not interested in intricate details.

"So off to Hindu Kush… aye… brother Zafar."

Chapter 20

US to India

The conference room of the ISHWAR facility was full. Nikhil Chowdhary was giving a seminar of the research project that he was working on.

"The bomber plane could launch the missile. The microwave emitter is installed in the missile. It's a jet-propelled cruise missile with pre-set coordinates of the target location," Nikhil explained the microwave emitter briefly. "The purpose is to hit the target with high-frequency microwaves to disrupt an enemy's electronic and data systems and make them useless before attacking them." He looked at the audience for questions. The person in the third row raised his hand.

"Yes Mr. Bhujang Iftkhar, do you have a question?" Nikhil asked. Nikhil never liked Bhujang. It was his gut feeling.

"How far are you from completion of the work so that you could demonstrate the actual results?"

Nikhil knew the answer but did not want to reveal the secrets.

"This is a high-powered electronic microwave concept, an alternative to traditional explosive and destructive weapons. A miniature microwave generator generates an electromagnetic pulse (EMP) field, which shuts down electronics. We are still working on software that could navigate a complex flight path by remote control. We also want to include the technology to turn the microwave on and off remotely. At this stage, it is difficult to assert an estimated completion date (ECD). We have to perform a few adjustments to selective functionality capabilities." Nikhil paused, looked at the audience, and continued, "The abrupt pulse of electromagnetic radiation results high-energy explosions. We are generating a non-nuclear electromagnetic pulse

(NNEMP). It is an electromagnetic pulse generated without the use of radiation. To achieve the frequency characteristics of the pulse needed for optimal coupling into the target, wave-shaping circuits and microwave generators are added between the pulse source and the antenna..."

Nikhil talked for another 20 minutes. There was a whopping applause. He answered a few more questions before returning to GEETA Research Facility in Greater Noida.

The company car was taking him back to Greater Noida. His lecture went well today, and he knew he had the full support of NSDI Chief Commander Bhosle. Today's seminar reminded him of the test that he did for his previous company in the US. On his way back, Nikhil started thinking about his old days in US.

The employees of the Ballistic Projectile Dynamics, Inc., cheered when the missile equipped with high-powered microwave emitter successfully completed the test. The planning for the next phase for jamming the electronic devices was in place. The CEO of the company congratulated Nikhil Chowdhary. His colleagues gathered around him, shaking his hand, and uttering words of praise. This was an outstanding achievement for the company and historic milestone in Nikhil's life. Nikhil worked at Ballistic Projectile Dynamics, Inc., for the last three years. This tortured soul from India rose to the rank of scientists.

After lunchtime, his manager, Tom Jenkins, Sr., invited him in his cabin.

"Congratulations Nikhil, this was great," he paused for a moment. "Would you like to attend a technical conference in New Delhi to submit a paper on your research?"

Nikhil had not seen Mai in many years. This would give an opportunity to meet with her. He could also visit his professors from Banaras, old friends from college, and the childhood friends with whom he grew up in the orphanage.

"I would love to go, thank you!" Nikhil responded with a twinkle in the eyes.

"Let me be frank with you. I had a discussion with our CEO. He was very much impressed with your work. We don't want to lose you. You are working here on an H1B Visa status. We are trying hard to process your visa status change from H1B to a Green Card through government agencies. However, it was becoming a pain in the rear because of the strict government regulations," he looked at Nikhil.

Nikhil did not say anything. He was aware of the situation.

"This prohibits you from working on major defense-related projects," Mr. Jenkins added. "Our CEO, Board of Directors, and I want to keep you in our employment. So this is the plan."

Nikhil joined The Ballistic Projectile Dynamics, Inc., in Seattle, Washington after completion of his Ph.D. at Berkley. Nikhil had seen many of his recent acquaintances and friends from India who came here on a student visa, lost their jobs, and had to leave the country. The funds that he had gathered over the last couple of years would not last long in India if he could not find a job immediately. He also knew that he was in a highly specialized field and there were not many jobs available for his specialization in India.

If you could sing or kick your legs and dance, then TV channels and masses would carry you on their shoulders and bestow money on you. Nevertheless, that fate was not available to a highly qualified scientist. That was the reality, that was the misfortune of secular India, and that was the grim and unfortunate situation of a scientist like him. The gleam from Nikhil's eyes faded away.

His manager saw, "Don't be disappointed, listen to what I have to say, the conference is in two weeks. We have been talking with our collaborators and arranging for you to present a paper. Go to the conference, present the paper, meet with our collaborators in India, and come back. In the meantime, we will arrange for your job in India with our collaborators until we get your visa status changed. It will take about a year and then you will be back to the US."

Nikhil saw some hope. Ballistic Projectile Dynamics, Inc. was involved with many defense-oriented projects. These projects required a security clearance. Although Nikhil Chowdhary was a valuable contributor and employee, he did not have the security clearance because of his H1B Visa status. The CEO of the company discussed this with his manager. They decided that he could work in India with their collaborators while they would be trying to get his visa status changed. The conference and the presentation was just an excuse for their collaborators to meet him.

His presentation went well. Commander Sitaram Bhosle from ISHWAR attended the conference. He listened to the presentation of this young scientist. The depth of his knowledge and analytical approach impressed him. He realized that GEETA Research Facility could use such talent. Commander Sitaram Bhosle took down Nikhil's details and his telephone number. He also made an appointment to meet Nikhil at the test facility.

The next day, Nikhil talked with the Indian collaborators of Ballistic Projectile Dynamics, Inc. He went to their facility for an informal talk. The discussion went well, but he realized the limited opportunities that existed there.

His visit to the GEETA Research Facility was far more exciting than the Indian Collaborator's Test Facility. He realized the unlimited opportunities and sources available to continue the research at GEETA Research Facility.

Commander Bhosle, Dr. Iyer, and other senior scientists from GEETA Laboratory talked with Nikhil about his work experience in the US and his Ph.D. thesis.

Commander Bhosle then asked Nikhil about his future plans, "So young man, would you like to stay in the US, or would you prefer to return home?"

Nikhil looked at Commander Bhosle and Dr. Iyer, "Well, sir, this is the most advanced and sophisticated setup with all modern equipment and facilities."

He looked at both of them. They wanted his acceptance.

"I would certainly love to work at a place like this." Nikhil answered.

"How long are you here and when are you returning?" Dr. Iyer asked.

"I am going to Kolkata to meet Mai and to see my friends with whom I grew up in an orphanage, and then I will meet with my professors from Banaras University where I completed my Master's degree." Nikhil responded.

"Who is Mai, your grandmother?" Commander Bhosle asked. Nikhil narrated the story of his childhood from the massacre of his parents and growing up in the orphanage. They were listening intently. It was a heart-breaking story. They were silent.

Looking at his credentials and experience, Commander Bhosle and Dr. Iyer both realized that Nikhil was the best physicist to work on some of the defense projects they had in mind for the Indian Military. The projects required complete secrecy and passion. Dr. Iyer requested that he should send a formal resume and application to the GEETA Research Facility and gave him the website to get the application form with the address of the location to send the resume.

Two months after returning to the US, Nikhil received an appointment letter from the GEETA Research Facility. He also received a letter from Commander Sitaram Bhosle, who personally requested Nikhil to join the GEETA Research Facility. The research facility was the part of the Institute of Scientific and Human Warfare Analysis and Research (ISHWAR) of India.

Nikhil took the job in the GEETA Research Facility. It took him a couple of months to undergo the required training and to become acquainted with the people. Slowly, he acclimated to the new environment. It was different compared to the US working environment. Nikhil had never worked in India before.

Almost three years passed since he joined the GEETA Research Facility. Mai retired from her job in Kolkata, and Nikhil insisted and brought her to stay with him in Greater Noida. She was getting old and was always after Nikhil to give her a daughter-in-law. Nikhil was in his mid-30s after all.

One afternoon, Nikhil came home and found Mai lying on the floor. Nikhil immediately took her to the hospital, but it was a severe heart attack. In the middle of the night, Mai passed away for a better afterlife.

The driver stopped the car when they reached Nikhil's company apartment in Greater Noida. With the jerk of stopping the car, Nikhil came out of rumination.

* * * * *

Mr. Tom Jenkins, Sr., the manager of the test facility at Ballistic Projectile Dynamics, Inc., got a call from the State Department. The woman on the phone was processing Nikhil's application to change the visa status to Green Card status.

"He got tired of waiting and eventually left our company," snapped Mr. Jenkins. He was pissed off at the State Department because he lost a valued employee.

"Do you know where did he go?" The woman from the State Department wanted to close his file.

"He got a job with the GEETA Research Facility in India and went back to India for good," Mr. Jenkins responded.

"Is he coming back or can I close his file?" The woman asked.

"I don't know, and even if he wanted to come back, he does not have a visa anymore, am I correct?" His tone was sarcastic.

"Ah...yes...I guess so." The woman exclaimed.

That afternoon, Mr. Jenkins again received a call from the State Department. The tone of voice was authoritative.

"My name is Mr. Padington. I am with the State Department, Special Branch. I am sorry to disturb you, Mr. Jenkins. I would like to talk to you about your past employee, Dr. Nikhil Chowdhary. I assure you that it's just a formality." His tone was now casual.

"Yes, what can I do for you?" Mr. Jenkins was a little apprehensive. The casual tone and façade of formality did not fool him.

"Well, I would appreciate if you gave me a rundown about Dr. Chowdhary, his background, his education, the project he was working in your company, etc." Mr. Padington asked him.

Mr. Jenkins was agitated. He did not understand the purpose behind the questions. Nikhil had already left for India. He provided as much information as he could to satisfy his appetite.

"I think that will do. This was just a routine inquiry. Now we can close his file, thank you for your cooperation."

With some additional words of formality and excuses, Mr. Padington disconnected the telephone line.

A couple of days later, Mr. Jenkins received an e-mail from Nikhil. It was an informal e-mail thanking Mr. Jenkins and employees of the Ballistic Projectile Dynamics, Inc., for their support and friendship. Nikhil also gave them his telephone number and address to keep contact with them. Mr. Jenkins immediately called Mr. Padington at the State Department and found out that no one by that name worked there. He was perturbed and did not know how to react.

Mr. Padington worked for the Department of Intelligence Oversight (DIO). He was a Deputy Assistant to the Secretary of Defense. His department conducted various questionable intelligence activities. He investigated intelligence activities that were not part of the organization's approved mission, provided intelligence services without proper authorization, and gathered information on US and non-US persons, of exceptional talents, as preventive measures though it was not part of the unit's mission.

After calling the Ballistic Projectile Dynamics, Inc., Mr. Padington made a few more telephone calls and got complete information about Nikhil Chowdhary and his talent. While talking with Mr. Gustav of the BAT Company, he made inquiries about the Ballistic Projectile Dynamics, Inc., and Nikhil Chowdhary. He almost cursed at the policy of the Immigration Department.

Mr. Padington was familiar with the GEETA Research Facility and its affiliation with ISHWAR and RAW, India's Intelligence Agency. DIO was aware of the GEETA Research Facility's Advanced Weapon Development (AWD) Department projects in collaboration with ISHWAR. He realized that because of the strict immigration regulation and delay, the Ballistic Projectile Dynamics, Inc., and the US lost a talented scientist to an advanced facility in India.

Although Mr. Padington did not tell him, Mr. Gustav found out about Dr. Nikhil Chowdhary and his employment with the GEETA Research Facility. He called his contact and narrated his discussion with Mr. Padington. He also informed about Nikhil, his extraordinary talent, and his employment with the GEETA Research Facility.

The US and India were allies. Occasionally, they exchanged scientists for sharing information and promoting technical development. Although the highly motivated purpose of the exchange of scientists was to promote technological and scientific advancement, both countries from time to time used this to spy on each other. In spite of this draw back, both countries mutually benefited.

Dr. Frank Muller was working in Germany with another laboratory and was busy until next year. The idea began to take shape. No one knew that Dr. Muller, a scientist, was also a part of the secret organization. They arranged to send Dr. Muller to Delhi under the exchange program after his return from Germany.

Chapter 21

Progress

During the regular weekly staff meeting, Dr. Iyer informed them, "Our guest scientist, Dr. Frank Muller, from the US will be joining GEETA Test facility in a couple of weeks on an exchange program. He will be working with Dr. Nikhil and Dr. Bhujang and will be with us at least for a year. I would like all of you to extend a warm welcome for our guest on his arrival."

After the meeting, he called Nikhil to join him in his office. Nikhil was surprised to see Commander Sitaram Bhosle sitting in Dr. Iyer's cabin.

"Good afternoon, sir," Nikhil offered greetings to Commander Bhosle.

"Sit down Nikhil," said Commander Bhosle.

"Thank you. Is everything okay?" He expected there must be some reason for Commander Bhosle's visit and Dr. Iyer summoning him to meet him. By this time, he was fully aware of Commander's high profile as the head of the Indian Intelligence. Naturally, his presence made him apprehensive. Commander Bhosle's penetrating look made Nikhil shiver.

"Have you made any progress on the project?" Commander inquired casually.

"Well, it is coming along," Nikhil looked at Dr. Iyer, who nodded. "The project phase of the mechanism to shutdown electronics through the microwave emitter is complete, I gave all the data to Dr. Iyer," he paused. "I am working with engineers on the construction phase of the mechanism. Dr. Bhujang is resolving some of the issues we encountered, but he is not up to the speed yet. I believe his field of specialty is different. I am sure he will pick up soon," Nikhil glanced at Dr. Iyer for approval. Commander Bhosle looked at both of them, coughed slightly to clear his throat.

"Dr. Iyer and Dr. Nikhil, this is confidential. Please keep it that way. Minister Naidu forced Dr. Bhujang Iftekhar up on us. Normally, I would have resisted but Mrs. Suvarna Khoja, head of the UFI, also pushed for his appointment based on minority, and it was awkward to refuse them. I didn't have much choice in the matter. You already know this, Dr. Iyer."

Dr. Iyer nodded.

"You all are aware that we handle sensitive and secret scientific projects here. I want both of you to be cautious and make sure you don't reveal any significant development to Dr. Bhujang. He also cautioned Dr. Iyer to keep the information secret of the project microwave emitter. I do not want Naidu and Khoja sticking their noses into our business." Commander paused.

"Any questions?"

Both Dr. Iyer and Dr. Nikhil were silent.

Commander Bhosle continued, "The United States and India are allies. We will welcome the arrival of Dr. Frank Muller. The US is advanced in technological areas. Let us watch and see what Dr. Muller can contribute. I don't want to sound too dubious, but let's make sure this does not become a fishing expedition for US. I doubt it, though. India and United States have a history of helping each other. I expect Dr. Muller to continue this trend. Do you understand what I am saying, Nikhil?"

"I'll keep that in mind, sir," Nikhil paused for a moment. He was thinking about his meeting with Dr. Patnaik from the Advance Material Development (AMD) Department. "Dr. Patnaik has some ideas about integrating a compound in an emitter mechanism. I am not sure whether the GEETA Test Facility would like to proceed in that direction. I'll discuss this later with Dr. Patnaik," Nikhil conveyed the information.

Commander Bhosle looked at Dr. Iyer, "We should venture into all directions and be ready. Look into it. I don't think Dr. Iyer should have any hesitation."

"By all means, if more funding is needed, let me know," Dr Iyer said approvingly.

"Is there anything else?" Commander Bhosle asked.

"Not much, Nikhil applied for a week vacation. He is working very hard. The break will do him well," Dr. Iyer replied. "Right, Nikhil?"

"I want to visit my friends in Mumbai," Nikhil responded.

"Well, then go now, before Dr. Muller joins us. You will not have time later," Commander Bhosle suggested.

"I think that's a good idea, Nikhil, I think it shouldn't be a problem getting a ticket on a Delhi Mumbai flight," Dr. Iyer said.

"It's Thursday today, I can fly this Saturday and be back by next Saturday. It will be convenient for my friend, Satish, to pick me up on Saturday since he is off that day. A Ticket shouldn't be a problem for early Saturday morning flight," Nikhil already started planning how he would be spending the next week with them, especially with his nephew and niece.

In the evening, Nikhil called Nirmala and Satish and informed them about his visit. Nirmala was excited.

"I will be staying in the hotel not far from your house," Nikhil added.

"There are no ifs, ands, or buts; you are going to stay with us, period. The children want to spend as much time as they can with their uncle."

Nirmala had two children, a four-year-old boy Prasad and a one year-old Rohini.

"I am not working now. Satish can also take a couple of days off," Nirmala insisted.

They had a nice three-bedroom apartment not far from the airport. Satish got it through his company. Nikhil had been there before, so he was familiar with the surroundings. The time flew by fast. He had a lot of fun with the children and, of course, a few heated discussions with Nirmala about the situation in India. The Sunday newspaper had this news.

The police revealed on Friday that nearly 120 precious statues of Hindu deities had been stolen from Orissa and Bihar in last two years from various temples and religious places. According to police officials, 74 statues of deities were stolen last year and almost 46 since the beginning of this year.

"Most of the statues stolen are made of *ashtadhatu* (eight alloys), an alloy of gold, silver, copper, zinc, lead, iron, brass and mercury, and added with rare marble. These statues are valued in millions of dollars in the international market. Theft in temples is a common occurrence in Orissa and Bihar. The temple administrators lodged more than 100 cases of theft last year. The statues were stolen from Deogarh, Bhubaneshwar, Baripada, Gaya, Bhagalpur, Vaishali, Begusarai, Nalanda, Rohtas, Sitamarhi, and Patna," the official said.

Except for a few cases, the police had been unable to recover the stolen statues. Mr. Abhijit Avasthi, a retired police officer, was angry at the inefficiency of the police department and demanded the government to take the matter seriously.

The news fueled Nirmala's anger, "This is outright conspiracy, you know, Nikhil," she blurted. "Police are helping thieves steal the deities, so they can have their cut in the millions of dollars of profit. Our secular government doesn't care about Hindu deities. We never hear the news that someone had robbed Muslim mosques or had stolen from the church. Why do they only steal Hindu deities? Can you explain this?"

"Calm down, Nirmala," Satish said trying to appease her.

"Calm down, my foot! You know Nikhil that our secular government controls the Hindu *Mandirs* (temples), and millions of dollars of donations given by Hindu devotees in temples like *Sidhhi Vinayak Mandir* and *Tirupati Mandir* channeled to help Muslims visit Hajj Pilgrimage. The money comes from *Hindu Mandir* coffer, to pay for their Hajj trip. Tell me why no one gives money to our Sandhya *Aji* (old woman respectfully addressed as Aji-Grand Ma), who leaves in *zopadpatti* (cluster of huts - dwellings for the poor in large cities like Mumbai) to visit Amarnath (Pilgrimage for Hindus) or Vaishnav *Devi Mandir* (Temple of Goddess Vaishnavi – a revered Hindu Deity)? Sandhya *Aji* is poor by all definitions. I will tell you why. It's all because of that Christian widow, Suvarna Khoja, and her corrupt Hindu retinue licking her feet for a few *lacs of rupees* or getting a position in UFI. This must be stopped."

Nikhil and Satish both knew that she was right, but words of frustration would not change the greed that induces corruption.

Nirmala and Satish both were planning a trip to Matheran, a nearby hill station, with Nikhil for a couple of nights. However, Monday morning they got the news of India Bandh (close) on Wednesday to protest against corrupt politicians and entrepreneurs about corruption and trillions of dollars stashed in Swiss accounts. All three of them were for such protest, but crippling the country for one day was not the solution. Stopping all services of the nation even for a day hurt the underprivileged society more.

"I don't believe Chhotu Gadkari is the right person for such movement," Nirmala expressed her opinion.

"Wait a minute Nirmala, he has millions of followers, everyone worships him," Satish said.

Nikhil interrupted, "I understand he has done a lot of good work for the community and helped a lot of people. However, this personality worship is harmful to India."

"You said it Nikhil, he is not the right person to lead the country of this size with diversified interests and variegated ambiance. He has no qualification or experience for such a job. I believe he has not even completed ninth grade in school. He is a good person, but mere sacrifice, selfless work and helping the people are not enough credentials for a leader," Nirmala paused.

"I am not sure about the people he associates with, either," Satish thought aloud. "Yes, that Rajasthani guy who is always around Chhotu Gadkari, I can't remember his name, he is more inclined toward Communism… well… I am not sure, don't quote me on it," Nirmala added.

The discussion would have continued like this whole day but Rohini, the baby daughter of Nirmala, started crying. She was hungry and it was a time to change her diaper. Seven days passed by quickly. All of them went to the Mumbai Airport to bid farewell to Nikhil.

Chapter 22

Theft

D r. Frank Muller arrived in Delhi a week later. He came to Delhi as an exchange scientist to work at the GEETA Test facility. Dr. Muller was a distinguished scientist, but no one knew that he was also a part of a secret organization. He worked before at the Boeing laboratory on a similar project that Nikhil was working. After arrival, he met with Dr. Nikhil Chowdhary, Dr. Bhujang Iftekhar, and other staff members and started working with Nikhil in AWD (Advanced weapon Development) Department. Bhujang Iftekhar was suspicious about this new arrival. It did not fit into his plan. However, after talking with SIMI's office, he realized that Dr. Muller might be an ally, though the staff from the SIMI office cautioned Bhujang not to reveal any information to Dr. Muller.

Soon after his return from Mumbai, Nikhil met with Dr. Patnaik and promised him that he would look into his suggestion. He read all the information provided by Dr. Patnaik. The integration may cause the abrupt pulse of electromagnetic radiation that could result high-energy explosions. Limiting the explosion to NNEMP level would require precise control in order to achieve successful integration. He remembered the paper he read about accelerating, transporting, and focusing ion beams where fusion could become the energy source. A small amount of fuel transforms into an enormously large output of energy and when nuclei fused together, the mass of the new nuclei becomes lower than the original converting the difference to energy. He thought of fusing compounds with isotopes of hydrogen, deuterium, and tritium at substantially lesser currents. The magnetic fusion energy (MFE) used to accomplish fusion in a doughnut-shaped reactor would require a powerful magnetic field. The triggering device would produce the magnetic field by modifying the design of the mechanism. He realized that the shell must be strong enough to withstand high temperatures. Both devices, the dough-shaped reactor and the triggering mechanism, would be bulky. The aircraft could carry this bulky device below the wings or below the aircraft and the pilot could remotely activate. However, there were a couple of problems – extremely high temperatures and finding the metal that could withstand such high temperature. He continued his research to lessen the effect of temperature and decided to go with the smaller experimental version.

The research took more than six months. As a test, he devised the plan to fabricate a miniature model with the help of lab technicians. Nikhil kept them in the dark about the true purpose of the research. The lab technicians had no idea about the projects. Then one night, he went to the lab when no one was around and introduced the small amount of the compound into the miniature dough-shaped capsule. The microwave emitter was in the device. After completion, Nikhil realized that he had created a formidable weapon. He named the device SHIV the Destruction. The miniature version could kill many people, and would isolate electronic signals, without damaging the buildings or surroundings. He fabricated four experimental miniature capsules with triggering mechanisms for testing and demonstration purposes – one for testing in the laboratory, one for demonstration to Commander Bhosle, one for military personnel, and one extra, just in case.

Dr. Muller and Dr. Bhujang had their portion of work cut out, but they both were watching Nikhil's work. Nikhil pretended to continue research and kept them altogether in the dark of this deviation. Dr. Muller continued to send periodic reports to the US. Nikhil took every precaution to keep this project secret. Nevertheless, he had a strange feeling that someone was watching his every move. He could not pinpoint it, but his gut told him there was something wrong. The warning of caution from Commander Bhosle about Dr. Bhujang and Dr. Muller was like a red light blinking in his conscience. Dr. Bhujang's curiosity about Nikhil's work was a part of his job. Nikhil was aware of that.

"Is it because Muslims killed my parents and I am taking that out on Bhujang," Nikhil pondered over the idea. The logic told him not to entertain such ill feelings toward a colleague.

He decided to be cautious. His laptop contained all information of the project SHIV the Destruction with detailed notes, reports, and fabrication information. The access to his laptop required the use of an encrypted password. The mainframe computer did not have the information about the new project development. He was apprehensive and restless, especially after fabricating those capsules. Therefore, he devised a scheme.

His authorized key could only open the cabinet. If unauthorized person tried to open the cabinet with a duplicate key to steal the capsules, the computer would automatically self-destruct the hard drive. The destruction of the hard drive would give a signal to explode his small lab. A couple of years back, when he was visiting with Commander Bhosle, one of Commander's agents taught Nikhil this technique of the tradecraft as a precaution to safeguard the secrets and gave him the necessary explosives. He was not worried over the loss of data because he could easily reconstruct the capsules from the information he gave to Dr. Iyer about the emitter and the partial information loaded in the main computer.

Nikhil then told Dr. Iyer about SHIV the Destruction. He also explained the problems of high temperature and metal.

"More research will be needed to complete the job. However, right now I have fabricated experimental miniature devices, SHIV the Destruction for demonstration. If it is successful, then I can request more funding and manpower needed to do the job."

Dr. Iyer arranged a conference with Commander Bhosle, Dr. Muller, Nikhil, and himself. Nikhil explained the device and the damage the device could cause. It could kill people, stop any kind of communication, jam electronic signals, no computer or phone would work; it would create a temporary devastation. He deliberately did not go into too many details. However, the information was enough for everyone to realize the potential of the death instrument.

"Are you sure that this project will work as you envision?" Commander Bhosle asked Nikhil. Nikhil looked at the Commander and paused; he didn't want to sound too optimistic. Due to the lack of test data, he could not positively commit to the success.

"I have fabricated four miniature grenade-looking capsules and triggering mechanisms for testing purposes."

"Why is a triggering mechanism required?" Dr. Iyer questioned.

"The mechanism would produce a high energy magnetic field and has a needle that penetrates and recoils the trigger to discharge a projectile at a specific destination. There is a chance that the internal parts of the triggering mechanism can obliterate after the use due to the heat generated. The handle is made of glass material with a small chamber of argon gas to isolate non-reactive heat effects and to prevent injury. It provides better insulation. I can test the device in a controlled environment, and only then I'll know how the device works and how much damage the triggering mechanism can sustain," he told them.

They all went to Nikhil's cabin to see the device.

"Wow, they are like hand grenades," Bhosle remarked.

"These are experimental miniature capsules and mechanisms. They are for test purposes only," Nikhil responded.

Commander Bhosle then requested Nikhil to arrange for a demonstration of the device. He consulted with Dr. Iyer and the others, made a couple of phone calls, and fixed the date for two days later.

Commander Bhosle was concerned about the security of the devices. When no one was around, he expressed his concerns to Nikhil about the security and the success of the endeavor.

"Are you positive about the success of SHIV the Destruction project?" He inquired.

"Only the test can tell us about the success," Nikhil told him. He continued, "I cannot say for sure, it is possible that a few adjustments will be needed, but I'll know that for sure after the test. I have also explained a few problems to Dr. Iyer, such as high temperature and availability of suitable material. More research will be needed once we get more funding and workers. I did not reveal this information in the meeting. These miniature devices would provide sufficient information to proceed. However, it is not a complete project; we still have a long way to go."

"How destructive are these miniature devices?" Commander Bhosle asked.

"They will still kill people and jam the digital signal temporarily in a localized area."

Then Nikhil explained to the Commander the contraption he installed to safeguard the project in his cabin. "God forbid, but even if the security is compromised and the data gets destroyed, I can easily reconstruct the whole project from the partial information loaded in the main computer database. The information about the microwave emitter is with Dr. Iyer. We didn't put that in the mainframe computer yet as per your instructions."

The Commander was not satisfied and he decided to transfer the capsule devices and the triggering mechanisms, including the data about the SHIV the Destruction project and Microwave emitter project, from the GEETA Laboratory to the ISHWAR facility immediately after the successful completion of the test.

After the conference, Dr. Muller called his contact in the US and briefly shared what he knew about the project and up-coming demonstration.

"It is really an instrument of death," The mysterious person expressed.

"Can you arrange pilferage after the demonstration and eliminate that guy, Nikhil?" He asked.

"It will be too obvious," Dr. Muller responded.

"Does the Muslim guy planted with the help of Pakistani Commander know about this?" The person on the other side inquired.

"I don't know. Let me see what I can do," Dr. Muller was thinking.

Dr. Muller talked to Dr. Bhujang about the meeting. Dr. Bhujang was not in the meeting, but he managed to listen and hear almost every word from the adjacent room. Dr. Muller's briefing helped him fill in the gaps. He immediately called the office of SIMI and informed them about the project. They devised the plan to pilfer the capsules and the computer before the test.

* * * * *

The shot fired. Nikhil's head dropped on the computer keyboard. The two men wearing janitorial uniforms entered the room. The smoke lingered from the pistol muzzle with a silencer that was just fired. One of them checked the pulse. Nikhil was dead. The file SHIV the Destruction was still open on the screen. The man who fired the gun put the 32GB flash drive in the computer to copy the files and quickly took the picture of the screen with a camera. The other man opened the cabinet with the duplicate key. He saw four devices with the triggering mechanisms inside the cabinet.

The self-destruct mechanism implanted in the computer activated. The smoke started coming out of the computer. He picked up the capsules and the mechanism and ran toward the door. While moving hastily, one of the triggering mechanisms fell to the floor. The second one removed the flash drive and ran toward the door. He noticed the mechanism on the floor, so he handed the camera and USB drive to other and turned back to pick up the mechanism. As he bent to pick up the mechanism, there was a bang.

DHOOOM... The room exploded. The explosion destroyed everything in the cabin. The man who bent to pick up the mechanism, the one who killed Nikhil, died on the spot. The other man dropped the capsules, camera, flash drive, and triggering mechanisms in the janitorial cart. The explosion created smoke and chaos. The other man disappeared out of the facility. The lab employees came running in when they heard the sound of the explosion, saw heavy smoke, and shattered pieces of furniture and glass all over. The smoke cleared out in few minutes. They saw two burnt dead bodies.

From the burned faces, they recognized one as Nikhil and the other was a stranger. They called the police.

In the initial crime scene investigation, the police inspector in charge saw a bullet wound on Nikhil's chest. He concluded it was not a simple accident. It looked like a planned murder. He secured the area. Dr. Iyer immediately called Commander Bhosle and informed him about the explosion and the murder of Nikhil.

The Commander cursed himself for not taking appropriate precautions after the meeting. He was sad about losing Nikhil. In last few years, Nikhil had made a good impression; he liked Nikhil. There was no way to know whether the project was a success or failure. Nikhil was vague; he never told Dr. Iyer or anyone about the project details. Only in the last meeting, he mentioned the project in detail. To confirm the results as Nikhil explained, they decided to conduct the test in a controlled environment.

Commander Bhosle was not even aware what India lost. It was one of the most dangerous inventions. It was best for all humankind that the Pandora's Box remained closed forever; otherwise, it would have caused havoc and chaos. The remains of the Pandora's Box, the stolen capsules, could still prove disastrous, and that was the price humanity would pay for the creation of technological monsters.

The Commander realized that he had to act based on the information from the meeting. He had to assume that the stolen capsules could pose a real threat to national security and take the necessary precautions to contain the damage and recover the capsules. Within half an hour, an entourage of secret service agents accompanied by Commander Bhosle flooded the facility. The wheels of tradecraft started to spin the web. No one knew how far it would go.

Chapter 23

Surveillance

The Police Inspector in charge of the murder investigation knew Commander Bhosle. He saluted him, gave the details of the crime scene investigation so far, and concluded that it was a case of a murder. Commander Bhosle sent the photo of the other body using an iPad to Suhas Gupta of EIW and asked her to investigate the incident. She searched the database and found that the body belonged to the known terrorist, Bahadur Khan of Harkat-ul-Jihad-al-Islami (HuJI).

She called and informed, "Sir, the terrorist organization HuJI is active in India. They are involved in a German bakery bombing in Pune, the bomb- ing in Varanasi, and the bombing in Delhi, among others. The US drone strike killed Ilyas Kashmiri, the Operational Commander of HuJI, in South Waziristan. The group also plotted to overthrow the Benazir Bhutto government. They are on the American terrorist group watch list. Their information is in the International Criminal Police Organization's (INTERPOL) database. Our agents from CBI are watching a couple of places in Delhi to keep an eye on Salamat Khan, and his cronies, Fahayat Khan, and others affiliated with HuJI." Commander Bhosle immediately requested the Police Chief to hand over the investigation to NSDI. The Inspector was relieved; he wanted to get out of this case because of the terrorist involvement. He passed all the information gathered by his team up until that point to the Crime Scene Investigation (CSI) team of RAW.

Commander Bhosle called Satish and Nirmala Joshi, Nikhil's closest friends, from Mumbai immediately and informed them of the sad news. He did not go into detail but informed that Nikhil died in an accidental explosion in his lab. He heard Nirmala's sobbing over the phone. Satish told him that they both would fly as soon as they got the air tickets. Satish immediately called Ruben on his cell phone and gave him the news of Nikhil's death. Ruben was shocked. Both Ruben and Kiran were in Middle East on assignment. Ruben did not have access to Kiran's number because of the nature of her job. So he called Lisa Hargrove, Kiran's roommate and her immediate boss, and told her the sad news.

Lisa had not met Nikhil, but she was familiar with their friendship and Nikhil's doleful story. She called Kiran and told her to call Ruben on his cell immediately. She also told her to pack her bag for few days visit to Delhi, and informed her that she booked the air ticket in her name at the Islamabad Airport. The office staff would pick her up at the Delhi Airport. Kiran did not understand all the fuss. Lisa informed Veronica that Kiran was taking time off to go to Delhi.

"Delhi? Isn't that place where the explosion and theft took place? I heard that some terrorist organization did that," Veronica needed more information.

She thought for a moment then said, "There may be more to it. I would like to find out. Coordinate with Kiran. Request her to look into it, emphasize that she should find all the details even if it takes more than a week. Ask her to coordinate with our agents in Delhi. I want to know everything about it."

Ramanuj Parmeswaran, an efficient agent of the RAW wing, was familiar with terrorist organizations. He was highly dependable and trustworthy. Commander Bhosle decided to put Ramanuj in charge of the investigation and assigned Pranav Chaturvedi from the TIW wing and Suhas Gupta of the EIW wing to help him. He dialed his office and immediately called all three agents to come to the crime scene as soon as possible. They all arrived with the van at the crime scene.

The van had all the necessary electronic gadgetry required for the investigation. The Commander updated them with the information and asked Ramanuj to take over. Miss Suhas Gupta had already started working on it when the Commander called and sent the photo to her earlier. She came with all the information about HuJI.

Ramanuj consulted with Miss Gupta and Pranav, went through the crime scene, examined both bodies, and reviewed the footage from the surveillance cameras. The footage showed the faces of two terrorists. Miss Gupta identified them from the database as Bahadur Khan and Salamat Khan. Bahadur Khan died during the explosion. The database also identified their third partner as Fahayat Khan. They took more pictures and reviewed the files that Suhasini brought with her. He requested Miss Gupta to send the photos of Salamat and Fahayat Khan to the airport security, and then he called the airport security personnel and requested them to be on the look out for these two suspects, as well as any other suspicious-looking characters. He also gave the copies of the photos to the Police Inspector and requested that he should put up roadblocks near the Border States like Rajasthan and Punjab.

The coroner's van came to pick up the bodies for autopsy.

"Would you please complete the autopsy of Dr. Nikhil Chowdhary as soon as possible? He has no known relatives. I have already called his closest friend from Mumbai and I will take charge of the body after the autopsy. Please hand over the autopsy report also," the NSDI Chief requested to the Delhi Police Inspector.

"Don't worry sir, I'll personally see to that, I promise," the Police inspector responded eagerly. He wanted to get out of the crime scene case as quickly as possible. Commander Bhosle thanked him. The coroner's van picked up the bodies. They all left immediately after they completed their investigations.

* * * * *

Fatima and her husband, Salman Akhtar, lived in an old, small three-story apartment building in Chandani Chowk, Old Delhi. Salman Akhtar moved to Delhi from a small village in Udhampur in Kashmir, near Jammu. Salman's *Begum* (wife), Fatima, came from a small village near Agra. Salman Akhtar, Salamat Khan, Bahadur Khan, and Fahayat Khan were childhood friends. Many times, Salamat, Bahadur, and Fahayat came to eat Monghalai biryani and kofta curry. Fatima never liked Salman's friends, but she did not say anything. Salman worked as a truck driver transporting merchandise.

His truck route was between Delhi, Agra, Jaipur, and Udaipur. He often had to go away for a few days at a time because of his job. Both Salman and Fatima were not aware that their friends were part of a terrorist organization.

The CBI agents had been watching the HuJI group members for a few years. In surveillance, the subjects are a list of details in an activity log, when they come home, when they leave, how many calls they make, where do they go, what are their habits, how they interact amongst their group, etc. Agents must discipline themselves to log their activities and watch them with hawk-like eyes. In recent months, the agents observed Bahadur Khan, Salamat Khan, and Fahayat Khan visiting the apartment quite often. Since then, CBI agent Malini Soumya started keeping an eye on this apartment.

Malini Soumya came from a low caste poor Hindu family from the southern part of India. Her father died of a severe asthma attack when Malini was 11 years old. He was a laborer working in a cement factory. Malini was the oldest child and she had two more sisters, age 8 and 6, and a brother, age 3.

There was no compensation given to the family by the cement factory owner in spite of the obvious fact that the cause of asthma was the below-standard working condition of the factory and the cement dust from the air. One of the *Panchayat* (local village administra- tor) members from their caste helped the family and requested the orphanage center in a nearby town to accept Malini and her sisters so they could continue their study. That was a great help for Malini's mother. She started working in nearby houses; cleaning utensils, washing clothes, and doing various odd jobs for survival. She also made a habit to visit Malini and her sisters at least every three months and kept in touch with them.

Malini was a good student. She was healthy and attractive. She actively took part in the girls' school *kabaddi* (Indian game) team and volleyball team. The school won a couple of championship games because of her. Five years passed. Malini just graduated. She was looking forward to go to college like some of the other girls from the orphanage. Her close friend Maya was in her second year of college.

During the middle of the week around 4 p.m., the orphanage matron sent a message for all girls to come immediately to the kitchen hall in nice clothes. They all came hurriedly. The matron, the administrator, and a couple of other employees were there with a tall man of about 45 years old. He looked at all the girls closely. The matron introduced him as a rich man from Saudi who donated a handsome donation to the orphanage for the occasion of the upcoming Diwali celebration. The girls clapped, and then left after just a few moments.

A week later, the matron called Malini and asked her to call her mother to the office. Malini thought that it was about her college registration. She was excited and left the message with the village shop for her mother. Sunday afternoon, Malin's mother came to the orphanage center. She was ushered into the office. The matron and the administrator were there. They explained to her that they found a suitable match for her daughter who is a rich Muslim from Saudi Arabia and Malini would be very happy with the marriage.

"He was here last week, liked Malini very much, and expressed his wish to marry her. Malini will be converted to become Muslim before marriage. The Saudi man will take care of all the expenses."

The matron asked her to go to Malini and convince her to become Muslim and marry the rich man from Saudi. Malini's mother was dumbfounded.

She went to Malini and talked to her. Malini flatly refused. She told her mother that she did not want to marry a 45-year-old man who was her father's age. Malini's mother pleaded with the authorities, but they gave her an ultimatum.

Ramesh Bhakhtiar, Assistant Deputy Director of CBI, was the younger brother of the man from *Panchayat* who helped Malini's mother five years back. He came to visit his family before Diwali. Malini's mother went crying to the man from *Panchyat* and told him the whole story. The younger brother from the CBI heard the story and told the mother that he would help.

He said, "Give consent to conversion and marriage and just before the conversion, I'll raid the place and catch all of them red-handed."

The local police sub-inspector was Muslim. He knew the place and the *Maula* (Muslim priest) who would be conducting the conversion and marriage ceremony. It was against the law and the police sub-inspector was also afraid of the CBI officer. He went along with the plan and caught all the culprits in action including the orphanage administrator, matron, and the man from Saudi wearing the Muslim marriage dress.

During interrogation, they found out that this man from Saudi visited India every two years, went to the different orphanage centers in the state, bribed the orphanage administrators and matrons, and married a virgin girl from a poor family for fifteen days to a month period, and then left for Saudi. He arranged the divorce from Saudi over the phone by uttering the word *talaq* (divorce), *talaq*, *talaq* three times in front of a Maula in Saudi to make the divorce official, an easy way to get rid of the mail-order bride, in this case the orphanage bride.

They were all prosecuted and given the maximum sentence as a deterrent for others. At the request of the Saudi Consulate's office, the man was deported with a heavy fine after spending six months in a hard-labor prison facility.

The CBI officer looked at Malini's credentials and sports activities and processed the application through the Indian administration to provide her with adequate financial support for her to complete her education until she reached the age of 21. He also promised her that if she would complete all the requirements, both educational and physical, he would try to get her a job with the CBI. Malini completed all the requirements and got the job.

One afternoon, Malini posing as sales girl, Farah Akram, went to the apartment to sell a raffle ticket to Fatima. Malini bought 20 raffle tickets to help an NGO organization. Those tickets came in handy for this purpose.

"The raffle tickets cost only one Rupee and is for a charitable organization helping orphan children from Kashmir," Malini paused. She looked at Fatima. She was listening. Malini continued, "If you win, you will get a free refrigerator. The second prize is a washing machine."

Malini told her how she started doing this work for an NGO organization. She also tried to recruit Fatima for the job.

"I would love to do the job. The work sounds appealing. I always wanted to do something like this when I was studying in the second year in Devaki Women's College in Agra. Then I got married and now I am pregnant. Soon I will be going to my village to stay with my parents for delivery. A couple of my husband's friends will stay here with my husband," Fatima responded. She thought for a moment and continued, "The refrigerator or the washing machine will be handy, especially after the baby is born. I'll buy five tickets."

Fatima liked talking with her; she also offered her a cup of tea. When Fatima went inside to get the money and to make tea in the kitchen, Malini quickly bugged the apartment. She realized that soon HuJI members would be occupying the apartment. Bugging the apartment could help them monitor their activities.

There was a tap on the door. Fatima's next-door neighbor, Mrs. Fayida Lodi, came to visit with her 10-year-old son, Hamid. Fatima invited her inside.

"Aunty, I want to eat the samosa that you prepared this morning," Hamid blurted.

They all laughed. Fatima also requested Malini, alias Farah, to have samosa (Indian spicy snack) with tea. They all talked for a while. Fayida also bought five tickets. Farah alias Malini made an impression on both. They exchanged their mobile numbers in case there was any work from the NGO organization. Malini gave her mobile number listed as Farah that she kept for such purpose.

Suhas called the CBI bureau and found out the names and mobile numbers of the agents watching the apartment. She also got the mobile number of the Assistant Deputy Director of CBI. Suhasini, known as Suhas for short, grew up in a warrior class of Punjabi Jat family in the army environment. Her father and grandfather both were in the army. She was the only child, brought up as a tomboy. She was also a black belt karate champion. She completed her degree in computer software engineering and applied for a job. After a few interviews with various companies, she eventually got a job at the ISHWAR Facility in the EIW Wing.

Suhas immediately dialed the mobile number of the Assistant Deputy Director Ramesh Bhakhtiar. He answered the phone, but did not want to give information over the phone. Ramanuj and Pranav decided to go and meet him and other CBI agents in their office. Ramesh was surprised to see Ramanuj and Pranav. He knew both of them well. When he talked with Suhas, he did not know that she worked with Ramanuj. Ramesh and Ramanuj Parmeswaran both came from South. They both belonged to a low caste. Ramesh and Pranav worked for the same MNC Company before joining the Secret Service agencies.

"My... my... my... a high-class Brahmin working with a low caste *Kshudra!*" Ramesh was aware of Pranav Chaturvedi's arrogance about being part of the high Brahmin caste. "How is that possible?" He smilingly passed the comment and greeted warmly both of them into his office.

Pranav completed his degree in computer science, received his MBA from Delhi University, and started working for the Multi National Corporation. The MNC did some work for ISHWAR and during the product demonstration session, the chief officer from the TIW Wing of ISHWAR noticed Pranav. He needed someone with Pranav's background and asked him if he would be interested in a position with ISHWAR.

Pranav's problem with the MNC was nepotism. He was not happy with the company. The new opportunity attracted him and gave him satisfaction knowing that he would be working for his country. He took the job. The pay was not as high as the MNC, but benefits and flat provided by the ISHWAR organization was a big plus for him and his wife. Commander Bhosle made sure all employees of ISHWAR were well taken care of so that they didn't become prey to corruption and greed.

Ramanuj described the sequence of events of the murder at the GEETA Laboratory and the stolen capsules that could be a threat to national security. The explosion destroyed the computer so no one knew the potential threat of the stolen capsules or what information the terrorist group HuJI had stolen. From the other burnt body, they concluded that it was a HuJI terrorist Bahadur Khan. Nevertheless, there was a chance that it could be any of the various terrorist groups. He informed Ramesh about the tightened airport security and the police putting the roadblocks on the roads leading to State of Rajasthan and Amritsar, Punjab State. Ramanuj also informed Ramesh that he made the Signal and Satellite Intelligence Wing (SSIW) and Analysis Synthesis and Imagery Wing (ASIIW) aware of monitoring communications, chatter, and analyzing intercepted messages.

Ramesh Bhakhtiar listened carefully. He checked the information on his computer and in his husky voice began narrating the available information of HuJI terrorist group.

"We are watching members of the HuJI terrorist group. They have a few terrorist cells in the city. We didn't notice any activities there. However, recently we came across a new place in Chandani Chowk, 24/3 Meher Bai House in Old Delhi. We have already bugged the house. According to our information, Fatima, the woman of the house, is pregnant. Her husband, Salman Akhtar, works as a truck driver. We checked his credentials with the trucking company. He is clean. According to our information, Salman Akhtar knew Salamat Khan and Fahayat Khan from childhood. They all belong to the same village. We are still investigating their connection. It is possible that Salman and Fatima are unaware of the association of Salamat and Fahayat with the terrorist group, HuJI." Ramesh Bhakhtiar paused and added, "We'll keep them watching. I get the information about their activities every day from our agents. They are on our active list because of the past bombing in Delhi and Varanasi."

One of the CBI agents came in and informed Ramesh Bhakhtiar, "Sir, one of our informants saw Salamat Khan and Fahayat Khan leaving Agra bus terminal. They separated and boarded different buses."

"Did you find out which buses they boarded? We can stop them," Ramesh said.

"The informant saw them from a distance and could not get the bus destinations. All he said was that the buses were going towards east," the CBI Agent informed.

"They are getting smart. They knew we would be watching the west side heading toward Pakistan so they headed toward Bangladesh," Pranav remarked.

Ramanuj added, "We'll alert our boys on the East Section. I would also appreciate it if you alert your CBI personnel to be on the lookout for them. They are carrying weapons that could cause devastation.

We'd like to arrest them quickly. I will arrange for the arrest warrant, let us move fast."

"Roger," Ramesh replied. Realizing urgency of the matter, he immediately alerted various divisions on both sides – east and west leading toward Pakistan and Bangladesh. Ramanuj was about to leave when he realized that HuJI members belong to a Pakistan terrorist group. They had no affiliation with Bangaladesh except being Muslim.

He was thinking aloud, "Suppose if they didn't intend to go to Bangaladesh, but want to mislead us, where can they go?"

Malini Soumya was entering the room and heard the conversation, "It is possible that they can cut through Darjeeling to Nepal and then head toward the west to Kashmir via border cities through mountains. It is a difficult journey, but it is worth it for them. In Kashmir, they have many HuJI members."

"And from Kashmir to Islamabad is not that far," Ramanuj uttered. "Well, boss," Malini addressed to Ramesh, "there is not much activity in the Chandani Chowk apartment. Salamat Khan, Bahadur Khan, and Fahayat Khan have not been there these last two days. It looks like the sleeping terrorist cell. Our investigation shows that Fatima and her husband Salman Akhtar are not aware of their friends' activities or association with HuJI. I am worried about Fatima and Salman, they are a nice couple."

Ramanuj interrupted and told her that Bahadur Khan died during the theft and asked her all the information of her surveillance on the apartment in Chandani Chowk including the address, names, etc.

"If it is okay with you and Ramesh, I can assign one of our RAW agents with you to help you in the surveillance. That apartment may turn out to be a key link in our investigation," pleaded Ramanuj.

Neither Ramesh nor Malini had any problem. His department was short on agents. The present economic crunch brought some personnel cuts and they had to reassign some CBI agents in other departments. Since most of the CBI agents were from the police department, there was no problem in reassigning them. Having extra help meant one less body and that equated to savings in the present economic system.

Ramanuj thanked Ramesh for the hospitality and the information.

"Thanks… aa…," Ramanuj looked at her.

She smiled. "My name is Malini Soumya," she said.

"Thanks, Malini, your information of the apartment is useful. I'll assign one of the RAW agents with you soon. The information of the Darjeeling Nepal connection is extremely valuable, we didn't even think of it, thanks for suggesting it," he complimented Malini and left the CBI office with Pranav. On his way back to the office, Ramanuj called Commander Bhosle, made him aware of the developments, and requested him to alert the Northeast Section. He also requested his permission to coordinate with CBI.

Ramanuj belonged to a Scheduled caste (lower caste) from Kochi, Kerala. His father was a Janitor who once cleaned latrines, collected garbage, and transported it to garbage collection point from Kochi. Ramanuj was a brilliant student. He loved sports; he was skinny but strong and nimble and won the championship by winning 100 m, 400 m, and one km running competitions for his school. The chief guest, Major General Singh, awarded the prizes. During the awards ceremony, the Major General asked Ramanuj about his aspirations. Ramanuj immediately responded that he wanted to fight for his country. Although the uniform Major General Singh wearing inspired his answer, the response impressed Major General Singh. He arranged for his scholarship and expenses through military funding.

Ramanuj's destiny took him away to a military career at Pune Military Academy, very different from his ancestor's line of work. During school years, Ramanuj's athletic body and agility made him popular among his peers because he always helped the team win many competitions. He was adept at mathematics and science.

After graduation, he joined the Indian Army Unit and fought in combat with Pakistan. At high altitude, his captain took a bullet in his leg. Ramanuj carried the captain and helped his unit get back safely. While retreating, he noticed an uneven camouflaged ground patch and discovered a huge stockpile of weapons and ammunition hidden under it by the Pakistani Army. His unit captured the stockpile and brought it back to the camp. The captain wrote a report that went to various divisions, including the Intelligence wing. Commander Sitaram Bhosle saw the report. Realizing the potential of Ramanuj, he arranged for his transfer to RIAW wing. In the beginning, Ramanuj had to face many derogatory circumstances because of his low caste.

"Can I come in, sir?"

Chaubeji did not even raise his head. "What do you want now? Don't you see I am busy," he shouted. "I'm not interested in wasting my time, looking at some stupid report. Complete your report by tomorrow and send it through the proper channels."

"Bloody *Bhangi* (one of the S.C.)... He comes here as if it is his Raj (domain) and I am supposed to help him," Chaubeji muttered so Ramanuj could hear him as he turned his back in frustration. "Damn the Keralite *Bhangis*," he cursed in a Punjabi dialect, "they grab the post claiming to be a minority class. Why do the minority low castes get the post, why not my candidate?" Chaubeji was expecting to hire his brother-in-law for that position. He was not happy when Commander Bhosle hired Ramanuj and put under him.

"Yes, sir," Ramanuj retreated. He burned inside. This upper caste officer was going to be his archenemy. He faced many such humiliations in the beginning.

The imprudent abuse meant for the low castes hurt Ramanuj's feelings. It was a part of the social system, a tradition of thousands of years without questions. It was his humble acquisition. A part of the Vedic scriptures, the Shruti (part of Vedas that directly came from God) had authorized this. *Manusmruti* (Hindu scriptures) placed his caste at the bottom of the social ladder. The Swamis and Mahagurus (teacher) had told his class to respect and obey the system and worship the Brahmins. Ramanuj was frustrated. He brushed the frustration aside and went to see Vinay Mehra, the immediate boss and his 'so-called' proper channel.

Kiran was at the Islamabad office growing bored with her mundane assignment, which was progressing at a slow pace. She never considered that her mundane assignment would soon go ballistic. When she received the call from Lisa, she was in the office. She immediately called Ruben, but his phone was off. She called the airport. Her flight was to leave in four hours, just enough time to go to her quarters, pack some clothes, and rush to the airport. Lisa had already called Ruben giving him information about

Kiran's landing time in New Delhi. She also called their local agent in New Delhi to pick up Kiran in case Ruben could not make it in time.

The day after next, four sad faces were sitting in Commander Bhosle's office at ISHWAR headquarters. Nirmala's eyes were red from crying. Kiran was sad but kept her composure. The Commander was surprised to see Nikhil's closest friends. He knew about the foreign correspondent, Ruben, though he had never heard his last name and did not envision him as Marathi. He was also aware of Miss Hopkins, the CIA agent, through his channels. Nevertheless, he could have never imagined in a million years that they were Nikhil's closest friends, or that one could say his closest family members, as in this peculiar case. The police inspector kept his promise and handed over the body two days later after the autopsy, along with the complete autopsy report and the bullet removed from Nikhil's body. They performed the funeral according to Hindu rites. Everyone present offered final prayers and then cremated Nikhil's body. Ruben pressed the button in the crematorium. The soul rose beyond to meet his parents – who were cruelly butchered in the hands of in- filtrators because of the irresponsible and reckless ruling of corrupt bureaucracy.

Chapter 24

Blow-Up

After the funeral, Ruben and Satish went to collect the ashes for immersion into the river Ganges. Nirmala stayed in the hotel room. Kiran stayed with Nirmala, calmed her down, and then went to see Commander Bhosle to get the complete information on the murder investigation. Ramanuj, Pranav, and Suhas were also there. Realizing their close-knit friendship, Commander Bhosle decided to share the information with Kiran, but did not include some details of the devastating effects of project SHIV the Destruction. He did not want anyone to know about it – not even his own agents – because a minor leak could cause major panic. He knew that the leak could be dangerous.

"I am sorry for your loss. Nikhil was also dear to all of us, so I understand how you feel."

"Do you know who is responsible for this?" Kiran inquired.

"We are working on it. A few leads show the connection with the terrorist group HuJI. I'll be frank with you, the matter is unusually grave and could become an international threat," Commander Bhosle responded.

"How are our friends at the CIA?" He suddenly asked.

The question startled her. She never anticipated that he would know about her work, but then realized that the Commander was the head of the Indian spy outfit, so, of course he would know her boss.

"Don't be surprised, during our joint operation in Pakistan, you worked with one of our agents," Commander added.

Kiran remembered the incident.

The Commander began narrating the events starting with the meeting and the brief information Nikhil provided about his project, the mechanism, explosion at the laboratory, and their findings.

"We'll do everything in our capacity to capture the murderers and recover the capsules within the boundaries of India. However, if we fail and they crossed the borders of India, it could very well become an international situation. My guess is that they will go into Pakistani Territory. If so, we may need help from the CIA. At this time, we have no knowledge whether the capsules are a real threat. The terrorist tried to copy the project information from the laptop, but I don't think they succeeded. Based on a talk with Nikhil, he assured that he had contrived to destroy the project details automatically in case someone tried to steal the capsules. I believed him. We lost the capsules, but I don't think the thieves got any secret information. Nevertheless, I will proceed with the assumption that the stolen capsules could pose a real threat to national security and will take appropriate measures as necessary to protect the Indian people," he paused and looked at Kiran.

"I am telling you all this because you are Nikhil's closest friend. He didn't have anyone in the world as close as you guys. I hope you will be discreet. Just one person could not organize a theft and murder of this latitude, neither a small organization. My gut feeling is telling me there has to be some international government influence behind this. I want you to be aware of that." He stopped.

Kiran got the gist of the seriousness. "May I ask you a question?" Kiran asked. Nikhil was her close friend and she wanted to be part of the investigation.

"Please, don't hesitate," Commander Bhosle responded.

"I want to be a part of the investigation team with Indian spy agents working on the case. Is it possible? Would you have any objections?" Kiran asked in anticipation.

"We would certainly appreciate your participation, it will help," Commander Bhosle hoped Kiran would ask to be involved.

"I suggest that you should call your supervisor and get approval."

Kiran was not sure how this would play out. The Commander was already thinking that Dr. Muller was a US scientist. He must have already communicated with his counterpart in the US by now and the CIA had to be aware of the facts. Therefore, there was no secrecy. She would be discreet and would provide needed help from the CIA if necessary.

Ruben, Kiran, Nirmala, and Satish left that afternoon for Mumbai with Nikhil's ashes.

* * * * *

Hamid, Fayida Lodi's son, spotted the strange men entering the apartment. His face expanded into a grin as he pointed to the open door of Fatima's apartment across the cluttered hallway to his mom. She had never seen these new faces. She was aware that Salman Khan had allowed his friends to stay during his absence. Fatima never liked the idea and tried to dissuade Salman of letting strange people stay in their home when he was not there. However, Salman could not refuse his childhood friends.

What a mess. Fayida wished the return of her friend, Fatima, with her newborn baby soon so these ugly looking faces would disappear. It would be fun to cuddle her baby; they are so tiny at that age. Fayida was daydreaming. She knew well it would not be that soon, Fatima was only four months into her pregnancy.

Recently, Salman's company changed his route between Agra and Jaipur. It was convenient for Fatima to move to her parent's house, so Salaman did not have to come all the way to Delhi to see her. Salman would be visiting Delhi every two weeks to collect his paycheck from the company. His friend found that out and decided to use his place as a temporary terrorist cell in his absence.

The two men were hanging posters of some semi-nude foreign actresses on the wall; the third guy was sitting across from them. Hamid watched them. Fayida did not want Hamid to see that. She glared at the two men, then, instinctively turned her attention away so as not to arouse suspicion. This time he tugged the sleeve of her blouse hard, she almost stumbled. She gave him a scolding glare, but he just grinned and wagged his finger excitedly toward them.

"They're bad," Hamid exclaimed. "They are carrying guns, Mom," Hamid said, still pointing fingers. Hamid was behind the apartment door, no one saw him from the other apartment.

Fayida craned her neck to stare almost straight up through the door. She glimpsed at the gun and some machines. She brought her attention back to her son, but she realized that Hamid was right. There was something fishy about those guys.

"I know – they're podicts!" Hamid was still looking at the guns and posters from behind the doors.

"What?" Fayida barked.

"Podicts…poster addicts! It's a quickie word." Hamid said with pride.

She smiled. Quickie was her son's latest preoccupation. The children got these ideas from the mobile phone messaging system. Over the last few weeks, Hamid bombarded her with his semisecret school language. Quickie apparently was the current craze throughout Delhi schools. Last month it was Harry Potter's magic wand and next month she was sure some different craze would emerge.

She thought again of those semi-nude posters and wished, not for the first time, that there was some way of making him grow up a bit slower. Such posters were becoming a part of the locale on the streets of Delhi. The Western influence and Bollywood mania were all around. There was no way to slow that down. The movie posters, depicting semi-nude dancing girls, or leading Bollywood actresses, barely covered, with actors showing the muscular six packs in the background, were hanging on the advertisement boards across the streets of Delhi. To add to the crass nature of the pictures, there were equally vulgar advertisements with semi-nude figures showing their legs or booty instead of the products that they were advertising. There was not an empty poster board left in the city. The harsh tone of filmy music filled the atmosphere almost day and night.

Over the past several weeks, all the local channels had been showing the stories of crimes and rapes. This disturbed Fayida, especially when she was raising a boy without a father. Hamid's father died in the Indo-Pakistan War. Hamid was only 2 years old. He didn't remember much about his father. Hamid was a late child. Fayida loved her husband. They were married for 14 years when he, the Muslim Indian, became *shahid* (martyr) in the war by the hands of another

Muslim-Pakistani soldier. She thought of remarrying again. The Muslim custom accepted it. However, raised in the old-fashioned Hindu surroundings, she had some reservations.

"What do you think they're doing?" Hamid asked, leaning out another precarious inch over the apartment door. Fayida decided the men had occupied enough of their time.

"It's none of our business." She gripped the nape of his collar and gently pulled him back into the apartment. "Come on, we've got some work to do. I want you to help me clean up the rooms."

"Awe, Mom! It's Saturday morning!"

"I know. Help me clean up and then haul garbage down to the garbage cans. After that, you can take off."

"I'm not a slave," he argued. "All my friends get to do whatever they want on weekends!"

"And so can you, as soon as you finish your chores."

"That's cruel!" Hamid whined.

She smiled with affection into the lively black eyes that reminded her of her late husband. He was a good-looking lad. He was still boyishly thin, but growing at a rate that sometimes startled her. Height wise, he was almost up to her shoulders. Moreover, the mop of tan- gled black hair added an extra couple of inches.

"Ya know," he began, in a subdued tone she recognized as being fraught with trickery, "I can probably take that junk down to the garbage can on the way to school Monday morning. It's almost in the same direction."

"No."

"It would make more sense to do it all in one trip. I could bike there in less than a half-hour and then cut straight over to the school."

Fayida slipped into one of her mildly disapproving frowns. "No. You've enough trouble waking up at the normal time on schooldays. Do it now."

He gave an exasperated sigh.

"Come on, let's get to work. The faster we get moving, the more time you'll have for yourself." She closed the apartment door.

It was one of those rainy season days in Delhi. Throughout the day, local news channels had been proclaiming the rain. The rain grew steadily throughout the afternoon. By 4 p.m., the air had become sticky and humid. It was cloudy with black and gray clouds across the sky, dissolving into one another and reemerging into shapes of an elephant or dinosaur. Sporadic thunderclaps roared between the glints of lightning. The lightning flashed, a large fissure blossomed in the clouds, scarlet-yellow lightning strobe the sky above.

"Did ya see that?" Hamid whispered.

Malini was watching the apartment in Chandani Chowk with Pranav. After the theft of the capsule devices at the GEETA facility, there was no traffic. The apartment was empty for two days. They heard some chatter today. Lightning flashed and another movement caught Malini's eyes. They were trying to hear the conversation. There was some talk about Salamat… Fahayat… north… pack… they heard the words weapon dealers... America... explosives. One of the guys mentioned explosion and something about copied information… computer… flash drive…, but due to severe weather, they heard the voice reception in patches. It was not that clear.

The rain slowed down and the wind-whipped downpour cascading in torrents across the porch stopped. They could hear the chatter from the apartment a little more clearly. The men in the apartment were talking about some mysterious plan. One of them mentioned Salman returning tomorrow and that they all had to get out of the apartment by early morning. Then another person appeared in dark clothing. He was carrying a bag in his hand. Malini's heart skipped a bit.

Fayida and Hamid heard the familiar voice of Salman from across the hall. Salman was mad to find people in his apartment that he did not know. He was arguing loudly. The discordant sound across the hall was audible through the rain. Malini and her crew also heard the argument. He caught them by surprise.

They heard the shot piercing through the evening clouds. It was loud and clear. Fayida grabbed Hamid's hand to prevent him from walking outside the door. The Secret Service agents from across the street rushed in fast. They all heard the exchange of gunfire. One of the Secret Service agents first in the door took a bullet and fell down, but before that, he shot one terrorist straight through his heart. From behind, Malini aimed and wounded another guy in his thigh, and fired again at the third guy. Her bullet grazed his leg, but the third terrorist grabbed a bag, threw a smoke bomb, and managed to escape from the back door in the midst of the smoke.

It was a mess in the apartment. Salman was dead, and so was the other terrorist. Malini checked the pulse of the Secret Service agent. He was dead, too. She called Ramanuj and heard the flashing siren of the police van. Ramanuj came immediately. They secured the area. The ambulance arrived. They bandaged the wounded terrorist and took him immediately to the hospital to remove the bullet. Hearing the sirens, apartment occupants came out like flies. Fayida recognized Farah Akram.

"What is she doing here?" Fayida wondered.

Malini came near Fayida, she was sobbing. Malini tried to console her, "I am Malini with the police, we were watching the apartment. Salaman and Fatima didn't know that their friends belonged to a terrorist gang."

Then Malini asked Fayida to call Fatima with the sad news.

Ramanuj told the inspector in charge to arrest the terrorist after they removed the bullet, put him in a secluded cell, and watch him for the night. During the surgery, they drugged the terrorist to remove the bullet, so Ramanuj decided to interrogate him the next day. Fayida immediately called Fatima's parent in the village and told them what happened.

Fatima could not bear the news; she had a miscarriage and lost the baby. One day later, with her parents, she arrived to claim the body. She was weak. After the funeral according to Muslim tradition, Malini talked with her and told her the story. Fatima became enraged. She wanted revenge and expressed her feelings bluntly to Malini.

"Is there anything I can do? I know Salamat and Fahayat and few other buddies. I also know their whereabouts in Kashmir. They leave in Dalsar Village near Udhampur in Kashmir." The rage was visible in her eyes.

Malini looked at her, "Wait here until I come back."

Malini went to Ramanuj and together they went to see Commander Bhosle. She described her conversation with Fatima to the Commander and Ramanuj and added, "Sir, she is young, healthy, and qualified. She has a strong motive. She wants revenge. She knows a few gang members of this terrorist group and their addresses. She could be useful in locating and identifying the culprits." She hesitated for a moment, "You told us the other day that there could be some international organizations behind this. Just in case, we could not recover the merchandise within our boundary, she could be an excellent double agent. She knows the language, the traditions, the mannerisms, and dress code of Muslims. She is mad enough. I believe it would be fair to give her a chance." Malini was convincing in her persuasion.

"How soon could she be ready?" The Commander asked.

"In a couple of days, she'll be okay."

"What about her parents?" The Commander inquired.

"I'll find out all the information from her, and make sure nothing gets compromised," Malini assured, Ramanuj also nodded.

Around 11 p.m. that night, *Mia* Zafar Ansari the deputy chief of the IBP called Balu Naidu at his house. He was drinking whiskey with his buddies. He excused himself and took the call in his bedroom.

"I'll deposit the $25,000 in your Swiss Bank account."

"What do you want me to do?" Naidu asked.

"Get rid of one of the prisoners in police custody," *Mia* Zafar Ansari told him.

"Make it $50,000 and consider it is done," Balu responded. He knew it was not a difficult job, things like that happened all the time to the people in police custody. The deputy chief accepted his demand – he expected Balu's greed.

Chapter 25

Timeline

New Delhi was warm and humid during midsummer, sometimes followed by torrential rains in the afternoon. Around
eight in the morning, the sun shined brightly outside the
prison. The atmosphere within the prison walls of the police station
was gloomy. The prison cells had a small hole to filter enough light
for inmates to know that the day had begun.

The prisoner brought in last night was in a secluded part of the
prison in the maximum-security section. The armed sub-
inspector accompanied the police constable that carried his
breakfast. What they saw when they opened the cell sent a chilling
shockwave through their spines. The prisoner was hanging from
the bar above.

"How could this happen? Where did he get the rope?" The sub-
inspector looked at the officer next to him. He called the inspector
in charge of the police station, secured the area, and informed the
RAW office about the incident.

Ramanuj arrived with his team quickly. He began the crime scene
investigation. They lowered the body on the ground. The medical ex-
aminer (ME), in his preliminary examination, determined the death
occurred around two to three hours earlier since the body was still
warm. Marks on the neck suggested possible strangulation. Someone
constricted his neck to suffocate him, and then hanged him after he
was dead. The ligature mark on the neck made by rope implied that
someone put the rope around his neck after he was dead. He ruled
out suicide. They took the body to the coroner's office for an autopsy
to determine the exact cause and time of death. The prisoner was the

only witness they had after the shootout at the apartment. Ramanuj thought, "It must be an inside job. Who could have done this?"

Ramanuj immediately called Commander Bhosle, "Sir, I have bad news to report. We found the terrorist that we caught yesterday hanging inside his cell. The initial examination concluded that it was a murder by strangulation. The hanging was done later to stage the scene of a suicide. I am looking at a prison log and interviewing everyone to find out about the killer. It looks like an inside job. I'll keep you informed."

Ramanuj looked to see who came last night in the prison log. There was one entry by the name Rangeela Pundu. He told the police inspector in charge to call every officer who was on duty last night.

The police constable that allowed Rangeela to go inside was a new cadre. He joined the police force only three months back. He was scared to death.

He told Ramanuj, "Rangeela had a note from Bada Sahib (big officer). He handed the note to me that I kept in the drawer. I thought it came from your office."

Ramanuj checked the drawer and found the note. The signature was unreadable. It was a fake note, and so was the name 'Rangeela Pundu.'

After carefully examining the fingerprints on the note and the artist picture drawn according to the police description, they found out that it belonged to a local hood, Jayaram Chauhan, a professional killer. The local businesspersons, leaders, and politicians usually hired this killer to clean their laundry. He lived near Dhobi Ghat, a slum area in Delhi, near the river Yamuna. They got his address. Ramanuj with Malini and other agent went to arrest him. Approaching his place near Dhobi Ghat, they heard some struggle. They got out of the car and ran toward his place. The place was on fire. They found his body lying on the ground and a couple of hoods running away in haste after hearing the sirens of the police car.

Malini and Ramanuj started to chase them. There were feces all around, the smell was too much to handle. Malini cursed the city developers. There were plans for beautifying slums in Delhi. Early in 2000, the government started plans for the Games Village to house the athletes and other sportspersons visiting Delhi during the 2010 Commonwealth Games. They started ambitious projects. The rays of hope seeped through the slum community. The games were over with a big bang. The politicians patted each other's backs and the hopes for the slum dwellers died. There was no progress. The project planners and organizers pocketed the money. Millions were left hanging to rot in their own feces on a long stretch of Yamuna floodplain.

Malini and Ramanuj began chasing the hoodlums between the huts, avoiding stray dogs, cats, half-naked children, and cows inhabiting the slums. There were too many bends and curves. Aiming shots at the hoods while avoiding innocents was a difficult job, even for a trained agent. But in that chaos, Malini managed to fire a shot at one of the hoods. He fell down and the other disappeared through the sectors of small huts. The bullet hit him in his abdomen, pouring his blood onto the pavement. Malini tried to stop the bleeding.

"Who sent you?" She asked him.

"B…al…u…S…a…h…i…b," he barely said before dying.

They immediately called the fire department. Fortunately, the fire station was not too far. The fire engine came fast and the fire fighters extinguished the fire. The police found Jairam Chauchan's mobile in the rubble – he was dead. The hoods strangled him. The fingerprints on his neck belonged to the same man, Kalu Pillai, shot by Malini. She took charge of the mobile and took it to Suhas of the EIW Wing.

The technician from EIW downloaded all entries from the mobile to his computer. It was one of those pre-paid unregistered mobile phones. A couple of entries belonged to Minister Balu Naidu's household. The cabinet Minister Balu Naidu was a strong suspect. However, that was not enough proof to arrest him. Based on their database, the Minister had no connection with HuJI. Sure, he had contacts with many hoods, but so had other corrupt politicians in India.

"There is no way to pursue all of them. After all, it is a secular country run by such politicians. That's the misfortune of the democratic secular India. The use of the word 'democracy' was a mockery," Malini thought.

The Inspector from CBI went to see the Minister to inquire about the death of Jairam Chauhan and Lalu Pillai. The Minister's PA answered that Jairam Chauhan was a worker for the United Front. They had no knowledge of his connection with the murder. That is the job of the police.

He chastised them, "Instead of asking a distinguished Minister question, you should concentrate on finding the killers." He also added a few more words the CBI Inspector didn't want to convey to his boss or Commander Bhosle.

The surfacing of Balu Naidu's name brought another name to Commander Bhosle's attention – Dr. Bhujang Iftekhar. He joined GEETA because of influence from Minister Balu Naidu and Suvarna Khoja, the Head of UFI. Suvarna Khoja might have supported Balu Naidu for the hiring of Dr. Bhujang to GEETA on a minority basis to appease him. Political favors like that were common.

"You scratch my back, and I'll scratch yours. That is the motto. Nevertheless, what could be the motive of Minister Naidu? Balu Naidu is a corrupt Hindu. I know that, but I cannot prove it," the Commander was thinking in soliloquy. "Is he under duress? Is some-one blackmailing him? What is the connection?"

He asserted from the beginning that this was not just HuJI's job; it was a much bigger endeavor. They had prior knowledge of the project. "Who could be better than Dr. Bhujang to provide information to HuJI? Is he the missing link? Dr. Frank Muller is here on friendly exchange. It is his job to report progress to his US counterparts. They have no reason to steal through HuJI, a Muslim terrorist organization." He discarded Dr. Muller from the suspect list. He decided to watch Bhujang and Minister Balu Naidu closely.

Dr. Muller called his counterparts in the US and gave them all the details. Since there was not much to do for him in India and his one-year term was completed, his counterparts in the US called him back.

"May I come in, sir?" Ramanuj stood outside Commander Bhosle's cabin, Room 911, the most coveted room in the ISHWAR Facility.

Bhosle twitched out of reverie, "Yes Ramanuj, come in."

"Is this a good time to talk? I have an update for you. You will have the report in a few hours." Ramanuj asked politely.

He started going through the sequence of events:

- Nikhil's murder
- The explosion
- Capsule devices stolen
- Possible HuJI connection with Fatima's apartment
- The CBI watching Fatima's apartment
- Salman and Fahayat of HuJI heading east
- Who has the capsules?
- Death of Salman and one terrorist in apartment
- Second terrorist with the bag escaped
- Third terrorist died in the prison cell
- His murderer killed in Dhobi Ghat slums
- Before dying, the terrorist/hood named Balu Sahib in his last breath
- Naidu's household denying any connection

"Based on this timeline, it is a fair assessment that it was a well-planned plot to steal the devices. They had the prior knowledge. The unrelated events like involvement of HuJI, murder of the terrorist within the prison cell by the killer who has no connection with HuJI or other terrorist gangs, the possible connection to the politician shows a much bigger conspiracy than we originally thought it was. The person or group of people behind this are making sure that the right hand does not know what the left hand is doing, and vice versa," Ramanuj looked at his boss for comments.

"I agree, there are too many variables. We need to examine them separately, what do you suggest?" Commander Bhosle looked at Ramanuj.

"They could be misleading us," Ramanuj added.

"Hmm...," Bhosle nodded.

"There are many loose ends," Ramanuj responded in frustration.

"Is there any recent news from the informants about Salamat and Fahayat Khan?" Bhosle asked.

"I am glad you asked that. The first spotting is in Patna where they met with others, including Latif Ahamadi. He is one of the local leaders of HuJI in the State of Bihar and he is from Kashmir." Ramanuj responded.

There was tap on the door. Suhasini Gupta, an agent from the EIW Wing, entered the room. She informed that her confidential informant (CI) told her Fahayat Khan and Salamat Khan met in Kalimpong before going their separate ways.

The situation was getting more complicated and they had no leads.

"What do you suggest, Ramanuj?" Bhosle asked.

"We should pursue our first two leads, Salamat and Fahayat Khan, and keep an eye on Latif Ahamadi. Being a HuJI leader, he could be important," Ramanuj stated.

"Let's start doing that," Commander Bhosle affirmed.

"Before that, I want to ask your permission to arrange for Malini to come aboard RIAW? I talked to Bhakhtiar of CBI. He has no objection. I would appreciate if you could call him and his boss to make it official. She is familiar with the job. She is a trained agent. She can train and take responsibility for Fatima," Ramanuj looked at Commander Bhosle. He was not sure about the Commander's reaction; he was known to be ticklish on such issues.

"That's an excellent idea. In fact, I was thinking the same, Let me call her boss."

The Commander called and made the necessary arrangements for Malini to join the RIAW on a temporary basis.

"There is one more task, Ramanuj."

"Yes sir?"

"Put a tail on Dr. Bhujang before you and Malini leave to chase the terrorists. Minister Naidu's name keeps popping up and Dr. Bhujang Iftekhar joined because of his influence. I do not know what the connection is, but you know my gut feeling for this whole affair. Who would have told HuJI? I am not implying anything, but better to be safe than sorry. Let us not leave any stones unturned. Be discreet, I don't want anyone to know."

"I'll do that, sir. Do you have any other suggestions?" Ramanuj asked.

"No. Not right now, go and get the terrorists," Commander Bhosle said.

He reminisced about the previous experience when he worked under Commander Badrinarayan Dwivedi, who was the previous head of ISHWAR. Bhosle arrested a young Muslim student. He thought the student was with a terrorist gang. During interrogation, the student broke down and confessed that some lecturer was trying to recruit him in the terrorist gang, but he was not willing. He gave the name as Lecturer Ulfatkahn. He also pointed to personal assistant (PA) of the Defence (Defense) Minister.

The previous Prime Minister (PM), Sundara Khoja, highly revered the Defence (Defense) Minister. The PA was a high caste Brahmin, and there was no reason to suspect him. Everyone thought the student was creating a story to save his skin. No one thought of putting a tail on this PA or talking to the lecturer. During the war with Pakistan, the Indian Army chief realized that the enemy already had the prior knowledge of the covert missions. It was a puzzle for him. Except for the Indian Army Chief and the Defence Minister, no one knew those covert missions. Even the soldiers had no prior knowledge until the final moment.

One evening, Bhosle was in Old Delhi perusing a suspect. He noticed the PA entering one of the sleeping terrorist cell houses. Bhosle was surprised to find him there. He followed him and saw that he was passing a sheet of paper to a known terrorist. Bhosle recorded the operation with a spy camera that he carried. Unfortunately, one of the local hoods recognized Bhosle and reported that to the gang inside the house. To save his skin, Bhosle had to run from the place. Immediately, after returning to the office, he issued a warrant, but it was too late. The PA disappeared. No one knew his whereabouts. His parents had no idea where he could be. Two days later the Rajasthan State police found the PA's body near Jaisalmer close to the Pakistan border. The mystery of the compromised covert operations solved. Bhosle wished he should have listened to the student earlier. He kept the name of the lecturer in the black list as a member of SIMI. Due to lack of proof, he could not take any action. It would have been considered harassment of a minority under the constitution of Secular India. Later, he released the student after getting more information about the local terrorist gang that resulted in arresting a few more members. The next week, they found the dead body of the student in the Chandani Chowk area of Old Delhi. They had a few suspects, but they could not prosecute them.

The next evening, they tailed Dr. Bhujang Iftekhar going to the house of Professor Haji Ulfatkhan. He was a professor of physics in Delhi University.

"Americans are asking about the capsules. They want to know our plans," Dr. Bhujang told him.

"You tell Dr. Muller in private that they will sell the capsules to BAT Company in the US. They will negotiate the cost," the professor told Dr. Bhujang.

The agent did not know what transpired in the meeting. He could not hear the discussion, but immediately reported the meeting back to Pranav from the TIW Wing. Ramanuj was somewhere in the Northeast region chasing after the capsules. There was no reason to suspect Dr. Bhujang because he was visiting a fellow professor from the same field. However, Professor Haji Ulfatkhan was another story. Commander Bhosle had a strong suspicion that Haji Ulfatkhan belonged to SIMI and helped recruit young college students into the SIMI organization. They tapped his telephone.

The news of Dr. Muller going back to the US spread through GEETA fast. No one was in a mood to arrange a send off because of Nikhil's death. Dr. Bhujang gave the message of Professor Ulfatkhan to Dr. Muller.

Chapter 26

Char Dham Pilgrimage

R uben called his father from the Middle East about the murder of Nikhil before leaving to attend Nikhil's funeral in Delhi. It was sad news. Both Pralhad and Olivia were fond of Nikhil and they could see the effect of this grief on Ruben. The summer was just starting. The school was running a few summer classes, but besides that, Pralhad was not busy. He and Olivia decided to go to India to be with Ruben. Packing was not a big problem, getting the ticket for Mumbai was a big problem, especially during summer. However, a couple of tickets in business class were available for the next day. Pralhad had close to half a million frequent-flyer miles in his account. Almost using twice the amount of frequent-flyer miles, they got the tickets on a direct flight from Chicago to Mumbai. They both left for Mumbai after calling his brother to come to the airport to pick them up.

Ruben, Kiran, Nirmala, and Satish were back in Mumbai with Nikhil's ashes. Ruben was surprised to see his parents. It gave him much needed solace. Nirmala collected her children from her parents, and they went home. Kiran went with Nirmala and Satish.

The next day, they all went to see Ruben, Uncle Pralhad, and Aunt Olivia. They all were depressed. No one said a word. Then Ruben talked to his father, Pralhad, about the immersion of Nikhil's ashes in the River Ganges.

He asked him, "Dad, do you remember how you used to tell me about *Char Dham Yatra* (a pilgrimage to four holy places as stipulated in Hindu scriptures)?"

"Yes, I remember. In fact, this is a perfect time to go there. Why are you asking?" Pralhad asked, he sensed the urgency in Ruben's voice.

"You haven't been there before, have you?" Ruben said.

"I went to few places but not all," Pralhad started thinking.

Ruben was depressed and this would be a good time to visit the holy places. He could perform the immersion ritual at the ghats (banks) of the River Ganges in Haridwar. It would provide peace of mind.

"Would you like to go? You can immerse the ashes in the waters of the River Ganges at Haridwar," Pralhad said.

"Can we go there? I would certainly like to do this with both of you," Ruben was emotional.

"That's a great idea. We'll go to the *Char Dham Yatra* of North. We can start from Haridwar; perform the immersion ritual at the banks of the River Ganges, then visit Yamunotri, Gangotri, Kedarnath, and Badrinath. Then we can return via Rishikesh," Pralhad was showing off his knowledge of the places in India.

Nirmala liked the idea, "Uncle this is a great plan, and while you are there, perform all veneration and rituals with Olivia *Kaku* (Paternal Aunt). I am sure Ruben and Olivia *Kaku* will enjoy."

"Why don't you all join us? It will be a nice company. I am sure Satish can take a couple of weeks off," Pralhad asked.

Olivia also requested, "Kiran why don't you come with us? You'll have Nirmala's company."

"I would love to, but I have to be at our Dubai branch to complete the seminar I started. I have to fly back immediately," Kiran excused.

As a CIA agent, she wanted to investigate the murder. From Commander Bhosle's account, it was a serious terrorist act so she wanted to return to Delhi as soon as possible.

Olivia looked at Nirmala and Satish.

"No, Kaku, this time the three of you go there. This is your time; spend it together. *Char Dham* pilgrimage is the perfect place to visit. Ruben will get peace of mind. *Kaku* you will love this. I know you had been to couple of places before, but this will be an excellent trip for you all. We Hindus have blind faith and these sacred places are always in our heart. For Ruben, it's an excellent study tour of Indian pilgrimages," tears started rolling from Nirmala's eyes.

She was thinking about Nikhil, her friend who was like her older brother. The monsters in Bengal butchered his parents, and then, years later, they killed him. At least his soul would travel with his best friend, Ruben, and visit all the sacred places from his motherland that he missed when he was alive.

Looking at Nirmala's tearful eyes and sadness on Ruben and Kiran's faces, Pralhad remembered some stanzas from Bhagavat Geeta.

Santosh was an expert on Bhagavat Geeta. Pralhad thought that the discussion of soul and theory of the Supreme Soul and its relationship to individual, the *Adhyatmic* discourse from Geeta would help them get the peace of mind badly needed.

"Santosh *Dada* (older brother), I have a request for you."

Santosh looked at him with a questioning gaze, "Yes Pralhad *Bhai* (younger brother), what's on your mind?" Everyone was looking at Pralhad.

"Ruben is familiar with Geeta. He heard about it in bits and pieces in the Indian Temple discussions in Chicago. This will be a good time to hear your comments on all chapters of Geeta to put everyone's mind at ease. This is also morning, perfect time to listen to the discourse on Geeta. Would you please?" Pralhad said pleadingly.

Santosh was an accountant by profession and also known as pandit (learned person) in the local community.

They all sat down. Santosh began, "Bhagvat Geeta is the essence of Hinduism or *Sanaatan Dharm* and covers various aspects of life. There are 18 chapters or *Adhyay* in Geeta. The knowledge and the theories presented in Geeta are stimulating. Geeta explains various doctrines of Hinduism and its applications. It briefly covers the theories discussed in Upanishad. It is a holy book for all Hindus. Geeta, the short form for Bhagvat Geeta, leads us through the conflict. It provides the supportive discussion for our conflicts and causes. It will unveil the ignorance for us to discover the path of truth through the darkness. The experience is unique. The satisfaction is ours to seek and enjoy. Geeta shows us the way of salvation."

Then he began describing each *Adhyay* (chapter):

The first chapter describes Arjun's dilemma on the battlefield. He had a conflict in his mind, whether to fight or put the weapon down.

He was indecisive. He questioned himself. He describes his dilemma to Shree Krushn (Krishna) and asks for his guidance.

In our day-to-day life, we come across many conflicting situations. We cannot decide. We are confused. We are in a similar situation like Arjun. We have the same dilemma like Arjun. Geeta is the advice from Shree Krushn to Arjun on the battlefield of Kurukshetra and to all the humankind. Shree Krushn kindles the path of ignorance and confusion with the light of knowledge.

The second chapter explains the doctrine of materialism. Shree Krushn talks about materialism, discusses the knowledge of Soul and body. It is the path of analytical study of matter, Soul, and   perception of God based on experimental knowledge and philosophy. Arjun is a symbol here. Shree Krushn knows that the whole world is looking for an answer. The indecisive conflicting situation on the battlefield of Kurukshetra is a metaphor for the struggle that we all face in our daily life. The answer is there, but we do not see it.

Shree Krushn discusses with Arjun, his problems that concerns life and death.

The death liberates the Soul from the ephemeral body. The Soul is indestructible. It was never born, nor, will it ever die. The Soul is unborn, eternal; it never ceases to exist. Body goes through this cycle of birth and death. For birth, death is unavoidable, for death, rebirth is inevitable. One is neither the cause of death nor the creation.

Therefore, Shree Krushn metaphorically, through the medium of Arjun, advises the whole world, "Do not grieve, do your duty."

Then to emphasize the concept, he focuses on Karm Yog, functions and duties, and explains the nature of rewards and retributions. We all work. We do not decide the remuneration. Someone else does that for us. Since we have no control, why should we worry over results? If we keep our expectations high, we are disappointed if they are not fulfilled. If we keep low anticipation, we are in for a surprise. In either case, one goes through extremes and loses peace of mind.

Arjun listened intently to Shree Krushn.

In the third chapter, Shree Krushn explains the Karm Yog (path of action). There are two ways to attain salvation, through the path of action (Karm Yog) and the path of knowledge (*Dnyan* Yog). Inaction is also a kind of action. Neither abstaining from action nor renunciation from it shall achieve freedom or perfection. Therefore, do your duties, do not expect the rewards (fruits) or retribution, bequeath the results of your action to God, and attain salvation; this is the path of action (Karm Yog).

Knowing thy Soul, that transcends senses of organ, minds, and intellect, overcome the enemies within. This realization leads toward the path of knowledge (*Dnyan* Yog).

The path of action (Karm Yog) eventually leads toward the path of knowledge (*Dnyan* Yog).

In the fourth chapter, Shree Krushn continues with the explanation of the transmigration of Soul and HIS purpose for incarnation as a restorer of law and order of *Dharm* (Religious Beliefs). There is a famous quote from Geeta. One will find the reference to this quote in various contexts. The quote - the revered statement states, "Whenever calamity (evil) occurs in Bharat (India), I'll reincarnate to protect people and restore *Dharm*, and law and order."

Then he goes on describing Karm Yog. The person who understands his duties and realizes the stage of equanimity is not liable for the results of his deeds because he is following his assigned path and performing his duties without attachments. The one who sees eqanimity in action and inaction knows the truth. Those who follow their path attain the divine knowledge, peace, and salvation. He assures equal chance to all of us to attain salvation based on Karm. He emphasizes the importance for the fulfillment of the obligations, and provides Arjun, and the whole world, the guidance to fulfill their duties and obligations.

In the fifth chapter, Shree Krushn goes on describing the difference between Karm Yog and Karm *Sanyas* Yog. The Karm Yog is where one follows the path of action. The one who follows this path with total detachment and complete faith is a Karm Yogi. In this process, Karm Yogi achieves equanimity of mind and renounces his desires with the realization of the True nature of God. This state is Karm *Sanyas* Yog. This is a repetition of what he said earlier. However, this reiteration emphasizes the concept.

In the sixth chapter, Shree Krushn explains the process of the eightfold Yog system that eventually leads to Self-realization and Salvation. He cautions that the wavering mind may need a longer time and more practice. However, in spite of this, one will eventually learn to detach oneself from the results of the actions by constant practice and achieve proficiency in Yog.

In the seventh chapter, he discusses the knowledge and beyond knowledge (concept of *para and apara*) that is not known.

The knowledge (*para*) is a day-to-day thing that we can visualize and experience. We visualize the perceptible nature of God through deities or through other similar iconic symbols. It is a mental concept of an unknown entity.

'I' (*Aham*) is the nature of the Supreme Soul, known as Almighty, omniscient, omnipotent, omnipresent in nature. It transcends all our imaginations. It is beyond our perception (beyond knowledge - *Apara*). It is not describable. The obscure phenomenon producing the effect of covering the Supreme Soul is the cloud of ignorance (*Yogmaya*). The cloud of ignorance (*Yogmaya*) covers the Supreme Soul. One can realize the imperceptible nature, the presence of the Supreme Soul (*BRAHMAN*), through manifestations.

Therefore, Shree Krushn advises Arjun to overcome delusion, tear the veneer of ignorance, and realize Supreme Soul's transcendental nature.

In the eighth chapter, he elaborates these notions in detail and explicates the primal creative aspect and nature (*Purush and Prakruti*). The primal creative aspect and nature are elements of creation. The incu- bation of the primal seed of desire with energy is creation. Henceforth, Shree Krushn is entering into the realm of the knowledge of Supreme Soul and its relation to individual known as *Adhyatm*.

In the ninth chapter, he shades light on *Rajyog*, Vedic Philosophy and more insight about salvation. Gradually, he propels Arjun toward the Supreme Soul. Here, Shree Krushn clarifies the Supreme omnipotent nature and the cosmogony.

In the tenth chapter, he reiterates the previous discussion with a stronger emphasis on voluntary approach and not desire to achieve salvation because desire has a connotation of greed. Through introspection, one knows the truth and can control the desire to continue the quest for salvation.

In the eleventh chapter, Shree Krushn reveals his universal cosmic manifestation. Arjun experiences the cosmic vision of the Supreme Soul – the perceptible divine appearance that was a billion fold radiant. He had no illusions or dilemma. Arjun realized the implied concept of soul. Neither the Soul is the doer nor have any desires.

In later chapters, Shree Krushn explains the path of devotion, the cosmic nature of existence, materialistic elements of body, and the material nature of Virtue, Passion, and Ignorance.

This is a short summary. There are many books available to get better insight." Santosh completed his commentary.

Olivia thought this was a brilliant religious discourse. However, she still had some doubts. She thought Hinduism was all about peace. However, the conflict described in Geeta was on the battlefield. Knowing the story of Mahabharat, she knew that Shree Krushn was asking Arjun to fight.

She asked, "If Hinduism is all about peace, doesn't this message conflict with the philosophy of Hinduism?"

Santosh smiled, "I am glad you asked this question. Let me briefly review some background here. Hindu culture is old. The Vedic Scriptures and *Purans* (Mythology) give some glimpses in this culture and philosophy. If one looks at the *Puranic Scriptures*, the main ones are Ramayan and Mahabharat, what do they allude? In Ramayan, Ram kills the evil Ravan who kidnapped his wife. He does not say to Ravan, okay you kidnapped my wife, now you can also kidnap my brother's wife who is in Ayodhya, does he? His *Dharm* is to protect good and destroy the evil. The message is, one has to destroy the evil. One cannot negotiate peace with it. In Mahabharat, Pandav destroyed the wicked monarchy of Kaurav. Yes, they did try to make peace with them. However, when wickedness crossed the limit, no mercy, no peace, they destroyed the wickedness. Arjun's

Dharm is to protect good and destroy evil." Santosh paused and looked at them.

Everyone was listening attentively.

He continued, "Let us go to Indian History. Chandragupt killed wicked monarch Nanda. Samrat Ashok was in the big battle in which almost 200,000 warriors died. To make the story short, let us come to recent history. In the sixteenth century, King Chhatrapati Shiwaji Maharaj fought with tyrant Muslim Kings to reestablish the Hindu Kingdom. In the eighteenth century, Queen of Jhansi fought for freedom with the wicked forces of British monarchy. Do you see peace in any of these examples? There are some stanzas in Vedic Scriptures as in all other religions throughout the world have about peace, that doesn't mean Hinduism tolerates wickedness and corruption.

The corrupt secular style government preaches peace. This is an extension of Lord Macaulay's teaching from the early nineteenth century to make Hindus impotent. Unfortunately, Hindus bought it. Our Swamijis and Gurus (Teacher) are supposed to defend the rightful edicts of Hinduism. Sure, peace is one of the edicts, but so is the elimination of evil. Instead of defending rightful edicts of Hinduism, they continue to preach the haphazard philosophy of peace only, in collusion with corrupt politicians for their own gain and popularity. That is the sad part. It supported politician's mission of secularity. They spread the philosophy all over the world to realize monetary gain and followers. People followed them blindly. They forgot the message of Mahabharat where Pandav destroyed wickedness by killing Kaurav. They forgot that in Ramayan, Ram killed Ravan. He didn't make peace with him.

Hinduism is not only about peace. Hinduism was never about peace only. It covers the pragmatic aspects of the reality of life. It covers various aspects. Like any other religion, it promotes peace, only after the destruction of wickedness and corruption."

Olivia nodded; she got her answers. The glimpse into Hindu philosophy and history was informative. Pralhad was glad Santosh summarized Geeta and Hindu philosophy in this short discourse.

Pralhad thanked Santosh Dada and added, "In the US, I attended seminars on Hinduism and heard discourses from Swamijis. They always preached that all religions are the same. Dada's lecture gave some answers. For example, take Hindu, Muslim, and Christian couples, say from Kashmir, Saudi Arabia, and Spain; and their wives just delivered babies. I bring all three babies out and ask the fathers to choose their own child from those three; you realize how difficult it would be. Let us look at another example. If I take a blade and bleed them a little, and then bring their blood back and ask them to select their blood, can they do that? No, they cannot do that. The color of the blood is the same. The question is if God has not made the difference, then why should we?"

Pralhad saw the puzzled looks of their faces.

"I agree we are all same. There are no differences. However, we forget we are born in different parts of the world, and for centuries and millennia, we were groomed in different cultures, traditions, practices, and customs. The God is the same, but we have different methods to approach salvation. Although our final goal is the same, not all religions are the same. Hinduism conveys concepts of Karm, Yog, Maya (Illusion), and Dharm. No other religion has these concepts. Methods and practices vary from region to region. Those variances coupled with greed, corrupt mind, and desire for dominance along with a few other undesirable human qualities eventually culminated into the fight for the territorial dominance and created the chaos that we see today. If we conceive these ingrained inculcations, it will allow us to realize our differences and help us to live in peace, instead of shooting the breeze about all religions are same. No matter how much we try, there are always some human tendencies, which will continue to make life difficult. Nevertheless, the statements like all religions are the same create confusion, and some take advantage." Pralhad concluded.

Nirmala got up, "Dad, I have a comment. It is not about violence or non-violence. Recently, I was watching a show about the Queen of Jhansi. There was a scene where she had been trying to make peace between Hindus and Muslims when the British were provoking the Hindus and Muslims to fight against each other similar to the present day communal riots that take place in India at regular intervals. What caught my attention was that she was holding two flags, one saffron-color Hindu flag, and one green-color Muslim flag. She was saying that one day Hindus and Muslims would unite and drive the

British out. The way she was holding the flags against the clouds from the sky gave an appearance of our national tri-color flag, saffron at the top, white in the middle, and green at the bottom representing both Hindus and Muslims together. I have two questions. The first question is if the intention of the flag is to have a united India, then why did they divide the continent of India in 1947 and why did our leaders allow that?

Second question is, after the division of the country in 1947, Pakistan became the Muslim Country, why didn't the remaining part of India be Hindu, Hindustan, or Hindu Rashtra? Why did they make itsecular?"

His daughter's question stunned Santosh. He was glad that the new generation is thinking about it, "Honey, I don't have the answer. We have been looking for the answer for so many decades."

He looked at Olivia, "Olivia, tell me, the United States of America is the only country to have defined itself as Judeo-Christian. It has always combined secular government with a society based on religious values. The administration supports all religion. You have churches, synagogues, Hindu *Mandir* (temples), Muslim mosques, and places of worship for other communities. You all live happily under one flag with one law like any other democratic country. No one bothers you, and officially, no one discriminates. Am I correct?"

Olivia nodded.

"Do they allow loud call for prayers (Adhan) five times a day?"

"I haven't heard," Olivia answered.

"In India, laws are different for different minorities. Muslims can have four wives. They can utter word Talaq (divorce), Talaq, Talaq in front of Mullah and divorce their wives. They don't have to go to court."

"Are you sure Santosh Dada?" Pralhad intercepted.

Santosh went to his desk and took a piece of paper out of the drawer that described the official copy of the Indian Muslim Marriage Act. He showed that to all.

The Indian Muslim Marriage Act is based on the Indian Muslim marriage law.

As per this act, marriage or *"Nikah"* between an Indian Muslim groom and bride is a civil contract that both the groom and the bride agree to.

Some key features of the Indian Muslim Marriage Act are listed below:

- The act applies only to Indian Muslim men and Indian Muslim women.
- A Muslim marriage is a civil contract in which there is a propposal (*Ijab*), usually by the bride and an acceptance (*Qubul*), usually by the groom.
- A Kazi (Qazi) is not necessary for the marriage to take place. The proposal (*Ijab*) and acceptance (*Qubul*) in the presence of two adults qualifies as a legal wedding under the act.
- Muslim marriage between certain set of people is not allowed. These include blood relatives, relations by marriage, with two sisters, with a foster mother, if the man already has four wives, if the man and women were previously married and have divorced, but the woman has not remarried, etc.
- Indian Muslim men can have up to four wives, provided he treats all of them equally.

Unlike the other Indian Marriage Laws, as per the Indian Muslim Marriage Act registration of the marriage is not compulsory. The Kazi who has performed the marriage can issue a "Nikahnama" which is a marriage certificate.

Olivia was shocked.

Santosh Dada Continued, "They allow Adhan, the loud call of prayers, from the mosque five times a day, but if a Hindu has to do a *Puja* and procession in the open with *mantra*, he has to take the permission from the police department. This disparity in law is wrong. Instead of secular India, this should be Hindu Rashtra-Hindustan known as Bharat Desh. All of us belonging to a different religion and culture can live happily under one law in Hindusthan or Bharat Desh like Americans live in US or Australians live in Australia. You don't need a secular country to live happily. A democratic Hindu Rashtra can achieve that just the way it is in the US, UK, Australia, or Canada.

This is all I can say. It is up to young generations to resolve and bring closure," Santosh concluded.

* * * * *

Ruben, Olivia, and Pralhad flew by plane to Delhi, hired an A/C taxicab with a driver, and went to Haridwar. Haridwar is a large and overcrowded city. Haridwar lies under the feet of Shiv's hills, called Shivalik. It is the doorway to the sources of the River Ganges (*Ganga*) and the River Yamuna. The Ganges emerges to touch the plains from the mountains. The water in the River Ganges was not that clear because the soil from the upper regions flowed down into it.

The next day, they went to a place called Har-Ki-Pauri to perform the ceremony and to immerse Nikhil's ashes in the River Ganges. It was the middle of the week and not so crowded. Then they visited *Mansa Devi Mandir* (temple) via cable cars that offered a picturesque view of the entire city. In the evening after sunset, they visited the banks of the River Ganges to witness the *Arti Puja* (the worshiping ceremony of the River *Ganga*). The floating ritual is a ritual of placing the lighted oil lamps on the river to float, a moving scene to watch. Olivia had never seen anything like this before.

In the morning, they started for Barkot via Kempty Fall, a stunningly beautiful fall. It is near the hilly tracks of Northern India near hill station of Mussoorie. The ravishing landscapes, gushing water of the sacred Yamuna River and apple orchards in the backdrop of the snow-covered Banderpoonch Peak of the Himalayan range radiating with a glint of faded orange shade in the morning sun took their breath away.

Suhas Gupta was tailing Latif Ahamadi, but near Kempty fall, two of Latif's hoods attacked her, and Latif dodged her tail. Ruben saw that and recognized Suhas from the EIW Wing of ISHWAR. He aggressively dodged forward and kicked one of the hoods. The crowd gathered around and chased the hoods away.

Ruben's parent did not see the commotion. They were climbing up the fall just coming up. She greeted Ruben and his family. Ruben introduced her as an employee of the laboratory where Nikhil was working. She made an excuse and left immediately to send an encrypted message to the office via her iPhone. Her message to the office confirmed Latif's whereabouts and his intention to head toward Kashmir. They alerted Udhampur Branch near Jammu.

The next day they traveled to Yamunotri, the origin of the sacred river Yamuna. After the holy dip in the thermal springs *Surya Kund*, Pralhad and Olivia performed the Puja Ceremony (Veneration). There is a rock pillar called *Divya Shila*. They offered their worship to the pillar before entering the Yamunotri *Mandir*. Later, they enjoyed the view of glaciers that surrounded the area.

Then they headed toward Gangotri. On the way, they visited *Prakteshwar* cave and *Mandir* of *Shree Vishwanath* where they saw the massive iron trident of *Bhagvan Shree Shiv*. They took a halt for the night at a place called *Uttarakshi*. The early morning drive brought them to Gangotri, the spiritual source of Hindu's most sacred river *Ganga* (River Ganges) in the backdrop of the scenery of Garhwal, which is the home of the Garhwali people. Garhwal is in the Himalayas, surrounded by Tibet on the north, Kumaon region on the east, Himachal Pradesh on the northwest and Uttar Pradesh in the south.

They all took a holy dip in the sacred River Ganga. The water was cold. Olivia and Pralhad just took one dip. Before coming out of the water Pralhad looked to the north, put his palms together (namskar) and offered prayers and reverence to Shree Shiv. For some inexplicable reasons, tears dripped down from his eyes. Ruben saw the tears. He knew the agony and pain his dad experienced for leaving *Matru Bhumi* (motherland). Ruben realized that those tears expressed his pain. It is a farewell to his ancestors from millennia back. Then they all went to the temple and performed *Puja* (Ceremonial prayers) and relaxed for a while in the heavenly surroundings of Gangotri Glacier.

It took them two days to reach Kedarnath from Gangotri, Uttarakshi via Guptakshi. It was a relaxing journey and a scenic drive. They were in a reverent mood, almost meditative. It was an incredible experience through the picturesque snow-covered peaks, lush green valleys, and the rivers snaking through. There are so many attractions on the way like Kashi Vishwnath *Mandir* and Ardh Narinateshwar (the image of dancing Shree Shiv in the half-female and half-male form) *Mandir*.

The morning drive to Gaurikund was refreshing. Kedarnath is near Chorabari glacier, the head of the river Mandakini flanked by breath-taking snow-capped peaks in the most remote side of the Himalayas. The Kedarnath *Mandir* (temple) is not directly accessible by road. They all had to trek from *Gaurikund*. *Bhagwan Shree* Shiv mani-fested in the form of *Jyotirlingam* (symbolic representation in a stone structure of God Shree Shiv). The Pandavas of the Mythological story of Mahabharat of unknown date built the original temple according to the folklore. It is an impressive stone edifice built of massive stone slabs over a large rectangular platform. The present *Mandir*, built by Adi Shankaracharya, stands next to the site of an earlier *Mandir*. It is more than thousand years old. Outside the *Mandir* door, a large statue of the Nandi Bull stands as the guard. They performed *Puja* in the *Mandir*. Standing in the middle of a wide plateau surrounded by lofty snow-covered peaks, the Kedarnath is a majestic sight.

The next day, in the early morning, they started for Badrinath via Pipalkot. It was a long journey. On the way, there are many sacred attractions. They reached Badrinath by evening and settled in a hotel. However, they encountered a slight glitch on their way. The car broke down. There was a passenger bus, taking pilgrims to Badrinath. The bus gave them a lift. It was uncomfortable, but they managed. By now, all three of them were in a revere state of mind. Small discomforts didn't matter much. Their driver told them that he would see them tomorrow in their hotel. These breakdowns normally happen on such tours, and the nearby garages can tackle such breakdowns with their welding hoods, metals, and rubber seals. On the spot, they can contrive the repairs. Many times, the parts are not original, but they are tough and durable. Once a large city is reached, repairs can be done with original or off-the-market manufactured parts.

In the early morning, they visited the Badrinath *Mandir*. It stands about 50 feet tall with a small cupola on top, covered with a gold gilt roof. A broad stairway that leads up to a tall arched gateway is the main entrance. The bird's-eye view of the town is picturesque. The two mountain ranges, known as Nar and Narayan, guard the temple on either side with the towering Neel Kanth Peak providing a splendid backdrop. Facing the temple to the back of Alaknanda River is a hot-water spring known as *Tapt Kund*. The view of the ice-covered mountain Neel Kantha in the first Rays of golden sunlight is   splendid. One can never describe the beauty of this wonder. It gives the aura of God Shree Shiv, and in veneration, one impulsively lowers his head to offer reverence to the Almighty.

Badrinath to Rushikesh was a long journey. It took two days to reach Rushikesh. There are so many attractions on the way. The driver/tour guide described them. They stopped at the confluence of Alaknanda and Mandakini River. The view is gorgeous. Ruben enjoyed walking down the stairs from the Mandakini *Mandir*. Pralhad and Olivia followed him. They all dipped their feet in the water. The water is cool and refreshing. The Rushikesh surrounded by scenic beauty of the hills on three sides is near the laps of the lower Himalayas with Holy *Ganga* flowing through. There are many temples, some ancient, and some new along the river Ganges.

During the return journey from Delhi to Mumbai, Ruben was under a spell, in the realm of awe. He felt proximity to the Supreme conscious. He never experienced such peace of mind.

It is surprising; a boy brought up in America still carrying the inculcation (*Samskar*) of his father's motherland. His heritage was innate within him. This is the Hindu character. It was there for many millennia, and it will continue to flourish no matter what anyone says.

Olivia never thought that she would see such exquisite beauty in the pilgrimage tour. She revered the proximity to the nature; somewhere within she felt the veneer of tranquility.

Chapter 27

Puppet

Fredrik Gustav called a secret number. He was discussing the annual report of the company and explaining the poor performance. He was whining about the various regulations that made his job difficult, and expressing his concern about the current administration and the President of the United States.

"After he became President his philanthropic nobility took over. He did not keep any of his promises that he made before he took the office. He wants to make the world a better place – make it more peaceful, cut down on the military budget, control the price of oil, put more regulations on offshore drilling, and new regulations on banking. Our illegal weapon trade, drug cartel, casinos, and other operations are in jeopardy," Fredrick continued like this for almost five minutes. The mysterious person on the other side was listening and taking notes.

"Is there anyone we could control?" The person wanted some definite answers, a decision he could depend on.

"Have you heard the name Henry Giarrusso, Governor of the State of Illinois?" Frederick paused.

"Yes, I've heard the name."

"I am talking about nominating him for the presidential election. Governor Giarrusso is the son-in-law of Senator Frank Fitzroy. The Senator is an influential person, and he is in our court. Besides, we have someone who is the Governor's eyes and ears. He can control him." Frederick felt a little elated.

"Who?"

"Robert Lange, he was working with the Mancini family before he started working for Senator Frank Fitzroy. Later he became the right-hand-man for Governor Henry Giarrusso, son-in-law of Senator Fitzroy. If we choose Governor Giarrusso to be our candidate for President, Robert Lange can rope him for us. He was his confidant for the last two terms and will be his campaign manager if he runs for the Presidency." Fredrik Gustav was expecting comments.

"We'll remain in touch," the mysterious person disconnected the line.

Mr. Chevalier and Mr. Richard Dalhousie were discussing the affairs of the present administrations while savoring the Filet Mignon in Mr. Chevalier's house in California. They were not that happy with the incumbent president.

Richard Dalhousie sipped the wine, cleared his throat, and said, "I think you're right. This Illinois Governor Henry Giarrusso character looks a suitable candidate. We have to spread the word around."

Senator Frank Fitzroy abruptly returned from Washington to Chicago and called the Governor, "Are you free for lunch today?"

"I have a couple of appointments, but I can move them. Is it urgent?"

Henry was wondering about the Senator returning so early from Washington, D.C. He knew Frank was revising the amendment to the US firearms and weapon policy. He wondered what he was doing in Chicago.

"Come over to the Antebellum Country Club, around noon. Can you make it?" The Senator asked.

"Yes, sure, I can," Henry wondered what was so urgent. He left the office and asked the chauffer to drive the car to the Country Club. The Country Club hostess ushered him to the table where the Senator was sitting.

Senator got up from his chair, smiled, and shook hands with Henry, "It's good to see you."

Robert Lange was with him, "Good afternoon, I am glad to see both of you."

Robert Lange said, "Good afternoon, Governor."

The Governor was puzzled, "Is there anything…"

The Senator looked straight into his eyes and smiled, "I have some good news for you, son. May we sit down? I have already ordered your lunch. Would you like a wine or whiskey to go with it?

"I'll have tea, pretty busy in the office," Henry could not figure out what was going on.

"Well, Washington is busy gossiping about you," the Senator spoke.

Chills went down through his spine. "Did someone found out about his affairs? That would be a disaster," he thought.

"In an influential echelon in D.C., there is a rumor that you're going to be our next presidential candidate."

The words "presidential candidate" relaxed the Governor and excitement took the place of the chill, "What... really... me... President!" "I flew down here to tell you that do not run for the third term.

I want you and Elena to join me at a party that I am throwing in Washington, D.C. on Saturday two weeks from today."

The Senator had a reputation for hosting parties for supporters, sports figures, entertainers, people with political influence, and visiting dignitaries.

"Sure, Senator, I'll talk to Elena. We will come." The thought of the presidency thrilled Henry.

Being Governor was exhilarating. Power was bewitching. Henry Giarrusso never expected the kind of power that could affect thousands of lives. He could make a difference by skillfully manipulating the legislature. He always remembered Senator Fitzroy's words, "This is just a stepping stone, Henry. Be prudent." He was always cautious. Women longed for him. He handled his affairs with discretion.

Senator Fitzroy said, "I had a talk with Elena this morning."

Henry tensed, "Did you?"

Senator Fitzroy looked at Henry and smiled. "She's very happy, excited with the news, and will be coming."

The Governor took a deep breath, as he was relaxed, "That's great."

"So I am, Henry, so I am. Just keep her happy. You know what I mean?" The Senator's nuance showed fatherly advice through warning.

"I will, you don't have to worry Senator," Henry assured.

"I do worry about you both, Henry. She is my only child," he was aware of the Governor's infidelity. Robert Lange kept him informed, "Just be discreet, don't hang it, keep it under the carpet."

That Saturday, at Senator Fitzroy's elegant apartment in Georgetown, Henry found himself shaking hands with some of the elite personalities, prominent politicians, and dignitaries. These people turned the wheels in Washington. It was a lovely party, and Henry was making a positive impression.

"Having a good time, Henry?" Senator asked

"Yes. Thank you. I couldn't wish for a better one."

Two weeks later, back in Chicago, Henry was working in his office when his secretary buzzed him.

"Governor, Senator Fitzroy is here to see you."

"Send him in," he said.

"I've just flown in from Washington," the Senator smiled. "It's begun. Your name is becoming a buzzword in Washington. We're going to start our campaign soon."

Henry felt a sudden quiver of excitement, but there were doubts, "Do you think I have a chance, Frank?"

"There is no such thing as a chance in Washington. We have already begun our work. Your name is circulating in the higher echelon. I am not a gambler and I don't believe in destiny. Let me tell you, we are going to do our best to make this a sure thing," Senator Fitzroy took a deep breath. "You are going to be the most powerful person in the world," he emphasized.

"I appreciate everything you've done for me, Frank," the prospect of presidency elated Henry.

"It's my duty to help my son-in-law." The emphasis on "son-in-law" was clear to Henry. He knew what Frank meant.

Henry thought about money, "Where is the money coming from? The campaign will be extremely expensive."

"Money is not a problem. I've convinced a lot of my friends, and they are willing to contribute. The generous donations are on the way."

He remembered the survey results, "Don't underestimate, Henry. The ratings listed you as the most likeable candidate in the country. You have something that the others don't have - charisma. You can't buy that with money. People like you, and they'll vote for you. This is a reality."

"I like it. This is truly exciting," Henry said.

"I promise, you we will get a strong campaign team. They'll start lining up delegates around the country." The Senator looked at Robert, "Let us start putting the team together; what is the name of those two pollsters who worked with Alderman... John Haskin and Ricky Benton, right, we will get them. Robert, you make sure about that. Let's start thinking about campaign strategy, number of campaign offices around the country, the advertising committee, and cyber committee..."

"What do you mean by cyber committee?" Henry asked.

"Well, this is the age of the Internet and IT. We'll need them and we'll push your name through social media like Facebook, Twitter, LinkedIn, and YouTube," the Senator was all excited.

"I am sure he will win," Robert Lange remarked.

Senator Fitzroy felt confident, he said in Soliloquy, "I'll have him in my pocket. He's going to be my puppet. I'll pull the strings."

Chapter 28

Deceit

The Republican Party's platform, GOP (for "Grand Old Party"), is based upon American conservatism. That is not to say the rejection of the political ideology of liberalism is the basis. Rather, the Republican Party's conservatism is based upon its support of traditional principles against the modern liberalism of the Democratic Party. The two times Republic Governor, Henry Giarrusso, was not comfortable with this distinction; he felt it was vague.

The handsome candidate was a lady's man, whether you called that a Democratic Modern Liberalism or Classic Liberalism of Republic ideology, it did not matter to him, though he liked to relate that to Classic charisma that emanated from him. It was a tough race; there were nine candidates in the primaries. Robert Lange built up a strong campaign team. The money was no problem; the donations were flowing from every corner of the US along with the Internet media adding contributions from middle and moderate-income families.

Three months after announcing his candidacy, Henry traveled from north to south and east to west. He went to fund-raising meetings, attended church gatherings, went to town hall meetings, and visited high school and college campuses. They went state by state. In Detroit, they praised the car manufacturers. In California, they talked about the integral importance of IT and aircraft industries. In Ohio and Pennsylvania, they praised the blue-collar laborers. In Iowa and Kentucky, farming issues took the prime importance. In Massachusetts, they supported same-sex marriages. On college campuses, they promised bright futures, more jobs, equal opportunity, and a lower interest rate on student-loan programs. He talked about International issues and bringing back the soldiers fighting in the Middle East. People loved to hear him. The pollster's survey showed the rise in popularity. Henry Giarrusso made his way to the top of the short list. Most of the others were trailing behind with seven and nine percent except Senator Adam Baker. Senator Baker from Massachusetts was a strong contender.

The debate was about to begin. The forum allowed five minutes for candidates to introduce their platform and views. The first two candidates were running on special-interest platforms. They emphasized the issues of gay marriages, green policy, and war on terror – there was no new material, same-old dirt. After a while, all you heard was a jarring discordant of the broken digital transmission blowing in your face in patches.

The third candidate was about to finish, and Henry interjected, "I perceive a sense of frustration, not hope." His interruption surprised the third candidate before he could finish his closing statement, not that it meant much. He was off-balance in a stage of stupor and his time was up.

The Moderator beckoned, "Yes, Governor Giarrusso, please continue."

"No one is talking about the American dream. The dream is dead. Sure issues are there; we need to take an out-of-the-box approach, not the old-callous approach. Let us talk about national purpose and national pride. We are the number one country in the world, aren't we? Asians are controlling the IT domain. Japan dominates the automobile industry and more than half of our consumables are from China. Where do you see the pride? Our troops are fighting far away from home. Do we have an orchestrated - return home - program for them? Folks' jobs are there. We have to bring them in. We have to have programs to recruit and put back our returning veterans to work, find ways to cut down the prices, no more specific issues, no more special platforms, why are our products inferior? We should be asking that question. I would like to discuss that. We need an integral approach. There are problems like our student-loan programs, same-sex marriage rights, and the immigration bill," he went on like this for the next three minutes. His voice was under control.

People across America heard him. The debates began. Governor Samuel Rothman turned out to be a tough opponent. Henry was vacuous. Senator Adam Baker was more subject-oriented. There were no solutions, but the voters were satisfied that they all discussed the issues. People liked what they heard. A few liked Henry for his charis- matic appeal; some made a case for Senator Baker for his focused and to-the-point approach. Pollsters gave both about a 32 to 33 percent approval rating with Governor Samuel Rothman trailing behind.

* * * * *

The Bianchi family moved to New York in the 1970s. The Mafia family was originally from the Midwest. Both Mancini and Bianchi families decided to shake hands and the Bianchi family moved to the East Coast. They owned many casinos in Atlantic City. New York was a perfect location for International flesh trafficking and drug business. The "plant," the law firm of Meijer Rosenthal and Associates, handled Bianchi family's accounts. It was a small firm, mostly handling tax and revenue cases. The firm transferred the black money to a Bianchi family's offshore account in one of the small banks on the Caribbean Island.

Senator Adam Baker started his career as Junior Lawyer with this law firm. Normally, Mr. Rosenthal handled these black money transactions, and Mr. Baker handled local Tax and Revenue cases. Just before Easter, Mr. Rosenthal took a day off to spend the Easter holiday with his daughter visiting from California. He received an urgent message from the Plant, Boss Jr. Meijer, to transfer $50,000 to the offshore account immediately. It was an instant payoff to some hoodlums on the island.

Mr. Rosenthal called the office. Adam Baker took the call. Per the instructions from Mr. Rosenthal, Adam prepared the transac- tion papers to transfer the money. Because of the small amount, and the intense workload, he missed checking the source or validity of the deal. Unfortunately, his signature was on the transaction. It was mafia drug money. A short time later, Mr. Rosenthal came to the office and handled the transaction. Baker was not aware of the deal. After a while, everybody forgot about it.

About two months back, Mr. Bianchi died. He did not have any children. Mancini family's accountants took over all of his business deals. While going over the old business transactions, the accountant accidentally came across the file and saw the old money transfer transaction. He recognized the signature of Senator Adam Baker and called Logan. Logan took all the papers and showed it to Robert Lange. Robert realized the significance and brought this to the attention of Senator Frank Fitzroy.

Senator Adam Baker was a good friend and an experienced politician. Senator Fitzroy knew him for a long time. He knew that this information could put a dent on his career. He decided to play the card delicately. Senator Baker was a good person to have on his side. He contacted Adam and showed him a copy of the paperwork. Senator Adam Baker had forgotten about his days with the Meijer Rosenthal and Associates law firm from Boston, Massachusetts. He saw his signature. Senator Fitzroy explained that it was a drug money transfer to the Mafia's offshore account. Senator Baker lost the luster from his face. He realized the consequences, the media frenzy, and the front-line news in the major newspaper. He looked at Senator Fitzroy; he did not know what to expect from him.

Senator Fitzroy cleared his throat, "Adam, you are a good friend. I respect you. I'll make a proposition, with which I am sure you won't be disappointed. My son-in-law, Henry Giarrusso, and you both are competing for the nomination. I would like you to ease out of the race. The last debate is next week. Let him win the debate. Then you drop out of the race. In the Republic National Convention, I'll make sure you will be nominated as the Vice Presidential Candidate. I would like you to work with him. He is a good boy, probably not as experienced as you are, but together you two will be a winning team. You will remain in the limelight, and it will give you a chance to run for presidential election eight years from now."

Senator Baker realized there is no option. The offered way out was decent. Presently, the race was 50/50; anyone could win. At least, the VP nomination gives him a definite chance next time. He accepted the offer. Senator Fitzroy was scheming that, if he played the game properly, then for next 16 years, the Presidents of the United States of America would be in his pocket, and he would be the puppet master.

Chapter 29

Convention

Robert Lange opened the door and let his strategists, pollsters, and campaign team in. John Haskin, Ricky Benton, Robert Dennison, Malcolm O'Connor, Robert Spears, Jessica Patel, Sandy Hoover, Josh Desai, the entire campaign team, was there except Louise Calvin. Louise was a well-built woman with a big bosom, a perfect body with 36-28-38, and ambitious nature. She was a Princeton graduate in political science, with a good reputation on policy research but not much concern for morality, which was a plus for Henry Giarrusso to have her under his wing.

Robert had to struggle to keep the lid on their secret meetings. He had left Louise off the list because more and more she had been fighting with Robert Lange for the center stage in strategy sessions. They made themselves comfortable around the conference table. They were tired, but they all had big smile. It was fun being on a winning team. Mr. Lange called a strategy meeting in the conference room of the downtown Hilton hotel. There were munchies on the table with water and soda.

The purpose was to look past Republican National Convention and start thinking about the democratic President Andrew Zoloft with a good record. Although recently he was losing popularity because of the falling economic trend, high rate of unemployment and unfulfilled promises for bringing deployed troops back to the US. It was not his fault. He inherited the budget deficit, loans from China in trillions of dollars, and the war expenditures from the Middle East fiasco.

President Andrew Zoloft had been promoting the same Democratic Platform. The recent developments made President Zoloft unsure about whether to continue concentrating on Senator Adam Baker, who was already leading in the polls looking like the candidate from the opposition, or to shift focus to the Governor from Illinois, Henry Giarrusso, with a not-so-known platform or policies.

Louise Calvin entered, "What's going on in here?" She asked, smiling at them and brushing her brown hair over her forehead.

"Getting ready for RNC and the election strategy," Robert said.

"Shouldn't the Governor be included? Does he know you're meeting?"

"The Governor is with Senator Fitzroy upstairs discussing the RNC and selection process for the VP."

"When did Senator Fitzroy come, wasn't he in Champaign visiting his daughter?"

"You mean Elena? The Senator came this afternoon with Elena," Robert cautioned Louise. He did not want to face unwarranted catapulting when they were so close to the election. Elena was unaware of the affair. He wanted to keep it that way.

"I tried to call you this morning, but you were unavailable," he hinted her. There was a sly smile on the team's face. Louise ignored it. "The Governor and Senator will be joining soon. There is a lot of work to be done, getting ready for the Republican National Convention, VP selection process, and the convention speech. Are you working with the speech?" Robert asked. He knew the Democrats were going to be looking for loopholes to put down Governor Giarrusso and his campaign after the Super Tuesday win and the latest tracking poll, so he had to plan the strategy to face that challenge.

"Okay, guys, we've gotta start looking ahead. All winning campaign polls are in our favor. Americans are optimistic about the Governor, but now the mud slinging begins. The next week we all will be at the RNC. James Spears and Jessica Patel, do you have anything planned to start from next Friday?"

"What about David Letterman or Leno shows? There are also many entertainment shows, they are calling us," Spears suggested.

"Let's start thinking about 60 Minutes and Nightline. They are hard news. Jessica, you help us with the gender gap and Sandy Hoover, you help her. Josh, you take over ethnic viewpoint. We'll keep Letterman and Leno for after the first debate, followed by entertainment media shows. Louise, you were looking into the Larry King show, any progress, feedback on that."

Senator Fitzroy and Governor Giarrusso entered the room followed by Elena. There was a pin drop silence for a moment. Elena came to a campaign meeting for the first time. Everyone welcomed her. Louise twitched a bit. She did not enjoy her presence.

"Carry on," Senator Fitzroy said.

"We can get on the Larry King show the week after next, but there is schedule conflict. That would delay the appearance on Nightline by two more weeks." Louise outlined the scheduled conflict.

"In the meantime we can do a 60 Minute piece," interjected Malcolm O'Connor.

"The Governor may like to go on the Letterman or Leno show earlier. They may have some spots open this week," Louise made a deliberate suggestion to tease Robert. She had no idea what would be available.

"I wanna do Jay Leno now," the Governor interrupted. "Robert, please arrange that, I would like to present myself as a normal guy, or better yet, I can go on David Letterman, a few laughs will be good for me."

Robert did not appreciate this. He thought that these shows could provide a better opportunity for a few laughs and jokes after the first debate appearance. Nevertheless, he let the suggestion go forward. Louise caused a rift between them. He did not want to be thrown off the wagon before it pulled into Washington.

Robert addressed to Senator, "Sir, the polls are running in our favor, we should do great in that setting. Do you have any suggestions?"

"Let's finish the convention first. Henry and I have made a short list for the VP selection. Later, we'll run that by you. How is the acceptance speech coming along? Remember, we have to lay our foundation there," Senator warned.

"Okay." Robert continued, "Malcolm, I need short policy statements on the key issues. We'll discuss those later; right now let us get ready to address any issue that the Democrats could throw at us.

Has anyone thought about international affairs, oil issues, the China loan, or the Middle East issue? We need the Governor to look good on foreign policy. Democrats won't hesitate to point out his weaknesses due to the lack of experience in these areas. You all know he hasn't had much exposure to international issues. That's President Zoloft's stronghold."

The RNC nominated Senator Adam Baker for the VP slot on the third day of convention and all States unanimously accepted the nomination. The atmosphere inside the convention center was dynamic. The combination of the young blood leading, supported by an experienced leader like Senator Adam Baker gave a new hope for winning the election. Senator Baker accepted the VP nomination. He gave the acceptance speech from the podium at the Republican National Convention Center.

Governor Giarrusso watched it from his hometown in Champaign, Illinois. Senator Fitzroy was sitting with the Illinois delegation. The daily pollster ratings for the last three days were on the rise showing voters' satisfaction. The next day, Governor Giarrusso flew in the early morning with Elena and joined them at the convention. He was ready for the evening speech. Last week, he was on one of the talk shows that went well. The campaign was picking up momentum.

Governor Giarrusso began his speech by thanking all delegates and congratulating Senator Baker, "Today, I see the vigor, American dream becoming reality. Let us not get relaxed, we have a lot of work to do. I need your help to re-energize the American dream, to bring the purpose back." His voice resonated in the dome.

He went on for almost 45 minutes and concluded, "We face many issues: rising unemployment, budget deficit, tax issues, immigration, racial discrimination, war in the Middle East, the North Korea challenge, and the Iran Nuclear threat. We'll work together, and resolve them. I am aware that we owe trillions to China. China manufactures more than half of our goods, and we outsource the IT task to the Eastern Hemisphere. This has to stop. We have to bring our GNP up, make sure our product quality is superior and our prices are competitive. Our entrepreneurs and labor force will have to work together to find the solution. The Government will provide resources; they will take back the system from the special-interest groups. Folks, this is a war, and we have to win it. This is our country. We have to take matters in our own hands and change them."

He took a sip of water and looked around at the rotunda, state by state. Then, he focused his eyes on the cameras, addressing the millions of viewers watching around the country, "This is what I want to achieve and with this, I am announcing my candidacy for President of the United States of America."

There was uproar all around the dome, clamor of clapping almost continued non-stop for the next five minutes. His wife, Elena, joined him on the podium and thousands of balloons, red, white, and blue, poured from the top. The political analyst criticized his speech as vacuous, but the crowd enjoyed it, boosting approval rating.

Chapter 30

Delhi Assam Waziristan

Taking a deep breath, Malini stepped once again into the Durbar Square of the town of Bhaktpur, an ancient town in the east corner of the Kathmandu Valley, Nepal. Many Hindu temples and Buddhist monasteries are in the city. The resonant sound of the bells and prayers filled the air with a sonorous and vibrant hum. The Nepali men, sari clad Nepali women, and wandering foreign tourists accompanied by English-speaking guides crowded the streets of Bhaktpur.

Malini felt like sending up a few prayers herself. It had been more than 15 days. She followed a man who was supposed to be carrying the devices. She felt as if she was following a shadow. The man was like a ghost, nowhere to be seen. She was afraid that she was being followed by more than just an icy wind brandishing down from the bulwark of the palace of Fifty-five Windows, a brick and wooden palace.

Malini took shelter at the gates of the palace. She stayed put behind the gates for few moments to find out who was following her. Then she exited the gates and headed for the square. She made a deliberate sound of her steps and then abruptly stepped behind the post next to a shop.

Each time she saw nothing but shadows. She knew that the two intimidating men she saw before were still following her. Ramanuj saw Malini and the two men following her. He sensed the danger. "I'll have to grab Malini before those two men attack her."

Ramanuj caught the flicker of glint. The gunman was using the silencer.

"*Are Deva* (oh God)!" Ramanuj murmured in a muffled voice the expression that he had learned when he was in Mumbai.

She looked and saw the face of the first terrorist. Ramanuj reacted quickly. Instinctively, he pulled her from behind the post. Malini missed the bullet by an inch. She felt the whiff of the bullet zooming past her shoulder. She didn't even realize how close she was to death. Ramanuj saw the look of surprise and shock on her face. He was out of sight, behind the post. The assassins did not notice him. Ramanuj slowly turned his head while attaching the silencer on his revolver.

Malini gasped as she saw the second face emerge. The second terrorist pointed the gun at her heart. Ramanuj's years of military training took over. He fired a shot; the second terrorist dropped to the ground. No one heard the shot. One of the Chinese tourists saw the man going down. He cried for help thinking that the man had a sudden heart attack. It became chaos on the street when people saw the blood oozing. Ramanuj and Malini briskly walked away from the crowd and the noise. From the corner of his eyes, Ramanuj saw the other terrorist running away. The crowd thought he fired the shot. They started chasing after him.

Malini was glad to see Ramanuj.

"Are you staying here?" Malini asked.

"No, I just arrived here, following the leads and chasing after the terrorists. When I saw you in Durbar square, I was about to call you. Then I saw those two strangers pulling the gun on you. Thank God, I was there just in time," Ramanuj shivered.

"Thanks, Ramanuj, I am grateful." Malini was shaken and trembling with fear. This is the first time she faced death so closely.

They both were out of the Indian Territory in Nepal chasing terrorists. Malini relaxed. After few minutes, away from the crowd and the commotion Ramanuj inquired, "What brought you here?"

"The lead was that Salamat Khan was seen in Assam going toward Arunachal Pradesh. I flew to Dibrugarh and then went by Jeep to Roing via Tinsukhia and Tezu. Roing was a small town; there was no place to hide. The terrorists who stole the capsules were nowhere. However, I could not ignore the lead. Then from Roing, I flew to Itanagar by helicopter where I met another agent who knew the secret hideout of the terrorist cell. We went together to the secret hideout. When we reached it, the place was deserted. There was a small tea stall. The agent showed pictures to the tea stall owner. He recognized the person in the picture and told us that he left the previous night. He didn't know where he went, but he had a Jeep and headed toward Tawang according to that man.

I followed the lead, contacted the police department in Tawang, and showed them the pictures. One of the informants recognized Salamat and saw him heading toward Thimphu, Bhutan. I contacted the SSIW Wing through normal channels using my laptop. Pranav received the message and responded. The encrypted message from him gave the latest Intel (Information acquired through intellegence by analyzing data) that they spotted Fahayat Khan and another terrorist in Darjeeling. Salamat was out of sight, no one knew his whereabouts.

I updated our office about my chase after Salamat. Pranav sent another encrypted message asking whether I was heading toward Thimphu. I responded that I was going there. I talked to our military personnel on my way over there. They gave the Intel about the Chinese incursion from the Northwest side of Arunachal Pradesh. I sent this information to SSIW and added that I would send another message from Thimphu. I did not find any lead for Salamat in Thimphu. On a slight chance, I went up to Gangtok in Sikkim. One of our agents in the Sikkim office told me that they recognized the man and raided the place, but he fled. I heard on the news about the Chinese military advancing in the Northern region when I was in Sikkim. I encrypted the detailed information including the advancement of Chinese troops and sent it back. Their return response informed that you were in Darjeeling. Therefore, I proceeded to Darjeeling and from there to Bhaktpur. You know the rest."

"Wow, that was a long trek," Ramanuj said mischievously.

"I didn't walk. I took the Jeep and bus," she said tersely. "Nevertheless, it was tiring journey. Especially in Arunachal Pradesh where 20 miles of travel could take three to five hours by Jeep because of the shifting bed of the River Brahmaputra. It was an experience. I admire the people. They have a tough life. However, I was surprised by their sentiments. In spite of the lack of administration of our irresponsible government, they still want to remain as Indians," Malini was thinking about her experience with the crowd she met in Tezu, Roing, and Ittanagar.

Ramanuj and Malini both traveled to Kathmandu in hopes that they could get the terrorist whom they saw in Bhaktpur. Kathmandu is a big place. Ramanuj had some information about the terrorist cell in Kathmandu. He knew the address and decided to watch that place. However, after 12-hour surveillance, they had no luck. They were tired and decided to return to the hotel. The next day, after breakfast, they sat down in their room and started analyzing the facts.

Ramanuj said, "What are we missing here?"

"Let us put the facts on the table that way we can analyze them more closely," Malini suggested.

"Right, I agree," Ramanuj asserted.

The first spotting at Patna

Spotted Salamat, Fahayat, Latif, and a couple of others

Salamat and Fahayat spotted at Kalimpong

From Kalimpong they went separate ways

Salamat spotted at Arunachal Pradesh

Fahayat headed toward Darjeeling to Bhaktpur

We met in Bhaktpur

One of the terrorists is dead

Terrorists are aware that we are chasing them

We are in Kathmandu

We do not know Latif's whereabouts

There is no credible information

Salamat and Fahayat disappeared

They both are in Nepal or Arunachal

They will not go to Lhasa

The airport security is too toght; they will not take that risk

There is no way to carry the capsule from Lhasa to Kashmir

Where could they go from here?

Ramanuj looked at the flow chart.

Malini blurted, "Do you see that?"

"What are you pointing at?"

"Salamat and Fahayat are in Nepal or Arunachal. They can't go to Lhasa or any part of China because they will be searched. That could mean that Salamat and Fahayat are not carrying the capsules. They are misleading us."

Ramanuj analyzed her logic, "It is possible that Salamat and Fahayat are traveling separately to mislead us. They all may be traveling by foot because we are watching all airports, railway stations, and bus routes."

Malini continued, "Latif disappeared from Patna. He never went to the Arunachal or Nepal side. Based on this flow chart, Latif could be our missing link. He could have already gone to Jammu via Lucknow, Dehradun, and Chandigarh with all the capsules."

Ramanuj said, "You are on the dot, Malini. We have agents watching Jammu and Udhampur areas for Latif. He may reappear there, let us call Delhi, and find out. I'll use my computer to communicate in an encrypted format."

MAKE SURE THAT AGENTS ARE STILL WATCHING THE DALSAR VILLAGE AND UDHAMPUR. OUR INTEL SHOWS LATIF AS MISSING LINK. SHIV THE DESTRUCTION IS STILL SOMEWHERE IN THE NORTHERN REGION. THERE IS A CONCERN ABOUT THE CHINESE INCURSION ON THE NORTHERN SIDE.

The SSIW wing picked up the communication and sent it to Suhas. She discussed it with Pranav, informed Commander Bhosle, and sent a message back to Ramanuj.

LATIF DODGED SUHAS AND DISAPPEARED FROM KEMPTY FALL. AGENTS SPOTTED HIM IN JAMMU. THEY RAIDED BUT HE DISAPPEARED. HE IS HEADING TOWARD HIS VILLAGE. HOWEVER, WE DO NOT KNOW HIS EXACT WHEREABOUTS. COME BACK.

After returning from Nepal, Pranav updated Ramanuj and Malini about various developments. "We put a tail on Dr. Bhujang. He knows many Muslims around. Other day, he went to see Prof. Haji Ulfatkhan. It could be an innocent visit. Up until now, we have no evidence about his association with SIMI. The professor is on our list of suspects as SIMI Member. We put a tap on his telephone and mobile. Fatima went to Arzoo Dairy Farm for further training. She will learn there how to use weapons and some of the basics of tradecraft. Since she is a Muslim, she does not need any training in that area. She will be there with another agent, Dabu Kadgul alias Farooq Khalid. He is in training there to become a perfect Muslim. They both will become a double agent and will go to Pakistan with proper cover. Dr. Muller left for the US. Miss Kiran Hopkins is still in Delhi. According to her information, there is no chatter about SHIV the Destruction devices in Islamabad or any other part of Pakistan. She may soon leave for Islamabad if the devices cross our borders. She has promised us to keep in the loop; she is equally motivated to find Nikhil's killers."

The next day, they received a conversation between the Professor and Habib Ansari. After the initial formalities, the conversation continued as follows:

ASIM AND AYESHA ARE GETTING MARRIED, KHUDA-WAZIR-E-ALAM. ASIM AND HIS FAMILY WILL TRAVEL FROM UDHAMPUR. AYESHA'S FAMILY WILL TRAVEL FROM ISLAMABAD. IT IS AGREED ON THE *MEHR* (DOWRY) OF THREE LAKH RUPEES. ARRANGE ONE-LAKH RUPEES FOR *MULLAH* FROM SAUDI. ASIM AND AYESHA WILL FLY TO US VIA LONDON FOR THEIR HONEYMOON. GIVE TWO LAKH RUPEES TO THEM FOR SPENDING MONEY.

The agents could not find anyone related by the name Asim or Ayesha to Professor Ulfatkhan. Commander Bhosle was familiar with the name Habib Ansari, the head of the Defense Supply Corps of Pakistan. They gave the conversation to the ASIIW wing for decipher. The interpretation revealed the plan for the devices stolen from the lab:

THE DEVICES WILL GO FROM UDHAMPUR VIA ISLAMABAD TO WAZIRISTAN. SOMEONE FROM SAUDI WILL COME TO COLLECT ONE DEVICE. REMAINING TWO DEVICES WILL GO TO LONDON AND US.

Ramanuj read the deciphered message, "The devices are still in Indian Territory. They are referring to three devices, which mean that the fourth is still in Delhi. Do we have any leads on the terrorist who ran away from Fatima's apartment?" Ramanuj looked at Pranav and Suhasini.

"The murder of Lalu Pillai in the prison cell and murder of Jairam Chauhan both point toward Cabinet Minister Naidu, but, we have no proof. The third guy who ran away from the slums of Dhobi Ghat has disappeared. We interviewed some of the other gang members from their circles. They are local gangs who worked for different politicians and builders threatening people to vacate their houses, distributing funds during the election to buy votes, and doing odd jobs for these corrupt groups. They don't have much power or brains to carry out such activities. We could not find any link between Naidu and the terrorists. We have no information on the last device," Pranav provided the details.

"Did you talk to the Commander and update him?"

"Not yet."

"Let's go and update him," Ramanuj, Pranav, and Suhas all went to see Commander Bhosle. Kiran was in his cabin talking with him.

"Come on in guys, Kiran just dropped in to tell me that Ruben went back to Kabul and may be coming to India with his crew to prepare a newscast about Chinese incursion."

"We also wanted to discuss with you about the Chinese incursion," Ramnuj said. He looked at Malini Soumya.

Malini continued, "I was in Arunachal Pradesh and Sikkim and talked to our military over there. Our Deputy Foreign Minister failed in flag meetings. They are very much concerned and ready for action."

Ramanuj asked, "Isn't our Deputy Foreign Minister, a Muslim? Could it be a conspiracy?"

Suhasini Gupta of the EIW wing interrupted, "I got similar feed-back from our military, and they are ready to attack. At present, we have some tactical advantage over them. There'll be heavy casualties to both sides, but that's the name of the game,"

Commander Bhosle interrupted the conversation, "Guys, be careful. This is a government office. Don't use politically incorrect language. We are all Indians, no Muslim, no Hindus, but secular Indians, supposed to turn the left cheek after you're slapped on the right cheek. That's our motto, right guys?"

"Secular, my foot," Suhas whispered.

Commander Bhosle pretended not to hear that comment, he continued, "The Cabinet has to consider how the masses will react. They have to determine whether the country is ready for war."

Pranav normally never gives his opinion so loudly, but this time he burst, "The country is busy watching TV operas, films produced by Muslim producers, and competitions with Pakistani singers and dancers in Bollywood. Actresses are busy vying over who is the best Muslim actor to marry. Our media is busy brainwashing the masses and keeping them engaged in music and dance. Patriotism is only becoming a showoff on TV during festivities, Prajasattak Day (January 26, when the Constitution of India was adopted) or Independence Day (August 15)."

"He is right, sir, that is the present-day India. We have a serious situation on our borders. Retaliation may be the only solution to wake up the masses from their slumber and unite them. If we don't retaliate now, the situation will become difficult. Don't you think our Foreign Ministry is deliberately procrastinating?" Suhas questioned. Ramanuj added, "We lost some land to China during Nehru Raj, and this is a repeat performance. Especially with the theft of SHIV the Destruction, Muslim involvement, Chinese incursion, and delaying tactics by our administration, all show a conspiracy of a sort."

Kiran felt uncomfortable with this talk. She said, "Commander Bhosle, I have a meeting to attend in 30 minutes, do you have any update on Salamat Khan before I leave India? I would like to see that the person who had his hand in Nikhil's murder is behind bars."

Ramanuj responded to Kiran, "We are not yet successful in catching Salamat Khan. He is eluding us. Hopefully, we will catch him in Udhampur or in his village Dalsar." Kiran thanked Ramanuj and left.

The Commander wondered about Kiran, how her office could let her stay here that long, she was in India close to a month. He did not know her boss Veronica Ivanovo's interest in SHIV the Destruction. In fact, Kiran was commuting between Delhi and Islamabad for her work and keeping an eye on progress in India. Since no one was monitoring her movements, no one knew that.

After she left, Commander Bhosle addressed the whole group, "One of my close friends from the US told me that Indian offspring from anywhere in the world, either both parents being Indian or a crossbreed between Indian and other nationals, all have love for India. I was glad to hear that. Nevertheless, be careful what you say in front of her. Let us remember that, although she has Indian heritage, she is an agent from another country. Whatever you said just now was okay. Kiran and Ruben were close to Nikhil, so they'll do whatever is necessary to get his killers. I have no doubt about that, but next time, watch."

I'll be discussing the Chinese incursion with the PM's office. It is a big fiasco. However, there are problems such as, interference from Foreign Minister, interference from Minister of External Affairs, interference from the head of the UFI (United Front of India)," the Commander tried to elaborate the political scenario.

"What does she know about India?" Suhas interjected.

"Let us concentrate on SHIV the Destruction. Let me have your update and trip reports," Commander Bhosle tried to shift the focus back to SHIV the Destruction.

They updated him. They also told him about the message deciphered by their SSIW Wing. Based on deciphered data, the SHIV the Destruction devices were in Udhampur or would soon reach Udhampur if they had not yet left for Waziristan. One device is still in Delhi.

The Commander listened carefully.

"I just got the news that the new agent, Dabu Kadgul alias Farooq Khalid has completed training, undergone the circumcision, and spent time in the Muslim community. He became a *Pucca* (perfect) Muslim, ready for deployment. Fatima took training in using weapons. She spent a little more than two weeks at the facility with Akabar Khan, alias Ajit Deshpande. They both are ready," Commander informed

Ramanuj added, "We have to send Fatima and Dabu Kadgul alias Farooq Khalid to Udhampur ASAP. If the circumstances change, they have to be ready to cross LOC to penetrate the Pakistan border.

Chapter 31

Operation Hind

TV channels were running the news of the explosion and the murder from the GEETA facility. The explosion and murder indicated terrorist involvement. Commander Bhosle's secretary, Miss Sarika Wadhwani, called Mr. Atul Chowdhary, the PA to the Prime Minister (PM) of India Mr. Kuldip Kaul. The Commander would like to have a meeting with PM this morning at 10 a.m. to update him on the recent murder and theft from GEETA. The Commander figured it was a good idea to tell the PM about the details before he was summoned to the PM's office.

Commander Bhosle arrived at 10 a.m. sharp and ushered into the PM's office. He was surprised to find Russian-born Suvarna Khoja - the head of UFI, Balu Naidu - the Minister of External Affairs, and Mr. Bhojwani - the Home Minister already in the PM's office waiting for him.

The Commander was not in the PM's best list. It is not that PM disliked him, but the unwritten edict was if Suvarna Khoja did not like someone, then that person was a black sheep. They would have gotten rid of him long time ago, however, considered as Chanakya (shrewd politician and advisor to the King Chandragupta Maurya of 4th century B.C.) of India, Commander was holding many secrets from their past. He knew about the girls serving cocktail in the Russian nightclub, and the madam of the escort service in Italy. He was aware of the coverup of the Asthana Project, the bridge construction fraud, real estate frauds throughout the country, voter bank fraud, the billions stashed in Swiss Banks from drugs and drug addiction of the young man being groomed for the next head of India, plus much more.

If revealed, the further investigations would open can of worms. It would make the position delicate. Once you start scratching, more rashes could emerge. The secrets have this uncanny tendency to blow up without warning. They were all aware of the fact. They also knew that the Commander had an exceptional ability to protect them from danger and had the loyalty of the staff to support him. Two hostile border nations on two fronts and bellicose ec- zematous on the mid-east side near Kolkata was a nuisance to face. They needed him.

Commander Bhosle briefly narrated the details of the theft of the project SHIV the Destruction, and the murder of the scientist, Dr. Nikhil Chowdhary, the inventor of the project. He also shared that the explosion destroyed the office cabin along with Dr. Chaudhary's computer. Their technicians could not retrieve any information from the burnt computer hard drive. The project SHIV the Destruction device was not tested; they had no record of the process by which to fabricate the device. He also agreed that, on hindsight, it was probably a mistake not to secure the perimeter immediately after the meeting. They simply assumed that GEETA was a protected and secured facility.

"You should have thought of that before the mishap," blurted Madam Survana Khoja.

The Commander nodded with an apologetic look. "One of the intruders also died in the explosion. Our database search revealed that the body of the intruder belonged to the known terrorist Bahadur Khan of Harkat-ul-Jihad-al-Islami (HuJI). The terrorist organization HuJI is active in India. They were involved in the German bakery bombing in Pune, the Varanasi bombing, and the Delhi bombing. Our agents are watching HuJI terrorists and their cronies Salamat Khan, Fahayat Khan, and others. We even caught one of the terrorists later in an attack on their hiding place. The next day, we found him hanging in his cell," Commander Bhosle paused.

He looked at Minister Naidu and noticed a slight twitch on his face at the mention of the hanged prisoner. He realized something was wrong and decided not to disclose the total consequences and the impact the SHIV the destruction could cause unless the PM specifically requested.

The PM was in a foul mood after hearing the account of theft and the murder of the young scientist. The investigation of the explosion and the murder pointed to terrorist involvement. He did not like the nuance of terrorism. That worried him. Already, there were many problems with the Muslim community due to the explosions caused by terrorists all around India. The dead victim and the stolen project were his concerns, too. Nevertheless, he did not want to irritate Muslim vote banks, either. That was one of the backbones of their party's campaign strategy. Madam Suvarna Khoja also realized the gravity of the situation. Her party could lose some seats in the upcoming election. The impending danger did not bother Naidu. All he was thinking about was how much he could extract from *Mia* Zafar Ansari Deputy Chief of IBP for such valuable information.

That evening, Minister Naidu called on the secured line of Deputy Chief of IBP.

"*Salam Alekum* (peace upon you) *Mia* Zafar, how are you doing?"

"*Wa alikom el salam WA rahmat Allah Wa barakato* (Peace, mercy and blessing of Almighty Allah be on you, too), Vazire Azam (Minister) Naidu, what is the reason for this honor?" Zafar Ansari responded.

"I have some information for you about project SHIV the Destruction," Naidu said cordially.

"Really, I don't think we are interested," Zafar tried to brush him off. He knew that one of the Pakistan terrorist organizations had already stolen the device.

"*Mia* (sir), listen to me, I know HuJI had stolen the device. The information I have, will surprise you even more and worth millions to you. It'll cost you only $1 million," Naidu sounded mysterious.

Zafar was wondering. He knew that Naidu was aware that the terrorists had stolen the device; still he was pushing some information and asking a high price. His curiosity made him say, "Remember I still have those photos. If the information is that important, then I'll give you half a million dollars. Go ahead, let me hear."

Naidu told him about the conversation that took place earlier in the Indian PM's office, "So you see, you have the sole custody of the weapon. India has no information on it."

Zafar realized that the information was extremely valuable. He didn't argue, and promised to deposit half a million dollars in his Swiss bank account. He realized that this was a lucky break and started to formulate a plan. The Pakistani battalions began marching on the other side of LOC (Line of Control - the de-facto military control line between India and Pakistan) ready and waiting for orders. The chatter began about Operation Hind. That night Minister Naidu checked his Swiss Bank account and saw the deposit of half a Million dollars.

"Sir, Mr. Atul Chowdhary is on the secured line. He wants to talk to you. He says it's urgent," Sarika Wadhwani's announcement through the intercom interrupted Commander Bhosle's bemusement about capsule theft and possible involvement of Minister Naidu. It had been less than 10 days since he had last talked to the PM, "Maybe he needs an update," thought the Commander.

The Commander pushed the red button. Mr. Atul Chowdhary, PA to the PM, told him to come immediately to the PM's office. "There are two officers from the Army Division of Intelligence (ADI) here with the PM. Come quickly," the PA cut the line.

It took almost half an hour to reach the Prime Minister's office through the heavy Delhi traffic. The two officers from the Army Division of Intelligence (ADI) were already there at the PM's office waiting for Commander Bhosle to arrive. The Prime Minister Kuldip Kaul seemed aggravated. Before starting the meeting, Atul Chowdhary announced the warning of utmost confidentiality to all present about the information that would be discussed in the PM's office. He added that it would be at the PM's discretion to disclose the information to the Parliament, if the circumstances warranted.

One of the ADI Agents took the lead, "There is a sudden increase of Pakistani battalions near the LOC, and they are spreading laterally. We are already haggard by the Chinese incursion, and on top of this, we heard the chatter of Operation Hind. Chinese incursion is on the news, but before this, we had no intelligence of any planned attack or any communication from ISHWAR or information from the Ministry of External Affairs on Operation Hind. This chatter of Operation Hind appears to be apocalyptic. We are taking measures to protect our international boundary and are here to appropriate funding for these operations."

The PM addressed Commander Bhosle, "Does this have any correlation to the theft and murder that took place in GEETA?"

The Commander was thinking, so the Minister took the bait, "It is possible. The SHIV the Destruction devices stolen from GEETA can cripple electronic gadgets, disable the communication devices, jam the transmission of signals, and cause human fatalities. It is a chemical weapon. No one knows about this project except Dr. Iyer, Dr. Frank Muller, and the participants from our last meeting with you. Even my agents working on the investigation are not aware of it except for the one who is in charge." He paused. He was in a dilemma whether to hint them about a possible leak.

He reconstructed his statement carefully, and uttered, "I believe, the emergence of the Operation Hind could be due to a possible leak of the information of the devastating effect of the stolen device SHIV the Destruction to our enemies. We have to be extremely careful. We do not know whether the source of leak is internal or external. It is better not to say anything to anyone until we investigate all the details." He paused, "There is also another concern I want to discuss with you, and since these two officers are here it may be prudent to discuss this now."

The PM nodded his head.

"The SHIV the Destruction theft, the Operation Hind, and the Muslim involvement, they all are interconnected. The Chinese incursion is a separate event. Based on the intelligence gathered and analyzed, my agents feel the Chinese incursion is far more serious than the Operation Hind and immediate retaliation is a must."

ADI agents agreed with the Commander's statement, and one of the ADI agents added, "Presently, we have some tactical benefits on the Northeastern frontier, once we lose that due to procrastination, we may lose more land to China."

Commander Bhosle phrased his words carefully to address the real concern, "News channels are alluding toward a communal web because of the failure of the Flag Meeting. The common masses are interpreting it as executive procrastination by politicians and that could be fatal. It is my duty to warn you."

The PM looked at them with his demure smile emanating through his bearded face, "You don't understand; we have to consult the cabinet, the Foreign Minister, the Minister of External Affairs, the Head of UFI, all Chief Ministers, and others. The public may not be ready for such an all-out war. It is against our policy of non-violence. Negotiation of peace is our motto. Then we also have to consider other nations; we have to preserve our image." The demure smile emanating through the white beard was a signal for others to shut up and get out. Commander Bhosle was familiar with that signal. He nodded to appease him like a Nandi Bail (Nandi Bull, a colloquial usage indicating stupidity).

"With your permission of course, I would like to take these two officers to Dr. Iyer for further discussion and technical updates," he looked at the PM for approval.

The PM had no problem. He knew he would not understand the technical details that they would be discussing.

Commander Bhosle called Iyer and requested an immediate appointment. He told Iyer that he was bringing two officers from ADI with him. No one said a word in the car. Dr. Iyer was waiting for them. He offered them a cup of coffee and began the meeting.

"I want you to swear to the absolute secrecy of what you'll hear today." Both nodded affirmatively and Dr. Iyer began his narration.

"Our scientist was not working on any chemical weapon. He was focusing more on the microwave emitter to disrupt the enemy's electronic and data systems useless before attacking them. This is a high-powered electronic microwave theory, an alternative to traditional explosive and lethal weapons. The focus was to produce non-nuclear electromagnetic pulses (NNEMP) without the use of nuclear weapons. One of our scientists suggested integrating chemical compounds in the microwave emitter. It was an experiment and there was no intention to manufacture chemical weapons. Our scientist was working on the project and keeping the information on his computer with very few details on the mainframe computer for security reasons. The terrorists murdered him. During the explosion, his computer burned. We merely have his oral statements describing the deadly effect of the device. Only three of us, Commander Bhosle, Dr. Frank Muller from the US, I knew about the project. Nikhil was a brilliant scientist. He updated us regularly. The final phase was a break by chance, and he promptly updated us. I doubt whether he had even the time to record the project in his computer before his murder. The last picture from the surveillance showed that he was updating the information in his computer when the terrorists murdered him."

One of the officers from ADI asked, "Can you update us how fatal the project is, and what are the precautions necessary to safeguard our soldiers?"

Dr. Iyer said the capsule could cause malfunction of the communication devices and create a risk of chemical warfare that will require wearing masks. He also told them about the parts for the masks.

"In my last conversation with Nikhil, he told me that he had only made a mini-version of SHIV the Destruction and a short-range throwing mechanism for testing purposes. Due to the thermostatic limitations, neither manufacturing of the large-scale capsule nor the fabrication of the long-range mechanism was possible and may require several years of work with the chance of discovering another element on earth or from outer space."

Commander Bhosle stepped in, "They have only four capsules. We do not know how they will use them. These capsules will cause damage, but it won't be catastrophic. With proper precautions, we can save the soldiers. During personal conversation with Nikhil, I understood that the disruption would be short term. Whether they can reverse engineer the devices to deliver more, I don't know. We should be ready. They don't know the details. Only four of us knew those details. Therefore, they will be relaxed musing about the victory. They'll take it for granted the destruction of Indian forces. Their ignorance is our gain. The element of surprise is with us. We'll be ready and alert when they attack."

"How do you know?" One of the ADI Officers interjected.

"That is classified. The sudden emergence of this exercise only implies that I planted the carrot and they bit it. The outcome is Operation Hind. I am more worried about Chinese incursion than

Operation Hind. Will you keep me informed about the development on the Northeastern frontier?" The Commander requested.

On their return journey, they were talking, "No wonder they call him Chanakya," they were referring to the reference of planting the carrot. "He is a damn good clever chap."

Chapter 32

Accident

B AM...DHOODUM DO...the screeching sound of brakes, the car coming from the other direction hit Sudarshan on the passenger side. The traffic on the road was normal for a Friday evening. Sudarshan Pillai was returning home from work at the Biochemical and Arsenal Testing (BAT) Company. He was thinking of his work and company business. He sensed something illegal was going on. When he confronted his manager asking for an explanation of the tests, he chastised Sudarshan. What is the matter with them? It was only a simple question.

In his reminiscence, he did not realize that the signal light just turned from yellow to red at the crossroad. He did not see the car approaching. Pedestrians who witnessed the severity of the accident immediately dialed 911. Within five minutes, wailing sirens of police cars sped toward the accident site. Sudarshan, the driver, and the passenger from the other car were dazed. No one was badly hurt. The damage to both cars was heavy and later, the tow truck towed the cars from the accident site. All three of them were taken to the hospital by ambulance and were admitted for examination and observation. Police checked street cameras for evidence. The video from the camera showed the light turning from yellow to red. It was Sudershan's fault. The police prepared the accident report, went to the hospital, and gave a copy of the report to both parties. The police also gave a citation to Sudarshan for reckless driving and passing through the red light.

Sudarshan had minor injuries and a concussion. It was not bad but the doctor decided to keep him overnight for observation. The attending nurse was Tania. She took down all his information, his name, the name of his employer, his address, medical insurance details, telephone number, etc., to complete the hospital registration formalities. She finished her shift at seven in the evening, and that was when James Montenegro called her. He was supposed to pick her up to take her to dinner, but he was running half an hour late. During the registration process, Tania found out that Sudarshan had no close relatives in the US. As a gesture of goodwill, she went to his room.

That night she talked to James about the accident and her patient.

"I believe he works for that BAT Company you talk about sometimes," she said.

James knew the company as a front for an illegal weapon and drug dealing business. The Mancini family, who destroyed his career, was part of that company.

"He seems to be a very nice guy. Poor fellow has no relatives here," Tania added a piece of information.

James began wondering. His detective instincts took over. "What is a nice fellow like him working for a company like that?" He smelled a problem and got interested.

On an impulse, before leaving Tania's apartment he blurted, "Is it okay if I come to the hospital to meet this young fellow?"

Tania was surprised. She never expected James to react like this, "Hey, I have no problem; in fact, I think it's an excellent idea. Tania knew that James was no longer an ATF agent. He was living on half-pension and doing some private security jobs that involved investigations. It paid adequately.

"No, I am not doing anything tomorrow. Times are slack. Since you are working tomorrow, I don't want to stay home alone and get bored," James replied.

James came to see Sudarshan Pillai. Sudarshan was thinking about the accident, the police report, and the citations. Moreover, he was thinking about the conversation he had at work. He was in a dolorous mood. He was anxious about how to get to work on Monday morning. He had no car now. The insurance would pay a little bit for the repairs and his job paid him well, so he did not worry about the cost of repairing his car. He decided to rent a car while he was waiting for his car to be repaired.

"Hello, how are you doing?" Tania entered the room.

"I am doing okay. Just wondering when the doctor will discharge me."

"Your reports are okay. I'll check with the doctor. I believe there won't be any problem getting you discharged by tomorrow, if not late this evening. But, you do have a visitor here today."

Sudarshan was wondering who that could be. He knew a few people, but he was not close to them, and he had not informed anyone about the accident.

"Meet Mr. James Montenegro. He is my friend. I told him about you last night, he just came to give you some company."

Sudarshan's eyes twinkled, he was happy to see a stranger. He did not want to go through the whole day thinking of the accident. He greeted James with a warm welcoming smile. They began talking.

Sudarshan rented an apartment near to the condominium complex where James lived. A few years back, James bought the condominium he lived in. To continue the conversation, James asked Sudarshan about his background and how did he ended up in this city? It was a mundane story.

Sudarshan's parents lived in Mumbai, India. He completed his degree in engineering at the University of Mumbai and applied for admission to universities in the US. He was accepted to a Master's program at Louisiana State University and came to the US on a student visa. Back home, he has one married sister and a younger brother. This year his brother will complete his degree in accounting.

While studying, Sudarshan met a girl, Laura, from Walker, Louisiana, who was working near the University in a coffee shop, a favorite student hangout. They started talking and gradually became friends. He dated her a few times. When she found out that he was on a student visa and might have to go back to India after completing school, she broke off their relationship, though she was decent about it. She made an excuse that it might not work out. She had family responsibilities and could not leave Louisiana. Sudarshan accepted the grief and concentrated on studies. After finishing his Ph.D., he started working for the BAT Company and moved to Chicago.

"I am still thinking of the accident," Sudarshan said.

"What happened? You didn't see the light turning red?" James asked.

"I was thinking about the testing project. Something is fishy; I cannot put finger on it. When I asked the boss, he chided me. I believe they are doing something illegal," Sudarshan replied.

James was right all along. He had a suspicion that the company was a front for an illegal operation. He decided to help Sudarshan and find out more about the BAT Company's illicit dealings.

On Sunday, James took Sudarshan home. He could not go to work immediately because the doctor ordered him to rest. James helped him get through the insurance paperwork. While he helped file the insurance papers, James found that Sudarshan does not have a rental-car insurance clause on his insurance. Sudarshan had to pay from his pocket for a rental car. James did not have any urgent cases. In fact, he had no case and was available. Therefore, he offered to drive Sudarshan to work until he got the car repaired or bought a new car.

After taking a couple of days off, Sudarshan returned to the office. The next day, after Sudarshan got out of the car, James saw Gustav coming out of the office building heading toward the parking lot. James waited and decided to follow him. Gustav drove to Noah's house. James waited, and an hour later, he saw Noah Mancini, Gustav, and Robert Lange exiting from the back door and Robert Lange immediately entering into the car. He saw Robert Lange on national television with the presidential candidate, Governor Henry Giarrusso. Noah Mancini was Mafia, and Gustav was in illegal weapons. He began wondering about their connection to the National Presidential Campaign.

Chapter 33

Domination

The octagonal mahogany table with a stone slab on top was built sometime in the Medieval Ages. Later, the slab was changed to a granite slab. This became the seat of the eight heads of the Clan of the Wolf Head. The Clans of the Wolf Head were the thugs, thieves, killers, pirates, and robbers in the continent of Europe that lived under the pretense of aristocracy. They formed a secret society. The mask of the wolf became a symbol of the Clan; they were richest in the world. The Clans of the Wolf Head do not belong to any country; they have no loyalty or fidelity to any nation. The black of the granite symbolized the wickedness of their hearts. Their purpose was to siphon money into their coffers. They used any means necessary to achieve that purpose. Every operation, every task, every acquisition was secretly performed.

The masquerade was the deliberation; the silence was the intention. They executed people who opposed, murdered the families when necessary to create fear, and robbed the poor mercilessly. Their motto was to accumulate… accumulate… and accumulate the wealth, no mercy, no fear. It was their nature. They called themselves the Clan of the Wolf Head, but no one outside their arena heard the name. No one knew the identity. Vagueness shrouded their character. The world began to grow in Europe. Few joined them by marriage, bloodline of Scythia, the daughter of Arthur the John of Scotland - lots of Camelot and Rudolophians from Germany. Intermarriages from the South of France and Spain brought another dimension to this secret society. Added to those were the cruelty and atrocities beyond the wildest imagination of the human race. The eight Chiefs occupied the eight sides of the octagonal table. That never changed; although the faces changed with time and death.

They sailed to America, spread through Canada, plunged Australia and the coast of New Zealand, and used the Crown Army, French Army, the Spaniards, or Dutch Monarchy to wipe out the aboriginals. No one even guessed. Most thought it was the British Army, the French Army, Spaniards, or the Dutch. No one had ever heard the name the Clans of the Wolf Head. Wiping out the indigenous population was the practice of the colonization. The game changed over the years. Novelty was necessary to protect their cloak; to keep themselves hidden so they could continue to conquest and accumulate. They did everything to hide their identity and purpose; they joined Illuminatis or became Freemasons to deceive the masses. Land was not their objective; they left their colonial conquest for immigrants to toil as the Clans of the Wolf Head continued to control them. Wealth, authority, and power – the trident of the New Age was their goal. They could not allow aboriginals to live because their way of life was different; it was more spiritual than materialistic.

They tried the same in India and China. They did not succeed in China. However, British Imperialism ruled over India because of the effective use of treachery. There were handfuls of British soldiers. Hindu and Muslim traitors made their entire army. This was how they were able to rule the country – using the axiom of divide and rule. McCauley's ideas took hold of Indian minds and corrupted them for centuries to come. Even after independence, the army, the police, and the administration continued with a legacy of the traitor mentality. The Indian leaders had no idea how to govern the country. Those who sacrificed lost forever. Indian constitution still carries many clauses that have their roots from the time of the British rule. To make the situation worse for Hindus, the amendments in the constitution geared toward fortifying the secularism. In a nutshell, these amendments to the constitution help Muslims and other minorities.

The concoction of the two world wars gave the Clans of the Wolf Head enough opportunity to accumulate more wealth and power, but also taught them a lesson. They learned new games. No more wars, but simply the lure of war could continue to help them dominate and achieve their goal to accumulate wealth, authority, and power. They were the maker of the kings, the presidents, and the prime ministers in the global arena. They were behind every endeavor, every contrivance, every fall of empires, the mergers of companies, the rise of corporations followed by bankruptcies, worldwide skirmishes, transfer of weapons, and supply of drugs. You name it and they had already practiced it. The key to power was in their hands, how to turn the key was for them to decide. They never held any direct positions in the cabinets of any country. They never held the positions of CEO or CFO of any corporations. They just manipulated the cir- cumstance to suit their purposes. The monarchs, the presidents, the prime Ministers… were puppets; the Clans of the Wolf Head moved the strings of manipulation to control them. The lobbyists, the entrepreneurs, and intermediaries from all four corners of the globe were in their grip. However, none of them ever realized or felt the pressure. The key of their operations was the indirect control so their identity would remain hidden. Manipulation was the weapon of their organization, so no one knew the Clans of the Wolf Head.

The octagonal table was in Europe before, that was transported to the US and sitting in the mansion of Josiah Baron in Los Angeles. The houses of various entertainers surrounded the mansion; a per- fect luxurious hideout in the open that no one would ever suspect. The meeting of the council of the Clans of the Wolf Head was about to begin in the residence of Josiah Baron of California. The remaining seven heads, Richard Dalhousie, Alexander Ferrari, Alano Aragon, Petrovsky Nikolaevna, Rothman Chevalier, Joshua Hamilton, and the latest addition, Sultan Akhmad from Saudi, arrived one by one. Sultan Akhmad is not an actual Sultan; this is his name. He is not a tribal chief or owner of any company. He knew most of the mem- bers of the Saudi monarchy and held vast wealth and influence in the Middle East.

The Middle East was rapidly becoming a lucrative center for wealth with its oil wells and reserves of oil. It was necessary to have a controlling presence over there. One of the heads of the clan died, and his seat became available. The ancestry of Akhmad was part of the Clan of the Wolf Head from the Medieval Ages through intermarriages from Spain. The daughter of the clan member from Morocco was married into the household of Akhmad. His name came up during selection, and they accepted Akhmad to add a new dimension to their expanding empire of wealth and power.

Josiah Baron started the meeting. He and Dalhousie, both in their late 70s, were the only two members alive since the last meeting. The eight heads meet every four decades. The faces change each time.

Josiah Baron began, "Welcome, Heads of the Clan of the Wolf Head. We eight heads meet every 40 years. First, let me take this opportunity to welcome all new members and introduce you to Sultan Akhmad, our newest member who joined us last year." Everyone cheered.

"Today we will discuss India. The Hindu civilization is the oldest civilization and an advanced culture that has been in existence from the dawn of humanity. Before I begin, I will give a short summary of our activities from the previous century." Josiah Baron paused and glanced at all of the seven heads of the Clan of the Wolf Head. They all nodded.

"This is a brief summary of discussion from the last two meetings for the benefit of all new members. At the end of the nineteenth century, we created the Durand Line on Afghanistan's border. This was good foresight on our ancestor's part. Today, the unrest continues near the Afghan border between Afghanistan and the newly created state of Pakistan and in the divided India. The two world wars brought us vast fortune. The global war fought in World War I centered in Europe. The incident of the Bosnian student attacking the heir of the Austrian-Hungarian throne ignited the series of skirmishes, which resulted in key players, the two opposing alliances, first - the UK, France, and Russia, against second - Germany, Austria-Hungary, and Italy. Several nations joined the war, faced each other, and chose sides. It was similar to the battle described in Mahabharat, the book of Hindu mythology. World War I created an extensive upheaval in the early nineteenth century. It took the authority of direct military rule away, and gave rise to the geo-political exercise of using capitalism, business globalization, and cultural superiority to run a country. It gave us a chance to redraw the map of central Europe into several smaller states, which was beneficial to us," he paused to sip water.

"World War II was unwarranted. Architecture wielded the mind of the Fuhrer to invade Poland. The idea was to prevent the spread of communism. The Fuhrer became greedy. He began dreaming of world conquest. The Second World War was not meant to be. Unfortunately, the end of World War I impregnated the seed of World War II. The main opponents used their entire economic, industrial, and technological capabilities to fight the war. The distinction between civilian and military resources vanished. The war escalated out of control, which was not the intention.

We struggled with this; on top of that, Subhash Chandra Bose unexpectedly arrived from India to Germany asking for help to liberate India from the clutches of British Imperialism. We never expected arrival of Subhash Chandra Bose from India. The Fuhrer welcomed him. Mr. Bose advised him to concentrate on Britain and France rather than to go after Russia during the winter. His advice was very sound. If he had listened to Mr. Bose, disaster would have been evident. Imagine if the Fuhrer had won, and the continent of an undivided India would have become the free Hindu nation under the leadership of Mr. Bose. However, for the Fuhrer, the Russian bear was far more important than the British sheep or the plea of Mr. Bose for the freedom of India. That unexpected problem worried us. That did not happen. Instead, a subdivided secular India under the leadership of the father of the nation and inexperienced corrupt leadership was born. That was a lucky break for us," Josiah paused. He saw the variegated streak of colors on the faces of the heads of the Clan of the Wolf. They all shuddered with the idea of undivided continent of India under the leadership of the strong Hindus.

He continued, "We got an unexpected break when the Fuhrer lost and Bose died in an accident set up by us. After the experience of World War II, we have prudently scattered the wealth widely all over the globe in various holdings. The CEOs and CFOs of these companies are on our payroll, some of them are also Clan members. Last century, the idea of a third world war emerged because we manipulated the situation in Afghanistan. However, we soon realized there was more profit in the lure of war to sell weapons on both sides, export drugs from their opium fields, and maintain control over oil production. The idea of a third world war is no longer lucrative, not now in this twenty-first century. It could bring destruction to our agenda. Our next heads will determine the course of action for the twenty-second century. This was the summary from the last meeting.

Now we will review the activities since the last meeting. In the last century, one of the presidents was synergetic. His attitude was rebellious. We tried to coerce him, but it was of no use. Our ancestors previously eliminated another president in another century in a similar situation for his love toward slaves; similarly, we also eliminated this president. The history tells us that it probably was an impulsive act on our part. We will never know. We have to keep a balance so all our operations will run smoothly," he paused looked at Mr. Chevalier and announced; "Now I will request Mr. Chevalier to share with us the latest development."

Baron yielded to Mr. Chevalier, who began, "Good morning to all of you. I thank Mr. Baron for providing the summary for continuity and a brief account of our activities. There is one more important event I would like to share with you all before I talk about the Indian situation. We will soon have our man in the White House. Governor Henry Giarrusso accepted the nomination of the Republican Party to run for the Presidency. He is the son-in-law of Senator Frank Fitzroy. The Senator is very influential man, and he is in our court. The Governor Giarrusso did a good job governing the State of Illinois during the last two terms and people are praising him. We have to make sure that he gets elected."

Every member in the room cheered, they forgot the thought of undivided India under the leadership of a strong Hindu nation. Mr. Chevalier waited to end the cheers and then added, "Recently, an IT spin brought many opportunities. I will request Alano Aragon to provide his input on the IT revolution," Mr. Chevalier looked at Alano Aragon and requested him to continue.

Alano nodded, "Good morning, Heads of the Clan of the Wolf. The IT revolution brought the opportunity to use the brainpower of Eastern countries for our benefit. Countries like India, Taiwan, and Thailand are providing IT-related services to Western countries. They help us grow. They feel that the American economy and IT-based structure depend upon their help and that make them relax.

They are paid for their services. The remuneration provides huge revenue to them. Based on that huge revenue and other technological initiatives, India boasts about the inclusion in first-world country status without the proper infrastructure to back it up. They do not realize their dependence on the US economy. One day, the IT spin will end. We can manipulate such a situation if warranted by the need of the time. They do not know that. Their ignorance will work in our favor. At this moment, we do not know where it is heading. I believe, Mr. Chevalier, you have something to add."

"Thank you, Mr. Aragon, for the report." Mr. Chevalier continued, "We were a little concerned about the brain drain from India in the beginning. After the independence of India, many Indians migrated to America, England, Canada, and Europe. While working with our corporations, they gained experience in advanced medicines, industrial processes, nuclear plants, manufacturing methods, design engineering, etc., and made a good name and money for themselves, as well as for India. We thought that they would take this knowledge back to serve India. That did not happen. There were riots, emergency periods, minority issues, and a race for the vote banks to win elections, and so on. The Indian Administration did not even give a chance to these highly trained intellectuals. The Indian government could have hired their own country's veterans and benefitted from their experience to advance to the next level to build a strong infrastructure. However, their leaders and entrepreneurs were busy stashing the money in Swiss bank accounts. They did not seize the opportunity to build the infrastructure of their country like China. Instead, the corruption and greed took hold of their politicians. This frustrated brain drain eventually became the citizens of Western countries and helped them to advance. That was good for us. Look at the American progress; the immigrants did it. Do you agree?"

Petrovsky Nikolaevna interrupted, "Why are we talking about India so much, is there any reason?"

"I am glad you asked that question. Presently, we have control all over the globe except India and China. In the last century, we managed to crumble Communism in Russia. As of this moment, China is strong. Our weak link is India – we failed in our mission during the Imperial Rule over India. We went to America, Canada,

Australia and New Zealand. We wiped out the indigenous population in those continents. We also went to India but could not wipe out the population. India always posed a challenge. Hinduism is still strong, however they failed in building the infrastructure needed for progress.

During our discussion today, we will address these issues. The China story is different. We thought we could make them depend upon us, but they have started building their infrastructure. China manufactures half of American products. The deficiency of the American economy is due to the money borrowed from China; America is indebted to China. We have no representative in that part of the world to exercise control. However, we shouldn't think about them right now because later we can devise a plan for China, similar to the fall of Communism in Russia.

We should also remember that in spite of the well-built influence of Communism, at heart, China is a Buddhist country. The Indian prudent scholars could have taken advantage of this religious situation. Hindu and Buddhist religious beliefs are not too much apart. Together they could dominate the world. However, India, the second largest demographically populated country in the world, became weak with the division of the country during independence. The most favorable fact is that it became secular by the grace of their pink leadership. We never expected that. We thought that Pakistan would become a Muslim nation, and India would become a Hindu democracy. Sometimes fate works mysteriously to help us," Mr. Chevalier responded.

They all laughed. He looked at all of them and then added, "I'll request Monsieur Alexander Ferrari to say few words about Indian Media."

Monsieur Alexander Ferrari coughed a little before beginning, "Another big joke is their Bollywood industry, controlled by Muslim money. They mimic the pattern of American Hollywood and TV programs, like dancing competitions, singing competitions and soap operas. How much is the percentages of Americans watch these dance and song competitions, and soap operas?

Hardly five or six percent, the number is a little higher for our younger generation; say about less than 20 percent. Almost 30-40 percent of Indians are crazy about Bollywood movies, shows, and singing and dancing competitions and the numbers are even higher in the younger generations, nearly 70 percent or more. What does that mean toward advancement of the nation? Zip..., there is practically not much contribution by the younger generation. Do you know what am I getting at?"

Ferrari paused, looked at the heads; there was still a puzzled look on Mr. Petrovsky Nikolaevna.

He smiled at Petrovsky and continued, "The nation as a whole becoming crazy after music, dance, wretched soap operas, and the actors and actresses. These temptations are luring the nation. Bollywood addiction, like drug addiction, is on the rise in the younger generation. Instead of Bollywood addiction, they can use their energy and time for the growth of the country.

Looking at Indian history, we know that whenever the monarchy became vulnerable to dance and music, downfall followed. History may repeat itself here. Instead of penalizing the country's corrupt leadership, thinking about bringing back the trillions of dollars stashed in Swiss banks by their leaders and entrepreneurs, trying to unravel the plots of the terrorist activities, these youngsters, the future hope of the country, are looking at Bollywood as their goal. The few remaining are either busy providing IT services to Western countries or building infrastructure for Middle East countries. This is the epitome of the present day India, who had a glorious golden past millennia back. I brought this up to highlight such archetypal behavior and see how we could benefit from it."

"There is one other aspect I would like to add," Mr. Arthur Hamilton interrupted. Hamilton's ancestors from East India Company almost ruled the country.

"Hero worship, they go crazy after this concept. To elaborate, let me tell you an anecdote from British history. During World War II, Churchill was the Prime Minister of Britain because he was most suitable for the job during the war. However, Mr. Clement Attlee became the Prime Minister as soon as the war was over. They did not continue with Churchill. India is different. They idolize the figure and continue to worship their families. Their ruling party leadership continues from generation to generation regardless of their capabilities. The club dancer could become the chief based on family worship. The people in the entertainment industry enjoy such worship. It is similar to monarchy. One will not find such celebrity worship in the West. There is a craze over celebrities in the West, but there is a difference between mania and worship.

It is vital for us to know this Indian attitude because we can use this to our benefit. We can manipulate India. The Indian masses never cared for those who had sacrificed for their country. Occasionally, after death, they will build the statue or give their names to the roads. In spite of all drawbacks, one wonders how this ancient civilization survived over the millennia," Hamilton paused.

All the heads of the Clan of the Wolf were looking at him in anticipation. Hamilton was knowledgeable about India. Hamilton cleared his throat, "You all must be wondering what it could be. It is their undeniable faith. They survived throughout all the catastrophes, surpassed all their pitfalls, rode over the inadequacies, and overcame the deficiencies, all because of their faith. Look at the millions of pilgrims at Kumbh Mela where they gather to take a dip in the cold water of the River Ganges. They visit the pilgrimages located in the high mountains, visit temples like Tirupati and Siddhi Vinayak, even the NRIs' (the Non-Resident Indians) of Hindu origin, who are no longer the citizens of India, go there with their foreign-born progeny and offer their reverence. The tradition continues no matter where the Hindu is.

They give millions in donations at these places. Now their secular government started controlling these temples, and I believe rerouted the funds to other activities. There are so many aspects with both pros and cons that I could go on and on, but Mr. Sultan Akhmad has some information on terrorism and Jihad. The attack on the World Trade Center was not in our agenda. Mr. Sultan Akhmad, I believe you have some information to share, so I will request you to proceed from here." Hamilton looked at Sultan.

Sultan began his report, "Osama was from Saud Family. He never expected the toppling of the two towers. The outcome was unexpected for him, too. There was a leak in Osama's organization; it was probably not the treachery, but showing off. However, someone in the US got the whiff of it and decided to use that information as an excuse to start a war with Afghanistan.

The reports indicate the presence of the explosives already planted inside the towers. The towers toppled straight down with the crashing of the plane along with the explosives already planted inside. Since all the terrorists who attacked the buildings died, we had no way to verify the information.

So, the question remains – who planted the explosives. However, after that event, the Afghan war started and it helped us. Finding out who planted the explosives was no longer our agenda. Our investors had a lot invested in the World Trade Center. The outcome was not profitable, however, I would add the Afghan war equalized the profits and losses," he paused and allowed the information to sink in.

Then he began his report about the new oil source in India, "Recently we received information about oil findings near Ahmadabad, in the State of Gujarat, in India. Presently, we have no knowledge about the quantity of the reserve, but rumor has been circulating that it is a huge quantity. We may bribe their Oil Minister in order to get one of our affiliates to install a pipeline. We are still working on the details."

Mr. Baron got up from his side of the octagonal table, "I think this was a very informative meeting. We learned that the plan of the third world war is not advisable. Instead, we fuel small battles and supply ammunitions to both sides.

China is still an uncharted territory and probably will remain like that for years to come. We did not discuss Chinese incursion into Indian Territory. However, this will benefit us eventually. That will keep India occupied for some time.

We did not discuss North Korea, Russia, or Chechnya, but our action plan about small battles also applies to these areas. The continent of South America has skirmishes going on all the time. The continent of Africa is still a machete monger. They take pleasures in cutting the limbs of their own brothers. Many times, we convert our funds to blood diamonds from Africa.

The main items that we covered today are the nomination for presidential candidacy and about the situation in India. Based on the informative knowledge provided by our colleagues, we know which direction to head to give us maximum opportunity to accumulate.

We can use Indians' 'Hero Worship,' their corrupt mentality, and the shortsightedness of their politicians who see nothing beyond their Swiss bank accounts to manipulate them.

A question that may occur in our mind is; what we will do with this accumulation, with this wealth? What is the future? I will direct your attention to sci-fi stories. The world is changing. The environment is probably deteriorating. Devastation is no longer a fantasy. It could very well become a reality. The science is working on galactic travel and building satellites. We cannot ignore that reality. Eventually, we will have to expand our horizons to colonize other planets. We will have to build a dome to make some part of Earth habitable and to build galactic ships to travel beyond Earth's atmosphere. No one knows whether there is another Earth like ours. We have to explore. Our vast amount of funds will help us achieve that. We have to find the scientists and pay them handsomely; we have to find qualified technicians. This will be the agenda for our next meeting after 40 years. So if no one has anything to add, we will discuss the action plans before concluding the meeting."

"Not so fast Baron," Rothman Chevalier interrupted him.

"Yes, Roth do you have anything on your mind?" Baron looked at him intently.

"We talked about India so much, but let me point out to you a line from one of their scriptures. The Geeta states that whenever there is a problem, God will arise to protect *Dharm*. In this case, we can conclude *Dharm* as the follower of Hindu *Dharm*."

Everyone was wondering what this statement from the scripture had to do with the present discussion.

Roth continued, "You may be wondering why I brought up this reference. It is just to caution you. Let us not take things for granted. In spite of their pitfalls, drawbacks, and treachery, the Indian civilization survived the harshest test of time and continues to live on."

He paused looked at them and began, "Let me start with the current invention that took place in India. One of their scientists from the GEETA Laboratory affiliated with the ISHWAR spy facility of India developed a product. I learned from one of our scientists that it could kill people and scramble any communications without destroying the facility or structure. It is a very innovative technology. A local terrorist organization in India stole the capsule and murdered the scientist. Our honorable new member Mr. Sultan Akhmad informed that the BAT Company, one of our American affiliates from Chicago, engineered this venture.

However, let us not ignore that even a very small percentage of awakened spies, scientists, and citizens could still create a problem. Their spies are chasing after the terrorist gang. It does not matter how much we try to belittle India, that one country always puzzled me. I believe our honorable new member Akhmad has detailed information about the invention."

Akhmad began, "Let me introduce all the details. The device is deadly. The plan was to steal all the devices, get them to Saudi and from Saudi to the US. Last night, I received more information that the terrorist gang stole four devices and the flash drive. The scientist is dead, the computer is burned, and from our reliable source, we found out that the scientist just came across this invention and he did not get the time to transfer the information to the mainframe computer. The laboratory does not have any information. The question is who else knows about this? Did the scientist transfer the information somewhere else? Who planted the explosion in the cabin? These are all unanswered questions," Akhmad paused.

Roth hesitated before asking, "There are four devices, but I heard that we would only get one device because of their Jihadist instinct and lewd desire for virgin hurries (nymph) in heaven."

Akhmad cleared his throat; he was trying to phrase his response, "Various factions of Pakistan and Afghanistan are not controllable. There is this promise of Allah and temptations of the Virgin Hurries (nymph) of Heaven, as you mentioned, to these terrorists. Their intent is to explode the devices in three cities – Delhi, London, and Washington. We will get the fourth device. I will try to get all the devices and the flash drive to us, but I cannot promise. If someone in GEETA got the information, the informant planted there would provide the information. In that situation, we have to either buy or kill that individual. Unfortunately, if the dead scientist had sent the information outside the GEETA facility, it would appear soon. In that case, the information may eventually reach to a politician or some government official. We have already contacted Dawood Khilnani from Dubai to contact the media. They can easily get into bed with these politicians or officers," Sultan paused, took a sip of wine from the table, and continued.

"In case the terrorists who stole the capsules decided to explode three of them, it could turn out to be favorable to us to produce more and jack up the price in the market for North Korea, China, Russia, and whoever else wants to buy. It is like a fear of nuclear attack. It never happens but just the thought of it deters it from happening."

"That's great," exclaimed Hamilton.

Sultan continued, "I am thinking of collecting the devices in Pakistan. Islamabad may not be a good place. India may have some double agents planted in Islamabad. One never knows. I have a few contacts in Waziristan and later I'll send one of my employees to collect the devices in Waziristan. No Indian RAW agent can reach that far. I will try to get all four of them but for some odd reason, if the perverted lust of these terror mongers makes them happy to have 50 hurries in heaven, so be it. I have my own harem."

The meeting continued for another hour with discussions about action plans and other details before concluding.

Chapter 34

Kidnapping

"This is foreign correspondent Ruben Joshi reporting for Independent Cable News Network-ICNN from the Ladakh Region. In recent years, there have been increasing reports in the Indian media of incursions by the Chinese along the border of India. The Chinese military incursion into Indian Territory is in the Ladakh Region. As the dispute continues, apprehension in the Indian capital is growing. The response by India's governing Party has been so far not so strong. The Prime Minister Kuldip Kaul refers to the incursion as a localized problem.

One of the sources from the Indian Foreign Ministry told us that the Foreign Ministry was considering resolving the issue through negotiations. They are downplaying negotiations as rubbing ointment over pus of a pustule. However, the political opponents, commentators, and political analysts have been pushing for much stronger action. They are accusing the ruling party as cowardly and incompetent. There is also a racial overtone attached to the negotiations owed to the government's procrastination because the person negotiating with China from the India's Foreign Ministry is Muslim by descent from this secular country.

Chinese Communists have been sending leaflets across their southern borders stating that Nepal, Bhutan, Sikkim, Ladakh, and the Northeastern Indian state of Arunachal Pradesh are the five fingers, with Tibet as the palm of China's hand, and China has to win the fingers (five Indian Provinces) back. Many Indians are publicly protesting that it is the same as the 1962 scenario, when China had seized almost 12,000 square miles near the Chip Chap River that was part of India. With the present progress, this territorial dispute may continue over a longer period. Military personnel state that it'll end like 1962 by losing some more land to China unless strong military response is implemented. This is Ruben Joshi of ICNN reporting from the Ladakh Region."

Ruben and his crew stopped overnight in Delhi and met with Kiran. He told her about the *Char Dham Yatra* tour. Kiran could see the light emanating from his eyes when he was describing the places they visited. He summarized the Chinese incursion on Indian soil in two sentences; Indian Government had tied the hands of their military, and the future of fingers depends on the "destiny" and the philosophy of non-violence of no action India since 1947.

Kiran did not comment. She updated him on the progress of the investigation of the theft and murder. The next day, he was about to fly back to Kabul when he heard the story about the hanging of the terrorist. He discussed the story with his cameraman and producer and decided to broadcast on the ICNN of US before living for Kabul.

He began his broadcast.

"This is foreign correspondent Ruben Joshi reporting for Independent Cable News Network - ICNN from Delhi. David Hakim, a convict of the August 15 attack in Baroda in the state of Gujarat, and the last attack in Kashmir, was hanged for his crimes early this morning. The credit goes to Gujarat Police and especially to Advocate Urmilesh Desai. During the trial, references were made to Article 370 and 238 of India's Constitution." Ruben did not read Article 370. The camera turned to the page to display the Article on the viewers' TV screen.

Article 370 of the Constitution of India

Temporary Provisions with respect to the State of Jammu & Kashmir

1. Not withstanding anything in this constitution:

a) The provisions of Article 238 shall not apply in relation to the State of Jammu & Kashmir.

b) The power of Parliament to make laws for the said state shall be limited to those matters in the Union List and the Concurrent List which in consultation with the Government of the State, are declared by the President to correspond to matters specified in the Instrument of Accession governing the accession of State to the Dominion of India as the matters with respect to which the Dominion Legislature may make laws for that State and such other matters in the Said Lists as, with the concurrence of the Govt. of the State, the President may, by order specify.

Explanation:

For the purposes of this Article, the Govt. of the State means the person for the time being recognized by the President as Maharaja of Jammu & Kashmir acting on the advice of the council of Ministers for the time being in office under the Maharaja's Proclamation dated the fifth day of March 1948.

(c) The provisions of Article (1) and of this Article shall apply in relation to this State;

(d) Such of the other provisions of this Constitution shall apply in relation to that State Subject to such exceptions and modifications as the President may by order specify; Provided that no such order which related to the matters specified in the Instrument of Accession of the State referred to in paragraph (i) of sub clause (1) shall be issued except in consultation with the Govt. of the State. Provided further that no such order which relates to, matters other than those referred to in the last proceeding provision shall be issued except with the concurrence of the Govt. of the State.

2. If the concurrence of the Govt. of the State referred to in para (ii) of Sub Clause (b) of Clause (1) be given before the Constituent Assembly for the purpose of framing the Constitution of the State is concerned. It shall be placed before such Assembly for such decision as it may take thereon.

3. Notwithstanding anything in the foregoing provisions of the article, the President may, by public notification, declare that this Article shall cease to be operative or shall be operative only with such exceptions and modifications and from such date as he may notify. Provided that the recommendation of the Constituent Assembly of the State referred to in Clause (2) shall be necessary before the President issues such a notification.

Ruben added, "Article 238, consisted of provisions dealing with the administration of states, in Part B of the First Schedule of Indian constitution (In 1950, the Constitution contained a four-fold classification of the states of Indian union --Part A, Part B, Part C, Part D states). This Article 238 was omitted from the constitution, by the 7th Constitutional Amendment Act of 1956 Part VIII about the union territories, in the wake of reorganisation of the states."

Dr Pravin Togardia, the local working President of Hindu organization said, "Hanging David Hakim is a welcome beginning for the war on terror that the Indian PM promises only on the foreign soils, and congratulates the CM (Chief Minister) of Gujarat. In Bharat (India) Hindus get arrested and jailed while terrorists get negotiations and free escape passes." He also criticized that the attackers of Delhi's Connaught Place, Afzul Khalid and other hundreds of Jihads are living happily in the Indian jails like parasites. "They are eating up Indian taxpayers' hard-earned money and are a burden on Bharat (Indian) Government. They also pose danger to Bharat's safety and security. Therefore, it is now imperative that the Government should deny Afzul Khalid's clemency petition and without any further delay, hang him per the Supreme Court's verdict."

He added that the Courts should also complete the cases for other Jihadis, and hang them, too. "The Mumbai blast convicts are still sitting in Indian jails, and some are at-large roaming free. The Union Government and all state governments should act in these cases faster and bring justice and peace to the relatives of the victims."

* * * * *

The Kabul Wall snakes along the Sher Darwaza Mountain running west and east from Babar Gardens over to Bala Hissar the oldest surviving structure in the capital of Afghan, across a flat arid steppe of scrub and rock toward the high flat-topped hill.

Down the road, on the outskirts of Kabul, was NATO's Camp Warehouse. Ruben and his crew were reporting the car bombing outside the warehouse compound. The car bomb blew an exterior wall of the compound apart, killed four civilians, and wounded at least 10 people. By the time, they had finished reporting, it was late evening.

They were returning to the hotel. Asif Basher, the cameraman cum driver, was driving the news truck.

Ubiquitous white pickups with militiamen operating machine guns cruised menacingly. These militiamen, said to be loyal to warlords controlling parts of the districts, were a part of the Warlordistan. Violence was frequent on these curvy roads, which slanted on both sides snaking toward the city.

Two SUVs trailed the news truck. Asif did not realize he was being tailed. Without warning, another Toyota SUV emerged from the side road. Asif slammed on the brake. The news truck stopped abruptly; Asif lost control, and the truck hit the tree and overturned. The impact was hard. The truck overturned on Ruben's side injuring him. All three were stunned but awake. The masked men from the other SUV quickly got out, pulled the news crew from the overturned truck, put them in the SUV, and drove away fast. The Toyota SUV continued to drive in the opposite direction.

Later, another Humvee carrying American soldiers back to the barracks saw the overturned truck with the ICNN emblem. They stopped, reported the accident, and checked for the news crew. No one was inside. They saw some blood.

The Military Authorities from Kabul immediately notified ICNN headquarters and the American Consulate. Secret Service agents came immediately to check for clues, but there were none. The DNA of the blood sample indicated it was Ruben's blood. The CIA, the State Department, and the Foreign Ministry were alerted of their kidnapping. The machinery began rolling.

The onsite CIA agents, friendly with the warlords, found out that one of his men saw the accident and noticed the SUV heading to Pakistan's border toward Khost. That was not good news. The north Waziristan-Pakistan border was near Khost. The deputy from the State Department flew to Kabul. The satellite watched for any signs of SUV. They identified suspected SUV and tracked them. It was almost more than 24 hours and there was no news. The American Consulate waited to hear demands for an exchange. State officials stood by along with ICNN network people. They tried to bribe some of the warlords in the area. Soon, the story became viral.

Chapter 35

Islamabad

"*D*adijaan (Grand Ma) *sambhalke* (be careful)," Fatima was worried about her husband's grandmother walking near the stream of water alone. She was a feisty woman in her mid-70s, still walking straight without using a stick. The crisp climate and the vibrant environment of Kashmir valley helped. The mountain peaks, covered with snow, edged against the skyline in the horizon.

According to the deciphered message, SHIV the Destruction may soon reach Udhampur, if it had not already left for Islamabad. Fatima's husband was from the same village where he grew up with Salamat, Bahadur, Fahayat, and Latif. Salman's grandmother was still living there in Salman's house. Salman's parents refused to join the Islam movement to free Kashmir. Terrorists killed them both. Salman's uncle brought him to Delhi. Fatima told Ramanuj that she could identify three of them and their houses in the village. So Ramanuj sent Fatima and Dabu Kadgul alias Farooq Khalid to Udhampur. They traveled separately. Fatima went to Salman's house in the Dalsar village and met with his grandmother. She had heard about Salman's death and embraced Fatima in tears, "*Beti* (daughter), stay here. This is your house."

Farooq Khalid came to the mosque in the Dalsar village near Udhampur. He saw the green string with crescent hanging on a big tree trunk as described by Fatima behind the mosque. He dug underneath and found the small tin. He opened the tin and found inside an encrypted message from Fatima giving details of the addresses of the three culprits that were left.

That night, there was a raid on those three houses. In a gunfight, the bullet hit Salamat in his chest. Fahayat saw him tumbling down, gasping for his last breath, and was scared. Farooq asked Salamat about the SHIV the Destruction devices, but he died before answering any questions. The military investigator searched the houses and surrounding area but could not find the devices.

Farooq Khalid aimed at Fahayat. Fahayat was sweating. He told them that Latif Ahamadi had the devices and already left with them for Pakistan. They took Fahayat Khan for further interrogation to Delhi. During interrogation, they realized that he was a fake carrier used to mislead them, a small pawn caught in the big game with mutual association. Farooq Khalid and Fatima stayed behind to get some leads on Latif or his plans from the villagers. The next evening, there was an attack on Fatima's hut. Farooq Khalid was in the vicinity. In a gunfight, terrorists shot Dadijaan and she died instantly. Fatima escaped safely.

* * * * *

Recently, Punj Bus service began to operate between India and Pakistan. Due to the present war circumstances, it was temporarily on hold. The Rajasthan and Gujarat borders also had the truck routes used for illegal trafficking that never stopped. The sea route for smuggling from Div Daman was still available.

"Latif could take any of those routes," Commander Bhosle thought and ordered the border patrol to increase security on all checkpoints and routes and his agents distributed pictures of Latif Ahamadi to the border patrol guards. Latif picked up the message from HuJI network about the tight border security and went underground.

Ramanuj discussed with Commander Bhosle about infiltrating Farooq and Fatima deep inside Pakistan. He explained his plan to his boss, "I'll go with Farooq and two other small-time local gangsters near the Gujarat-Rajasthan truck route. Give some drugs to those gangsters to carry with them to Karachi. All three will travel to Karachi and the two hoods will come back from Karachi, that way no one will suspect. However, I have created a twist in this endeavor," Ramanuj paused to hear any comments from Commander.

"What kind of twist?"

"You must have read about recent raid in Mumbai to arrest one of the top Bhai (gangster) Kala Vinchu (Black Scorpion)."

"He died during the raid," Commander said.

"Yes, he died, but his right-hand man escaped. No one saw this man. His name is Farooq Khalid. Our team apprehended him. During the search of his place, we found the stash of money and the name of Zillat Pathania. Further investigation indicated that Zillat Pathania is Kala Vinchu's counterpart in Karachi. This Farooq was a tough guy. We could not break him. The daredevil tried to escape. We killed him in the encounter that night. We kept that a secret even from Mumbai police. For the underground world, he is still alive and has the black money of Kala Vinchu. We gave his identity to Dabu Kadgul." The Commander understood.

Ramanuj continued, "For Fatima, I have a different plan. A prominent Pakistani singer is here as a judge with two Pakistani participants for Bollywood singing competition. The competitions are over and one of the singers won second place in the competition. They are returning tomorrow to Islamabad. Fatima will travel on the same plane with them using a fake passport and identity. You know how crazy people are on both sides of the border. There'll be a lot of the crowd at the Islamabad Airport to welcome them. Fatima can slip through the security posing as an assistant to the singer. She'll wear make up to have a different look. The moment she gets out of the security, our agents will pick her up."

Commander Bhosle approved both plans. He was pleased with Ramanuj. He also updated Ramanuj of the current development in Kabul and ordered him to use his full force if necessary.

After Ramanuj had left, Bhosle dialed a number in Kabul, when Kiran entered his office. Commander Bhosle updated her of the developments. He told her that Nikhil's killers were dead and told her to call the Washington office immediately. Kiran called and updated Lisa Hargrove.

"Nikhil's murderer died on the spot during the robbery. The other man involved in the theft was killed during the raid, and the third man is being brought to Delhi for interrogation. HuJI operative Latif Ahamadi is transporting SHIV devices. However, he is nowhere to be found at this moment."

"There is an assignment... waiting... for you in Islamabad. Go back to Islamabad. Our agents will be watching for SHIV the Destruction." Kiran sensed the temerity in Lisa's voice, "What is the matter, why are you so tense Lisa? What is the assignment?" Kiran thought it must be some dangerous undertaking and being a friend, Lisa was worried and anxious.

Lisa hesitated, then decided that it is better she should hear this from her, "Anthony is ready and waiting for you in Islamabad. You fly from Islamabad to Kabul immediately undercover. You'll be given a Muslim identity. We just received the message that the terrorists kidnapped three American journalists."

Kiran's heartbeat skipped, "Are... are you talking about Ruben?"

"I am afraid so. The State Department is doing everything to negotiate their release. We have satellite details. A full team of agents is working on this task in Kabul. They are heading toward Waziristan. I don't want you to be scared. Go to Islamabad, Anthony has the details." Kiran was dazed and despaired, but as a trained professional, she controlled her emotions. Her job was to rescue them, and she was going to do it. She was resolute.

Kiran told Commander Bhosle, "I am leaving immediately." She gave him the details of Ruben's kidnapping. Commander Bhosle saw the determination of a trained agent in her eyes.

"I have heard about kidnapping. Some of our agents had already penetrated in Pakistan are working on it. Ramanuj is also helping them. Americans don't have access to that part of the world. Be aware we'll not spare any efforts to rescue Ruben. Someone will contact you in Kabul or Islamabad. They'll use the password 'Op Nikhil *tayyar hai* (Ready)' and you'll respond '*Ji nahi, abhi nahi, kabhi nahi* (No, not now, never).' Take their help; do not hesitate. Either they'll give you good news, or they'll be extremely useful in the rescue operation. Go with them, they could penetrate that area."

Kiran thanked him... she did not know what to say. Just for a moment tears formed on her sclera near the cornea. She turned and left.

* * * * *

The front office of Bhudev Lohana's garage had two dilapidated sofas, two chairs, a desk, and a high chair. Bhudev occupied the high chair behind the desk. His family lived for centuries near the village Mithi just inside the border of Pakistan near Gujarat. After partition, Mithi became part of Pakistan and most of the Hindu community migrated to Gujarat a few miles from Mithi.

His grandfather, Jaydip Lohana, resumed the life of peddling fruits and vegetables. With the money offered under the refugee resettlement plan and the money earned through his peddling business, he purchased a garage on the truck route between two countries. They realized new business opportunities in illegal trafficking between two countries. New opportunities like drug trafficking, illegal immigration, and flesh trade provided a lot of *moola* (money). Bhudev was the "transportation" link between the two borders. He was very careful in handling the business. The raw agents caught some of the trucks carrying women and girls, drugs, and illegal weapons, but could not apprehend Bhudev due to the lack of evidence. He rented his trucks.

The truck route thrived during Katch and Pakistan's skirmishes on cross-border smuggling. The petty thieves and troublemakers running away from the police from both sides of the border did cross-country running between two countries. The border runners smuggled gold, silver, and foreign fabrics. They carried back Indian liquor, pan (*betel*) leaves, *bidi* (leaf-wrapped native cigarette) and acetic anhydride, very much in demand in the heroin refining industries of Afghanistan and Pakistan. Flesh trade was also booming. Thanks to respected leaders like Naidu who took it upon themselves to provide a better life to poverty-stricken young girls from Indian villages by throwing them to the wolves and warlords of Pakistan, Afghanistan, and Saudi Arabia.

"Be careful about the Border Rangers and the Pak Intelligence Bureau. It's important that you take *Mia* Khalid to Karachi," Ramanuj was instructing Bhudev, he found Bhudev at the *tadi* (local wine) place in Jalor, a musty old town on the southern border of Rajasthan. Bhudev knew Ramanuj as Rajaram a small-time hustler and a smuggler, fallout from *thuggee* (cutthroat robbers) tradition. He was a good customer who paid without quibble, and his money was good. Bhudev was under the impression that the people he was transporting for Ramanuj, alias Rajaram, must be hustlers like him running away from the police. No one asked questions in this business.

"Rajaram Sahib, this time the security is too tight. I can take your guys through different trucks each night. This will cost you. I have to offer more bribes to *Jamadars* (officers) and his *lavande* (slang for sepoy)," whined Bhudev. "And it's too far to travel to drop them off in Karachi. I usually deliver the load a few miles inside the border."

"Don't bicker. I know last week you dropped the consignment of gold in Karachi."

Bhudev was wondering how, the hell, he knew about the consignment.

"*Kya Janab, Mazak Karte ho* (you are joking man). I only deliver. I don't see what is inside," he pleaded.

"I am paying more money to do this."

Ramanuj's primary concern was the successful penetration. They could have sent Dabu Kadgul alias Farooq Khalid with the false passport via air that leaves the trail behind. This was the safest route. No one would suspect. The security was too tight, especially on the Indian side of the border because of the strict orders from Commander Bhosle; they were looking for Latif Ahamadi. The border patrol already received the copies of his photos.

"Make it double," Bhudev pleaded.

Another 20,000 rupees will not make much difference. Ramanuj agreed for additional payment.

"Only after you deliver them safely," he added.

They were getting ready to go. They had to cross the desert on both sides. Before starting the truck, the driver and his mechanic drank a few glasses of water, mixed with salt and sugar, and asked Farooq to do the same. It was a long drive and the body has to retain the fluid. Bhudev warned him not to speak a word during the journey until they reached the destination. He did not want any locals to get suspicious.

Before starting, Ramanuj talked to Farooq of his present assignments, including rescue operation of American journalists and the whereabouts of the SHIV the Destruction devices.

"We have to get those devices back. Jahangir or one of our other agents will contact you in Karachi and stay in touch with you. Your code word to respond will be *Mausam Hasin Hai* (weather is fine) when the agent will say *Janab garmi bahut hai* (hey man, it's hot). After this exchange of responses, the agent will introduce himself and give you instructions. Fatima will be joining you in Islamabad. She will reach Islamabad tomorrow. You'll get the details later."

He also gave Farooq a pillbox containing tiny capsule of Cyanide, "Use this only if torture becomes unbearable. Death could be a blessing. You learned that in training."

Ramanuj waved him goodbye.

He did not know whether he would see him or not. Most of these deeply penetrated agents did not come back. They accepted the thankless job in the name of their country. No one will ever know of his or her sacrifice. If they are exposed, the Inter Services Intelligence (ISI) or the Pakistan Intelligence Bureau (PIB) will slit their throats.

Few escaped and those who did escape were working desk jobs in India. A few lucky ones established as business people in Pakistan making millions from Pakistanis and supplying information back home. That money is theirs to keep, no questions asked. Some might have a bungalow in Morocco or a villa in Spain with a beautiful dame they could find in the Jannat of Afghanistan or Nooristan. He did not know what fate the destiny would bring for Farooq and Fatima. However, somewhere inside he felt a twinge of remorse.

The truck was running through the desert. The crescent-shaped moon was shining in the sky. Soon Farooq fell asleep. Arnakulam was a distant memory for Dabu Kadgul. The bittersweet memories from his childhood haunted him in his sleep, the love for his little sister, the raid, and the bullet-riddled bodies... so remote. Dabu completed his schooling. He was one of the few from the lower caste of that village to complete the schooling.

That week, he went to Nellore to find out about a job. When he returned, he found his parents and his little sister all dead. He went to Thanedar's office to file FIR, when he heard some police talking about the raid. He realized that the police were also part of this conspiracy. He was dejected and despaired. After completing the final rites for his parents and sister, he left town and went to Bangalore. He had no job, no money. He did not eat for three days and was too ashamed to beg for food; all he wanted was to die. He was tired and hungry. He lost consciousness and fell on the street.

Ramanuj was in Bangalore. He was giving a seminar in the college on various opportunities available in the Indian Army. Dabu almost missed him while falling. Ramanuj took him to the nearest hospital. The next day, he came to see him in the hospital. They were about to discharge him from the hospital when Ramanuj talked to him. His story made him extremely sad.

Ramanuj himself was from the lower caste and experienced similar atrocities when he was growing up. He told Dabu about the possibility of a career in Indian Army. Dabu accepted it. Ramanuj kept in touch with him during Army training and offered him the opportunity to become a double agent.

There was a run-down tea shack, Dhaba Qureshi, on the outskirts of Karachi. That was the delivery point. The truck driver woke up Farooq and dropped him there. Farooq was now in Pakistan. There was an old guy in the tea shack serving tea and Kabob with *roti* (Indian bread). He was the contact point. A few minutes after the truck left, he approached Farooq and told him to follow. About 100 feet from the shack, the taxi was waiting for him. The taxi took him to the hotel in Karachi, the driver handed him a suitcase and a briefcase full of cash. The room was already booked.

In the hotel, he took a bath, called room service, and ordered breakfast. He rested for the whole afternoon and then changed into Farooq Bhai, a Don from Mumbai with diamond-studded gold chain around the neck, a diamond ring, and Rolex gold watch.

That night, after a good rest, he came down, kept the brief case in the hotel safe, and then called a taxi to take him to the night-club *Manzile Jashna*, Zillat Pathania's fortified stronghold. Farooq told the barman to inform Pathania that Farooq was here. Zillat had never seen Farooq, but he heard of the raid and encounter of Don

Black Scorpian. He also heard that Farooq escaped with cash. He was expecting him.

Police had a file on Black Scorpian and confiscated a lot of information during the raid. Ramanuj made Farooq memorize the information. The memory training given at the camp by Akabar Khan, alias Ajit Deshpande was helpful. He memorized the information. The information came in handy while conversing with Pathania.

"What are your plans now?" Pathania asked.

"I am thinking that I can start a small business venture, I think... weapon and parts supply business. You keep your turf in Karachi, I will move to Lahore or Islamabad to set up a business. Once I am established, I can also convert your black money to white and that way we both benefit. What do you think?"

Zillat Pathania instantly liked the idea. He had heard before that the guy was dangerous and deadly and equally clever. He was worried about him moving in on his Karachi turf. However, instead Farooq decided to move away from him, leaving his turf alone. He was safe.

With Black Scorpian's money, it would not be too difficult for him to get into the Defense Supply Channel. He could also be helpful in the illegal weapon supply business. Most important, he could turn the black money to white money. In an excitement, he did not even bother to check Farooq thoroughly.

"That's great Farooq Bhai, *Aish karo abhi* (have fun now), tomorrow I'll make an arrangement for you to go to Islamabad. That's a better place than Lahore. I'll make a reservation for a week in Islamabad Serena Hotel. Then you decide what you want to do. My *Khabri* (informant) will help you find a luxurious apartment close to nightclubs. Don't forget to visit *Mohabbat-E-Masti* in Islamabad. Remember that is important for business, especially Military Supply Chain business. Many of your clients will be there and you can have some masti (fun) on the side."

Later, that afternoon, an agent contacted him, *"Janab garmi bahut hai."*

"Mausam Hasin Hai," Farooq responded.

After the exchanges of passwords, Farooq told him where he would be staying in Islamabad. Because of Pathania's unexpected help, Farooq was ready to be an effective operative much earlier than expected. Ramanuj received a message that both packages are intact, Islamabad *Zindabad* (long live). The next step began.

In the morning, Farooq left for Islamabad by plane. He stayed in the Islamabad Serena Hotel reserved for him by Pathania and that afternoon, as prearranged, he met Fatima in the bar below. She was eating lunch in the hotel. She was staying in an Islamabad hotel near the civic center. She gave him the details then excused herself so no one became suspicious. After lunch, he took a map of Islamabad from the hotel concierge desk, called a taxi, and went around. He stopped at the Bazaar, went to few shops, and ate in a local restaurant, *"Des Pardes,"* before returning to the hotel.

The next day, he met the Pathania's informant to find a place to rent and signed a short lease. Normally, they do not allow short leases, but because of Pathania's informant, he had no problem. He also inquired about renting or leasing a car. Later, he came back, dressed in plain Muslim dress, and left the hotel from the back door. No one noticed him.

He made a couple of stops, went through the bazaar, and from there he took a small street that he spotted yesterday to make sure no one was following him. On the other side of the lane, he took a taxi and went to Hotel Islamabad. The agent who met him in Karachi gave him two phones; one was a prepaid that he could discard at any time. He used that phone to call Fatima and told her that he would be meeting her in her hotel. Imran Quadree was there with her.

Imaran was a muhajir. His grandparents were Hindu Brahmin from Lahore. After partition, Muslims converted them by force. Later, Imran's father got married to a muhajir girl from another con-verted family. In spite of the atrocities, many converted Hindus in Pakistan kept their Hindu culture alive.

Officially, Imran was working as a peon in the Indian Consulate. One of the officers found out about his dislike for Pakistani Muslims and decided to use him for doing some odd work requiring secrecy. They tested his fidelity over time and found out that he was loyal, efficient, and innovative. He hated Muslims because of the stories he heard from his grandfather. He helped the Indian Secret Service to recruit more muhajirs like him. Imran updated both, of the latest development.

One of the local guys from Islamabad, a *khabari* (informant) of Pathania, called Malika Husaini Shafi earlier to inform that an important client *Mia* (Mr.) Farooqji will be arriving at her house, and requested to make him happy. She also received the hefty sum of money in advance. Pathania did not want to take any chances. He wanted Farooq to enjoy and make the new place as his turf.

Pathania called a few contacts and arranged for Farooq to meet with *Mia* Murad Hamid, one of the assistants to the head of Defense Supply Corporation. Pathania already greased heavily Murad's palm with a large sum of money to take Farooq to the courtesan house, *Mohabbat-E-Masti*. Murad jumped on the opportunity. He and Malika Husaini both liked such customers who paid in advance.

Murad contacted him in the afternoon in his hotel. They both went to see Army Supply Division and discussed few business prospects. Later, that night they went to the courtesan house, *Mohabbat-E-Masti*. Malika Husaini Shafi was expecting him.

The elite courtesan house was an elegant place. Surayya was the best singer in the house. Farooq was shocked to see Surayya singing and recognized her as Sunayana… he remembered that she was also kidnapped along with other girls that night in Arnakulum. He thought his cover was blown. There was no way out. Later, Sunayana alias Surayya took him to her room for a private treat while Murad was busy with other courtesans. Farooq kept a finger on his mouth and cautioned her not to utter a word.

She recognized him, and whispered in his ear, "I know you, Dabu, did you come to help me?"

"I didn't know you were here. I am here on a mission… well, I…" Farooq, alias Dabu, paused.

Sunayana recognized the hesitation and timidity, "Don't worry, tell me, Dabu, is there anything wrong, and is there anything I can do for you?"

"Well…not really."

"Look Dabu, I am still the old Sunayana. Don't hesitate, please be a friend. I need a friend in my barren life. I have lost a lot. I miss my parents, my little brother, and our village. Now I am a woman of pleasure, and since you are here, I guess something drastic must have happened to you also. Consider me your friend and trust me. I'll help you any way I can," she pleaded.

Dabu looked at her and held her hand, "I give my life in your hands. I hope I am doing the right thing," he narrated his whole story and told her how he became an agent. She was surprised at his venture and her eyes became moist when she heard about the death of his parents and little sister. She knew his sister.

She also told him her story. It was a heart-breaking story. Dabu did not know how to respond. Before leaving India, Dabu visited his village and informed Ramanuj and Commander Bhosle about the old incident. Both guaranteed him that such kidnapping would not repeat in the future. He also told her that her parents were doing okay, and her little brother will soon finish his schooling. She was happy to hear that. They both decided to meet each other regularly. He also told her about Fatima and his immediate tasks of the rescue operation and recapturing the SHIV the Destruction device.

"What is SHIV the Destruction'?"

"It's a deadly weapon. Terrorists stole it from Delhi and might be bringing it to Islamabad or Waziristan."

"Who are you rescuing?"

"They are American journalists. One of them is from Indian descent, Ruben Joshi."

"Marathi guy…"

"Yes, his father is from the state of Maharashtra"

She was trying to recall yesterday's conversation. She heard from two Pakistani Army Officers of Tochi scouts of Pakistan's Frontier Corps. She knew that from the badge on their military uniforms. They were stone drunk and blabbering about, "*Hum… America ko… dikhayenge, sale…* (We'll show to America, bastards). They are… are sending… journalist… spies."

"*Chalo… aaj maza… karenge* (Let's have fun today). We will kill… kill… them Friday."

"*Friday… nahi… nahi…*, Saturday… (Not Friday, we'll execute them on Saturday)," the other said laughing hoarsely. He was also drunk.

Surayya took one of them in her private room. She was trying to make him drunk, so she would not have to sleep with him. "*Abhi aish karo* (Now have fun), don't think about *katle am* (execution)."

The officer was in boasting mood, "*Aish to ... karenge ... meri bulbul* (We'll have fun my beautiful bird), then I'll ... I'll ... go to Miramshah ... Bazar ... to watch the fun ..., execution ... behind the Mosque." The officer was drunk, sleepy, and just blabbering.

Although she was no longer a virgin, she learned with experience that this technique always worked.

She told Farooq her conversation with the Army Officer from Tochi scouts of Pakistan's Frontier Corps.

They spent some time together. Before parting for the night, she told him that she would help him with any information coming across. She got a new purpose for her life, and India got another valuable deeply penetrated agent.

Chapter 36

Rescue

This was an unexpected break. The information was extremely critical, and it was necessary to communicate to the ISHWAR head quarters immediately. Farooq returned to the hotel in the early morning, called Fatima, and then went to see her. He followed the protocol and took all the necessary precautions. Fatima called Imran Quadree. He took the information and gave it to one of the agents at the consulate, their regular channel to contact ISHWAR and the Commander. The agent immediately encrypted the message and sent it to the SSIW to deliver to agent Ramanuj Parmeswaran.

After initial formality and greetings the coded message read:

"BEHIND THE TEMPLE, SAHIB'S MATERNAL AUNT MARIUM JI SHAH GOT THREE RARE BIRDS. THEY WILL BE SOLD ON SATURDAY IN THE BAZAAR BEHIND THE TEMPLE. PLEASE TELL AUNT TO SEND THE CAGE TO HIS DAUGHTER IMMEDIATELY"

Ramanuj immediately went to Commander Bhosle and gave him the deciphered message.

"Three journalists are in Miramshah Bazar in Waziristan. They will be executed this Saturday behind the Mosque in Miramshah Bazar. Immediate rescue operation is necessary."

The Commander told Malini to fly to Kabul immediately, get in touch with Kiran, and give her the message verbally. He did not want anyone to intercept it. Malini also requested his permission to participate in the rescue operation with Kiran. Malini knew the Pushtunwali language and was an excellent shooter. He called Kiran and told her that Malini was coming to meet her in Kabul. He also called a number in Kabul and gave instructions.

Malini left immediately and reached Kabul late that afternoon. Kiran came to meet her at the airport. Malini gave her the message and told her that the Commander was sending help. By the time they reached Kiran's hotel, Barkat Niazi and Hadith Abu were waiting for her.

Barkat approached Kiran and said 'OP Nikhil *tayyar hai*' and Kiran responded '*Ji nahi, abhi nahi, kabhi nahi.*' After the exchange of the code, Kiran greeted them.

Barkat Niazi and Hadith Abu were Pathans (Pushtun). During the first American attack on Kabul, they were running through the streets near the Indian Consulate. Bhosle spotted them, saved their lives, and took them inside the consulate.

Both thanked him and said, "We are in your debt, and our life belongs to you from now on."

Pathans are famous for honoring their word. There is certain finality in their promise. They never break it. From then on, they both ran several small errands for him and were very dependable. Commander Bhosle made them both promise that they will accept payment for their errands. He always paid them well. He knew the scarcity of money for poor families in Afghanistan.

Earlier, Commander Bhosle called and gave them instructions to help Kiran and Malini. "Consider I trust my daughters' lives in your hands."

That was enough for those two Pathans. The Commander knew very well that once a Pathan gave their word, he would sacrifice his life to protect without a second thought.

Immediately after calling those two Pathans, Commander Bhosle called his friend in Israel to request his help.

The Israeli Commander understood the gravity. He didn't ask any more questions.

Kiran called Anthony Hurtz, introduced him to Barkat and Hadith, and gave him the location of Ruben, Adolph, and Basher that she received from Malini. They sat down and worked out a plan

Kiran began, "We all will go to Khost and the operation will begin from there. The United States has a camp in Khost. Miramshah is 100 miles from Kabul and about 25 miles from Khost. I will travel to Miramshah, Waziristan with Barkat and Hadith by Jeep from Khost. The population is about 10,000 so it won't be that hard to find them."

Malini interrupted, "I'll accompany you in the rescue mission. I speak proper Pushtunwali and I am a sharp shooter. Two men and two women might make a better team."

Anthony agreed with her. Malini was a trained agent. Kiran agreed.

"The three helicopters will accompany; one AH-64 Apache Helicopter and two UH-60 Black Hawks. AH-64 Apache helicopter packs radar-guided Hellfire anti-tank missiles to destroy targets with precision strikes. The Target Acquisition Designation System (TADS) linked to the head movements of the pilots, so the cameras point where they look, convenient for instant action when needed. The helicopter gadgetry includes a night-vision sensor, a laser range finder and laser target designator, a thermal imaging infrared camera, and a television camera. Images from TADS superimposed onto the crew's helmet-mounted optical sights and the M261 rocket launcher with 19 tubes armed the Apache Helicopter. I'll send the signal once we identify the target area. Anthony, please make sure we have satellite coverage." Kiran said

"Yes, I'll make sure we have a satellite coverage and we'll also use a scrambler to scramble Pakistani troops' signal monitoring devices so we can catch them by surprise," Anthony added.

Malini was thinking.

"Pennies for your thoughts, Malini," Kiran said.

"I have a suggestion if you would like to hear it."

"Go ahead, Malini."

"Since we have satellite coverage, we can use drone. The drone will fly first at a low level, drop some bombs around the periphery of the mosque to disperse the soldiers, and then fly east toward Pakistan before making a u-turn back to Khost. The soldiers will think it is a drone attack and turn their guns toward the drone's direction. There will be an open space. Then the helicopter attack will begin. You guys will have at least 60 seconds before they can turn their attention to you," Malini stopped.

"That is excellent suggestion, Malini," Kiran complimented and began planning the mission, but the events did not go as planned. The satellite informed them of heavy security and another battalion of 2000 more Pakistani Tochi Scouts of Frontier Corps with heavy artillery and anti-aircraft missile launchers. Al Qaeda decided to make a big show of their prized prisoner execution. The American State Department contacted Pakistani officials, but they pleaded ignorance. Kiran and Malini had to abandon the idea of carrying any weapons because of the physical security check.

Barkat told Kiran that she did not have to worry. "Commander Sahib warned us of something like this happening. We already have two men inside Miramshah with the weapons."

Commander Bhosle called Anthony and informed him, "Israeli commando squad is flying on El Al Israel Airlines or similar career with American passports. They'll meet with Indian commando squad in Kabul. The Indian commandos will have helicopters ready for action for both Israeli and Indian commandos."

"Malini suggested an addition of drone attacks at the beginning to clear the space for helicopter attack as soon as we get the message from Kiran," Anthony informed the Commander.

"That's great! Tell Malini on behalf of me that she will be recognized for this," the Commander informed.

With this information, there was a change to the plan.

The next day, Ramanuj was at the Kabul Airport waiting for the arrival of the Israeli commandos. The Commander called and told him about the microwave emitter.

"You know it is Nikhil's invention. It's a jet-propelled cruise missile. The microwave emitter is installed in the missile attached to the MI-8 helicopter. You pre-set the coordinates of the target location. The microwave emitter will hit the target with high-frequency microwaves to disrupt Pakistan's electronic and data systems and make them useless right before you attack them. This will be a good time to test the device. If it fails, then the American scrambler will still do the job, but if it succeeds, then the US scrambler may not work. The effects of jamming is set to last for 10 minutes only, enough time for you to disable Pakistan's army and Kiran to find the prisoners and send the message back to you after 10 minutes. So, remember to fire the emitter missile after 24 minutes, once you get the message from Kiran," Commander paused.

"Any questions?"

After arrival of the Israeli commando squad, Ramanuj met with Kiran, Malini, and Anthony and gave them the complete account of the logistics including the number of people and the ordnance. With the additional information, Kiran, Anthony Hurtz, Ramanuj, and Malini discussed the new plan and wrote down the steps.

They all met in a US Embassy conference room in Kabul and after the initial introduction of the newly arrived Indian and Israeli commandos, Anthony conveyed the revised plan.

"We all will go to Khost and the operation will begin from there. The United States has a camp in Khost. Miramshah is 100 miles from Kabul and about 25 miles from Khost. Malini and Kiran will travel from Khost to Miramshah, Waziristan, with Barkat and Hadith by Jeep. The population is about 10,000, so it won't be that hard to find the prisoners.

The four helicopters will accompany on the rescue mission; one AH-64 Apache Helicopter and two UH-60 Black Hawks and one Russian-designed Mil MI-8 helicopter.

AH-64 Apache Helicopter will hold two crews, a pilot, and co-pilot gunner. AH-64 Apache, both Black Hawks, and MIL MI-8 will carry armament such as rockets, missiles, and gun pods. The UH-60 Black Hawk can carry 11 crews. There are seven on the ground. I'll be in one of the Black Hawk with the two gunners at the center to pull the seven people up and the crew of eight on the second one with the two gunners. Eight Indian and eight Israeli commandos will be ready with Russian-designed Mil MI-8 helicopter. We'll use a scrambler to scramble Pakistani troops' signal monitoring devices so we can catch them by surprise," Anthony paused and looked at Kiran.

"Thanks Anthony," Kiran continued, "Today is Friday. We all will fly to Khost immediately after lunch. Miss Malini - the agent from India, Barkat, Hadis, and I will start at 1700 hours from Khost. Because of the tight security, we cannot carry arms. The two of Barkat's men will provide weapons to us and then mingle among the crowd. They'll be providing hand grenades as well as smoke bombs.

For some unexpected reason, if they have to participate, then MIL MI-8 will pull them up.

After reaching Miramshah, we'll start looking for Ruben, Adolph, and Basher. Once I identify the target area, I'll send the message. It's essential to make sure the moment you get the message about location, you all will start from Khost. There should be complete signal silence, no more communication. Fly low and synchronize operation on a minute-to-minute basis starting with time zero. I'll expect you there in 25 minutes.

Exactly, 24 minutes after you receive the message, the drone sent first flying at a low level would drop bombs around the periphery of the mosque to disperse the soldiers and create confusion and chaos. It will then fly east toward Pakistan before making a u-turn back to Khost. The Pakistani Army will think it is a drone attack and turn their guns toward the drone's direction. They will use their guns to attack a drone flying eastward.

That will provide space for Apachi, Hawks, and MI-8. Then the helicopter attack will begin. You will have at least 60 seconds before they can turn their attention to you. All four of us on the ground will start throwing grenades and start firing synchronizing with the drone attack. If possible, Barkat and Hadis may even throw grenades at a couple of missile launchers. That will create more confusion. Make sure drone attack starts at 24 minutes after you receive the message to synchronize with the ground attack.

After a couple of minutes of confusion, we all four will be targets for Pakistani Army. You will all come with heavy firepower and land the men as necessary to help us rescue. The Apache would do the initial job of disabling enemies and clearing the area. The Black Hawk with Anthony will position to pick us up. Another Black Hawk will encircle the area, blast the perimeter, and shoot at the sight if someone enters. Apache will provide firepower, and MI-8 will supplement the firepower around to keep the troops away. The MI-8 will concentrate on disabling anti-aircraft missile launchers. There are 24 men in four helicopters all wearing bulletproof vests excluding Anthony, the pilots, and the gunners. If a fight breaks out, the American Marines from another Black Hawk will land to help and rescue Ruben, Adolph, and Basher. The commandos from MI-8 are a back up if necessary except the two gunmen remaining will land, finish the clearing operation, and then get back in the helicopter. The entire operation shouldn't take more than 10 minutes to rescue and get out. Do you want to add any thing," Kiran looked at Anthony.

Anthony nodded, "The silence will be broken the moment the prisoners with Kiran, Malini, Barkat, and Hadis are rescued, and up- loaded in the Black Hawk. Then everyone on the ground will retreat to the helicopters and fly back." Anthony handed the copies of the plan to all commandos.

Kiran and Malini wore burqas and underneath regular Afghani dress of Shalwar Kameez. They started sharp at 1700 hours from Khost with Barkat and Hadis Abu.

It was Friday night. After sundown, Pakistani soldiers began their feast in celebration of tomorrow's execution. No one bothered them. Barkat's two men gave the weapons and ammunition to Kiran, Malini, Barkat, and Hadis and pointed them at the house next to the mosque. Kiran and Malini did some reconnaissance to identify the weak spots. The three prisoners were inside the house.

Most of the troops were busy eating. She called at 1900 hours sharp. At 1924 hours, the low level-flying drone started dropping bombs. Barkat and Hadis threw their grenades at the launcher and Kiran and Malini threw grenades outside the house. All hell broke loose; no one suspected two females running for the cover near the house.

The next second, the whole area was covered with shells and missiles shot from the drone followed by the microwave emitter jamming the entire electronic system of the Pakistani army below. The microwave emitter-jamming device was programmed for the location so it did not jam the electronic system of the helicopters or drone flying above, although it created a chaos on the ground. The Pakistanis had to operate the launchers manually because none of their electronic systems worked.

Barkat and Hadis came back to the Mosque. Kiran and Malini killed the two guards at the door and broke the door open. There were two soldiers inside pointing a gun at them and no sign of the prisoners. The soldiers shot at the two women. A bullet grazed Kiran's shoulder causing a sharp needle-like pain. Malini dodged the shot and fired back killing both.

Seeing no prisoners, they were stunned. One of the room doors opened and a soldier came out pointing the gun at them. Kiran shot him in the stomach. The other was inside the small room pointing the gun at the prisoners. Malini saw and fired. He fired one shot at the prisoner while falling just missing Adolf's torso, but Ruben got the bullet in his leg. Kiran got hold of Ruben while Malini and Barkat helped the other two. Marines surrounded the house. The 50 soldiers from the other side rushed in. It was a close fight. The Marines, Kiran, and Malini had the advantage of the walls of the house; however, it was difficult to rush to the Black Hawk. The MI-8 dropped another eight soldiers and kept on firing.

The Pakistani Launchers were not that effective since they had to operate them manually. Anthony noticed that from the helicopter, he had no clue why that was happening. He thought that it could be a temporary mishandling because of the chaos. He didn't know anything about the microwave emitter.

All seven climbed back into the helicopter. The signal for retreat was sent. Just before that, the Apache and MI-8 both dropped missiles to cover the area and to help pull the remaining Marines and commandos back in the helicopters. There were no casualties on American, Indian, and Israeli sides. In the next 15 minutes, the whole area cleared, and helicopters were heading back. Anthony sent a signal to the American Unit in Khost. The two aircrafts headed toward Miramshah from Khost to prevent advancing Pakistani troops and aircraft tail.

The rescue operation was successful in spite of the unforeseen pitfalls encountered and the last-minute changes and surprises. It was a classic example of performance anxiety. The team rescued the prisoners. Ruben and Adolph both barely missed death. There were no casualties. A few wounded Marines, who after dispensing the initial medical care and patching, went to Germany for treatment. Indian Commandos went to Delhi and Israelis to Jerusalem.

Ruben went to Germany along with Adolph and Basher for de-briefing and further treatment. They were tortured for confession before execution. Ruben could barely stand because of the bullet wound. The Pakistani Consulate officially filed a protest against the attack on their soil in the Islamabad American Consulate, but there was not much air to it because of the evidence of the prisoners and the planned execution as community entertainment by Al Qaeda. The US State Department rebuked Pakistan because of the presence of the Tochi Scouts. Kiran was in Kabul preparing the report and tying up loose ends. Anthony Hurtz returned to Islamabad.

Chapter 37

Subterfuge

Anthony Hurtz got a call from Veronica Ivanovo about the involvement of Indian and Israeli Commandos. She admonished him for calling them and not informing her.

He said to her that he did not call them, "In fact, the Indian Security Head took upon himself to find out about the whole saga of elaborately planned execution and formation of additional troops of Tochi Scouts. Because of him, Kiran, Ruben, Adolph, and Basher are still alive. Further investigation and analysis of satellite images indicate that we had the information but no one bothered to tell us. Why did we not get the information? I called Lisa Hargrove before the planning of the operation and left a message for her to call me back. I called her again to tell her about the help we were getting from Indian and Israeli commandos, but she never returned the call. Now I found out that she was on another assignment. She was our handler. Everybody in the agency was aware of the mission. The information from satellite images was available for our office, but no one bothered to tell us about it or gave us the temporary contact information. Isn't that the protocol? Is our office waiting for another Daniel Pearl or Isaac Edmond to happen?"

"Don't say such rubbish," Veronica slammed down the phone.

Anthony started wondering after the phone call from Veronica Ivanovo. He called Lisa again and found out that Ivanovo sent her on a routine task that was unnecessary. He reviewed the satellite images again. It was clear from the images and time stamp that the satellite had the images much earlier. He checked with his friend in the satellite unit and found out that satellite images informed the CIA about the additional two thousand troops much earlier before the planning of the mission. Luckily, the captain of the Marines called them as a routine check before starting the operation. As a result, Anthony found out about heavy security and additional reinforcement of the 2000 troops. Was this a perverted plan by the CIA to have another "Isaac Edmond?" He knew that the CIA sometimes had other motives and people like Isaac Edmond and Ruben were just collateral damages. Kiran might have become a causality of war in this operation along with Ruben, Adolph, and Basher. Thinking about it gave him the chills.

Commander Bhosle's foresight and thoughtfulness impressed him. Without the help of Indian and Israeli commandos, the opertion would have never succeeded. He called Kiran to enquire about Ruben and others.

"Ruben is headed to the US. He will need at least another month to get back on his feet. Adolph is also going with him. For the time being, ICNN will send another team. Ruben may take some time off, but he'll decide after going home. The day after tomorrow, I'll be heading back to Islamabad and I'll meet you there. I already called Commander Bhosle and thanked him. He was a great help and a real leader, don't you think? Commander Bhosle's actions and decisions showed a sign of great leadership."

She knew this operation would not have been successful without his help.

"Not like ours for sure, without his help and foresight, we would have never succeeded in this operation," Anthony responded. He was hesitant about giving her all the details and decided against it. He decided that he would probably talk to her in Islamabad after analyzing the whole chain of events.

* * * * *

There was not much nightlife in Islamabad. Pathania's man showed Farooq a couple of places to go. Those were secret places not open to the public. Twice, he took Murad with him to grow a deeper relationship, good for business. He also rented a warehouse. Pathania's khabari introduced him to a weapon dealer in town. The dealer was short on cash. Farooq agreed to provide the capital. Commander

Bhosle had the money that Black Scorpion stashed. Farooq was setting up the business with the flow of cash available. This was a decent start. Murad helped him start with a few small contracts, of course with a hefty commission. Unless one greases the palm heavily of the recipient, one cannot get a foothold in such business in Pakistan.

Well, India is not any different from this, Farooq thought. He also visited couple of times the courtesan house, *Mohabbat-E-Masti*, and decided to go there at least twice a week. Malika Husaini Shafi was happy for such a client. She found out that he was a Don from Mumbai. She understood his interest in Surayya's singing. It worked well for her as well as for Farooq and Surayya. Farooq found out about the successful rescue mission and heard the commotion in Islamabad newspapers cursing Americans as usual.

After a couple of weeks, Farooq moved into a rental apartment that was more convenient for him. This was an elegant apartment with a large hall and two bedrooms. The hall area was big enough to hold parties for clients, customary in many Pakistani cities because of the lack of nightlife. Fatima also found a small apartment in an impoverished area with the help of sleeper agents and kept a low profile. Farooq took her to nightspots where she befriended a few other women of the night. Pathania impromptu got the report and was happy to hear of his connections with the women. Real daredevil and horny Don, he thought. He didn't think there was any more need to watch him.

Just after moving into the apartment, Farooq went to the courtesan house, *Mohabbat-E-Masti*. Surayya told him that she heard the device of destruction arrived in Islamabad and may soon go to Waziristan.

"Your friend, Murad, would handle the transfer," Surayya said.

That night, he went to see Fatima and gave her the information.

He called Murad in the morning, *"Kaise ho Murad Mia* (How are you Mr. Murad), what's the plan for the weekend?"

"Apka kya mijaj hai? (What do you have in mind?)"

"I am thinking to have a party to celebrate our friendship."

"Well... not this weekend, I am delivering some supplies to Waziristan."

"Thik, phir kabhi (It's okay, next time). Oh… I remember… we talked about the supply route via Waziristan. Can I accompany you? After we come back, we'll visit *Mohabbat-E-Masti.*

Murad was hesitant; he was doing the job for Al-Qaeda members. For reasons unknown, they did not want to involve his boss or army personnel, but they offered him good money, so he decided to take it. The temptation of *Mohabbat-E-Masti* melted his resistance.

"Okay, we'll start tomorrow."

He went to see Fatima and told her the conversation between him and Murad, "I'll be accompanying Murad to Waziristan and try to recover the devices. Please inform the Commander and pass the word to Jahangir and others in Pakistan to provide backup. In case everything fails, tell the Commander to keep a backup plan ready."

Fatima encrypted the message to Commander Bhosle and sent to SSIW via the proper channel. The machinery began rolling. The Commander arranged for the squad of commandos ready at Kabul. After the last episode of prisoner rescue, he knew that Al Qaeda in Waziristan would be ready and may expect such action. It would be a difficult operation and could become bloody.

The next day, Murad and Farooq started late in the afternoon with a small squad of terrorists. They couldn't make an early start as planned because Murad was meeting with Habib Ansari, head of Defense Supply Corps. Habib was not happy with the new guy. He wanted to know more about him. Commander Bhosle anticipated this would happen and told Farooq to give more money to bribe Habib.

"Huzur, mafi chahata hu (I am sorry sir)," he put the envelope on the table.

The envelope revealed a wad of high-value dollar notes. "Don't worry about the new guy, he was a Don from Mumbai and ran to Pakistan."

He shared Farooq's story, "He is well connected and has many international contacts with dealers of weapon suppliers. We don't want Americans to know that we buy weapons illegally from other sources. So you see, this guy could be useful for our operation."

More than Murad's explanation, the wad of dollar bills convinced him.

The distance between Islamabad and Miramshah is about 190 miles. Because of the late start, they decided to stop at Banu. Farooq was carrying a bottle of Chivas Regal. At night, after dinner, when he and Murad were alone, he opened the bottle.

"*Mia*, we two will finish this today, party *nahi, yehi sahi* (this'll do in the absence of the party)," Farooq said to Murad.

After finishing half the bottle, Murad was in a boasting mood, "*Ye maut ka dibba hai* (This is a box of death), can you find something like this?"

He opened the box but there was nothing inside. He looked and looked, thinking he was just too drunk, but Farooq also said there is nothing inside.

"*Ya Allah, ye kaisa gajab hai* (Oh God, what is happening)?" He sobered up from his intoxication. He couldn't believe what he was seeing. He closed the box, decided to pretend that nothing had happened and to hand over the box to Miramshah as agreed.

After the setbacks of the rescue operation, Al Qaeda became alert. They thought the leak might have come from someone in Defense Supply Corporation. Al Qaeda staged a false transportation mission of SHIV the Destruction as a trap for intelligence. They spread the rumor about transportation of the device among the defense Supply Corporation employees assuming someone within the group is the informer. If the Indians took the bait, then the leak is within the Defense Supply Corporation, and they'll deal with them.

Farooq returned to his hotel room in Banu and called Fatima, "It's a trap. SHIV the Destruction is not here. Request to abort the mission. I am destroying this mobile." He disconnected and destroyed the mobile. The message was immediately relayed, and the operation was aborted.

The next day, Murad delivered the box in Miramshah and returned. Al-Qaeda wondered, if the leak was not from the Defense Supply Corps., where was it from?

Chapter 38

Dubai Zurich Islamabad

R amanuj was waiting for Jahangir at Le Camille Noir on Wednesday night. Jahangir Singhania was a prominent name in the Pakistani underworld and the defense supply organization. He had eyes and ears everywhere. He was the owner of the Jahangir Allied Industries. The company was a front for many illegal operations. The defense supply organization to the Pakistani Army depended on Jahangir Allied Industries to get weapons from Tashkent, Istanbul, Japan, Germany, and France. He secured nuclear weapons for them from Russia after the fall of Communism. No one knew whether those weapons were usable. The Geiger counter indicated radiation. Not only he was paid well for the job but his reputation also grew.

The army was not aware that punching the code would begin the activation mechanism of the nuclear weapon and detonate on the spot. Once they took one of the weapons on the border to use against Indian military in Kashmir, the device detonated killing an entire Pakistani squad. The inquiry conducted by the international organization found small traces of nuclear radiation. They questioned the chief of the Pakistani army, but he pleaded ignorance. The supply division hid the weapons and attributed the incident to untrained Army soldiers. The Pakistani army was just happy to have those weapons. The word on the street was that Jahangir Singhania has contacts in America also.

The terrorist cells in every major city in Pakistan and Middle East countries knew him. They depended on the Jahangir Allied Industries for illegal supply of weapons, ammunition, explosives, and drugs. Not only did he provide them the illegal supplies, but he also helped them transport between Afghanistan, Pakistan, Turkey, and Europe. His motto was peace between terrorist organizations was not good for the weapons trade. Instead, let them keep fighting and killing each other.

Sometimes the terrorists used those explosives on Indian soils. Jahangir did not like, he hated the word collateral damage as a way to justify the killing of innocents. His mentor and previous chief of the ISHWAR explained to him the inevitable lesson that if he doesn't do it, someone else will do it, but if he does it, at least the Indian Secret Service will know about it and be proactive to help minimize the damages. Not that it convinced him, but that was the game and he could not turn his back.

A few years back, when Jahangir was doing some business in the French Rivera, he met Alexandria Xinthas at the casino table. The stakes were high and Jahangir was winning. Alexandria was watching the game and this handsome young daredevil attracted her attention. Jahangir noticed her beauty. After the game, Jahangir approached her and offered her a glass of wine. They began talking and met a few times later on. They never realized when their mutual attraction turned to love.

Alexandria was the last heir to the Xinthas dynasty from the South of France. Xinthas migrated from Greece to Spain and eventually settled in the South of France. The family had connections to the Clan of the Wolf Head. They had a large shield with an emblem of the wolf in their mansion. Alexandria once asked her mother, Isabella, about the shield, but she didn't know anything about it or the Clan of the Wolf Head.

Isabella was a beautiful Muslim woman from a Moroccan-Muslim family, and her husband was a handsome man. His death was sudden, whether it was an accident, or a murder remained a mystery. The rumor said that he had fallout with some unknown organization; no one quite knew the truth. Alexandria was a late child, and her mother never remarried.

Jahangir met Isabella, a sweet old lady. A sophisticated Muslim boy from Morocco was enough for her to give consent for their marriage. Jahangir and Alexandria had two boys. Nana was a very happy grandmother playing with her grandchildren. Jahangir made a point not to touch the Xinthia family fortune. However, after marriage, his reputation multiplied tenfold.

The BAT Company conducted background checks on him and found his roots to a village in Morocco. The previous chief of the Indian spy agency made sure that Jahangir visited the small village in Morocco often and donated to an orphanage house. The background check indicated him growing up in the orphanage house as a Muslim boy of unknown parentage and married into the wealthy family of Xinthas with a severed connection to the Clan of the Wolf Head. After this revelation, BAT Company did not want to pursue the background check any further, but they did not want to do busi- ness with him either.

The Jahangir Allied Industries was not a manufacturing facility. It was just a name for the business with small warehouses in major cities like Lahore, Islamabad, Karachi, Peshawar, and outside the country in Kabul and Istanbul. He also maintained a well-furnished elegant apartment in each of these cities and a beautiful house in Islamabad to entertain his clients lavishly.

Because of his business, he had to travel all over the world and visit his wife and children in the villa in the South of France every fort- night. This also gave him an excellent cover and opportunity to meet and exchange information with Indian spies globally. Sometimes he brought his family to Islamabad during his children's summer va- cation. His wife never liked Islamabad. She was happy to stay in the villa in South of France. Jahangir visited her every other weekend.

Every second weekend as prearranged, Jahangir would fly to Paris to meet his contact to give the progress report before heading to meet his family. They would normally be meeting in one of the nightspots on Wednesday night in the Montmartre District of Paris.

At Le Camille Noir Night Club, the evening entertainment was glamorous and the dinner was delectable. After the show, Jahangir and Ramanuj moved to a secluded spot near the corner and discussed the business at hand and followup on SHIV the Destruction.

"We don't have any news about the location of Latif Ahamadi. He turned out to be a real pain in the ass. We caught only one conspirator alive. All others are dead. However, the one we captured is a pawn. We only found out from him that Latif Ahamadi is the carrier. Latif must be getting some help from the Pakistani side. The Commander thinks that if we don't succeed catching him, he will either cross the border from the northern part of India or take a boat ride from Div Daman (a smuggling route for many). Right now, we have tight security of the Rajasthan border and Gujarat border truck routes," Ramanuj paused to get some comment from Jahangir.

"It is better if you could catch him on the Indian side. The situation in Pakistan is tough. Nevertheless, I'll have my informants watching for him if he comes to the Islamabad side."

"That'll be great. We have covered the Karachi side. Farooq told Pathania to watch for him, Pathania had an excellent network in Karachi Province."

"Do you have anything else on your mind, Ramanuj?"

"Well, ASIIW analyzed data received through our network, interception of satellite communication, and e-mail messages and they came across interesting information. There is going to be a meeting in Zurich. Some big shot is flying to Zurich from US to meet someone coming from Saudi. The person from Saudi is associated with a Saudi terrorist organization called Clan of Harabi. Many from Al-Harabi's clans are steeped in terrorism. Normally, we would not have given this so much importance; it caught our attention because one of our sleeper agents have collaborated the story. He heard one of the leaders of the terrorist gang from Islamabad boasting about selling and making a very high profit. Based on various clues, ASIIW concluded that they are talking about SHIV the Destruction, and the organization from America is buying it. The Commander was right from the beginning, in fact, he did express his thoughts that it is not just the work of a small organization like HuJI, there must be some bigwigs involved."

"Do you think that has any connection with Operation Hind?"

"That is what we have concluded. We see movement across the border. Pakistan is busy with their election and new leader. They don't have the manpower or weapons to fight India at this time, unless they are backed by the weapon like SHIV the Destruction."

"You said there are only four devices. How could they manage that kind of threat with so little?" Jahangir expressed his doubts.

"Only if they could do reverse engineering and produce more devices. We do not know who is behind it, what information they copied from the computer, or what type of facility buys this and does the reverse engineering. There are so many questions, and we do not have the answers," Ramanuj said in frustration.

Now, Jahangir realized the gravity of the danger. For a moment, he shuddered.

"The original plot was to steal and reverse engineer the devices, but the terrorist group that stole the devices may have become greedy. The meeting probably could be to negotiate a higher price. Who knows?" Ramanuj blurted.

"You told me about the meeting in Zurich, do you have any plan for that?"

"We know the terrorist who is going to the meeting. He is just a negotiator. They don't know him. One of our double agents befriended him and attached a bug to his phone to hear all the conversations. There is a small computer chip inside the bug. Remotely, we can manipulate the chip software to divert his calls to our office or call him from our office. We got the code word they'll use upon meeting."

"So you know the hotel and other details," Jahangir enquired.

"The meeting will be in Hotel Widder in Zurich. We plan to re-place him with our agent. The Commander wants you to be there on the plane with them."

"Do you have the names of these big shots from US and Saudi?"

"No names were mentioned during the conversation. We checked the reservation record and found out that Mr. Chevalier and Mr. Akhmad are wealthy businessmen from US and Saudi."

"Do you have the flight details?"

"The terrorist will fly from Islamabad to Zurich. The plane leaves early in the morning. There is a three-hour layover in Dubai. That is the place to replace him."

"How will you change the identity?" Jahangir was unsure.

"That's where we got lucky. I have already told you that they have no idea, what his name is nor do they have a picture of him. The recognition will be by using the code so replacing him shouldn't be a problem. We had already planted our agent in the Hotel Widder. One of our agents will replace the terrorist and travel to Zurich. Since, we are sure that they will search before entering the hotel suite; he will not carry any weapons or bugging devices. Once inside the room, he will order a desert like banana split with chocolate and almonds. Typically, these big shots order either liquor, hard drink, or iced tea but they do not order desserts like a banana split with chocolate and almonds. However, a person from a third world country is more inclined to order a dish like this, common in Pakistan and Middle East. That'll not raise any flag. Our agent in the hotel will bring the dessert with a bug attached below. They'll search the waiter for weapons but will not conduct an electronic search for the bug. That will look suspicious. Our man in the room will plant the bug."

Jahangir listened carefully, "What about SHIV the Destruction?"

"We do not know. We'll monitor the progress. This meeting will give us a much better idea of their plans and culprits behind such operation."

They ironed out all the details before going back to their rooms.

Jahangir was looking forward to the weekend. He was supposed to fly to his villa to meet his family via Paris. However, the plans changed. He called his wife.

* * * * *

Zurich becomes a tourist spot in July and August. The weather was chilly but pleasant. The magnificent view of the snowcapped Alps on the horizon offers a picturesque backdrop. It is the largest city in Switzerland. The Hotel Widder is located close to Bahnhofs within the halls of nine historic homes in Old Town. Mr. Chevalier booked a suite in the hotel and arrived in Zurich by early afternoon. He arranged a meeting in his hotel suite.

The passenger *Mia* Ebrahim Quasim in seat 48A of Arab Airline flight #615 was in a good mood. It was his dream to visit Switzerland. He read so much about it in a travel brochure. He was daydreaming that, after the meeting, he would extend his stay in Switzerland. He was going to Zurich to negotiate the price of the device. His peers already coached him enough about price and haggling techniques.

Liyaqat Habib alias Surendra Varma occupied the seat next to him. They began a cordial conversation. The flight attendant brought coffee, soda, and snacks for the passengers. Both Liyaqat and Ebrahim preferred coffee. Liyaqat also offered Ibrahim Egyptian sweet toffee. It was a short flight to Dubai. There was a three-hour layover at Dubai. The drugged Egyptian toffee was making Ebrahim drowsy. Liyaqat helped Ebrahim get off the plane and to the gate. Ebrahim sat down on the chair, after that, he did not remember anything.

Liyaqat continued his journey to Zurich by Arab Airline flight #87 and arrived by 2 p.m. in Zurich. The car was waiting for him outside. After exchanging the codes, the driver took him to the Widder Hotel for a meeting. On arrival, they first searched for bugs and weapons, and then they sat down in the room and ordered lunch. The late lunch was delicious. They started with Krug Grande Cuvee, an excellent 1988 bottle of wine. For starters, they ordered green pea soup, mountain cheese, and truffle, "Croque Monsieur," followed by entrecote of Piedmontese beef with wild mushrooms, green asparagus, shallots, and later Liyaqat ordered a banana split with chocolate and almonds to finish the lunch. Liyaqat took the dessert but dropped the napkin on the floor. While picking up the napkin, he pressed the bugging device below the chair.

The meeting lasted for a little over an hour. Sultan Akhmad and Rothman Chevalier wanted to buy all four devices for $5 million. Liyaqat explained to them that the group was divided over the issue. They could only sell one device, haggled over a price, and eventually settled for $2 million. He assured that he would try to convince the group to sell all four devices for $5 million, but could not prom- ise unless Loya Jirga, a large assembly of elders, initiated the talk. Sultan Akhamad was familiar with the process. He explained that to Rothman Chevalier. Akhamad told Liyaqat that his man would come to Waziristan to pick up the devices. In front of Liyaqat, Sultan transferred $500,000 to the account number of their leader in good faith, for the promise of delivery and gave bribe of $100,000 to Liyaqat in advance to convince others.

After the discussion, Liyaqat left and Mr. Akhmad called the PA of the Oil Minister in India from the room. The agent in the hotel recorded all of the conversation and sent the encrypted information of the meeting and the conversation with the PA of the Oil Minister of India to the Delhi office. Jahangir and Liyaqat traveled separately from Zurich to Dubai. It was just a precaution to make sure no one would be following them. They both knew they were dealing with a very dangerous organization.

They reached Dubai around midnight. In the Dubai air terminal restroom, Liyaqat gave Jahangir the complete account of his meeting and divided the $100,000 between them. It was their money to keep. Jahangir typed an encrypted message of the details on his computer and sent it to ISHWAR Facility.

Then he called his men in Dubai to bring Ebrahim out. Jahangir's men kept Ebrahim drugged for two days and then just after midnight, they brought Ebrahim near the Dubai airport terminal. He woke up from his sleep not knowing where he was. It was nighttime; slowly his memory came back.

"Hi Allah, I missed the flight," He ran inside the terminal. As he was entering the terminal, his phone rang. The voice on the other side said, "Sir, you missed the meeting. We were calling you all day. Our boss discussed and decided on a price of $2 million. You'll deliver the device in Waziristan. We deposited a $500,000 in the account as discussed with your leaders prior to the meeting. Understood …"

Ebrahim listened without a word then checked his telephone. There were a few messages. He checked the date. It was time to return. He did not understand what happened to him. He was scared. If Loya Jirga found about this, he knew he would surely meet his fate, probably in hell for not doing Allah's work. He decided to keep his mouth shut and deliver the message upon returning to Islamabad. He reached Islamabad early in the morning; his compatriots were at the airport. He gave them the message, made an excuse of jetlag, and left. The organization did not want to leave any loose ends. Ebrahim's travel to Switzerland was a documented fact. Later that night, Pak police found Ebrahim's body in the back alley.

Chapter 39

Aftermath

"Careful Ruben, don't stand, you are putting too much weight on your leg." Olivia chided him, pretending to be angry.

The tension of the kidnapping was too much. They lost all hope hearing the stories of past kidnappings. It was a miraculous escape because of Kiran's bravery. Ruben never mentioned Kiran's name to his parents to maintain the secrecy of her job as CIA agent but told his parents how the US Marines, Israeli, Indian commandos, and Commander Bhosle of the Indian spy agency ISHWAR, helped with the rescue.

"Mom, I am using crutches, and the doctor told me to move my legs. I am bored sleeping in bed for the last two days," Ruben complained.

His real problem was the strain of memories of torture popping into his mind now and then with bright lights and electric shocks, not to mention hanging upside down and the beatings when he slept. He had not had a good night's sleep since his escape. He did not mention that to his parents, because he did not want them to worry. During debriefing and later in the local hospital, the psychiatrist explained the situation to him and arranged therapy to help him heal.

A week later, he received a call from his boss, Elizabeth Penelope. Elizabeth had already spoken with Adolph and gathered information about their health.

After the customary exchange of greetings, Ruben told her, "I think in a couple of months I can go back to work starting with office duties before going full time to the war zone."

Not many in his situation would like to get back to the war zone so fast, she thought. Elizabeth admired his spirit.

She told him, "Ruben, I talked to Adolph and had an idea of what you guys went through. It was a gruesome experience. I am sorry. Adolph is thinking of taking six months off. He is undergoing therapy. I suggest you should do the same. It was traumatic and you may need more time off than you think. We have the insurance plan in place for a situation like this. I'll put you on a long-term disability. I suggest you take it slow. I have also made similar arrangements for Basher in Afghanistan. I would like to keep your team together. But, for now, relax and get better."

A month later, Ruben got a surprise. Without any announcement, Kiran, Nirmala, and Satish were at his doorstep. Ruben's kidnap story was all over the news. Satish's boss knew that Ruben was Nirmala's cousin and could imagine what they went through. A temporary assignment came up in the Chicago office and his boss decided to send Satish. Nirmala communicated with Kiran's office and left the mes- sage. Kiran returned her call and they both decided not to inform Ruben or his parents and surprise them with their sudden visit.

There was a knock at the door. Ruben was relaxing in the living room watching the news. He got up and opened the door.

"Surprise…!" Kiran and Nirmala both said in unison.

Ruben could not believe his eyes. He was ecstatic to see two out of three beautiful women in his life, third is his mother, at his doorstep when he was feeling lonely, and fighting off the apprehension that surfaced now and then at random. He choked with an emotional outburst, tears drizzling down.

He frantically said, "Hi… Kiran… Nirmala… glad to see both of you, what on earth are you doing here?"

He saw Satish behind them. Hearing the clamor, Olivia came out from the kitchen and was equally surprised; she had happiness emanating from her face by this unexpected visit.

"Hi, come on in." The children ran in and hugged Aunty Olivia.

"We decided to surprise you."

"Ruben and Aunty Olivia, it was Kiran's idea, not mine," she looked at them both. They all laughed.

Nirmala told them about Satish's temporary assignment in Chicago by his company, which arranged for their executive apartment. However, Olivia put her foot down and insisted that Nirmala and Satish, and their children will stay with them. She told Nirmala, "Ruben needs company. He would love to have you here. This'll be great therapy for Ruben. Children also need open space. They'll have fun in the backyard." Neither Niramla nor Satish resisted. In fact, they both liked the idea. Kiran left a couple of days later to see her parents in Ohio.

Sunday afternoon, Pralhad, Olivia, Ruben, Satish, and the chidren, Rohini and Prasad, were returning from the temple in Chicago. Kiran was also there with her parents. She was following them from behind, Nirmala sitting next to her. Last night, Kiran came to Chicago with her family. After the rescue, her parents wanted to visit Ruben, so they joined her.

Her return flight to Islamabad was the day after tomorrow. They were staying in a hotel. Before leaving for temple, Olivia took a promise from Priyanka that they would spend the whole afternoon with them and go to the hotel after dinner in the evening. Both Priyanka and Professor Hopkins agreed.

Today, the temple was crowded. There was a discourse by a well-known Swamiji from India. The subject was comparative religion. Swamiji had many followers in India. Nirmala was not so keen, she and her husband were skeptical about his teaching in general and the band of followers. However, Pralhad was to give a vote of thanks, and this was an opportunity for Kiran's parents to visit the Temple in Chicago after a long time, so everyone went.

It was a typical lecture. Swamiji's idea of comparative religion is to parrot few aspects from each religion that were available in any text-book. He stated that the concept of all religions is the same, and went on without elaboration or shred of evidence. Later, he talked about Hinduism, a concept of peace, and on vegetarianism.

Nirmala was so mad, couple of times she almost confronted Swamiji. Ruben and Kiran had a hard time holding her down. It was getting boring. Half the crowd was yawning; no one was saying anything out of respect for the tradition. It seemed that there was no way to stop him except by rudely intervening. The President of the temple sensed the restlessness and took the opportunity to intervene when Swamiji stopped to drink a glass of water.

"Thank you, Swamiji, it was an enjoyable discourse. Now, I request our distinguished professor and scholar to give a vote of thanks, and then we'll proceed for lunch."

Professor Pralhad had a difficult time expressing words of thanks. He was already bored. As a courtesy, he thanked Swamiji on behalf of the community for spending his valuable time and giving the opportunity to share his company. He was almost tempted to say invaluable time, but he controlled himself.

After reaching home, Nirmala exploded. "The most boring discourse, all religions are the same... my foot! That is preposterous. He has no real knowledge of any religion, not even Hinduism."

Professor Hopkins, Aunty Priyanka, and Aunty Olivia had demure smiles upon their faces. However, Ruben and Kiran were openly laughing and supporting Nirmala. Satish calmed Nirmala down. Satish politely asked Professor Hopkins for his opinion.

"I agree 100 percent with Nirmala, but the subject is controversial," he took the middle ground.

The shameful parroting without substance about the glory of yesteryears by hypocrite swamis, with the help of few wealthy NRI's (Non Resident Indians) who were lost in the materialistic world of the West, was a sad performance. These NRI's are searching for self-salvation in the realm of ignorance from people with self-interest and their own agenda to get foreign followers. Babbling chants of peace, Hare Rama, Hare Krushn, and Radha Krushn, they are degrading themselves. Even the younger generation from India was revolting.

Kiran interrupted, "Come on, Nirmala, now I want a full hour of commentary from you. We already had our food."

"Dad, you know Satish and Nirmala are very knowledgeable. You would love hearing her. Am I right, Aunty Olivia?" Kiran asked. Both Ruben and Aunty Priyanka pushed Nirmala for her commentary.

Nirmala looked at Kiran with big eyes, "You are putting me on the spot today."

"Don't worry, you can't be any worse than what we heard today," Professor Hopkins said jokingly. Everyone laughed.

"Dad, don't underestimate Nirmala Didi, you'll find her analysis very intriguing. Nirmala, start with comparative religion, I remember the last time you had an interesting argument when I was in college and visited you guys," Ruben pressured her.

"You don't want to hear that, not in front of them," she meant his parents, Olivia and Pralhad.

"Yes, we want to hear," Priyanka forced it.

Nirmala saw no way out of this quagmire and bowed for sacrificial offering.

"What I am going to say is not out of disrespect or to hurt anyone's feeling. These are just few observations and the disarray of thoughts. It is mixed, and you may find it disorderly because they flow in all directions," she paused trying to compose some order to present her thoughts.

"Before I begin, let me tell you one analogy that I saw on the Internet about the place of worships and the sacred religious scriptures of Hindus, Muslims, and Christians. The places of worships are Mandir, Masjid (Mosque), and Church – each word carries six characters. The sacred scriptures are Geeta, Quran, and Bible – each carry five characters. This analogy surprised me when I read it; I think you'll like it." She paused, looked around, and continued, "Every religious philosophy spread the same message of peace for the welfare of humanity. It provides guidance to become a good human being. Every religious philosophy has its own place in everyone born into, brought up in, or belonged to those respective religious faiths. The teaching of Hinduism has its value for Hindus, Christianity for Christians, Islam for Muslims, Judaism for Jews, Buddhism for Buddhists, and so on. You remember, Ruben, what your dad told us last time during the Geeta discourse. I am going to repeat his words. Hinduism conveys concepts of Karm, Yog, Maya (Illusion), and Dharm. No other reli- gion has these concepts. We are born in different parts of the world, and for centuries and millennia, we are groomed in different cul- tures, traditions, practices, and customs. The God is the same, but we have different methods to approach salvation. Although our final goal is the same, not all religions are same; methods and practices vary from region to region.

The greed, the corrupt mind, and the desire for dominance coupled with few other undesirable human qualities eventually culminated in the chaos that we see today. Nevertheless, we humans always have this urge to prove superiority and establish dominance, whether it is religion, politics, football, company, establishment, and so on. We are all the same, in spite of it, we fight for territorial dominance. Comparative Religion is a vague term. I found out that the Universities and Institutes offer grants for the study of the Comparative Religion. However, the scholars and professors curtail their studies and research and limit the focus to a particular reli- gious philosophy or aspects to satisfy the objectives of the Institute and to make the Dean or Institute authorities happy. The biased en- vironment does not do justice to the goal for the study or research on the subject of Comparative Religion."

She paused to gather her thoughts and continued, "I am not a scholar of religion, and it is difficult to study each of them in detail. They are sciences of Philosophy. Out of curiosity, I used the easy way. I am Hindu and I have read the Geeta and some parts of Upanishad and Ved. I got most of these scriptures on the Internet and read a few paragraphs at random, attended Bible classes in the Library of California, borrowed the Quran from a friend of mine, and looked through it. What surprised me, during this random reading is that all of them gave a similar message in different words. Not all religions are the same; each one has its own pattern, traditions, rituals, man-nerism, and methods with different names for their gods, deities, and symbols of worship. The interesting fact is, the Christian Bible states that Jesus said come to me for salvation; in Geeta of Hinduism, Shree Krushn iterated the path of *Karma* and *Bhakti* (Devotion) for salva-salvation; in Quran, Islam preached Allah is the one and only. Each one is frantically saying the similar goals of Almighty in different forms of devotion and worship and ready to kill for it.

One cannot compare the religious morals, values, and teachings inculcated on everyone since birth. There are many idiosyncrasies in every religion. I am sure there are lot of written essays in modern literatures of Christianity, Judaism, and Islam; the logical thought processes of Geeta, Ved, and Upanishad go way back millennia.

The blind faith, the caste system, the rituals, those are all tradi-tions mingled with the corrupt nature of humans and manipulated by them to satiate their needs and desires. That is the aspect of Hinduism used today by corrupt politicians to incite people, by religious leaders to sway people, and by foreigners to criticize Hinduism. However, we tend to ignore that similar aspects more or less are present in all religions.

It is difficult to say whether one is better than other religion. Last time we were talking after the terrorist blast in India, I made a statement to Kiran that the terrorists who are human explosives are doing this so they can have a better afterlife with fifty hurries (nymph) in heaven. This is the bribe offered to execute jihad if you blow yourself up in the suicide bombing to kill non-believers in the name of Allah. I jokingly made a statement to Kiran that this is a perverted concept from Hindu and Greek Mythology about King of God Indra or Zeus and their court of Apsaras or nymphs.

However, apart from mockery, there are many references in the Quran in Surahs about degrading non-believers, treating them as enemies, and killing them. Their founder's life is an illustration of lust, multiple marriages, molestation of children, raping of women, using slaves and concubines, and reaping the conquest of war booties. There are numerous references by Muslim historians about the life of the founder.

The religious concept of Islam is a scathing blend of perverted forms of Hindu mythologies, Paganism, and twisted Bible stories. If one looks at the Quran verse by verse, one will certainly find good advice in some Surahs as in Hindu Vedic Scriptures or the Bible, no one can deny that. Nevertheless, it is also blended with the message of hate, destruction, forceful conversion, or killing of non-believers - death to Infidels. This is evidentiary from the Quran; no one can deny the evidence. These are few observations about Islam with ref- erences to Surah in Quran and the life of their founder. Satish, do you have the list that you showed me once?" Nirmala asked.

"Let me check," Satish checked his wallet and found a torn piece of paper. He gave that paper to her.

Nirmala looked over the torn paper, "Satish showed me these numbers of some sample Surahs, Surah 9 Ayat 5, 28, 37, Surah 4 Ayat 56 and 101, Surah 33 Ayat 61 that he got from his Muslim friend. His Muslim friend boasted in justifying the reason for the Jihadis committing jihad and killing the non-believers. He gave these numbers as evidence. It is in the Quran. I checked these Surhas; it was all there. These Surahs mentioned here give the message that the non-believers are enemies, they are not clean, kill the non-believers, throw them in fire, and seize them and slain. These are just a few examples, not a complete list."

"I have some Muslim friends back home in Mumbai. I grew up with them. They are likeable people; they are honest, trustworthy, kind. However, some communal flare ignites them to other extremes. According to them, there is no God but Allah; either you believe in Allah, convert to Islam, or die," Satish added.

"Conversion is also a Christian concept. Only two religions are doing the conversion even in twenty-first century, Islam by force and terror, and Christianity by force and bribing and using missionaries. The Christians believe in Christ. They would like to see the whole world converted to Christianity. Of course, they don't use terror or suicide bombers. There is a message of peace in the Bible.

The question emerges, when Vatican authorities with their immense funding visit countries like India to convert the people or missionaries visit third world countries and start the campaign to convert people to Christianity. Sure, they offer incentives like free food, clothing, schooling, and medical help to entice people to convert. You know our religious book Geeta states, do charities without expectations. Offering charities as a piece of bone to a dog is not a charity, it's called taking advantage," she hesitated, was not sure to mention the fact of the visit by the Pope to India in the last century, then continued, "At the end of the last century, visit by the Vatican just did that."

"That's true, Lawrence. In fact, Mother Teresa did the same thing in Kolkata. Our family hated that. Now the Vatican wants to give her Sainthood...," Aunty Priyanka intervened.

Professor Lawrence looked at his wife and daughter. They were his life. He was well qualified and knowledgeable; he could look at the discussion from the universal objectivity. He believed in God, but he or his parents hardly went to the church. He was not that religious. After marrying Priyanka, his outlook on religion became universal.

He thought that what this young woman said does make sense, of course one could argue back and forth on some of the issues, but this was not about issues or argument, or right or wrong. It was about the bleeding heart revealing the wound that could never heal with ointment.

Nirmala looked at Satish, "I think Satish would like to say something."

"Yes, Nirmala, I would just like to add that I had a discussion with a colleague of mine in the US. We were talking about Mother Teresa, conversion, and the opulent and exquisite monumental city of Vatican. I just happened to ask him a question about the expensive outfits of the Pontiff and the display of wealth. How did that compare with Jesus, who, as we all believe, lived in poverty?"

He was mad, "Who said Jesus was a poor man. Jesus was a wealthy person and it is the duty of Vatican to convert the world to Christianity."

"This person was qualified, a regular churchgoer. I didn't argue with him. There was no point."

"Are you serious, Satish?" Olivia asked.

"I am not chaffing, Ruben knows him, but the name is not important," Satish replied and looked at Nirmala.

"There are a couple of observations I have on Jesus' life ... Jesus went towards East as a child. There was no documented evidence; no one knew where he went. He began performing baptism when he returned. Have you seen people dipping in holy waters of the River Ganges, and other rivers? That is an age-old Hindu custom. Isn't this act of dipping the head in the river apparently similar to what you call as baptism? He also performed many miracles. They are in the Bible. It is apparently similar to the power of Yogic Manifestations."

"One parallel I noticed in Judaism and Christianity versus Hinduism and Buddhism.

Jesus was born a Jew, spread a message of peace, and disclosed knowledge of religion to common people, which became known as Christianity. Jews didn't accept Jesus or his teaching.

Siddhartha was born a Hindu Prince. He also spread a message of peace and translated Hindu scriptures in simple vernacular language for the benefit of common folks. Brahmins didn't accept him, and he had to go away. He never thought of forming another religion just as Jesus Christ never thought of forming Christianity.

Both Buddhism and Christianity revived after the death of their founders. In reality, Buddhism is an extension of Hinduism, and one can say Christianity is an extension of Judaism. I know many of you will disagree with this logic, but these are some baffling questions and observations." Nirmala paused. She was trying to recollect the statement from the article of Vedic Civilization.

"Yes, I remember the statement from Ruben dada's (cousin) article on the Vedic Civilization where the author Edmund Leach reference implied that the versions of Buddhism, Jainism, and Brahmanical Hinduism were concurrent and transformations of a single system of ideas and practices. I would say that system of ideas and practices was the Vedic Civilization or Sanatan Dharm, now known as Hinduism," She stopped. She was thinking about a thought that came to her mind. She was hesitant.

"The Bible claims that everything started with Adam and Eve; but if that's the case, what about their sons, who did they marry? How did procreation continue? This just baffles me," Nirmala paused to see if anyone had questions. "I think this is enough for today."

"You didn't say anything about Sikhism, the thing that you told me when we all were in California," Ruben asked.

"Some other time, Ruben, I know there are many questions you all may have. I don't think I have all the answers or adequate justifications. This is just a thought to tantalize the brain.

However, before I finish, I have one last comment about the usage of word Lord for our icons. We have a beautiful word Shree. We can say Shree Ram or Shree Krushn, or Shree Saraswati, Shree Ganesh, and so on. I know the word Lord denotes reverence to God as in Lord Jesus. Nevertheless, I feel the word Lord has a connotation of slavery forced upon Indian minds through Lord Macaulay's system of education. It is okay to say Lord Macaulay, Lord Cunningham; the British Crown conferred the title to them. However, I do not like using the word or title Lord in front of Ram or Krushn. It gives me a shiver as if the British Crown conferred Ram and Krushn with the Lordship when they bowed in front of the queen or king of England and monarchy put the sword on their shoulder and conferred them with the title of Lord." Nirmala finished her discourse.

The entire room burst into laughter. Professor Hopkins appreciated her thought process and expressed his admiration to her.

Her children, Prasad and Rohini, were restless. They were tucking at Nirmala.

"I think they both are hungry," Olivia said.

Olivia, Priyanka, and Nirmala went inside to get the dinner ready.

"Nirmala, I enjoyed what you said today, you gave me a lot to think about. Thanks," Olivia said.

"Uncle Pralhad and my Dad are more knowledgeable about these issues than me," Nirmala uttered.

"But he never says anything, you know," Olivia blurted.

Logan came to see Ruben once after his return. He heard that Ruben was taking time off from the ICNN channel. He thought it was a good idea for Ruben to join the presidential campaign during his time off. It would keep him occupied, which was a good therapy. He is a public figure, just returned from the war zone, wounded. His presence could be useful to the campaign. He also thought that it would be a brilliant idea to have Ruben on the campaign team. He could be useful in the publicity department. Logan knew that the campaign office was looking for a manager for the publicity department because the previous manager had a problem with one of the campaign team members, Louise Calvin. "She was a real bitch," he thought. He informed Robert Lange to approach Ruben.

Robert Lange called him, "Hello Ruben, my name is Robert Lange. I am the campaign manager for the presidential campaign of Governor Giarrusso. Logan gave me your name."

Ruben knew Robert Lange well from the experience of that night when Logan murdered the hood a few years back. He had not forgotten that experience, "Yes, I remember you. What can I do for you?"

"I know you from your news cast, and you had probably seen me in the Mancini house when you were young. Mrs. Sophia Mancini and your mother Mrs. Olivia Joshi were good friends. I heard the story of your kidnapping. It was all over the news. I am sorry that you got hurt. How are you doing now?"

"I feel much better. In a week I'll start walking without crutches," Ruben responded. He wasn't sure why a campaign manager of the presidential campaign was calling him and inquiring about his health.

"You must be wondering why I called you. Logan told me that, for the time being you had taken a leave and will not be returning to the war zone soon."

"That's true."

"I have a proposition for you. We are looking for someone to work as the manager in our publicity department. It is a short-term job until the election. It will fit into your calendar. You are a journalist and I think you can handle that department well. We'd love to have you on our team. This temporary assignment will be an ideal spot for you if you are up to it. You don't have to answer me right now. Think about it for a couple of days and then call me."

Both Logan and Robert had no idea that Ruben had witnessed the murder. Ruben thought over the offer. He was getting bored anyway. This will keep him occupied for a time being. He had heard some stories of the campaign and about this Governor and his character before. From experience, he knew these stories could be rumors also. He was an investigative journalist. This would be an excellent opportunity to find out firsthand what kind of President Americans would be getting. He decided to accept the job with his own agenda. He never thought the job would land him into a web of conspiracies.

Chapter 40

Dalliance

*"*__A__re you all right, President Zoloft?"

The moderator was concerned; he noticed the President was uncomfortable.

Democratic incumbent President Andrew Zoloft and the Republican candidate Governor Giarrusso had agreed to three debates; one on domestic issues, one on foreign policy, and one on any topic on television before studio audiences.

The League of Women Voters had sponsored today's debate on international affairs. The coin was tossed and the moderator asked the first question to Governor Giarrusso. The question was the readiness of the American troops to retaliate nuclear warfare with North Korea and Iran. Each candidate had five minutes to answer the question and the opposing candidate had three minutes to respond and rebut the arguments. That was the debate format. The forum also agreed that, at the moderator's discretion, the candidate could extend the discussion by one minute.

Rebecca Mateson, the camerawoman, was taping the debate for Ruben Joshi, the publicity manager, to edit later for campaign advertisements and to show at campaign funding dinners and receptions. The edited video shows the high points of the campaign as well as a better side of the candidate to inspire donors and TV viewers to donate. The campaign advertisements, with the aggressive approach of the orchestrated cuts, influence the voters.

Governor Giarrusso talked of the problems the country is facing and his answer to unite them in case of war instead of answering the question about the readiness of the American troops to retaliate nuclear warfare with North Korea and Iran. He brought in the defense budget and talked about balancing the budget with war efforts. He went on for more than five minutes. The moderator tried to warn him that his time was elapsed. However, Governor Giarrusso's etiquette and adherence to the rules were far from normal.

This was only the first question and he did not even start the debate by thanking the University for allowing the use of their auditorium or the League of Women Voters for sponsoring the debate. He was in his own world trying to confront and resolve the issues. The five minutes time extended to six and a half minutes. He mesmerized the audience by his colloquialism from the start, but eventually they also became restless to his insensitivity to stick to the time at the podium.

President Andrew Zoloft began with a smile, "My colleague is very enthusiastic. Let me first take this opportunity to thank the moderator and the audience." He also thanked the University for allowing the use of the auditorium and the League of Women Voters for sponsoring the debate. Then he briefly stated the limited capabilities of North Korea and Iran, the American troops' strategy to respond without revealing sensitive information, and a one-line foreign policy directive of the US. It took him less than three minutes.

The debate continued with questions on China, Middle East, South America, and immigration policy. Both candidates were doing well. Andrew Zoloft's response was organized, brief, and to the point. Governor Giarrusso was theatrical, befitting his charismatic appearance.

Both had their appeal. The President was appealing to a knowledgeable audience while Governor Giarrusso was appealing to a macho mentality. The President's response was pragmatic and sequential but lacked the vitality due to sensitive nature of the issues and the dominant influence of the lobbyists. It was somewhat ineffective. In real life, even an honest person has to take the middle-of-the-road approach to get things done. The response of the Governor, on the other hand, though vacuous, was more aggressive and charismatic.

The previous debate on domestic policy was favorable to the President, but there was not much point difference. The topics discussed during the previous debate were controversial.

No debate exposes just how far both parties have sold out the American people to a group of lobbyists in suppressing vital issues that warranted careful scrutiny by the discerning voters. Both were aware that the elections have been practically decided by these debates and trying their best to be the excellent performer, while the lobbyists orchestrated the show.

This is the melodrama of the debates where both actors and directors in the role of candidates and lobbyists presented the show for the entertainment of the nation while the world watches the drama through the remote balconies of TV media. A good actor before the camera can pocket millions of votes while a faux pas could ruin a candidacy. The televised presidential debates are the perfect political dramas at the height of election season. These debates are the Super Bowl of politics. The dramatic effects of the debate could be crucial in winning the trophy

Almost more than half an hour into the debate, President Zoloft had heart troubles. Last week, his doctors had warned him about abnormal heart rhythms and suggested implanting a pacemaker to treat his arrhythmias. The President was clutching the lectern. There was a pin-drop silence in the auditorium; the moderator realized the seriousness. He got up and ran toward the President. Governor Giarrusso abruptly stopped and went to the lectern. They had to stop the debate; the ambulance arrived; Secret Service agents cordoned the area.

After the debate, Elena was mentally exhausted. She loved her husband, but she could see through his charisma, his disregard for the time, aggressive but irresponsible behavior, interruptions, vacuous responses, and the promises made during debates; this was all a mental torture for her. She could see that he was lying outright, but convinced herself that these lies are just a campaign strategy, and the phase would soon pass. She was determined to insist on that.

Her experience in the peacekeeping force in the Eastern Kivu province of Congo, the hard-working masses trying to survive, the misery that surrounded the area, and the false promises made by the native administration and the international groups revealed to her a new face of life that she was not aware of before. It taught her lessons, the value of integrity, a code of morals, and honesty. She loved her father but never liked his ways. She loved her husband and thought they both could make a difference. She did not like this new face.

After becoming Governor, many of her thoughts helped her husband thrive to become a successful Governor. He presented her thoughts to the council members and staff and they in turn successfully implemented them. The public benefited, the staff and the council got compliments, and the Governor got the glory. That was the key to his success. He spent most of his time having affairs with various damsels of the administration. His Chief of Staff, Robert Lange, kept it secret and the staff averted their eyes because of his success. No one was getting hurt; at least, it was not visible.

Governor Giarrusso, Elena, and his campaign staff immediately returned to the hotel. They decided to hold a campaign staff meeting in the conference room. Governor Giarrusso wanted to take advantage of the situation. Elena decided to retire to the presidential suite. Ruben and camerawoman Rebecca Matheson entered the conference room together. They both did not like the entire fiasco of the debate, and in the conference room, they saw Governor Giarrusso gloating. It was not a victory, but intoxication of ignorance clouded his sense of reality.

He asked his campaign team pollsters, John Haskin and Ricky Benton, about how this will play in public polls. Both cautioned him in unison to slow down and play it cool. Jessica Patel, Josh Desai, Malcolm O'Connor, and others from his campaign team agreed. They all agreed to return to the Campaign headquarters early tomorrow morning and wait for the update on the President's health, which all TV news channels were focused on. They were waiting anxiously for the report from the hospital. The news of the debate and the performance of the candidates took the back seat. The current poll results did not show any drastic changes. At the capital, the cabinet was busy deciding whether to carry out a temporary swearing-in of the Vice President to the Presidency.

Up until now, the Governor was behaving normally. However, in spite of the warning of caution from his staff after the abrupt halt of the debate, he illusively became more confident and relaxed. Everybody left the conference room. Outside the conference room, Louise Calvin whispered words of praise in the Governor's ears, the words he wanted to hear so badly tonight, and dropped the duplicate keys of her room to his pocket then left. Ruben, Jessica, and others decided to go for a quick nightcap in the hotel lobby. Rebecca was tired; she left the meeting early and decided to return to her room it was just after 9 p.m. She was next to Louise Calvin's room.

Rebecca woke up just after midnight by the sounds of the loud moaning and hissing. The sound was coming from the adjoining room. A door connecting the two rooms was open; she thought, the maid probably forgot to close the door. Rebecca cautiously got up and went toward the door. It was slightly ajar. She pushed it a little. The light in the other room was dim. Louise Calvin and Governor Giarrusso were rolling around and around in delirium, kissing passionately. Her dress had fallen down, and there were octaves ending with a gurgling breath. It was a crazy scene.

Rebecca had her iPhone in her hand. She decided to capture the whole scene with it. She filmed for few minutes and then decided to go back to sleep. The moaning was still in high octaves and it made her restless. She could not fall asleep. She thought, "What kind of man I'm working for, he is married; his wife is sleeping upstairs in the hotel, and he is banging another woman here."

She was not happy with the campaign to begin with. She had heard stories of his philandering adventures. There was no substance except bombastic rhetoric in the last debate, the speech before at RNC, and the tonight's performance at the podium. His insensitivity to stick to the time… if someone like him is elected… something was wrong. "Is this guy going to lead my country?" She asked the question to herself. "This is not right," she thought as she drifted to sleep.

Chapter 41

Agenda

S itting in the café, looking across Lake Superior, Ruben was thinking about his old friend, Logan, and the murder he saw at the Mancini mansion many years ago. He saw Robert Lange in the Mancini mansion, and linked the presidential candidate to the mob; that was an obvious link. Being an investigative reporter with war-zone experience and witnessing so many examples of treachery and deceit, he knew that things are not always, what they look like.

He was wondering what could be the link between a mobster and the candidate, there had to be something more. He admitted to himself that he did not like the candidate because of his superfluous acts and philandering activities. However, as a Governor of Illinois, he did not do a poor job. The people of Illinois praised the Governor and the First Lady of Illinois, Lady Elena. He also read about her humanitarian work in Congo.

She grew up in an elegant environment, actively engaged in many charitable societies, and she had an excellent career record. Why does this horny son of a bitch go after other women when he has a gem of a wife at home? Ruben could not understand. He knew it was none of his business. Something did not make sense. His journalistic instincts told him there is a story behind it, there is some connection between the mob, the murder, and the President, and he would certainly uncover it.

After returning from the debate, Ruben and Rebecca decided to meet at the café in the late afternoon. Rebecca knew of a place in downtown Chicago where they could go and rent the equipment to edit their projects. In the midst of this complex digital revolution, there was a madness that could create an illusion in the realm of media advertising, and Rebecca had a lot of practical experience in editing and Ruben in journalism. Together, they could produce an image to make nobody to somebody.

The monitor flickered as they started their work. The picture of the Governor appeared on a screen, "Look at this asshole," she murmured.

"We have to finish this job by this evening, so stop grumbling and start concentrating," Ruben said.

They both knew the debate was a no win situation. They were helping a man with no moral etiquettes.

"Robert Lange is feeding the information, and the Governor is parroting it, doesn't that bother you?"

"Yes, you bet, it bothers me," he snapped.

Rebecca was in a bad mood. She ignored Ruben's rude response.

She hesitated and then decided to come clean, "Last night I was sleeping in my room, and the moaning from next door woke me up. The sound was coming from the adjoining room. I decided to check it out and found the connecting door open. I saw this moron was jumping and rolling on top of Louise Calvin, sucking her mouth and what not. I captured them on my iPhone. Their huffing and puffing kept me awake. I kept saying, "This guy could be my next leader, no way!"

She turned and focused a withering gaze at him,

"He may be our next President."

"Damn it, Ruben, you know that really pisses me off?"

There was no way to stop her, Rebecca was downright mad. What aroused his attention was the captured video clip on the iPhone. This smut could be crucial, he thought, "Let's get it on tape what you filmed last night."

She handed him the phone that he hooked to his computer and downloaded the file. He also made an extra copy for safekeeping. "What really makes me mad is that I'm helping this imbecile," she said.

They looked at each other in the darkroom on the second floor above the shop. It was summer; the weather was blowing outside with pouring rain. The raindrops tapped rhythmically on the window, disrupting the silence between them.

Ruben could sense her anger. She shut down the editing machine. "I quit," she was pissed off.

"Let this go to hell, don't bother paying me. I am not going to finish the job. You know what; I don't want to be paid at all. I wouldn't be able to spend money with a clear conscience," Rebecca said. She picked up her briefcase and camera equipment, leaving the tape behind. "Do whatever you want with this tape. It's yours and that assholes," she said.

Ruben had the same feeling, but he had an unusual agenda. He wanted to expose the whole mystery. It was a dangerous task and he could not take Rebecca into confidence.

"Let me ask you… if the Governor is a puppet, has no courage, and is morally corrupt, how can you make these advertisements for him; how can you get up in the morning and look at yourself in the mirror?" Rebecca questioned.

Ruben had an answer for her question that he couldn't reveal.

"You're a good man, Ruben, with an international reputation; they are using your reputation. They want you; you are a showpiece. I tell you, one day you are going to regret it," she said, verbalizing his thoughts.

"Calm down, Rebecca, I fully agree with you. Please let me think for few days; for heaven's sake, don't be too hasty." She walked out of the shop. Ruben stood there, thinking about what she said. The gusting wind was roaring outside replicating the storm brewing within. The rain falling against the window, tap-tap-tap… the rhythmic sound was transferring to his brain making him restless. He knew he could not let Rebecca go. He needed her.

The next morning he saw the newspaper,

President Is Doing Fine

The news ran that the doctor checked the President's health. It was a mild attack of arrhythmias. The hospital spokesperson told the reporter that all the test results came back negative. The hospital kept the President overnight for observation and would discharge him late that afternoon. Under that, the subheading read:

Concern about President's Health
Nation Prays For Speedy Recovery

Last night's sudden heart attack created concern nationwide about the President's health. In spite of the abrupt end, the President's rating had not changed. His opponent, Governor Giarrusso, had a tough fight ahead.

Robert Lange expected this reaction. He decided to call a staff meeting to warn them not to make an issue of the President's health. He wanted the reality to sink in for the time being.

Chapter 42

Journey of Shiv

A big title appeared in the Pakistani News TV Channel with the photo of the victim.

IBP Successfully Killed Indian Spy

Kiran and Anthony were monitoring the chatter on the digital box. They noticed the sudden increase in chatter between Waziristan, Peshawar, and Saudi Arabia. The TV story ran that Indian spy, Latif Ahmadi, was found sniffing around for information on the streets around Peshawar Army Camp. The IBP spotted Latif and in the exchange of gunfire, they killed him. The crowd gathered around mutilated his body and fed the pieces to the street dogs. The Pakistani Embassy lodged the official protest to the Indian Embassy in Islamabad. The Indian Embassy immediately responded that Latif Ahamadi was a known terrorist belonging to the HuJI terrorist network and Indian authorities were seeking him about the theft.

After watching the news, Kiran said to Anthony, "Finally, Latif Ahmadi successfully crossed the border and delivered the SHIV the Destruction device in Peshawar. The increased chatter also indicated the same. What a fate. He worked for the terrorists, took a risk for them, completed the task successfully, and now the street dogs devoured his dead body while his soul began enjoying those 50 hurries (nymphs) on the gates of heaven as promised for participating in terrorism."

Latif was dead. No one knew who had the possession of SHIV the Destruction. They began communicating with other terrorist organizations to find out information. Kiran and Anthony heard all about the aborted mission of Indian intelligence agents in Miramshah, but they did not know that Al Qaeda did not have the device.

Surayya was waiting for Farooq's visit to *Mohabbat-E-Masti*. Last night, she heard an important communication from Karim Abdul. He was a local member of the terrorist cell in Islamabad. Since the last fiasco, she was a little bit hesitant, but Farooq explained to her that no matter what the information was, she should pass it to him and let his people worry about relevance.

Karim was cursing TNSA (Tehrik-e-Nafaz-e-Shariat-e- Ahamadi) and IBP. He was drinking and babbling. He was mad because they killed his relative, Latif Ahamadi, from India who bravely crossed the border to deliver a package. He was babbling about IBP, mobs, and body fed to dogs. When Farooq entered *Mohabbat-E-Masti*, Surayya narrated the whole episode to him.

"Did he say any name or place?"

"Yes, he blurted that he was going to kill the fellow. I believe he babbled something about money… and sell…, and '*Chaman-E-Baksh*,' but I am not sure. The place must be in Peshawar because he was talking about Peshawar," Surayya replied.

Farooq relayed the message with setup protocol next morning to Jahangir and Commander Bhosle insisting that, based on the new intelligence, they must negotiate the deal immediately to buy the devices.

There was a mosque to the north of Islamabad within the Islamabad city limits and behind the mosque, there was a tree. Jahangir dug into the west side and found two boxes with messages. The message in the first box was in Urdu containing references to Surah from the Quran. He used the Quran and deciphered the message by using the first and last words of each Surah. The message was about SHIV the Destruction and Chaman-E-Baksha.

The second box contained a message to pay for three stooges from Chaman-E-Baksha. Jahangir understood the message. *Chaman-E-Baksha* was a dilapidated building on the outskirts of Peshawar. It is a local quarter for TNSA members to get together. The TNSA was mainly involved in illegal weapon smuggling. Jahangir had little luck doing business with them. The three stooges meant three devices. They were at Chaman-E-Baksh, in Peshawar with the TNSA terrorist group. The message was to buy SHIV the Destruction devices.

"Oh hell… it'll be goddamned difficult to get SHIV the Destruction from them," the words blurted from Jahangir's lips.

He destroyed both messages by burning them to ashes before going back to his place.

Jahangir contacted one of his CIs that happened to be a TNSA member. The CI confirmed that devices were in Peshawar with TNSA. He also confirmed that they would be selling it to the highest bidder to get money to free their leader and TNSS is very much interested in acquiring the device.

Jahangir had two options: first, negotiate a deal to buy the devices at a high cost; and second, if negotiations failed, arrange a raid as a backup plan. Jahangir decided to ask Farooq to handle this job.

Farooq was a rising contractor and supplier of weapons and drugs for the Defense Supply Division of the Pakistan army. No one would suspect him if he contacted TNSA. Jahangir also thought of getting help from the CIA to raid the place as a backup if negotiations failed. He prepared two messages and dispatched them via different channels, one to Farooq, and other to SSIW for Ramanuj and Commander Bhosle. He asked for immediate confirmation from both since time was running out.

He sent message to Farooq requesting him to visit *Chaman-E-Baksh* at Peshawar and to negotiate a deal with TNSA to buy the devices, Shiv the Destruction. In a message to Ramanuj and Commander Bhosle, he requested help from the CIA. He also added that TNSA was willing to sell the device to the highest bidder since they needed money to buy the freedom of their leader. If the negotiations failed, Farooq or Fatima could signal the CIA to raid the place after confirming the presence of the devices at *Chaman-E-Baksh*. Commander relayed the message for help to Anthony.

It was a perfect plan. Anthony immediately called the CIA office in Virginia requesting satellite help for monitoring and permission for raid. They flatly refused the request with a stern warning from the higher-ups that they should not interfere in the country's internal affairs or help the intelligence agencies of other countries.

Anthony was furious, "Intelligence agencies of another country, my foot…, they assigned you to monitor the progress of SHIV the Destruction. Indian Intelligence Agency accepted your participation. Now, it is somewhere in Peshawar. They also knew that it was a personal issue for you. You want to find the device that your dead friend Nikhil invented, and still they are refusing, and on top of that with a warning…," Anthony said to Kiran and informed her CIA decision.

The last few days, Anthony was agitated ever since his talk with his bosses, Veronica Ivanhoe and Lisa Hargrove. He did not mention that to Kiran previously because he knew it would upset her. However, today, after talking to his office in Virginia and denial for the permission to raid the place, he was even more aggravated.

He expressed his suspicion and narrated her previous conversation and comments from the boss, "I am mad, Kiran. They chided me for taking help from Indian and Israeli commandos during the rescue operation. I also found out about satellite images and the CIA having the prior knowledge about the gathering of 2000 more Pakistani Tochi Scouts with heavy artillery and anti-aircraft missile launchers in Miramshah. Veronica deliberately sent Lisa on a routine task so she could not communicate with us or warn us. It looks like another Isaac Edward or Daniel Pearl situation. I wonder about their motives. They treat us like collateral baggage that they can sacrifice to fulfill whatever ulterior motives they may have."

Kiran was shocked to hear. It aggravated her, "We'll discuss this with Lisa and Veronica when we get back to Virginia. Right now, I'll call Commander Bhosle."

Kiran informed Commander Bhosle about the CIA's decision and apologetically conveyed their wish to help. Commander Bhosle knew the meaning of subordination and possible consequences. He pacified and convinced both of them not to violate the direct orders.

"In fact, the raid may not be necessary, they are eager to sell the device."

Kiran and Anthony were not convinced but unwillingly decided to go along.

* * * * *

The intoxicated man was talking about certain gang rivalry. It was a common occurrence of gang rivalry among these terrorists belonging to different provinces and tribes.

"*Ye lavandia kuchh nahi janti* (these women don't know a damn)," he was cursing.

The man was agitated. Surayya was listening and trying to squash his anger with *sharab*. Putting his piecemeal babble together, she gathered that some female terrorist gang member, a rival gang of TNSA from Kabul, would be taking a parcel to America from Dubai. He gurgled the name of the group that sounded something like *Hizb-I-Is*…she wasn't sure. She realized this must be important and was hoping that Farooq would come to *Mohabbat-E-Masti* to see her today. She had his number, but it would look suspicious to call him.

The madam, Malika Husaini Shafi, already knew that Farooq was a big Don from Mumbai with lots of cash. She also heard about him buying a warehouse and setting up a business in Islamabad; had a *mashooka* (lover) on the side, and had an ongoing fling with Surayya. She liked such customers; they were safe, paid a lot, and presented no danger for stealing their merchandise.

"Is *Farooq Mia* coming today?"

"*Muze nahi malum* (I don't know). I have his telephone number," Surayya responded.

"Call him, *dosti badhai ye. Business ke liye achha hai* (be friendly; good for the business)," she enticed her.

Surayya telephoned Farooq, "*Mia juldi ai ye* (come soon)."

In the evening, Surayya conveyed the message to him. Farooq relayed the message with setup protocol next morning.

Chapter 43

Avian of Death

Shots fired…Fatima was lying in the pool of blood. She was counting her last moments, whispering, "Laa ilaaha illa-Allah (there is no true god except Allah)," her last words. The other person opposite to her was also dead. The gunfire in *Chaman-E-Baksha* injured two of Pathania's hoods and three TNSA guys. No one knew exactly what happened, where the shots came from, and why they were fired. Farooq heard the noise of a motorbike starting.

Farooq, Fatima, and Pathania, with two of his guys and four TNSA members were sitting in the room negotiating a deal. They wanted more money. The TNSA was a mixed group of terrorists that included Muslim men, women, and children from the Punjabi Pushtun origin. They were a deadly combination of suicide bombers ready to blow up any target for the cause of Jihad. Their local leader was a 22-year-old boy. The police arrested him during the political demonstration. In his absence, his mother, Begum Jamia Kazi, was the acting head of the group. Her husband and brother-in-law blew up the Consulate in Germany, and, as a result, the family had earned the respect of the local members of TNSA.

Latif Ahmadi was supposed to deliver the devices to a Saudi terrorist organization called Clan of Harabi, which was connected with the international Jihadi group Tehreek-e-Nafaz-e-Shariat-e-Salafi (TNSS). Some of them are also members of Al-Qaeda. Sultan Akhmad had ties with the Clan of Harabi and TNSS, the followers of Wahhabism. Salafists are considered the hybrids between Wahhabism and other Jihadi movements. Salafism, depicted with strict and puritanical approaches to Islam, considered violent Jihad against civilians as a legitimate expression of Islam.

Latif's friend *Mia* Mamood Massood, was a member of the TNSA group. He helped Latif cross the Indian boundary to enter Pakistan. Latif mistakenly took *Mia* Mamood Massood as part of the Harabi group, not knowing the difference between TNSA and TNSS, and gave him the bag of SHIV the Destruction devices, narrated the whole saga of theft, murder, the deaths of their friends Salamat and Bahadur, and the capture of Fahayat. He cautioned him that these items were extremely valuable and to hand them over immediately to his boss.

Mia Mamood did not know anything about SHIV the Destruction. The only word made an impact on him was "valuable," which meant cash, the badly needed *moola* (money) to buy the freedom of their young leader. He promised Latif that he would take care of it and give it to Begum Jamia Kazi. He knew Begum would know what to do with it. Latif then called Karim Abdul, his relative in Islamabad, and narrated his adventure. He told him that after collecting the reward money, he would come to see him in Islamabad and they would go together to that place, *Mohabbat-E-Masti*, that Karim always bragged. He went to the house of the merchant to collect his reward for bring- ing the devices safely to Pakistan.

At the house, they were all waiting for delivery. Latif introduced himself, told them that he delivered the devices, and asked about the money.

"What device, where is it, what the hell are you talking about?" The man took his pistol out.

Latif was confused. He knew he was supposed to deliver the device to something like Tehreek-e-Nafaz-e-Shariat. He did not remember whether it is Ahmadi or Salafi. He did not know the difference between TNSA and TNSS. By mistake, he handed the device to the wrong person. He opened his mouth to explain, saw the pistol pointed at him, and tried to flee. Shots were fired and he was killed before he could divulge the information.

Mia Mamood Massood found out about his friend Latif's death from the TV news. He did not understand all the fuss; however, after hearing the news, he realized that the bag containing the devices must be valuable. He took the bag to Begum Jamia Kazi and told her the story of his friend's gruesome murder. She could not figure out the function of the SHIV the Destruction device; it looked like small toy. Begum realized that the device must be expensive so she kept it in a safe place. They needed money to bribe the police to free up their leader and decided to make money out of it. For a couple of days, they remained silent to find out who would be interested in the devices. Then they spread the rumor alluding to the mysterious items.

One day earlier Farooq called Pathania, "Pathania *bhai, gustakhi maf* (sorry for disturbing).".

"Farooq Bhai *banda hajir hai, hukum farmaie* (Brother Farooq I am at your service, what can I do for you?)."

"I need your help to do business with TNSA Group in Peshawar."

"*Bas Hukm kare* (your wish is my command)," Pathania answered.

Farooq hesitated for a moment, "I am negotiating a deal to buy weapons from TNSA group. I do not know them. I believe you know a few people over there. I'll pay you $25,000 for your trouble if you come with few of your men. If the deal goes through, I'll add another $100,000."

Pathania thought, "Wow, $25,000 is a lot of *moola* (money) for the one-night job. Farooq is new to the territory; he needs protection. All I have to do is to be there with a few of my men. There is no danger, no fighting, I know the people, and if the deal goes through, another $100,000, and if the deal doesn't go through, I still have $25,000 in my pocket. Not bad at all."

He liked the idea more and more as he thought about it and was pleased with Farooq for asking his help. Knowing Farooq's reputation, being a friend to him was helpful for Pathania and, if that came with a bonus, then that was even better.

"*Banda apka gulam hai* (I am at your service), I'll be there," Panthania responded.

Time was running out. SHIV the Destruction could leave Peshawar for Saudi anytime. Farooq explained that to Pathania so he immediately arranged the meeting for the next night giving enough time for him and Farooq to travel to Peshawar. At first, Farooq was reluctant to take Fatima with him, but she insisted. She wanted to see the device for which her husband died, and Pathania told him that they would be negotiating with *Begum* Jamia Kazi. Therefore, Farooq agreed to take Fatima along with him. Fatima wore the *burqua* and they all left.

The TNSS was frantically searching for the device. They heard the rumor of the mysterious items. They also heard about the meeting between Defense Supply Contractor, Pathania, and TNSA members from their informant. Knowing the reputation of Pathania, involvement of the bigwig, and from the intelligence gathered, they planned an attack on *Chaman-E-Baksha* that same night during the negotiations when the device would be available for exchange.

It was a dark night. There was no moon in the sky. There were only two dim streetlights on the entire road. Al Qaeda and TNSS terrorists stealthily entered the area and saw two men guarding the door. Two Al Qaeda men came from the side; the two men guarding the door didn't even notice them, and before they knew it, their throats were slit. Two women were standing with a motorbike on the side of the house. The terrorists entered the house and saw four TNSA members gambling with a card game. The stakes were high; they were concentrating on the game and did not notice the entry of strangers. The terrorists captured and disabled the three of them, the fourth one, *Mia* Mamood, escaped and ran toward the adjacent room.

Begum Jamia wanted to jack up the price. Farooq was ready, but Pathania decided to haggle. *Mia* Mamood Massood entered the room to warn them. Fatima turned her head and saw him; she removed her burqua and her face contour was visible under the dim light. *Mia* Mamood did not know what shocked him, her face, which he knew to be that of Salman's wife, or the movement at the door. Fatima knew him from the Dalsar village as her husband's friend. *Mia* Mamood attended their *nikah* (marriage). Fatima realized that he recognized her. Her cover was blown. She realized *Mia* Mamood belonged to the same terrorist group who killed her husband. She was mad and burning with revenge.

He said, "Mo ...," no one knew whether he was cursing or saying Motarma (Madam) to Begum Jamia Kazi.

Fatima did not care. She took her pistol out and shot. *Mia* Mamood fired back before falling.

The Al Qaeda men entered the room firing. Farooq was behind the desk. He heard the whispering moan *"Laa ilaaha illa-Allah* (there is no true god except Allah)" from Fatima's lips. Fatima took her revenge; she killed the terrorist from the village she thought had his hand in killing her husband. *Mia* Mamood was dead. The gunfire injured Pathania's hoods and TNSA guys. Pathania was holding others at gunpoint, but it was too late. One of the TNSS men grabbed the bag, ran out, and delivered them to the two women riding the mo- torbike. Farooq heard the noise of the motorbike starting. The bag disappeared with SHIV the Destruction. Everything happened so fast, it was chaotic. Farooq and Pathania grabbed Fatima's body and left the place with the injured hoods. The stealth returned with the smell of death.

Chapter 44

Return

The second page of the English version of Pakistani Daily had a small caption about the murder and fight in the outskirts of Peshawar. Kiran read the news.

Fight Erupted - Gunshots Fired
In *Chaman-E-Baksha* Peshawar

Last night, gunfight erupted in *Chaman-E-Baksh*, a rundown building in the dilapidated area of Peshawar. Two people killed, four others wounded in the gunfight were taken to the local hospital for treatment. One of the wounded is still in critical condition. The police suspect that the building is a local quarter for the TNSA terrorist group. However, wounded claimed it was a random attack and refused any connection with TNSA. There have been no arrests yet. The matter is under investigation.

Kiran was waiting for news from Fatima. She was hoping that they had already negotiated the deal and secured the devices. After reading the news in the Pakistani Daily, she became restless. There were no names mentioned in the news. She called Fatima; someone answered the phone. Kiran posing as a friend of Fatima asked in Urdu about Fatima. The person answering the phone cut the line. Kiran called repeatedly, but there was no response.

Imran Quadree, the peon from the Indian Consulate's office in Islamabad, came to see Kiran in the American Embassy. He gave her the awful news of Fatima's death and disappearance of the SHIV the Destruction devices. She felt remorse.

"Fatima's death is a great loss to us," Imran paused, hesitated, "The Commander would like you to monitor the chatter about SHIV the Destruction; I hope you don't mind doing that. No one has to know."

"Not at all," Kiran said, but she knew that Commander would find out long before them about SHIV the Destruction.

Jahangir got the news of Fatima's death immediately from Farooq. The next day, he tried to contact his CI, but there was no word. He left a message for him. Two days later, his CI called and gave him the complete account.

Local Al-Qaeda members attacked the TNSA quarters and stole the devices before the deal. Their leader, Begum Jamia Kazi, survived. The two women on a motorbike headed toward Waziristan and they would deliver the package to someone coming from Saudi Arabia. Jahangir had no contacts in Waziristan. The isolated and sparsely populated area was the most dangerous zone. The people knew each other well and they would detect any new arrival or suspicious activities easily.

Miramshah was the headquarters of the Khost Battalion and was heavily guarded. From the account of the secret meeting in Zurich, he knew that the two women on the motorbike would go to Banu to deliver the package to Akhmad's man. He encrypted another message suggesting to send Barkat Niazi and Hadith Abu to Waziristan. Barkat and Hadith both were in Kabul at that time when they received the message from Commander. It took them one day to get to Banu, Waziristan. Banu is not a big place. One of the relatives told them that a new face did arrive two days back from Saudi and had already left. The two female terrorists left for Dubai on the motorbike this morning. Barkat and Hadith passed on the information. Both Jahangir and ISHWAR facility got the news. The Commander told Suhasini to inform Imaran so he could convey the news personally to Kiran.

After delivering one package to the messenger from Saudi Arabia, the two women, Jahanara Hakim and Shabanam Mallika, rested for a day in Banu and then left for Karachi. Shabnam dropped Jahanara at Karachi and returned. Jahanara took a small boat and went to Dubai. She did not take a chance to fly from Karachi because her leader told that IBP would be watching for the parcel at Karachi and Islamabad Airport. It took her about four days to reach Dubai. Jahanara was to deliver the devices to London and to Washington D.C. At the Dubai airport, Jahanara met another terrorist who was working as a baggage porter at the airport. She gave him the bag and went inside the airport.

In the second week of August, Kiran received a call from her immediate supervisor, Lisa Hargrove, around 9 p.m. in her hotel. The weather in Islamabad was hot. The hotel air conditioner unit was running on emergency generators due to the loss of power in Islamabad. This was common in Pakistan due to the lack of enough power generation. It was not comfortable in the room at all.

"Good evening, Kiran."

"And good morning to you, too, Lisa, what can I do for you?"

"Veronica Ivanhoe called this morning and she wants both you and Anthony to return."

"What do you want to do with the present investigation of SHIV the Destruction?"

"The department wants to put that on hold. Based on your intelligence, I believe the device is no longer in Pakistan but probably left for Saudi. We have agents in Saudi and they'll monitor. Besides, more work is piling up here, especially in your specialty, information analysis. If you want to take a few days off to visit your family before joining, let me know so I can arrange the ticket accordingly. Check with Anthony, I am also sending him an e-mail."

"Okay," Kiran said curtly. She was still mad about what Anthony told her before and wondered about the sudden change. Nevertheless, she was also excited that she would get a chance to see Ruben soon. She immediately called Ruben to inform him about her homecoming. The device had vanished from Pakistan. Based on the intelligence received, it might be somewhere in Saudi Arabia. She wanted to pursue and retrieve the SHIV the Destruction device for Nikhil's sake to provide peace to his soul, but realized that the plot is becoming too thick and the conspiracy much bigger than she thought.

Kiran called Commander Bhosle and told him about her return to the US. She requested that the Commander continue to look for the device. While talking to her, the Commander began thinking about the message he received from Farooq. He realized that Indian intelligence did not have much control in either Saudi or the US. The device from Saudi would be delivered to US soil or someone would come to Saudi from the US to pick it up. The female terrorist taking the other devices to the UK and the US would be traveling from Dubai. Suhas found out that HII, short form for Hizb-I-Islam, was Afghan-based and TNSS was the offshoot of HII in Pakistan. The SSIW Wing gathered the chatter received from various Al Qaeda, TNSS, and HII (Hizb-I-Islam) quarters and passed the intelligence to the ASIIW to process and analyze. They analyzed the information along with the intelligence received from Jahangir and Farooq and approximately determined the day the female terrorist would reach Dubai. The Commander decided to reveal the intelligence to Kiran.

"We received some intelligence about the device. One device is in the hands of Saudi executive, Sultan Akhmad. Either he will arrange for delivery to US or someone from the US will come to pick it up from him in Saudi. The woman from Hizb-I-Islam (HII) will be carrying the remaining two devices to the UK and US tomorrow. See what you can do," he instructed.

Kiran and Anthony knew about the terrorist gang Hizb-I-Islam (HII). They checked the flight passenger manifesto, but could not identify any name. Anthony checked with his local CI and came up with a couple of names. One was Jahanara Hakim, who was an Afghani national with ties to HII. She was traveling on the next day's flight to Washington D.C. under an assumed name. The CI could not provide the assumed name. He was a little hesitant when Anthony asked. He said Jahanara did act as a messenger a few times before. She always traveled with different passports to places like New York, Chicago, and Baltimore. She had never been to Washington, D.C. However, the rumor had been circulating that she wanted to quit. He had no idea whether she was traveling to Washington, D.C. for a cause or for requesting asylum. There was no photo available. She regularly traveled with make up, changing facial appearances each time, and wore burqas.

Kiran and Anthony flew to Dubai late that afternoon. Since they did not know which flight the woman would be on, they kept a watch on the departing passengers. Flights to the US from Dubai always departed early in the morning, before sunrise. Anthony noticed a woman with a burqa and an American passport presenting the reservation voucher at the ticket counter. She gave the bag to an airport baggage porter and went inside the airport. Her behavior looked suspicious. Anthony beckoned Kiran. The woman was passing through security for boarding flights after she got her ticket voucher.

On the other side of the security checkpoint, Kiran saw someone handing her the bag. That act confirmed their suspicion. It was a British carrier. Kiran and Anthony decided to board that flight. Getting a seat was a problem because the flight was booked. The ticket agent, a fair-looking English woman, was about to announce the names of the standby passengers. Anthony showed his badge to her. Without any question, she issued them the two tickets. There was a three-hour layover in London.

"Do you think one of the devices will change hands in London and the other will go to the US?" Anthony asked.

"That could be," Kiran said.

They decided to watch her movements. Nothing happened in London. Neither Kiran nor Anthony realized that Jahanara left behind one device under the seat where she was sitting.

Normally, airport security was tight in the US and UK. However, due to the present budget cuts of the administration, there was considerable slack in security on all US airports. The Democrats and Republicans were fighting. The lobbyists were trying hard to get those cuts for the reduced airport security. The UK always followed American guidelines. This gave the opportunity to the terrorists to bring the devices inside the country. At both airports, Heathrow and Washington, D.C., there were many Muslims working as porters and Customs Officers. Most of them were honest and trustworthy, but one could always find a couple of rotten apples in any lot. Due to the security slack, no one noticed the device left under the seat.

In Washington, D.C., Kiran and Anthony signaled Customs to detain her. US Customs took her to a room. She requested to go to a washroom. The male Customs officer accompanied her to the rest room as she carried her fabric tote bag. The officer waited outside. Jahanara discarded her burqa inside the latrine and a beautiful woman emerged underneath wearing an American outfit. She still had her tote bag. Inside her tote bag was another designer boutique signature Salvatore Ferragamo handbag. Her passport, ticket, a large sum of cash, and a parcel were inside the handbag. She expected a disaster like this to happen and was ready for it. She threw the Tote bag in the garbage.

She walked out, right past the officer waiting for her. He was so stupefied by her elegance and beauty that he did not realize she was the same woman in a burqa he escorted to the restroom. After 10 minutes, the officer called for a female officer. She went inside, searched, but there was no one. She found the burqa hanging in the latrine along with her purse and the tote bag in the garbage. The female officer came out empty handed.

When Kiran and Anthony found out that the suspect had fled from the airport, they went through her purse but could not find any clues, except a note pad. Anthony used the carbon from the pencil to smear the front page from the pad. An address from the remote part of Manassas, Virginia appeared.

The car was waiting for Kiran and Anthony outside with an agent. They drove to the address. It was a rundown place with a for sale sign hanging in front. There was no movement inside. They called the real estate agent. She was cooperative. She opened the house for them. She was not expecting anyone inside the vacant house. She entered…, a scream shrieked through the emptiness of the house.

The woman's body was hanging upside down, knife protruding from the chest, blood dripping. The body was warm, the eyes were open, and the area desolated. No fingerprints were found on the knife. Somewhere in the outskirts of Washington, D.C., a couple of men were getting ready for action. Kiran and Anthony returned to the office, updated Lisa, and then Kiran left D.C. to visit her parents in Ohio.

She had no idea what dreadful consequences the device would bring in the near future. Destiny plays a game that humans will never fathom. Nikhil would have never dreamt of this. Ideas from two scientists intermingled and created a monster. The technology is a coin with two sides. One side is God to make life easier for humanity with new inventions, flip it and other side is the Devil with horrible corollaries.

* * * * *

The dreadful evening of August 21 drew near. The police cleared the roads near India Gate, Delhi, and they took bodies to the morgue. Delhi, the capital of India, was in a panic. Throughout the entire evening, TV channels were broadcasting news. The names of the dead appeared with soulful stories about the families left behind. The media blamed the police, the Secret Service, and the politicians, whatever the reporters could conjure.

News that was more shocking blasted again. The TV channels and radios roared news by 8 p.m. about the similar dreadful event. A blast, a blur... hit Trafalgar Square in London, the capital of England, and more than 50 people died. The panic became intense. Where would the next attack be? Security was tight all around the world. Every airport, every major city on the globe was on RED ALERT in capital letters.

It was almost midnight. After four to five hours of toil, Ramanuj and his colleagues at ISHWAR identified the person from the film retrieved from the pole. His face was visible. He was wearing normal clothes. The film showed that he threw away something and then entered the car. The agents identified the car by which the terrorist fled from the scene and concluded that it was a one-person operation.

RAW's database had no information, but the Interpol database confirmed that he was a known terrorist on the Interpol wanted list belonging to the Salafi Jihadi Movement, the group known as *Tehreek-e-Nafaz-e-Shariat-e-Salafi* (TNSS). That surprised them.

Unlike the US and the UK, the TNSS was not so active in India. First HuJI and then TNSS, the terrorists used two devices and there were two left. They realized the incidents that took place in Delhi and London were the work of SHIV the Destruction.

From the license plate, police identified that the car was a stolen. They found the car deserted near the nightclub *Bahar-E-Noor* in Chandani Chowk. The agents from the ISHWAR Facility requested both the CBI and the police department not to interfere, and they raided the nightclub the same night. It was a lowlife nightclub screaming loud filmy music, tobacco smell, cloud of smoke perme- ating all over, and half-naked girls belly dancing on the stage, a few flirting with customers.

Agents were carrying photos of a few suspected terrorists with them but they did not find any clues or see any faces resembling those photos. One of the agents went out from the back door and found a dead body in the alley. This was the same guy who was seen running earlier from that catastrophic scene. They realized that someone was making sure there were no clues left behind.

The Commander called the head of the Secret Service GCHQ of the UK, and informed them about the SHIV the Destruction devices that terrorists stole from the GEETA Laboratory. He also informed them that there were two more devices still out there and requested their help to locate them. He cautioned them to keep the information secret to avoid global panic. The GCHQ was exasperated about re-ceiving the information after the fact. They realized the gravity and danger, and communicated with CIA. The Commander informed them that the CIA was working with ISHWAR on the recovery of the devices. His main concern was if the terrorist organization, in collaboration with the specialized laboratory, could manage to re-en-gineer the device, then it would have a devastating impact. Such a laboratory could be anywhere – Switzerland, Germany, US, Russia, or China – there was no telling.

This was a catastrophic situation. The two secret agencies had in-formation; they and the other nations could put tremendous political pressure on Indian technological advancement. However, there was no such move, no repercussion yet.

Why…?

Who could be behind this…?
Who are these conspirators…?
What is their motive…?
Big question marks, the Commander began wondering.

The police cleared the streets near Trafalgar Square after removing the dead bodies from the streets. Soon, the evening turned to night. Scotland Yard was alert and looking for suspects everywhere. Later that night during their normal vigilance, Scotland Yard spotted a scuffle under the bridge on the banks of the River Thames. They noticed one person running away from the scene. The officer from the passenger side of the car got out. He shouted and started chasing after him but it was too late. The guy disappeared into the woods.

The other person was lying in a pool of his own blood. He was wearing the same clothes; there was no identification except a burnt mechanism in his hood pocket and a wad of loose bills. The police identified that this was their guy based on the pictures that were taken that afternoon at Trafalgar Square. He was dead now. The GCHQ identified the dead body as the terrorist from the international terrorist organization, TNSS.

The scene in front of the Crystal City Shops was devastating. The squad cars, ambulances, and coroner cars surrounded the area. Adding to that devastation was the pile-up on the highway next to the Crystal City Shops. Kiran was standing next to the handcuffed suspect. Blood was oozing from his leg. Kiran showed her badge to the police and informed them the injured person was a terrorist. She handed the motorbike to the police to return it to the owner. She also requested the police to thank the motorbike owner for letting her use it, and to tell him that the agency would pay for any damages. The agency car approached her.

The terrorist received medical treatment. The police were reluctant to hand over the terrorist to her. The detective argued with her about jurisdiction. He told her he needed clearance from his superiors. He was aware of the disaster at the Crystal City Shops from his police scanner. However, he created an illusion in his mind that with the terrorist in custody, he could resolve the matter fast and take the credit for it. He conveniently forgot that the CIA agent caught the terrorist. The internal politics and the glory took precedence.

Eventually, Kiran called her office and talked with her boss. Within a few minutes, the inspector received a call. He turned around to pick up the call from his police car. No one knew where the shot came from. The shot missed the terrorist, but the bullet grazed his shoulder. Kiran found the bullet in the back seat of the police car. She took it for evidence. The ambulance came, treated the prisoner, and took him to the hospital.

The triggering mechanism appeared to be intact. Kiran took the mechanism and followed the ambulance to the hospital. The police officer was angry but he could not do anything to stop her. Kiran called the office, gave them the news that she caught the prisoner, and requested Lisa to send the van to the hospital.

The doctors treated his wound and patched him up in the hospital. They gave him sedatives and painkillers and discharged him. The CIA van was in the parking lot. There was no way to interrogate him that night. Kiran handed over the mechanism to Mr. George Austin for record keeping along with the bullet to analyze. It was a bullet from the .45 magnum.

Next morning when Kiran went to the office, she found the prisoner hanging in his cell. It looked like the prisoner had committed suicide. Later, the autopsy indicated that the death was by suffocation staged as suicide. The federal security did not know how that happened. Kiran was upset.

Three incidences of the blur, three dead terrorists, and yet no suspect was identified. This was the third incident on August 21, one in India, another in London, and a third in the US. August 21 was not a holiday. It was a mundane day. Everyone was wondering. The machinery began rolling, looking for pictures, videos, information, and leads, but nothing surfaced except the dead. The alert level was raised to orange.

Chapter 45

Windfall

A round 9 a.m., Robert Lange received a call. The mysterious caller conveyed to him the instructions. Robert Lange immediately called Senator Fitzroy. One and a half-hour later, he called a meeting of all the campaign staff in the Oxford Conference Room of the hotel in Chicago. The purpose for the meeting was to decide the Governor's activities henceforth until Election Day. Everyone was in the room, John Haskin, Ricky Benton, Robert Dennison, Malcolm O'Connor, Robert Spears, Jessica Patel, Sandy Hoover, Josh Desai, Ruben Joshi, even Louise Calvin. Except for Rebecca, the entire campaign team was there.

Ruben made an excuse for Rebecca, "She is under the weather," he said.

Governor Giarrusso and Senator Fitzroy also entered the conference room.

Elena was not there; she had already left. She was caught between her love and her own convictions. Elena grew up in an affluent family with a Catholic upbringing. From childhood, she was taught to control her emotions, avoid public scenes, and not to become the center of attention.

After the unexpected ending of the debate when media gathered around and asked questions, she remained silent. Her press secretary had tried to arrange interviews, but she declined the requests. She hoped that Henry would lose the election and this whole media frenzy would unwind on its own.

Robert got up and addressed the staff. He did not mention the incident at the debate either, and he cautioned all of them not to talk about the President's health.

"Let the facts sink in. Few sympathy votes may be with him, but let us not fuel the issue of health and give media more to frenzy over. That could turn against us. We have already planned a few interviews on national networks," he looked at Malcolm.

"Malcolm, do you have those policy statements on key issues that we discussed before? I would like the Governor to go from north to south and east to west across the country; those policy statements will be handy. Remember there is one more debate left in 20 days."

Senator Fitzroy interrupted, "Although, in the last debate they could not discuss the foreign policy issues because of the President's heart trouble, the issues may certainly come up in the next debate."

Robert looked at Senator Fitzroy and then addressed the campaign team, "What do you think about a short trip abroad for the Governor to visit the UK, France, Germany, Italy, and Saudi Arabia? I have already talked to the Senator. We can easily plan little over a week-long trip that'll give badly needed foreign exposure to our Governor."

Everyone agreed that was a brilliant idea.

"This'll also give an opportunity to the Governor to go away because this is not really a good time to talk about the campaign to American people," Jessica Patel added. "So, it is settled then," every one nodded.

Robert looked at Ruben, "Ruben, you have worked as the foreign correspondent, how about you joining the Governor to cover the publicity aspect?"

Senator Fitzroy blurted, "That's a great idea."

"Can Elena join?" Robert Dennison asked. He was the one responsible to make all travel arrangements and similar logistics for the campaign.

"This'll be a quick trip with discussions and strategy management of foreign policies, let's leave her out of it," the Senator spoke.

"What about Rebecca?" Robert addressed the question to both the Senator and Ruben.

"Well, Rebecca is not here, let me think about it," the Senator responded. He had some other ideas. He would call his friend in the

CIA to send an agent as a cameraman to help them for more security and as a safety concern.

Robert was thinking that Ruben had undergone a traumatic experience only few months back in the Middle East, so he wanted to make sure rather than assuming, "Are you okay going abroad, Ruben?"

Ruben nodded. He was more interested in getting to bottom of the mystery. Ruben knew that the tape that Rebecca showed him would destroy the Governor's career, but there was more at stake here. He met Kiran just after he returned home from the second debate. He had talked to her in detail before she left for Washington, D.C. Kiran told him about Fatima's death and the disappearance of the SHIV the Destruction device probably to Saudi Arabia amongst other things. He did not know Fatima, but the news of the device and Saudi Arabia intrigued him.

The morning campaign meeting announced the sudden planning of a trip abroad including the visit to Saudi Arabia. He thought about Robert Lange's association with the Mafia and the Mancini family. "Is there any connection?" Ruben still vividly remembered the murder that he saw as a boy, the conversation that he had heard at that time about arms, weapons... Karachi and the latest information coming from Indian intelligence, there had to be some connection. The ringing telephone interrupted his thought process.

"Hello, Rebecca... we were looking for you this morning. You have to hear the latest news. The Senator and Robert Lange have planned a trip abroad to give our Governor the foreign exposure he needs. You were not there; I made an excuse for you. I don't think they are replacing you. I won't allow that, but I believe they are temporarily bringing someone else as a cameraman to go abroad. We are leaving tomorrow. Where are you?" Ruben wanted to give all the information in one breath.

"I showed the video clip to Elena."

"You... what? What are you saying? Are you out of your mind?"

"I called to let you know that I am resigning. I called the office but no one answered. No wonder, everybody is busy getting ready for the trip. I'll give my resignation tomorrow," Rebecca was resolute.

Ruben murmured, "Good luck, Rebecca, best wishes to you in whatever you do. See you upon return," he did not know what else to say. She already did the damage.

Kiran was busy preparing the trip report and the report of the Blur incidents. It took her the whole morning. There were so many details to remember. She also processed the information on the dead guy. From the database, she identified him as a member of the TNSS terrorist organization. They were an off-shoot of the Clan of Harabi from Saudi. She remembered that the people who conducted the Blur attack in the UK and India belonged to the TNSS terrorist organization. She realized that all of this pointed to Saudi.

Just after lunch, she received a call from Ruben. Ruben told her about the latest campaign development of the Governor's trip abroad and him accompanying the Governor as a publicity manager.

"He is also going to visit Saudi. I told you before about my friend, Logan Mancini, and the Mancini family. What I didn't tell you is that Robert Lange and the Mancini are closely connected. There is something fishy here. Now this trip to Saudi, and according to your information, SHIV the Destruction is in Saudi. There has to be some connection, don't you think?"

Kiran listened to him carefully. It made her realize there were more to the theft of the SHIV the Destruction devices than met the eye. The connection to the Mafia family, the campaign, Robert Lange, the trip to Saudi, SHIV the Destruction devices in Saudi; she could not figure out how to connect the dots, but there was a lot of coincidence. She warned Ruben to be on the watch-out.

While she was on the phone with Ruben, there was another call. Mr. George Austin picked up the phone. On behalf of Senator Fitzroy, Robert Lange was calling for Major Bartlett, the CIA chief. Neither Major Bartlett nor Veronica was in the office. Kiran told him to take the message and give it to her supervisor, Lisa Hargrove. Lisa discussed this with Kiran, "They want someone to accompany Governor Henry Giarrusso immediately on his foreign trip as a cameraman. Do you have any suggestions?"

Kiran was thinking of her conversation with Ruben. Suddenly, an idea occurred to her. "Wow, this would be a good break," she thought.

She realized that if there were something fishy going on in Saudi, then this would be an excellent opportunity for Anthony Hurtz to join them as a cameraman and film everything.

She pretended to be thinking and said, "If it's okay with you and Anthony, then Anthony can join them. It's going to last only for a week to 10 days. I'll talk to him right now."

Lisa had no problem with the suggestion. Anthony was in the office.

Kiran immediately went to his desk and requested that he accompany Ruben and Governor Henry Giarrusso on their trip abroad. She also told him her discussion with Ruben and her suspicion about SHIV the Destruction.

Anthony Hurtz was familiar with the entire scenario. He accepted the assignment and booked a ticket to Chicago. Kiran cautioned Anthony to keep the affair secret until they got the concrete proof. Lisa asked Anthony to call Robert Lange to convey the message, and to get the time and place to meet.

Chapter 46

Darkness

E lena was happy with her marriage. She knew Henry was not fit
to govern, but she loved him. They did well; they governed the
State successfully. She enjoyed her first two terms as the First
Lady of Illinois with Henry, but his new façade scared her. She wondered, "What's happening with Henry? He is engulfed by arrogance
and fallacy; does campaign phobia do that to a person?" She was des-
perately waiting for the election to end. She decided that win or lose,
she would get her old Henry back to the man she loved.

Rebecca knew Elena from the college days where Elena was a
lecturer and Rebecca was her student in Black History class.
During those days, the two of them developed a bond of friendship.
Rebecca discussed the situation with Ruben. He tried to persuade
her from showing the telephone clip to Elena. Rebecca knew that
the content of the phone clip would almost kill her. At first, she
was reluctant, but her conscience would not allow her to rest,
keeping the secret from her friend and mentor tormented Rebecca.
It was nagging her. Eventually, she became vulnerable to her
mental acuity. The agony of keeping the secret from her friend
was unbearable. She went to Elena's house in Chicago to visit her
where Henry and Elena moved after finishing the second term as
Governor.

Elena was surprised to see her and mildly happy to see an old friend
in the time of her conflict. She welcomed her. They chatted about old
college days and Elena's experience in the Congo. Then they talked
about the campaign. Elena openly expressed her unhappiness about
Henry's imprudent behavior, irresponsible attitude, and the vacuous

promises. She was furious. Rebecca sensed Elena's utter displeasure toward imprudence, falsehood, and irresponsible behavior.

"Elena didn't know anything about Louise," Rebecca felt sorry for her. Tears gathered around her eyelids. The clip that she was about to show her would intensify her agony. She felt her pain and hesitated for a moment.

"Do you have anything on your mind Rebecca?" Elena sensed her hesitation.

"Well…," Rebecca was not sure what to do.

"Come on, you didn't come here just to visit me."

Rebecca showed her the telephone clip. Elena was dazed; she was never so belligerent. She tried to avoid confrontations, but she did not know how to fend this monster. From college days, she knew he lacked moral strength, but she thought he came out of it. She thought that maturity took over the hormonal desires of his youth. Her dreams shattered with the clip she saw. The demon was not dead; he was just hiding. The more she saw of him during the campaign, the more she drifted away from him. The campaign phobia, the offensiveness, the irresponsible behavior, she tolerated it all. However, this reality she could not ignore. Rebecca tried to console her but Elena excused herself. Rebecca left.

She poured two shots from the crystal decanter from the wine bar and sat down on the quilted sofa. She was furious; she thought about the events of the whole campaign. Up until now, there was a dilemma. She consoled herself by pampering the thoughts that time would pass and the election would be over. Win or lose, she would still have her beloved husband. That was no more. The dreams would never return. The cloud of deception shattered all hopes of mending. Was this the man, she loved? She poured two more shots. She saw no way out of it. She could not stand with him on any podium after this. Eventually, she gathered enough courage to tell him she was going to leave him… she drifted to sleep.

Henry came home from the Chicago campaign headquarters by 11 p.m. He wanted to get ready for the trip abroad. He found her asleep on the sofa in the study. He looked down. She was beautiful, but her facial contour revealed a taut expression. The usual serenity was no longer there. He saw the glass on the table and the bottle almost half empty. She was a social drinker, but this surprised him. He did not want to wake her up, so he went straight to bed. The next day, he woke up early to pack.

She heard him. She sat up.

"When did you come home?" She asked.

"Last night."

She was not ready to fight with him, but she had to do it. He began walking toward the bedroom.

"Henry!" She screeched his name.

He suddenly turned around, not knowing what to expect,

"Yes, Elena, what's the matter?"

"I want to talk to you."

"Not now, I have to get ready for the trip abroad."

"I want a divorce."

He looked at her, "Come on, Elena, what are you talking about?" She was walking out of the study toward her bedroom.

"I can't do this anymore, Henry. I'm going to see a lawyer tomorrow."

"Honey, cut out the nonsense."

"That's what I wanted to tell you."

The Governor was baffled. He never expected this bombshell. He was getting ready to go abroad.

"Do you know I can actually win, do you realize what's at stake? I am talking about Presidency of United States of America," he said.

"I don't care!" She walked to her bedroom and slammed the door.

"Why? Please tell me what's wrong," he knocked, she would not respond. He pleaded, but it was of no use.

The phone rang. Robert was on the line. Henry picked up the phone and told him about her being mad and wanting to divorce him.

"Shit, this is bad timing Governor. If she files for divorce, it'll create a scandal and media frenzy."

Henry did not say anything.

"What happened?"

"She wouldn't tell me, she shut the door."

"Governor, a lot of press is at the airport right now. We have arranged a jet for this trip abroad. This is going to be a paparazzi fest, do you understand?"

Robert called Senator Fitzroy and told him his conversation with the Governor.

"What the hell is happening?" The Senator blurted in rage.

"I have no idea, sir. I'll pick you up," Robert said.

Robert had some inkling. He always kept it a secret from everyone about the Governor's extramarital affairs. He was also aware of his secret meetings with Louise Calvin. The reason he was sending Louise Calvin with him on the trip was so the Governor would not be venturing any new scandals abroad and gives the media any new fodder. She could keep tight control and satisfy his hormonal flings secretly. It was possible that Elena probably found out about Louise Calvin or some other sordid affair.

Robert then dialed the airport. Robert Dennison answered the phone.

"Delay the flight, Dennison; we have a problem," Robert ordered.

"But sir, the Boeing is ready for takeoff. The passengers are already boarding."

"Disembark them from the plane."

"What? What is the problem? Is it serious?"

"I can't tell you over the phone. Just hold the flight. Make some excuse, mechanical check, wheel alignment, something," said Robert.

"Gosh, man you are kidding. If we delay, they may think something is wrong. They'll be all over me asking questions. This is the press we are talking about."

"An hour or two is not going to kill them. Keep them busy with free booze, those suckers will enjoy it. I'll call you in an hour."

"Whatever you say, boss," Dennison disconnected the line. Robert started the engine.

The Governor was in the study. Elena's door was closed. He turned and looked helplessly at the Senator and Robert, "She's locked in there."

Robert and the Senator asked the Governor, "Why is she mad?"

"I don't know."

He repeated the whole episode.

"She is not opening the door and wouldn't tell me what's bugging her."

"Did you fight with her?" The Senator asked.

"No, the chauffeur just drove me straight home and dropped me off. She was sleeping on the sofa. There was empty glass on the table."

The Senator went upstairs. Robert and the Governor went to the study so they could listen.

"Elena, please open the door, I just want to talk to you." The Senator knocked on her door.

"Please leave me alone, Dad. I don't want to talk at all."

"At least tell me what happened," he said quietly.

"Elena, it's Dad," the Senator said, tapping again on the door.

There was no movement from the other side. The Senator was baffled. Elena was thinking that her father would be devastated if she told him, but keeping her mouth shut was not an option. There was a long pause and then she unbolted the door.

The Senator went in. He put his hands around her and looked into her face. She was like a statue, expressionless.

"Must be something serious," the Senator thought. He wanted to pamper her, soothe her, and calm her down.

"Honey, this is not the time to get mad. That man has a bright future, he can win this race."

"He is a cheating piece of sh... he doesn't deserve the Presidency."

The Senator understood. He was aware of the Governor's horny nature and told Robert to keep everything under tight control.

"No, Elena you mustn't listen to gossip. People talk nonsense about public figures."

"Go away, Daddy, leave me alone."

"Listen... uh, I will. I'll go, but first I have got to know you're okay."

"Just go. Leave me alone."

The Senator closed the door, "Look honey, he is about to go abroad. The press is waiting at the airport. I don't know what happened. Please think it over for few days. We'll talk it over later. He is a man. Mistakes happened. Presidency comes only once. I am not defending him. All I am asking for is to give some time; you do love him, don't you? Don't do this. Doing anything rash when you are angry will be media frenzy, don't give media a chance. You don't want your face to be plastered all over front pages. Cool down. Why don't you come home? Your old room is waiting for you."

"No, I'll be okay here, Daddy. Go, just leave me alone." Elena said.

"Okay then, I'll be in touch every day. If you still feel the same, just say the word."

She looked at her Dad for a long time and finally nodded her head.

Chapter 47

Decision

Robert heard every word of the conversation. "Cheating ... doesn't deserve the Presidency."

It was clear that Elena found out about the Governor's extramarital affairs. The words that caught his attention were the words from the Senator's mouth, "Give some time, and if you still feel the same... just say the word." The Senator is very powerful and influential. Elena is his only daughter. Emotion and love for a child could take priority over ambition. He could side with Elena. Elena could divorce Henry, and then there would be no campaign. If, for Senator Fitzroy, his daughter became priority, then the Governor's Presidency is in jeopardy. He started thinking. This did not sound good. He was looking forward to becoming Chief of Staff in the White House. He was dreaming for the power behind the throne. His dream could shatter.

On the way to the airport, Robert told Governor about the package to be picked up from the Saudi businessman.

That afternoon, Rebecca went to Robert's office. She had her resignation letter in her hand. Robert thought that Rebecca had come to complain about not letting her go on the trip abroad as cameraman. Robert decided to calm her and welcomed her inside his office.

"Hello, Rebecca, I hope you are not mad at us for not letting you go as camerawoman. It is a hectic trip with Saudi and the Middle East and all the clothing restrictions for women, etc. We just chose a man temporarily. You and Ruben will do all editing and publicity as you see fit."

"Thank you for thinking about me, but I don't want to work for a person like Governor Giarrusso," Rebecca said sternly.

Robert was bewildered, "What ...? Why don't you want to work here? Is there any problem? Is someone bothering you? Just say the word."

Rebecca looked at him; this guy did not know anything about what the Governor does behind his back. She opened her purse, took the iPhone out, and showed him the clip. Robert was jolted when he saw that video.

"Where the hell did you get this?"

"I captured it on my iPhone. You might remember I went to my room early because I wasn't feeling well after the debate. I was staying in a next room to Louise that night in the hotel. The connecting door was open. I heard the noise in the middle of the night. I had the iPhone in my hand. Now you can put two and two together," Rebecca said.

"Elena knows about it, right."

"Of course, I told her, she is my old friend. I didn't want to hide that from her. She had to know," Rebecca did not flinch.

"Who else knows about this clip?" Robert asked casually, trying to keep his anger under control.

"Ruben knows; he copied it. I don't know who else. I don't think Ruben told anyone." She put the resignation letter on his table and left.

The revelation crept into his cerebral cortex. The water is too deep. "Something has to be done swiftly," he pondered. Logan and Noah Mancini's name popped up. He called and arranged to meet at one of his nightspots with a back door entry.

It was around 8 p.m. when he met with Logan and Noah Mancini. He told them about the Governor's affairs.

"Oh, so he is a horny asshole," Logan said laughingly.

Robert nodded, "Elena found about it."

"What is the problem here? That bitch may stay mad for few days, God… it happens all the time, why are you so worried?" Logan did not understand why Robert wanted to make this a big deal.

"Well, you don't get it, do you?" Robert said.

Noah Mancini understood the situation and explained it to his son, "She is not just an ordinary bitch. The Senator is a powerful and influential man. His daughter could make the difference. She may not even care for the Presidency and may file for divorce."

"If that happens, the campaign falls apart. No campaign, no election, and then there is no Presidency. No Presidency means no power, no agenda; our profit goes down the drain," Robert said.

"Now, do you understand?"

"Kill the bitch," Logan blurted,

"She is the Senator's daughter, son. You can't just kill her," Noah said in a conciliatory manner.

"How did she find out about it?" Noah asked. Seeing the expressions on Robert's face, he realized there is more to the story.

"That's the difficult part and that makes the problem even worse," Robert narrated the story.

"That makes it rotten," Noah said.

"Everything revolves around Elena. If she keeps quiet, then Rebecca will not create trouble," Robert said. "And I'll make sure Ruben will not be a problem," Logan said.

"Let me call Gustav from the BAT Company and run the story by him," Noah said.

Robert left from the back alley. Later, Noah called Gustav and told him the whole story. They both went back and forth discussing various options. Logan thought that he could persuade Ruben so he would not be a problem.

In their business, the tools they used are persuasion, corruption, punishment, or alienation. The only option they saw plausible, was persuading or getting rid of the cause, the punishment. Getting rid of the problem meant murder. If Senator Fitzroy could persuade Elena, then they could convince Rebecca and Logan could persuade Ruben. If they killed Rebecca and Ruben even smelt murder, he could be a dangerous enemy.

Acknowledging the severity, Gustav dialed the secret number and relayed the story. The person on the other side listened carefully. Gustav also told him that Ruben is traveling with the Governor abroad and Rebecca resigned from the campaign. The next day, Gustav received the call from him. The instructions were specific.

"The stakes are high. We cannot take chances. Eliminations are inevitable. We have to wait until we get the confirmation about the package delivery. After that, eliminate Elena also." The person on the other end of the phone disconnected the line.

Chapter 48

Suicide

The screeching sound of the brake and noise of collision woke up the building security guard from his day slumber. It was around 4 p.m. He rushed out from behind his desk. There was a security camera in the lobby. A man entered the building. He was wearing a hood. He noticed cameras and was cautious to hide his face. The security guard was more concerned about the accident; he did not notice him entering the building.

The accident was minor. Both cars were drivable. The guard was thinking of dialing 911 and jotted down the number of the license plate that banged the other car into his iPhone. He recently bought the new iPhone. The various functions that came with the phone intrigued him and he made a practice to write small notes to become familiar with the phone's functions. The action of jotting down the number was purely spontaneous. The drivers from both cars got out and exchanged names. The driver with a rugged beard who banged the car in front of him offered the man a wad of bill to avoid a police complaint. No one was hurt. They both drove away. The guard dropped the idea of calling the police and went back to his slumber. It was a modern nine-story apartment complex with cameras on each floor in an affluent Chicago community. Rebecca lived on the sixth floor.

Rebecca heard the knock on the door. She looked at her watch. It was five past 4 p.m.; yesterday she resigned. This was her first day off from work and she was already bored. She thought it must be the woman from next door. She welcomed the opportunity of having someone to talk. She never realized the death was standing behind the door.

Logan sent Bartoli Mendoza, the Super Fixer, to stage a suicide scene. She opened the door and saw a strange man standing. Super Fixer pointed the gun at her, pushed her inside, and grabbed her. He injected a high dose of heroin into her veins that made her drowsy. She fell on the bed and almost lost her senses. He was careful and meticulous, wore gloves, made sure there were no signs of struggle. He searched for her phone, found it on the table, grabbed it then opened the window, removed the screen, and pushed her body out of the window.

The fall from the sixth floor was terminal. It made a crashing sound against the rooftop of the car she fell on. The people walking on the street ran toward the car and saw the mangled body, legs hanging from one side, blood dripping down. The security guard woke up again hearing the uproar outside the apartment building, saw the people rushing, and came out. When he saw the body, he was aghast. He knew Rebecca and recognized her body. He immediately dialed the police. The hooded man exited the apartment, joined the crowd to see the body fallen on the car rooftop, and left the scene. The police arrived with an ambulance. They saw her body, there was nothing they could do but to process the crime scene. Rebecca did not feel any pain. Her soul left the body.

Police took statements from the bystanders and talked to the security guard who gave them her name. They went to her room but did not find anything indicating a struggle. The guard told an officer that she worked as a camerawoman for the Governor's presidential campaign. The police realized that this death could become a high-profile case, but when they called the campaign headquarters, they found out that the campaign fired her from the job.

They went through her apartment to look for any clues and addresses for the next of kin. They found some campaign photos, her parents' and aunt's address, and Ruben Joshi's card in the drawer. The police knew the foreign correspondent, Ruben Joshi. He was the high-profile international news anchor. Since they did not find any evidence of struggle or any other suspicious clues, they closed the case as a suicide and took her body to the morgue for autopsy. The police officer who found the addresses informed her parents and made a mental note to inform Ruben Joshi.

Chapter 49

Heaven and Earth

After Fatima's death, Farooq was depressed. He started visiting Surayya in *Mohabbat-E-Masti* more often. Surayya consoled him; her soothing words were like an ointment. It is not that he loved Fatima or knew her for very long. She was his partner; the difference was that she was his partner in a foreign land where he was alone. Her mere presence helped him a lot during loneliness. They both knew the risks of their work, and now she was gone.

One night he came to *Mohabbat-E-Masti*, the lights in the room were dim and soft. He did not know when his loneliness turned to passion. For the first time, he softly held Surraya's hand close to his heart and embraced her. Her breasts touching his chest, she could hear his heart beats beckoning her; strong and vivid desires streamed through her. He put another hand around her slightly caressing, pressing her close, and kissing softly against her mouth; she could sense his nervousness.

"I want you Surayya, I …," there was an inviting hunger in his words.

She looked at him with longing.

He whispered her name. She put both her arms around him in a tight embrace; she was breathless, her lips parted. His lips touched her compelling mouth. His tongue slid into her mouth. Savoring the sweetness, he kissed her passionately in a sensuous movement. A wild surge of pleasure ran through her. His hands roamed pressing and caressing her. She trembled, a starburst of ecstasy, starting deep inside; the final explosion of physical sensation climaxed in harmony. Bodies relaxed and flesh was satisfied. She was a courtesan with countless sex encounters, but for the first time in her life, she offered herself willingly – her body and mind. There was no hold, no bar; it was passion in veneration. She felt completeness within.

Farooq looked at her; her eyes half closed, the goddess of love; emanating tranquil delights; "I…," he began. She put her palm on his face.

"No… don't say anything," she said. "Let us enjoy the moment." Words had no meaning. They were beyond. She was a courtesan, a goddess of pleasure. He was a double agent in an enemy land. They both knew each other's fate. Words of love were meaningless. However, they both understood the eternality of love; they bonded together forever, if not this life, the next.

* * * * *

Though she had forgotten long ago, that day was Surayya's birthday. The first time she met Farooq in *Mohabbat-E-Masti*, she told him her story of the kidnapping. While narrating her story, she mentioned they just celebrated her 16th birthday a Saturday before. Farooq made a note of it. He wanted to celebrate her birthday with her. He called Surraya and told her that he would be coming. She had some information, but she did not say anything over the phone.

He was going to bring a cake and a necklace, but he knew that would look suspicious. Muslim men are not accustomed to such emotionality toward the courtesan. Although, after that night, he decided that when they grow old, and if he is still alive, he would buy her freedom and they both would disappear together to Europe or some remote island.

As soon as they were alone in the room, Farooq embraced her and wished her happy birthday. Surayya was surprised. She had completely forgotten that while telling the story of her kidnapping, she mentioned her birthday. He remembered! She was extremely happy. Together they celebrated her birthday in bed in each other's arm.

"Yesterday, I saw a new face walk in here. He was completely drunk when he came and wanted more wine. I took him to a room. He had a wad of money in his hands, but he was agitated and raving about dropping a dead body of his friend in some river for the company.

They gave him money to do the job. I consoled him and extracted information. He told that they wrapped the body in a shielded material. He uttered the words nuclear weapon and the name of the place."

Farooq listened, making a mental note of the information. He just struck the pot of gold; the Commander was looking for this information.

Chapter 50

Contamination

Veronica Ivanhoe entered the office softly chanting some melodious tune from an old 1938 children's movie *Rebecca of Sunnybrook Farm*. Shirley Temple was the child actress in the movie. Her daughter, Alina, was turning 8 years old today. She was celebrating her birthday. She invited a few friends, including a few of her friends from the school. Veronica was going to leave the office early.

There was a call from the outside to the higher echelon of the CIA. The information received needed immediate action. As soon as she entered the office, the department head summoned Veronica and instructed her to act on it. She was supposed to leave for Islamabad via Kabul immediately with a layover in London for information. She called Lisa Hargrove, Kiran Hopkins, and George Austin to her office and explained to them the nature of the job.

"Tonight is my daughter's birthday party. I guess I have to cancel that," Veronica said.

Kiran, without showing any enthusiasm, indicated her willingness to accept the assignment. Ruben left yesterday with the Governor, "If I leave tonight, I can still catch him in London before they leave for Paris," she thought.

Kiran looked at Veronica. Veronica was glad that Kiran willingly accepted the job.

A body surfaced in Jhelum near Jammu in Northern India. The Indian authorities found the contaminated body. The cause of death (COD) was determined as exposure to radiation poisoning. This was strange and baffled Indian police. They referred the case to ISHWAR.

The Commander realized that somewhere within the borders of Pakistan, Pakistani scientists were doing research for nuclear weapons or nuclear testing.

Rosemary Hutchinson, the niece of the British Attaché Major Edward Hutchinson, came to the steps of the British Consulate in Islamabad coughing up blood around 7 p.m. She parked her car farther away and walked toward the British Consulate. The British Guard at the door noticed her coughing and vomiting. Realizing that she could be in trouble he immediately rushed forward to pick her up.

She told them in a muffled voice, "Please get my uncle, Major Hutchinson, and a doctor. I have some information." She signaled them toward her car, "The car may have few traces of contamination, so be careful."

The other guard called Major Hutchinson and the Consulate doctor and they started walking with her toward the Embassy.

Both Major Hutchinson and the doctor were in the Consulate building. Edward rushed to the doors followed by a doctor. He knew his niece was working on a research project in Karachi, Pakistan. She was the exchange scientist from Great Britain. He could not figure out how and why she ended up in Islamabad. The British guards, along with Miss Hutchinson, were in front of the Consulate building gates when Major Hutchinson was coming out of the gates toward them; the car zoomed in front of the consulate and gunned her down. Everyone thought the target was British Attaché Major Edward Hutchinson, who was exiting the door. There was confusion, one guard rushed toward Major Hutchinson to cover him while other covered Rosemary, but bullet hit her and she fell down, still breathing.

The doctor rushed toward her. She whispered in his ears, "They may have poi... soned... me, but... I have...very import... ant inform..." She dropped her head. She was dead. The doctor tried to revive her, but it was of no use. There was no pulse; the life already left her body. The doctor retold her last words to her uncle the British Attaché Major Hutchinson.

Rosemary Hutchinson came to Islamabad to discuss her project with a scientist in the Islamabad Test Facility and to complete some tests. In the laboratory, a Geiger counter gave the alarm just before she could start the test. She was surprised. There was a breach somewhere outside the test laboratory.

Following the breach, Rosemary Hutchinson traced the source of contamination to the terrorist cell. The terrorist cell adjacent to the test facility was secretly manufacturing the nuclear arsenal with the help from China. When the terrorists found out she knew, they captured and gave her a slow poison, dimethylmercury. Somehow, she managed to escape. She was going to the British Consulate's office to see her uncle to give the information. When they realized she es- caped, terrorists followed her to the British Consulate. They took the shot when she was just in front of the building and killed her at the doorsteps before she could pass on the information.

The Pakistani police arrived at the site immediately. Since the murder took place outside the British Consulate on Pakistani soil, Pakistani police took over the investigation and they took the body to the morgue to conduct the autopsy. The police also took the car into their possession because the doctor told them that the car might be contaminated.

Major Hutchinson called the research facility in Karachi and he was told that Rosemary Hutchinson came to the Islamabad Test Facility for her project. He made the report of her death, her last words, and the possible contamination of her car and wrote down the name of the research facility in Karachi. He sent the report to his head office in London. Reviewing the report with the mention of contamination, they forwarded the copy to MI6, the British Intelligence Service, for further investigation.

Later, after decontaminating and thoroughly examining the car for evidence, the police returned the car to the British Embassy in Islamabad. When asked about the contamination, the guy told them he had no idea, he was told to bring it back to the Embassy. The British Embassy never got a straight answer from the Pakistan police, either.

Dr. Rehmat Mudliar was a Muslim from Delhi. His grandfather migrated to Delhi just before the partition and chose to live in India after the partition because all relatives of his grandmother were in Delhi and his grandfather owned a huge house near Chandani Chowk in Old Delhi. After graduation, Dr. Rehmat joined a medical facility in Greater Noida who offered medical services to the employees of the GEETA and test laboratories in the area and employees from ISHWAR.

Rehmat was always fascinated with spy stories while he was growing up and read all the spy novels he could. During one of his visits to a patient, Commander Bhosle met with Dr. Rehmat Mudliar. Rehmat was impressed with Commander Bhosle and indicated his fascination toward spy activities and his inclination to work as a spy. Commander Bhosle was looking for someone with a medical background who could work as a double agent in Pakistan.

After doing a thorough background check, the Commander made Rehamat a proposal, which Rehamat immediately accepted. As a boy, he visited his relatives in Islamabad. After training, he secretly migrated to Islamabad and Jahangir found him a job in the Morgue. Many of the Indian prisoners of war were brought to the morgue after severe torture resulting in death. Having a spy on the morgue staff was essential to keep tabs and Rehamat was ideal for the job.

At night, Mudliar was the only doctor on the staff in the morgue. The police handed over Rosemary's body to him with instructions of donning properly from head to toe before conducting the autopsy in order to protect him from the possible contamination. During the autopsy on Rosemary Hutchinson, Mudliar found a note with a Muslim name, local residential address in Islamabad, and the scribbled message about fabrication of nuclear arsenal.

He took the note out and hid that in his pocket. Then he began the autopsy and gave the report to the Pakistan police indicating the cause of death (COD) due to the poison dimethylmercury. The dimethylmercury was a slow killer, highly toxic, and had a slightly sweet smell. He also wrote in his report that he found some traces of contamination in a low quantity. He made a copy of the report for file and one for himself.

The next day, he gave the copy and the note to Jahangir's men. He did not mention anything about the note to the Pakistani police.

The revised autopsy report handed over to the British Embassy mentioned only the name of the poison as the COD.

Gustav's operation in Pakistan found out about the test facility, which was a front for the terrorist cell. The facility was officially under the Pakistani government and working with the British and US liaisons, but they were secretly manufacturing nuclear and other types of weapons with the help of the Chinese government using materials from France and Germany. The intention of the Pakistani government, if exposed, was so deeply covered that fingers would point to European nations.

This was a competition for Gustav's operation, and his company was losing control over weapon exports to the Middle East while the Chinese were gaining more business. Gustav informed his contact of this development by dialing the secret number and giving all the information. Duly higher echelons of the CIA got the call and machinery began rolling. Kiran was sent to analyze the encrypted data found by the local CIA field office and Satellite Monitoring System, determine and identify the cause of contamination and source, and destroy the location with the help of the US military and CIA field agents.

Kiran arrived in London early morning and went to MI6 Head Quarters. The Assistant Chief of the MI6 was surprised to see a CIA agent at their doorstep asking about the murder of Rosemary Hutchison. They never asked for the CIA's help, although the news of her murder was in all the Pakistani newspapers and on the wire. MI6 and the CIA always cooperated with each other, so they welcomed her and gave her whatever information they had. Kiran never got the complete story from Veronica. She left the MI6 Head Quarters before noon, called Ruben in London, and met him at his hotel for lunch.

Ruben was there with Anthony Hurtz. He was surprised when he saw Anthony Hurtz joining them as cameraman and he expressed his surprise to Kiran when they met. Although he welcomed Kiran warmly, Ruben was not cheerful. He already received the news of Rebecca's death from the police officer working on the case in Chicago.

After exchanging a few words, Anthony excused himself and left. Ruben discussed the suicide of Rebecca with Kiran, told her that Rebecca did not commit suicide and she never used drugs. He said that she left the job on her own and he told her about the missing iPhone with the clip on it. The police report did not mention the iPhone.

"I am now worried about Elena, too. Rebecca showed Elena the video clip and Elena must have confronted the Governor. That is how Robert found out about it or Rebecca may have told him while handing in her letter of resignation," Rebecca's suicide left a heavy burden on his mind.

Kiran told him that she would look into it upon her return to the US and in the meantime, she would call George Austin and request him to keep an eye on Elena.

On an impulse, Ruben asked her about Commander Bhosle.

"The last time I called him was after your rescue to thank him for his tremendous help. I already told you that because of his help, we could rescue you. I have not spoken to him since."

"Can we call him?"

"You mean right now?"

"Why not? It's not too late," Ruben said.

Kiran thought for a moment. "It's not a bad idea," she also wanted to talk to him.

The Commander was working late and was about to leave the office when he received the call from Ruben and Kiran. He was happy to receive the call. They exchanged formal greetings. Ruben told him about his temporary new assignment, his trip with the candidate to European countries and Saudi Arabia among other things and expressed his gratitude.

"Without your help, I know that my rescue was almost impossible. I do not know how to thank you, but I am indebted to you, sir," he said and gave the phone to Kiran.

"Hello, Sir, I'll say Namskar (formal Indian greeting with respect)." "Whatever you say, dear, I always love to hear your voice. How are you doing? By the way, I heard Ruben is leaving for Saudi with the candidate."

"Yes, he is. I know what you are driving at, I have not yet told him, but with your permission, I can."

"Go ahead, tell him everything. We are waiting for this opportunity. Tell him Akhmad's name and ask him to check the Governor's schedule." Then, the Commander inquisitively asked her about her being in London.

"You must have heard about the death of Rosemary Hutchinson," she said.

"Yes, I did hear. I believe that she died of some poison, I think it is dimethyl... something and they found some traces of contamination, isn't it?"

Most of the information was in the news and on the wire, so Kiran was not surprised.

"That's true, the poison is dimethylmercury. The source of contamination is a mystery; we don't know where those came from. Based on intelligence received from MI6, there could be a possible endeavor to manufacture nuclear arsenal by these terrorists. Do you have any idea?" Kiran did not mean to fish for information, but the words just sprang, "I am sorry, I didn't mean to prod."

"That's okay, dear, you don't have to be apologetic," the Commander was about to ask her whether she had any clue, but stopped abruptly. She was a foreign agent and questions like this mean poking, which is unethical and unprofessional.

"Will you be dropping in to Delhi?" He asked. The Commander was thinking about the incidents on Indian soil. The Indian police found a contaminated body up north that caused havoc.

"I am going to Kabul and then to Islamabad to investigate. I heard that Indian police also found a contaminated body in the River Jhelum near Jammu," Kiran said.

"Yes, we did. It caused considerable havoc. A few people are still in the hospital recovering from contamination and the ambulance nurse died due to the exposure. I believe these two incidences are connected."

"I think you are right, I'll investigate the cause of the contamination when I am in Kabul. Our office in Kabul is better equipped with modern technological gadgets than Islamabad to do research and analysis, so I'll be going there first."

"Go to Islamabad. Someone will contact you if I get more information," the Commander decided that if Jahangir or Farooq could get some information about the terrorist cell producing the nuclear arsenal; he could pass that information to her. If Americans could destroy the facility, that would help India also.

Kiran gave him her contact number in Kabul and Islamabad and the name of the hotels where she would be staying. She shared the Commander's message about SHIV the Destruction with Ruben.

"Look for any contact with Akhmad and delivery of the parcel containing the device. Please also inform Anthony. He can watch over things, and if possible, film the delivery."

After lunch, both Ruben and Kiran left for London Heathrow Airport. Ruben joined with the Governor's staff to go to France and Kiran found a seat in business class on the flight to Kabul.

The note found during autopsy on Miss Hutchinson gave a Muslim name and local residential address in Islamabad along with the message about fabrication of nuclear arsenal. The Commander asked both Farooq and Jahangir to look into it. Jahangir sent one of his men to check on that address. When he was near the house, he saw police cars and a coroner's van. They were bringing a dead body out of the house. The men had donned protective clothing, and police cordoned and quarantined the area. That note and the body confirmed the nuclear activity. Farooq communicated the information he received from Surayya to the Commander that also provided the name and address of the terrorist facility.

Adventure

I t was a comfortable flight to Kabul. Business class had sleeping arrangements on the plane. Kiran reached Kabul the next day. It was warm; the temperature was close to 100 degrees Fahrenheit. She first went to the hotel and took a bath. Then after lunch in the hotel, she went to the CIA office in Kabul. She went through the encrypted files and database and satellite reports. It took her almost two days to sort out and analyze the information.

"That's interesting… it can't be true…," she went back and forth through the encryptions, satellite reports, and database. She could not believe the CIA's involvement in something like this under-the-table business. She came across names like Gustav, the BAT Company, weapon deals, and distribution. She copied it to a flash drive she was carrying with her for later examination back in the US. Her whole trip was a plan to eliminate the competition to make room for the US-based illegal ventures. She hated the idea of someone using her, but was also aware that it was a necessary evil regardless because it was a terrorist nuclear weapon venture with Chinese conglomeration. However, the purpose was different from what she thought, "I guess the end justifies the means," she convinced herself.

The information, the encrypted files, the satellite information, and the database were only for the eyes of the elite group. No one changed the access code. Otherwise, Kiran would have never gotten access to it. She thought for a long time. She knew Veronica would not be involved in something like this; she must be another gear in the cogwheel of this mesh and equally innocent, just like her. She realized how dangerous it was to be involved and how venomous it would be for her if someone found out. She heard rumors and stories of CIA operations and their cruelty. She decided not to utter a word of this to anyone, not even to Lisa Hargrove or Veronica Ivanhoe.

During her analysis, she found the information about the body found in Jhelum. A closer look revealed different information. She was in deep thought and began connecting the dots based on her analysis, information from the MI6 office, and possible travel path of the body from satellite pictures. She suddenly woke up from her thinking when the phone rang. She heard the familiar voice.

"Hello Imran, how are you?" She asked.

"Memshib, Salam-Ale-kum, Commander Sahib has information for you, when are you coming to Islamabad?"

Her work was almost finished there and her next stop was Islamabad, "I'll be there tomorrow morning after I finish work here."

He abruptly disconnected the phone.

"Hello, hello?" There was no response. The call lasted less than 25 seconds. Kiran was perplexed and suddenly her tube light illuminated. The information must be an absolute secret; he did not want anyone to trace the call.

The next day, in the morning, she reached Islamabad. She went straight to the office, chatted with other agents, and gave them her findings. She also called the CIA office in Delhi and got information about the path of travel of the body.

Production of nuclear arsenal was serious. The data triangulated from the satellite narrowed on the few places and based on intelligence received from Delhi, she narrowed down the four possible areas of interest. However, in Pakistan, you cannot go on prodding based on suspicion. They needed facts.

She brought a couple of Geiger counters from the Kabul office with her, which she gave to two field agents. They left immediately. She was going through more files still trying to analyze the facts to divert her attention, but the conspiracy theory would not go away from her mind. The crucial question mark 'WHO' in capital letters took a giant leap.

Her phone rang, "Memshib, *Salam-Ale-kum.* I am bringing two men along to see you. Can we meet at the corner restaurant?" Imran asked.

"Wale-Kum-Asalam, sure, I'll see you there in 15 minutes."

"That'll be great, *shukran* (Thank you)." He disconnected the line.

Based on the analyzed information, she gathered that the terrorist cell is nearby and they may have to attack the cell immediately after the positive confirmation. She told the local agent to wait for her in the office and be ready with target elimination preparation.

"It should happen sooner than we think if I get information from the CI." Kiran carefully closed all applications, gathered her things, and left the building.

In a café, she met Barkat Niazi and Hadith Abu with Imran. She never expected them to be there. Nevertheless, the site of them pleased her and implied that this was going to be a big bang. They exchanged greetings and sat down. Barkat gave her the name, location, latitude, and longitude for the terrorist cell and asked her how she would like to proceed.

"This test facility is an alliance between Pakistan, US, and British governments. First, we have to confirm that the location is active," she said.

She carefully studied the address and the map coordinates. The terrorist cell was in a building next to the facility warehouse. Precise attack at nighttime would not harm civilians or scientists working in the building. She was aware that sometimes the scientists work 24/7. Therefore, before planning an attack, she had to be sure about the target, having latitude and longitude coordinates for the target does help.

Her brain started spinning quickly, which was the sign of a well-trained agent. He or she exactly and precisely knows when and how to proceed and the logistics required for the operation. She started putting things together in her brain.

"I need a Jeep with a GPS that can accurately indicate latitude and longitude to reconfirm the coordinates and then I have to confirm that it is an active working facility. I have to be there to do that. I can pose as a buying agent of some Middle East country. Any transaction would require money. The CIA always keeps that kind of sum available at the office."

Barkat interrupted her thought process, "Commander Sahib (boss) told us that the CIA had a paper-thin microchip that can be attached to anything and can be remotely activated."

"That is good information," she thought. "The microchip can be attached to the currency note. Since it is not active, no one can detect it. After I leave the target area, I could activate the microchip to send the signal for attack from the Jeep. This eliminates any need for communication. We'll accomplish the operation with complete telephone silence. Even if the coordinates turn out to be slightly inaccurate, the activated microchip can provide an accurate signal for attack," she thought highly of the Commander's capability and foresight.

She thanked Barkat for the information and was about to bid goodbye, when Barkat told her, "Sahib (Boss) told us to be with you throughout the operation and not to leave you alone for a second. This is a dangerous place. You can't go there alone or with other CIA agents. We can arrange the meeting tonight if you are ready."

Kiran sensed the resoluteness in Barkat's voice.

Quietly, she thanked the Commander. She knew she could depend on these two Pathans from her last experience. She gave them adequate instructions and asked them to wait for her outside the café.

"We'll start sharp at 2000 hours. Set up the meeting for 2100 hours. Insha Allah, if everything goes all right, we shall be back by 2300 hours." She thought she could still catch the 2:45 a.m. flight to the US.

She went back to the office. The two agents were back with the Geiger counters and informed her that out of the four places only one indicated an existence of contamination and gave her the address. The address matched with the address provided by Barkat and confirmed her suspicion. However, visit to the facility was required to pin point the precise location because of the test facility next door. She asked the agent, "Do we have a paper-thin microchip device that can be attached to currency?"

"Yes, it is a passive device and can be activated remotely by radio waves. When the radio waves are off, it's impossible to detect the hidden device," he replied.

"That's great! In the Virginia office we have the device but I wasn't sure whether you guys kept it here."

"We try to keep up with all the modern technology in this day and age; we can't do without it," he smiled.

Then Kiran gave specific instructions to the agent. "Can you arrange for a Jeep and mount a gage on the dashboard to check latitude and longitude? Also, keep ready $25,000 in $100 bills with the paper microchip attached to one bill that could be activated from the Jeep. The Jeep should be equipped to activate the microchip. I also need a Muslim dress with burqa."

"Yes, that can be arranged."

"How long do you need?" Kiran asked.

"It shouldn't take more than one hour."

"That's great, thanks."

"We should attack from a high altitude flying jet. The jet will get the signal from the microchip once we activate. Encrypt and transmit these coordinates to the jet pilot only. They should zero in the attack on the signal transmitted from the microchip attached to the currency. The attack should be precise. Tell them the building 200 feet from the given coordinates may have some British and American scientists working inside the building. I have planned the meeting sharp at 2100 hours; we'll start at 2000 hours. I'll go there as a Tunisian agent to buy nuclear arsenal. The $25,000 is only goodwill money upfront. We should be out of there by 2200 hours. Is that clear?"

The agent nodded his head, "How many agents should accompany you?" He asked.

"No, I do not want any agents. I have my two CIs with me. Once I leave the premises, there is complete telephone silence until the jet pilot receives the signal from the activated transmitter."

"Understood."

The CIA agent hesitated, "But, Miss Hopkins..."

"What's on your mind?"

"What is the backup plan? How can you plan a big operation like this without a backup plan?" The agent looked at Kiran. She was thinking.

"Please tell me you have one," he pleaded.

"Yes, I do have a backup plan. Success of this operation is vital to us, right?" She said.

He nodded his head.

"God forbid if anything goes wrong. We cannot carry any weapons. If they suspect anything, we have to depend on our wits to escape.

Satellite can monitor, but don't forget that it's probably an active nuclear facility. Satellite cannot discriminate the signals accurately to differentiate," she paused.

"Yes, but I still don't see the backup."

Kiran's face was blank; there were no expressions. She looked through him and said in a steely voice, "If something goes wrong, and we couldn't escape, I won't let them catch me alive. I'll be dead, and so will my informants. If we are not out by 2200 hours, give another 30 minutes and bomb the place. The Jeep parked close to the facility has a GPS monitor. Satellite can get the coordinates from the GPS to instruct the jet pilot. That is the backup plan. In that situation, consider this as the final farewell, adios, goodbye…"

The agent could sense her resoluteness. Kiran did not say that she always carried a cyanide pill for emergencies. The agent was astonished; he never expected this response. Now he realized, "No wonder she has such a high esteem and respect from others. This is the woman with nerves of steel." The agent prayed for her safe return.

Kiran wore the Muslim garb with burqa and met Barakat and Hadith outside the café. They traveled for the next 45 minutes to reach the outskirts of Islamabad. She saw the Test Facility Compound. The warehouse was on the backside and next to the warehouse was another long building. That was the terrorist cell with facilities to manufacture nuclear arsenal. She checked the gage; it showed the correct reading. From the outside, the building looked deserted and unoccupied. The outside walls gave a deplorable impression with withered paint. However, the moment you stepped in, it was a well-equipped facility.

Upon entering the building, Kiran removed the Naqab, the veil face cover, from the top of the burqa. They met a young guy with a goatee. He only gave his first name as Usman. Kiran looked beautiful in her Muslim outfit. Her beauty mesmerized him. Kiran saw an open door with stairs leading down toward the warehouse. She guessed the facility and this warehouse were connected.

Hadith introduced her as the agent from Tunisia and explained that they wanted to buy the arsenal on a regular basis and would like to negotiate a price. They would like to see whether the facility is equipped to supply their demand. Hadith also told them that if they are satisfied, they could negotiate a deal and start ordering on a regular basis. As a gesture of goodwill and promise, the woman will give $25,000 up front.

Two other men and a woman came out and thoroughly searched them. The guards made sure no one was following them. Usman did not see any problem and told them that he would take them inside, but they could not wait too long. He gave them only 15 minutes and accompanied them. Upon return, Kiran handed him the $25,000. He did not even bother to count it.

They left the building and got in the Jeep. She drove for two minutes before activating the signal and saw a missile explosion a minute later. She was in the office by 2300 hours. The mission was accom- plished. She profoundly thanked Barkat and Hadith and offered them a cash reward. They would not accept it. After bidding *Khuda Hafiz*, they left.

Chapter 52

Saudi Arabia

T he Governor arrived in Riyadh, the capital of Saudi Arabia
with his entourage late at night. The limousines took them
straight to the hotel. The presidential suite and nearby rooms
were booked for the staff on the same floor. It was convenient having
a jet at your disposal. It was a hectic weeklong trip with many meetings and shaking of hands with dignitaries and delegates in various
European countries.

The trip started by visiting England first, then France, Germany,
Amsterdam, Italy, and Jerusalem before arriving to Riyadh. Riyadh
was the last short stop before returning to the US. There were only
two items on the schedule. A get together with the business moguls
of Saudi and a welcome dinner arranged by the Prince of Saud to
welcome the would-be American President, Governor Henry
Giarrusso, at the palace.

Ruben remembered what Kiran told him in London, SHIV the
Destruction is in Saudi Arabia. He saw Akhmad's name. He was
organizing the first meeting with business moguls of Saudi. Ruben
realized that Akhmad would deliver the package during the
meeting. He told Anthony to keep a close watch on the
Governor and Akhmad.

Ruben was close to the Governor for the last few days. He did ob-
serve that the man was a womanizer and lacked the moral strength
and character to be the President of the United States.
Nevertheless, there was a fine line between weakness and
treachery. Whatever he was, Ruben could not put him in the

category of a traitor. There was good record for him as Governor of Illinois and he did some good work to help people. Elena was his strength during the Governorship. In spite of being a womanizer, he did love Elena. His connection with Robert Lange was through his father-in-law, Senator Fitzroy, who himself was a Congressional Representative for a long time. His record as a Congressman was not bad. Every politician has a Robert Lange to do his dirty laundry; that is politics. So, how did this device SHIV the Destruction fit into the equation? He decided to wait and watch.

The get together was in the Kingdom Centre located on Al-Urubah Road around King Fahd Road. After freshening up in the morning, they came down to the hotel lobby for breakfast. Akhmad, a businessman whose company arranged their stay and transportation in Saudi Arabia, came to greet them after breakfast. He escorted them to the limousines and the retinue proceeded to the get together in the Kingdom Centre.

The place was in the business district of Al-Olaya. The street was very busy at that time in the morning. Kingdom center was the tallest building in Riyadh with a shopping mall, business offices, and state-of-the-art apartments. There was a large opening in the middle of the building. The conference room was a very large room to accommodate close to two hundred plus people. It was almost near the top, approximately 10 to 12 stories below the top floor. The panoramic view of Riyadh was spectacular from the room. One of the guests told the reporter that the round opening in the middle of the building is illuminated at night.

When they reached Kingdom Centre, Akhmad whispered in Governor's ears, "I have package for you."

The Governor remembered that on way to the airport, Robert told him about some package to be picked up from the Saudi business-man. Before the luncheon meeting with the business moguls of Saudi Arabia, Akhmad invited the Governor and his staff to his penthouse. They did not allow the press to come inside the penthouse and re-quested that Anthony Hurtz keep his camera outside with the guard. It was near the top floors of the Kingdom Centre. Akhmad seemed to be a very hospitable and jovial host, gave a warm welcome, and shook hands with all of the campaign staff, noticing Louise, Jessica, and Sandy clad in burqa with face cover down.

"Someone trained you well about Muslim customs," he said with a wide smile on his face.

Every one laughed. Immediately after that, Akhmad offered small gifts, souvenirs from Saudi Arabia to each member of his campaign staff to take home. He also handed a package and gift to the Governor. Louise Calvin took the package and the gift from the Governor. Anthony was standing next to her. He also saw the package. Louise handed the gift and package to Anthony so that she could open her purse. With the garb of burqa, it was difficult for her to manage the simple movements like opening a purse.

Anthony quickly attached the microchip to the package; no one noticed it. She took the gift and package from Anthony and kept that in her bag with her gift. Ruben had his iPhone in his hand and he took video of the entire scene which no one noticed either. Later, Ruben called Kiran in D.C. and told her that, after their arrival, Kiran should arrange to separate him and Louise Calvin along with a couple of press members from the crowd for a random courtesy custom check. Louise would be carrying the SHIV the Destruction device in her purse and he had the video clip of the entire scene on his iPhone that she could download. The video clips were important because they contained evidence of the device delivery and it would expose the whole scandal and save the country from another Blur attack.

The luncheon business meeting was about to begin. Akhmad's secretary ushered them downstairs to the conference room. Akhmad joined them a few minutes later after calling the US to inform about the delivery. They allowed the press in the conference room but without cameras. They were not happy.

The table arrangement was in a crescent shape with a large open space in the middle. The business owners and the executive officers of various construction or oil-oriented business companies were standing in the open space to greet the Governor. This was more like a shaking-of-the-hands type of gathering. There were no presentations or discussions. They were more interested in handshaking over the deals and trying to extract information from the Governor. They wanted to ascertain how much he would help the Middle East if he were to win. They discussed topics like oil deals, getting weapons from the US, Israel policy, and similar topics.

Throughout the trip, Ruben noticed that the Governor was not really equipped to answer questions or deal with the foreign issues. In the US, Robert Lange coached him every step of the way and he parroted very convincingly. During two terms as Governor of Illinois, Robert Lange and Elena were the policymakers and the Governor accepted the role of presenter. No one cared; the results were good. Chicago was famous for its Mafia activities. During the Governor's administration, because of Robert's influence, although the Mafia profits were growing, they kept a low profile and maintained peace in the city. That became a plus for the Governor. A common person does not care or not even aware of what happens behind his back as long as he gets his bread and butter, and peace.

Senator Fitzroy warned Robert that they have a big agenda ahead and asked him to maintain the veneer of tranquility in the city and the state. The big agenda was the Presidency of United States of America. Robert was fully aware of that. He was an excellent administrator. It is the misfortune for any country when people like him choose the wrong path. It is a loss.

Ruben felt bad for the Governor and he tried to help him communicate with the official guest and visitors, not for his sake, but for the country's sake. In functions like this, no one notices much. Because of Ruben's quick wit and ability to provide non-committal but adequate answers to complex issues and guidance, the Governor came to depend upon Ruben during the trip. The Governor was aware of his background as a war zone journalist and familiarity with foreign issues. He knew more about the issues than the Governor did. Ruben knew very well that in all the questions, answers, promises, and assurances, there are many ifs, buts, probabilities, and innuendos.

After about an hour of mixing and shaking hands, they all sat down for lunch. Akhmad told them that he had ordered a light lunch so they could enjoy the evening dinner in the Saudi Palace. The lunch included some Mediterranean and Muslim delicacies with American sandwiches. After lunch, they all left for their hotel.

The Saudi Prince arranged the welcoming dinner in his palace. The Governor and his staff freshened up and got ready for their visit. Around 6 p.m., a representative of the Saudi Prince called them from the lobby. The limousines lined up in front of the hotel to take them to the palace. They did not allow all press members to come inside the palace. Only a couple of them joined with Ruben and Anthony.

After entering the palace grounds, the Governor and his staff were ushered inside. The ground was at least one square mile and was surrounded by high pinkish walls. The Prince, the Governor of Riyadh, and other delegates and dignitaries, including the members of the Saudi Royal Family, were present to welcome the Governor. There were many rooms inside the palace, all lavishly decorated. Ruben noticed that women working inside the palace didn't wear burqa, and few of them were clad in American dress. The female staff members of the Governor's campaign removed their burqa inside. The Governor had met the Prince in Washington, D.C. during an official dinner party a few years back. They sat next to each other.

The dinner included various Mediterranean and Muslim preparations and American dishes. The Governor noticed that the Prince only ate the diet food. The Governor asked him about that and he said with a wide grin that his American doctor had prescribed light food for his health. The belly dancers accompanied by music entertained the dinner guests while dinner was served. The Governor profoundly thanked the Prince and the Saudi Royal Family for their warm welcome and hospitability.

As soon as the dinner was over, the Governor told his staff to pack up to leave for the US. Another debate was nearing soon. He got the message from Robert that the President was in a good health and to come home soon to get ready for the next debate.

Chapter 53

Collision

Tea is very special in India. They call it Chai. You boil water with tealeaves and add some tea spices. The main ingredients of the tea spices are ginger, clove, nutmeg, cinnamon, and cardamom powder. Instead of powder, one can also use small pieces of raw ginger, cinamon stick, couple of pieces of clove, and couple of cardamom with nutmeg, and boil the mixture in the water with tealeaves. After boiling, strain it in a cup and add two tablespoons of milk and one or two teaspoons of sugar, or if you are a diet freak, you can substitute Splenda or some other sweetener for sugar to the de- light of your taste buds. People in India drink the tea throughout the day, whether it is good for your health or not, let the dietician worry.

Sudarshan Pillai made James Montenegro a tea-aholic. James would drop in at Sudarshan's apartment often and Sudarshan would offer him tea. The first couple of times, he did not enjoy the taste so much, but after that, he grew accustomed to it and now he loved it. It was late evening; Tania was working the night shift. James was bored; he felt like having a tea so he dropped by Sudarshan's apartment. Sudarshan was busy making a dinner, the aroma of curry diffused in his apartment. He was happy to see him and invited him to join for the dinner. He also made tea to serve with the homemade dinner.

During casual conversation, Sudarshan told James that he was going to test a new weapon soon. His boss was excited about it.

"They are negotiating a deal with some foreign outfit for collaboration and waiting for the arrival of the item. The boss also assured that he would help to get the Green Card and make me a project manager for the task. I am not sure; I don't trust them. I'll see what happens. Right now, I am getting paid, paying my bills and paying off the loan of the Reserve Bank of India (RBI)."

"Why do you have to pay to the Reserve Bank in India?" asked James.

"The scholarship money only paid for tuition and hostel, but there are other expenses like transportation, clothing, occasionally eating out, buying over the counter (OTC) medicines, etc., that required money. The RBI loan helped meet just the bare expenses for a couple of semesters. Then I got an internship."

James realized how much hardship and struggle foreign students go through. American students do not realize that. They just take everything for granted; they do not appreciate. To them, all help is offered on a silver platter. He knew some cases where some of them do not even pay their loans back to the Federal government. The more time he spent with Sudarshan, the more he liked the guy.

James knew about the association of the BAT Company with an illegal weapon industry and the connection of the owner Gustav with Mafia families. When Sudarshan told James that he would be testing the device, James became suspicious. Could this be the device, they had been talking on TV? He did not say much to Sudarshan. On the way home, he was thinking about the whole situation. Somewhere in his mind, a caution bell rang.

The weapon manufacturing facility, new weapon testing, weapon and drug dealers, old Mafia family, offshore account with $200,000, the murder of Suleiman, his frame up, Governor Henry's association with Robert Lange and participation in the presidential election… there were too many confusing coincidences, events, and questions that needed answers. The detective in him began to investigate. He decided to continue to watch over Sudarshan.

By the time he left Sudarshan's apartment, it was after 10 p.m. On his way home, James passed by the Mancini mansion. The streetlights illuminated the street. James saw Carlos Garcia, also known as Point Blank, a known killer on the FBI black list, coming out of Noah's house. Point Blank was a sharp shooter in the US Army. While serving in Iraq, he got involved in an illegal weapon transport operation handled by Gustav. He never mentioned Gustav's name during the interrogation. No one knew what actually happened, whether someone manipulated the chain of evidence or the evidence was not enough to incarcerate him. The Army dishonorably discharged him. Gustav introduced him to Noah Mancini and since then he worked for Mancini family.

James's car was behind him. Point Blank parked the car on Bloomfield Avenue in a fire zone. Point Blank knew he would get the ticket for parking there and that would be his alibi that he was at Mancini's house. He walked for a block and found the Nissan Sentra. He looked around; no one was watching. He put the gloves on and opened the door with the bar he was carrying, got in, hot-wired the ignition, and drove the Sentra away. James became suspicious; he decided to follow him.

Point Blank drove the stolen car near the Governor's house, abandoned the stolen car on a nearby street, and walked toward the house. There were two security guards. Point Blank was carrying a gun with a silencer. He shot both of them. No one noticed.

James parked the car and waited for him. It was dark; he did not see Point Blank shooting the guards. James knew it was the Governor's house. After a while, the garage door opened and a white Cadillac slowly started to back out of the garage and into the driveway. Point Blank drove out, closed the garage door, and started driving away from the house. James noticed Point Blank driving the car, and the woman next to him seemed drugged.

James followed the car. All of a sudden, he became aware. The Governor is abroad; the woman must be his wife, the wife of the presidential candidate. He immediately dialed 911 and told them his suspicion that someone was kidnapping her.

* * * * *

Kiran called the home office to speak with Lisa. It was close to lunchtime in the US.

"Hello Lisa, Kiran here."

"Hi and congratulations! We just got the news. How did you do that so fast?"

"Thanks Lisa, I guess we were just lucky."

Kiran talked with Lisa, gave her the briefing, and told her that she found a seat on a plane leaving at 2:45 a.m. from Islamabad. Lisa got the report of her adventure and successful completion of the task from the satellite report.

She was not expecting her call. She thought Kiran would like to rest for a day. She earned it.

"Why don't you relax for a day or so, you did extremely well. I never expected such a fast turn around."

"No Lisa, I would rather go home. It is too muggy and hot here. The AC doesn't work half the time. The business class has sleeper coaches that are decent and cool. If I leave in half an hour, I'll reach the airport two hours before the flight time giving me enough time to check in. I reach Washington, D.C. tomorrow at noon."

"Why are you not going straight to Chicago to meet Ruben and Anthony?"

"They are all returning on Thursday morning. Wednesday I'll see you in the office, give you the reports, and then fly to Chicago by late evening. Is George Austin around?"

"Hold on, he is here, and bon voyage, see you soon," Lisa transferred the line to George.

"Hello Kiran, congratulations!"

"Thanks, George. How are you doing? Is Elena okay?"

"She seems to be doing okay. Her father visits her every day. My man is watching over her off and on. I am sorry it is not 24-hour surveillance as you wanted, but I haven't heard anything adverse."

"Thank you, George, I'll see you tomorrow."

Kiran disconnected the line.

Kiran reached the airport in time and got on the flight. It was 18-hour flight from Islamabad to Washington, D.C. with a short layover in Dubai. There was a slight delay in the Islamabad airport, but the plane reached Dubai in time to catch the flight straight to D.C. She had a lot of time to think. She told the flight attendant not to disturb her for the next eight hours so she could sleep.

She was thinking about Elena and Ruben's suspicion. Kiran did not tell anything about Elena to Lisa; she did not want her boss to get involved on such an unfounded suspicion. Ruben might be right, but it was his gut feeling. George was her colleague. He was also from

Chicago and had many contacts in the police department. He arranged for surveillance without arousing any suspicion.

She knew the terrorists stole the devices and the attack was a demonstration. The satellite information and analysis of data provided useful information to fill in the gaps. However, some of the information was disturbing. The formula and the information that terrorists might have from Nikhil's computer was to produce more devices. The Blur attacks in Delhi, London, and Washington, D.C. meant three devices were gone. The explosion in the GEETA Laboratory in Delhi destroyed the fourth triggering mechanism. Therefore, there is no immediate danger from the fourth device. However, the terrorists or a qualified physicist could reverse engineer the device from the information and the fourth device. Someone in the US had to be pulling strings. Who could that be? There were many questions, Elena, Rebecca, the puzzle of the presidential candidate's overseas trip to Saudi, SHIV the Destruction, were all pieces of the same puzzle. "Is there a link or am I just imagining?" She kept asking herself. Soon she fell fast asleep. The flight attendant woke her up three hours before arrival to Washington, D.C.

Kiran went to the office immediately and completed her trip report. Veronica came to her desk and personally congratulated her. She praised her for the good work and told her that she would put in a word for getting her commendation. Kiran thanked her.

George pulled some strings so that Kiran could access Rebecca's suicide file from the Chicago Police records on the Internet. The medical report did say there were drugs in her system. She remembered the conversation with Ruben. Rebecca never used drugs, and she resigned her post, she was not fired. She was not happy with the job and the low-life character Governor Henry Giarrusso. However, the report indicated that the campaign fired her, and therefore, she committed suicide. That was fishy; there was more to this than meets the eye.

Kiran was thinking about looking into the flash drive that she had copied in Kabul to confirm some of her suspicions, but by the time she finished her work, it was almost 3 p.m. She had a reservation on a 7 p.m. flight. She decided to look into it later and hurried to the airport to catch the flight to Chicago. Kiran's plane was late, arriving in Chicago just after 10 p.m. She left the airport, rented a car, and drove to the hotel.

Point Blank was driving the Governor's white Cadillac. Elena was next to him. He heard the sirens of the police cars and increased his speed. James was on his tail. Point Blank noticed another car had been following him and was closing in on him. He was nearing the crossroads, saw the lights turning yellow, and stepped on the gas so he could beat the lights but he saw another car coming from the left side and slowed down. Just then, James crashed into him from behind. Point Blank got out with the gun in his hand. Elena was under the influence of a drug and not wearing her seat belt; the crash was not hard enough to inflate the airbag; but she banged her head on the dashboard.

Kiran was on opposite side of the crossroad. She saw a car coming in front of her and another car crashing into it from behind. She heard the bang and the police sirens. First, she thought it was an accident. Then she saw the man and a woman, her head banged on the dashboard. She thought of helping the woman in the front car when the man got out with a gun in his hand. He fired the gun at the other car. A bullet grazed James near the head, crashing his car windows and hurting his face and left arm. It looked like a kidnapping attempt. There was no time to think. Kiran drew her gun out and shot below the belt line to disable the culprit. Point Blank bent to avoid the shot, took the bullet in the chest, and dropped. James heard the gunshots, saw Point Blank lying in blood on the road, saw a woman at the crossroads with a gun in her hand, and heard the police sirens behind.

The police car arrived. They saw the collision, and a man lying on the ground in a pool of blood. The Chevrolet crashed into the Cadillac; glass shattered, the wounded man inside the Chevrolet, and a woman beckoning them from the other side of the crossroads with a gun in her hand. They pointed the gun at her. Kiran immediately dropped her gun on the road and made a hand gesture to surrender. There were four police cars chasing the Cadillac when James told them on the 911 call about his suspicion. Kiran also heard the helicopter hovering above. Other police officers came where Point Blank was lying and checked his pulse. He was dead.

Both James and Elena were hurt. The police immediately called the ambulance and a coroner's van. They checked Point Blank's pockets, but there was no license or any identification. They approached James and the drugged woman. The police immediately recognized the woman as the wife of the presidential candidate.

When they received the 911 call, it was just a suspicion, but now after recognizing her, suddenly the whole scenario became a very high-priority situation. Kiran was also surprised to see Elena there. "Ruben's gut feeling was right," she thought. Kiran told the police that she shot the man. The police officer in front of Kiran was startled and immediately put his hands on the gun; she showed them her CIA badge. It was all a mystery, an accident, woman shooting a man, man with no identity laying dead, cars colliding, and the wife of the presidential candidate getting hurt in an accident. They could not figure out what was happening. Kiran told the police officer what she saw. The police were glad that the CIA agent was there to help them. Another police officer came forward to help James and Elena. He recognized James Montenegro the ex-ATF agent.

He was astonished, "Wow, a CIA agent and an ex-ATF agent, am I in some kind of spy thriller?" He exclaimed.

James told him that the dead guy was Point Blank and he worked for the Mancini family of the Mafia. He asked who the CIA agent was and the police officer pointed to Kiran. James came forward and thanked her.

"Is there any reason you were following them?" She asked.

"I just saw them coming out. She seemed drugged. That aroused my suspicion."

He looked around and the ambulance was there. The police and the paramedics were taking care of Elena and another medic was coming to help James.

"Come with us to the hospital, I'll tell you."

The police took statements from James and Kiran, and called Senator Fitzroy since Governor Giarrusso was out of the country.

The ambulance took both of them to the hospital. Kiran followed them.

Chapter 54

Shoot Out

James had a minor injury. The nurse patched him up in the hospital. They were still waiting for his blood test and X-ray report. James Montenegro's girlfriend, Tania, was a nurse in that hospital. She heard the story and came running. At first, seeing him in the bloodstained clothes shocked her, but after looking at his smiling face, she relaxed.

"My hero, saving the life of our first lady," she praised him; the adoration was exuding from Tania's eyes.

She also cautioned him, "Wait until they get the blood report and let the doctor look into it, but be ready to spend the night here. You do have a head injury, doesn't look that bad, but we can't be sure about a concussion. Overnight observation is a good idea. I'll run by your place and get you some clean clothes."

Elena was hurt and had to stay in the hospital. Kiran realized that it was a murder attempt to kill Elena, just as Ruben had told her. Kiran went to see James in the hospital emergency area. The police were still waiting outside to get the blood test and doctor's report. They recognized Kiran and let her in. James was sitting on a chair.

"Do you know who the woman is?" She asked.

"I was not sure at first when I was following the car, but I had my suspicion. I am glad that I actually saved the life of the presidential candidate's wife," James said.

Then she asked why was he following Elena? James told her that he was not following Elena; he was following Point Blank.

"To be honest with you Miss Hopkins, it just happened. I wasn't on any mission. In fact, I was returning home after visiting my friend Sudarshan, who works for the BAT Company in their engineering department. We talked about some tests that he would be doing. As a former ATF agent, I had some experience with their illegal weapon operations, and when I left, I was thinking about that. On the way home, I saw Point Blank exiting the Mancini house, the Mafia family. My car was behind him."

BAT Company! The name was familiar. Kiran remembered that during her analysis of the data in Kabul, that name surfaced few times. Now she was interested and made him tell her the whole account from the beginning. He told about his casual visit to Sudarshan's apartment for chai and his talk with Sudarshan about some weapon testing. He also expressed his thoughts relating to the weapon and the attack at the Crystal City Shops.

"My car was behind Point Blank's car, and I saw him leave his car in a no-parking zone and steal another car from the street. That caught the attention; I smelled a crime about to happen so I followed him. Then he came near the house, abandoned the stolen car, and went inside the house. I recognized that it was the Governor's house, the presidential candidate. I became curious. What is a Mafia hit man doing in the Governor's house? I waited outside. I did not see any sus- picious movement. After few minutes, the garage door opened and a Cadillac rolled out. I saw a lady in the passenger's seat and Point Blank driving the car. At first, I didn't realize it was the Governor's wife. I remembered reading in the newspaper that he was abroad. Then, I sensed that it must be a kidnapping attempt and followed the car. You know what happened next, you saw the accident."

"You didn't find any surveillance or a guard at the house."

"No, why would I?"

"Because I requested someone to watch the house and Elena," Kiran said.

Later, police told Kiran someone shot those two guards surveilling the Governor's house.

Senator Fitzroy was angry because of the murder attempt of his daughter. He talked to Kiran and the police. The police described the accident and told the Senator that the guy in the other room saved his daughter's life. The police confirmed the identity of the dead man,

Point Blank, as Carlos Garcia, a hit man for the Mafia. The Senator knew he was working for the Mancini family.

He called Robert Lange, told him about the murder attempt on his daughter's life by the Mancini family's hired gun. He wanted Robert to get rid of Logan for attacking his daughter. Robert called Gustav and told him about the failed attempt on Elena's life and the Senator's anger and his order to kill Logan. Gustav told him to hold on about Logan until he delivered the device. They would think about Logan later.

Kiran realized that Elena was in grave danger. The planned attack at night unveiled a strong chance for another attack. She cautioned the Senator to beef up security in the hospital. The Senator arranged to move Elena to a special room, and with the help of police, arranged to tighten the security. He was going to stay in the same room with her.

This was a matter of national importance. The guy lying in the hospital bed was an ex-ATF agent. He did save Elena's life risking his own. She saw that what he did was dangerous and showed his valor. Kiran thought that by conversing with him, she could get more information. She remembered the warning by Ruben about Elena's life and her deductions from the database and reports. The guy in front of her, James Montenegro, had all the dots, digging information from his past could most likely help.

"May I ask you a personal question?" She asked.

"Yes, Miss Hopkins, go ahead."

"Why did you resign?"

"It's a long story," he began the story of the events that led to his resignation.

The BAT Company, Mafia connections, Robert Lange, and Gustav, his story not only gave her more leads, but also confirmed her confidence in him. She was glad she decided to poke.

"Do you think there may be another attack tonight?" She asked him.

"Yes, there is a very strong possibility. The hospital security is adequate, but it won't deter professional killers."

"You are right, James. I cautioned the Senator about it. He has more weight than we do. I am sure he can arrange more security. If you remember anything call me," She gave him her mobile number.

"May I make a suggestion?" He asked.

"What do you have in mind?"

"The FBI has some places for the Witness Protection Program (WPP) in Chicago. I know an FBI agent. I worked with him. I can wake him up and make a request to authorize, and there shouldn't be any problem arranging a safe place."

"Well, the Senator knows best. I have already cautioned him. I am sure he'll take care of it," Kiran said.

Just then, Tania and the emergency room doctor entered. The doctor studied the report, examined James, and suggested he should stay until morning for observation. Since Tania was there, James had no complaints. Kiran talked to the Senator before leaving the hospital, stating that James's life could be in danger too for saving his daughter's life. The Senator understood the gravity of the situation and was kind enough to arrange a special room for James next to Elena's room.

The police were guarding the room. No one knew exactly what happened. Around 3 a.m., James woke up to a hissing sound. He recognized the sound as a gun shot with the silencer attached. James got up from his bed, he saw the two police officers lying on the ground in a pool of blood. There was no sign of life in them. The hooded guy was at the door of Elena's hospital room. Senator Fitzroy opened his eyes. The hooded guy saw the movement and shot him point blank. The Senator died instantly. James shouted at the top of his lungs. The third police officer around the corner took his gun out and shot. The bullet grazed the gunman. The gunman was startled and fired two more shots. The first bullet grazed Elena's arm but the second one hit her in the shoulder. There was no time, the gunman sprinted and disappeared. With the noise, other staff came running. They found the two police officers and Senator Fitzroy dead. Elena was unconscious. The doctor and the nurse took her to the operating room. The hospital was well equipped. They saved her life, but with the trauma, Elena fell into coma.

The shrilling sound of the police sirens pierced the still of darkness through the neighborhood. The police immediately rushed to the hospital. They took a statement from James and the third police officer. The lights were dim. The officer described the gunman wearing black hooded jacket and jeans. They found the gun outside the hospital in the bushes; there were no fingerprints on the gun. James swore that it was Mendoza Bartoli, known as Super Fixer, who was the henchman for Mancini's drug lord. The police had his file on record. They went to his apartment. He was drunk and fast asleep when the police arrived. The police could smell the drink. He had an alibi – he spent the whole evening until the closing time at a night-club, drinking and flirting with the women. The police had no choice but to release him.

The telephone bell rang. Kiran was just getting up from bed. She picked up the phone.

"Did you hear the news?" James was on the line. He was calling from the hospital.

"I just got up, what news are you talking about?"

"Senator Fitzroy and Elena were shot last night. The Senator died on the spot. Elena is in coma," James shot the information without stopping for breath. Kiran switched on the TV. The news of the event was on every TV channel. Kiran cursed herself for not listening to James.

"How did that happen?"

James narrated the whole sequence that he told to the police.

"I am sure it was Super Fixer."

"Who is Super Fixer?"

"He is a head basher and terminator just like Point Blank."

"I'll tell the police," Kiran said.

"I already told them, but they said he was in the nightclub all night and many people saw him. I don't believe a word of it."

Kiran didn't comment. James decided that after discharge, he was going to watch the Mancini house. Tania informed him that his test results, X-rays, and blood tests were normal and that the hospital would discharge him soon.

Kiran could not figure out what happened. This was the second time the Mancini family's name appeared. Kiran began connecting the dots. Earlier, Ruben told her of the connection between Robert Lange and the Mancini family. Robert Lange was also a trouble fixer for the presidential candidate Governor Henry Giarrusso. It did not indicate an outside job. There may be a Mafia connection as James suggested, but the Mafia was a hired gun. Someone was orchestrating the strings to manipulate this puppet show. Elena is the wife of the presidential candidate. She just found out about her husband's affair. It was possible that she could divorce him. If that happened, the election would go down and the Governor would lose. Someone was extremely nervous.

Chapter 55

Touchdown

T he fascinating speed of the electronic age makes one wonder. The news of gunshots in the hospital caught by wire in the police station was now all over the Internet and had the attention of the world of journalism. In the next half hour, the news of gunshots, the murder of Senator Fitzroy and murder attempt on his daughter, Elena, the wife of the presidential candidate, spread through the news media like wildfire. The newspapers started rolling on the machines and news editors replaced the first page immediately with the news of the murder.

Senator Frank Fitzroy Murdered

Attempt to kill First Lady of the State of Illinois

Mrs. Elena Giarrusso, wife of the Presidential Candidate

Ex-Governor Henry Giarrusso

The newspapers on the East Coast were already out so all the major newspapers came out with the second edition. The 6 a.m. and 7 a.m. news reports on the East Coast roared with the news of the murder.

The Governor got the news on the plane. The news shocked him. The doctor on the plane gave him a mild sedative to calm him down. Elena was his college sweetheart; she was his mate, the inspiration to guide his lost soul. He thanked God that she was still alive and prayed for her fast recovery. He felt bad for his father-in-law, Senator Fitzroy. He helped Henry a lot. Henry was indebted to him. However, more than an obligation, he also admired and adored the old man.

The Governor's plane touched down at the Chicago O'Hare International Airport just around 11 a.m. At the airport, Robert Lange and the VP candidate, Senator Adam Baker, along with small crowds and hoards of news channel reporters came to receive them. They all exited through Customs and the security checkpoint after going through a baggage check.

Kiran saw Ruben at the Customs checkpoint and an officer beckoned Ruben. He gave Kiran the iPhone and told her to download the footage. He also signaled toward Louise Calvin who has the package. Because of the sad news, Louise Calvin stayed behind. The Customs officer took Louise, Ruben, and a couple of other reporters for a random custom check to the separate rooms. Customs checked her baggage and handbag for the device, but they did not find it. Kiran was surprised; she did not know that the Governor took the package back from Louise on the plane. The Governor was already out of Customs.

Robert rounded the entire campaign staff from the airport and they went straight to the hospital. Anthony activated the microchip immediately after they boarded the bus. The Governor handed the package to Robert Lange.

"I am sorry, Henry. This is bad. I don't have exact words to express my sorrows. I knew the Senator for a long time. I feel like I lost a father," Robert said.

"Who killed him?"

"We do not know the details. It was all very sketchy. First, they kidnapped Elena, and then there was a car accident. One of the CIA agents happened to be passing by and saw this. It looks like an old vendetta against the Senator combined with extortion," Robert tried to explain as briefly as possible to alleviate Henry's grief.

The police told him the name of the CIA agent who was coming home for vacation and the name of the rescuer. Robert had no idea that Kiran and Ruben were friends, and he did not know James, either. He told the police to thank them both on behalf of the Governor. He was not interested in getting involved any deeper.

The Governor went to her hospital room. Elena was sleeping. She was out of major surgery.

The doctor told him, "She will recover soon. Her vitals are okay, but she is in a coma. She will come out of it in a day or two, a week or maybe a month, we cannot say for sure. We'll know soon."

Henry waited there for an hour or so. He was extremely tired. The doctor saw his condition and told Robert Lange to take him home.

Robert Lange told the staff to go home, take a rest, and come back at 7 p.m. for a quick meeting. The staff expressed their sympathy to him and wished for a fast recovery for Mrs. Elena Giarrusso and left.

Although Senator Fitzroy supported President Zoloft's opponent, he was the President's long-time friend and associate. President wrote a personal consolation expressing grief for the loss of Senator Fitzroy and sent his Chief of Staff to convey sympathy to the Governor's house in Chicago in person. He also wrote an obituary and read it in the White House Press Conference. Then he asked his campaign manager to gather the campaign staff at the White House to discuss the strategy.

He first expressed his grief for the loss of Senator Fitzroy and the sympathy for the Giarrusso family and speedy recovery for Mrs. Elena Giarrusso and requested his campaign manager, Denise Wilson, a woman with a heavy figure in a black suit, to conduct the meeting. Denise asked the campaign pollster, Dave Patterson, about the latest poll results. Dave Patterson, wearing a tuxedo vest and plaid trousers with a moping look, had the latest telephone tracking results in his hand.

He got up holding his spectacles in his hand, "Let me express my sympathy to Governor Giarrusso and his family. The tragedy is shocking, and I pray for the speedy recovery of the Governor's wife, First Lady of Illinois, Mrs. Elena Giarrusso," he paused for a moment. "Now to the business at hand, the quick poll conducted indicates huge political fallout. We may have to change our strategy. I want to point out there is a feeling this tragedy was a deliberate attempt by someone, no one is pointing fingers at us but it looks odd and embarrassing. It sounds cold blooded but thank God his wife is not dead," Dave saw some glances interchanging, with strange and nervous uneasiness creeping.

"The police are coming up with a Mafia angle and I put my investigator on the case to look into it. He told an interesting fact that one of the CIA agents, Miss Hopkins, happened to be at the spot at that time. It was a mere coincidence. I checked on her background. She is an excellent CIA agent with high credentials and just returned from a covert operation in Pakistan. I requested the Chief of Staff to request the CIA to keep her on the case to help the police investigation."

"Good job, Dave, a really proactive approach," Denise commended him.

"The survey is demographically scattered. The accuracy is moderate. However, I believe it can impact our strategy."

"I agree with you," President Zoloft nodded.

"The sympathy factor is playing a big role. The common folks are leaning toward him. Some did express disgust when we tried to conduct a survey. This is just a preliminary survey, but the fact is the Governor is receiving wide support and we have to deal with the fact. I cannot say for sure that it's just a week-long scenario that can eventually drop or gather more strength." Dave Patterson sat down.

"What about Ava Daniel, the Governor's previous press secretary, and the Emily Gauthreux incident?" Teddy Millican asked.

Some of the investigations done by the President's campaign staff dug up some dirt about the Governor's womanizing behavior and found a couple of women willing to confront him upon his return.

"We better not do that. It will do more harm than good," Denise Wilson snapped sharply.

The campaign meeting lasted for another half hour. The Democratic campaign decided not to take a personal attack approach anymore, and just take the wait and watch approach.

Chapter 56

Damage Control

West Town, Chicago is a busy place, especially in the afternoon. The traffic was heavy near the Auburn Gresham neighborhood; it was two-lane traffic. This was one of the areas, where the risk of violent crime was high. Every other day, Chicago TV news channels reported stories about a rape or gang shootings in the area. Murder was a common occurrence.

Robert told the housekeeper that he was going to a department store. The weather was cloudy and windy. He was casually dressed in jeans, ragged top, and a hooded navy windbreaker. The media approached him and he avoided and drove past them to the Shops at the Mart in the River North neighborhood of downtown Chicago, parked his car, and went inside to look for a phone booth. He noticed a couple of reporters were still behind him. He pretended to visit a few shops to escape the reporters following him, and then he went down and took the subway to the Auburn Gresham neighborhood. Before getting off, he made sure no one is following him, and just before the closing of the door, he got off the subway.

He walked to the gas pump, checked around; he didn't notice anyone watching. He called Logan from the public phone.

"Hello, Logan, Robert here, I got the package from the Governor."

"Great, thanks."

"The Governor is very much shaken by Senator Fitzroy's murder and Elena being in a coma. There is a lot of media outside the Mansion. You may have to wait a day or two, let the media attention subside, and then I'll call you again. The package is safe with me."

"I'll call and find out. They may not want to wait that long," Logan was thinking that it might not be a smart idea for Robert to go to the BAT Company. It could cause suspicion.

"We have a campaign meeting in the American Legion Hall from 7 to 9 tonight. So, I'll call you tomorrow. Let me know when I call how they want me to deliver the package." Robert said.

"That'll do," Logan replied.

"Police know the name of the kidnapper, the dead guy, Carlos Garcia. He was on your payroll. Did they come to see you?"

"Yeah, the police lieutenant was here inquiring about him and asking a lot of questions. I told him that he did work for me as a boxer in one of my nightclubs. I don't know what else he did or whom else did he work for. They asked for his address. I gave it to them."

"Ruben is back. He knows about the video clip, the one I sent you."

"Yeah, I watched it. The Governor is a really horny guy!"

"Yes, the video clip is a real scandal. If Ruben suspects that Rebecca's death was not suicide but a murder, then he'll blow the whistle. Urgent action is required. What do you say, Logan?"

"What time is your meeting tonight?" Logan asked.

"Around 7 p.m. and will last until 9 p.m. Ruben will be there, too," Robert replied.

"Ruben is a problem, I agree with you. Super Fixer can handle the Ruben job."

"I am sure he can," Robert disconnected the line and left.

Logan watched the video clip again. The reality struck him that, if the video clip went viral, then all the sympathy and empathy would disappear, and the Governor would never win the election. Logan called Gustav.

"Ruben is back in the country. We have to fix him. Super Fixer can clean the mess and make him disappear. No one will find his body."

"Go ahead and finish it. Did you get the package?"

"Robert got it."

"We need delivery," Gustav gave him the instructions.

Kiran received the call earlier from Lisa Hargrove, "Hello Kiran, you'll work with the Chicago PD to help them solve the murder of Senator Fitzroy."

"Why me?" Kiran tried to play cool.

"The request came from White House. You are in the big league now," Lisa said.

"What, the White House! What's the connection there?" Kiran asked.

"The Senator was a long-time friend of our President. The request came from his Chief of Staff. Anthony is still in Chicago working as the cameraman with the Governor's campaign. He'll help you. I am going to call him."

On an impulse, Kiran said, "Call him to help me but don't withdraw him yet from the campaign. We still need an inside man on the campaign. Aye...Lisa, does that mean the CIA will be picking up my hotel tab?"

Lisa laughed, "Yes, it is official, I'll make arrangements. I am also booking Anthony in the same hotel. Are you still staying there or are you at Ruben's place? I understand that he is now renting an apartment downtown near the campaign office."

"Lisa, Ruben's father and my mother are Indians. They are not orthodox; however, what you imply is off limits, you know that."

"Are you telling me that ...?"

"Don't ask," they both giggled.

The friendly game of poker turned into a high-stakes bet. The excitement culminated in games like this, but today, there was no excitement, just fear. Super Fixer was not in a good mood and he was playing recklessly. The other three players at the table realized his awful temper. They were aware of his violent rage and let him win the game. No one wanted to become the victim of his rage.

His friend, Point Blank, was dead and his body was still in the morgue. Last night, he barely escaped. The bullet fired by the police grazed his upper arm. It was not that bad. His street doctor outside the club fixed him, but someone recognized him. That was bad. Logan chided him. Later, the police came looking for him at his apartment. Super Fixer shivered with the thought that if they had searched him, they would have noticed the fresh wound. The police that fired the shot did not realize that the bullet actually grazed him.

Super Fixer was about to raise the stakes to $500 when the ring tones chimed.

"Don't say anything. Are you alone?" Logan asked him. He excused himself and went out on the streets. "Can you come right away?" Logan said

"Yes boss, give me 15 minutes," Super Fixer replied.

"Park the car a couple of blocks away and enter through the back door. Police could still be watching the house."

"Okay, boss," he collected his share of money from the table and hurried to the house.

He parked the car two blocks away.

"I have a job for you," Logan said to the scarred face with heavy brows.

"You know Ruben Joshi."

"Yes, he is your friend."

"Get rid of him today, but before that, go to his apartment, and search for DVDs, I don't mean the movies. Then go to American Legion Hall after 9 p.m. By that time, they will finish the campaign meeting and he'll be coming out," Logan said.

"No problem boss."

"No traces, no body, just make him disappear."

"Got it?"

Super Fixer grew up in Chicago's North Lawndale neighborhood. It was the worst area, known for high crime rate. His mother never remembered the name of the guy who made her pregnant. She worked in a club as a striptease dancer at night and used drugs during the day. She died when he was 13 years old. He had moved through a couple of foster homes before he ran away. After he turned 16, he started doing odd jobs and robbing houses. Police caught him and he served time in jail for two years. While in jail, he learned many tricks. He was muscular and he developed his body by exercising. After his release from prison, one of the jail mates introduced him to Noah Mancini. Since then, he worked for the Mancini family. He was adept and creative for getting things done, and so he got the name Super Fixer.

He immediately left the Mancini house. In a hurry, he forgot to go out of the back door and exited through the front. Montenegro was closely watching Logan's house and saw Super Fixer exiting.

He went to his car, wore a hooded jacket and gloves, and returned. He looked around and saw a Malibu parked on the street. The door was unlocked so he got in, hot-wired the ignition, and drove away. James followed him. Super Fixer went to an apartment building in an affluent area with security guards and cameras. He went to the backside of the building making sure to avoid the cameras. James was wondering what he was doing there…, Super Fixer was not the kind of guy who would rob apartments, attempted kidnapping or killing was a possibility, but not robbery. James did not know Ruben personally; he only saw him on TV and certainly did not know he lived there.

Super Fixer went inside the building, fiddled with the lock, and entered Ruben's apartment. He looked for the DVD and found it on the bookshelf hidden inside a book. He broke the DVD, put the pieces in his pocket, and left. James was still waiting outside for him. He was expecting Super Fixer to come out with someone under duress but he exited the building alone. He then went back to the club. James was on his tail.

He got a shovel from the back room. He knew a construction site downtown where they were going to pour concrete in a couple of days. James was behind him. It was past 8 p.m. No one was around. It was a new site; there was no security.

Super Fixer dug a hole, put some debris around it, and left. James had binoculars and he watched what Super Fixer was doing. It became clear to him that he was going to kill someone and throw the body in that hole. James was thinking of calling the police, but he had no proof. There was no point in alerting them. James had the advantage of surprise. Super Fixer never suspected that someone was following him. He drove to the American Legion Hall parking lot. James stopped his car on the other side of the road. Just after 9 p.m., a few people started coming out of the building and left. James was watching them through the binoculars. Then he saw the foreign correspondent Ruben Joshi, the anchorman from the TV news channel. He recognized Ruben. Ruben was calling for a taxi; he still had not bought the car after returning from the war zone.

James turned the binoculars to Super Fixer and sudden realization struck him. Super Fixer was going to kill Ruben. James kept his gun ready. He began thinking, the secluded place of the construction site, the man-size hole in the ground; the dots started connecting.

Ruben saw Super Fixer and recognized him.

"Logan wants to talk to you immediately about the campaign due to the latest development. He sent me to pick you up."

James heard that and was surprised. He could not figure out the connection between Ruben and Logan. He did not know that Logan and Ruben were childhood friends. The car began rolling. Near the construction site, Super Fixer stopped the car, drew his .39 caliber out, and told Ruben to get out of the car. James was not far from them and could see their every move. Ruben got out of the car, while Super Fixer still pointing the .39 caliber at him.

"Get your briefcase from the car and walk there," he said indicating to a pile of debris. Ruben moved slowly, hoping someone could see him and rescue him. They walked to the hole.

Super Fixer wanted to ensure that the DVD was inside the brief case. He spoke harshly, "Let me tell you straight, Logan said not to hurt you. He wanted those video clips of the Governor. I am not going to hurt you, but give me those clips and copies."

"Look man, what does Logan want to do with those clips? Is he going to blackmail the Governor?"

That's none of your goddamn business, just give it to me, or...,"

"Or what ...,"

Without warning, Super Fixer fired the gun over Ruben's shoulder. It had a silencer on it so it only made hissing noise and then entered the wooden plank near his head. Ruben looked at it in horror, astonished by his sudden reaction. He realized that death was near, even if he gave him the DVDs. He knew Logan's wickedness. Mendoza Bartoli was even worse.

"Come on, Ruben, this is not a TV script. Put the combination in and open the briefcase," Super Fixer ordered. The DVD was inside. Ruben knew that once he got the DVD, it was over for him.

"What's the combination?" Super Fixer asked.

James was watching them. His conclusion was correct. Super Fixer brought him there to kill him.

Ruben knew this was his only chance to escape. He pivoted on one foot and threw the briefcase at him, hitting him hard on his left ear.

Super Fixer fired his gun but he fumbled and missed the shot. Ruben was about to jump on him as Super Fixer aimed again. Ruben heard the shot. Super Fixer put his hand on his chest as life drained out; the lifeless stupor dropped into the hole. Nothingness crept.

Chapter 57

Analysis

The sharp sound of the gunshot panicked Ruben. He turned around and saw a strange figure. James introduced himself. Seeing the lifeless body of Super Fixer falling in the coffin-shaped hole, which he dug, made Ruben wonder about the mockery of destiny. For a moment, he was speechless; he could not utter a word. James realized his anxiety; he knew Ruben's story and his recent abduction by terrorists. James thought it was probably PTSD. He held Ruben's hand with a firm and warm grip, then dialed 911 and Kiran Hopkins.

"Hello, Miss Hopkins, James here, I am in a precarious spot," he explained the situation.

Kiran was shocked to hear Ruben's name but Ruben was even more surprised that James knew Kiran? He thanked James for saving his life and decided to ask Kiran later about him. They heard the police sirens. Kiran and Anthony arrived immediately following the police van. They showed their badges to the police and told them that they were assigned to work as CIA liaisons for the Chicago PD.

Logan was anxious; he was waiting for the call from Super Fixer. It was getting late. He dialed his number but there was no answer.

"He should have been back by this time," Logan thought. He also dialed the club. He was not there either. "Did he get hold of some dame on the way home?" He was familiar with Super Fixer's horny nature. "That's probably what happened."

The police officer recognized Ruben Joshi. He described what happened. James also confirmed that Super Fixer worked for the Mancini family. James saw from a distance that Super Fixer was aiming a gun at Ruben so he ran toward them and was there just in time to fire the shot that saved Ruben. The Police took the statement from both of them. They traced Super Fixer's telephone records. The last three calls on his phone were from Logan. However, that was not enough to file a case against the Mancini family, so instead; the police put them on the radar.

After CSI finished with the crime scene and took Super Fixer's body to the morgue, Kiran, Ruben, and James all went back to Ruben's apartment to talk. The apartment was a mess. They found a couple of broken pieces of the DVD and concluded that Super Fixer was there. They reported the forced entry to the police. They responded immediately. Although nothing was stolen, the place was a mess. Finally, they concluded that the burglar came to rob but was suddenly alerted by some noise and fled.

Kiran did not say a word to the police but she began connecting the pieces together. Saudi, mole in the CIA, involvement of Mafia, BAT Company, Gustav, the presidential candidate bringing SHIV the Destruction from Saudi, Point Blank's kidnapping attempt, murder of Senator Fitzroy, attack on Elena in the hospital, Super Fixer attempting to kill Ruben, connection of Mafia family to Robert Lange - the conspiracy was getting much thicker.

What could be the connection between the Governor and the SHIV the Destruction device? From Ruben and Anthony's observation, the Governor was not aware of the significance of the package he received in Saudi.

Whatever the connection was, two things were crucial: the saga of SHIV the Destruction and the safety of Ruben.

Anthony asked, "Hey, Kiran, what is bugging you? You seem to be in a vacuum."

"Well, Ruben cannot stay in the apartment tonight. His life is in danger."

Ruben nodded. He was numb because of the attack and attempt on his life, death of Super Fixer in front of him, the mess in his apartment, and the destruction of the DVD. Slowly, realization took a grip over him. Logan wanted him out because of the video clip. Ruben spoke, "Now, the connection between the Governor, Robert Lange, and the Mafia family are clear. We don't have all the pieces, but this is the first segment of the conspiracy. They murdered Rebecca for the same reason." His investigative journalistic instinct began working.

"What are you implying… what reason?" Anthony looked at Ruben. He narrated the whole sequence of events that he never told anyone before. He started with Rebecca's filming of the sexual encounter between the Governor and Louise Calvin and the copying of the video clip to discredit the Governor. He told them about Rebecca showing the video clip to Elena. He expressed his suspicion that Elena might have threatened to divorce the Governor and if that happened then there was no campaign or presidency. It would be a scandal.

After that, someone murdered Rebecca and made an attempt on Elena's life. He also told them the connection between Robert Lange and the Mancini Mafia family, narrated his childhood friendship with Logan, and finally he described the murder event of Suleiman Quasim by Logan that he saw.

"What? That son of a gun killed Suleiman and put the blame on me to ruin my career and you never told this to anyone!" James interjected with anger.

"Sorry, James, I didn't know you got blamed for it. At that time, I was just finishing high school. I was scared and confused and was not interested in talking to anyone. I didn't even tell that to my parents. I had known Logan since we were kids. My mother and Logan's mother grew up in the same neighborhood. From what I heard, Suleiman was also a hood equally as dirty as they were. However, now I can clear your name if we can reopen the case."

"James, calm down. Ruben was just a kid at that time, try to understand," Kiran said in a conciliatory voice, paused to see any reaction, then continued, "We have much bigger problems to solve. Let us list in order of priority:

- Find SHIV the Destruction
- Identify the thieves and culprits behind the conspiracy
- Presidency of our country
- Rebecca's murder
- The brain behind Elena's murder attempt
- Senator Fitzroy's murder

Once we resolve these questions, it will be easy to reopen the case of Suleiman Quasim and clear James's name. If we try to do that now, we are alerting them and missing the crucial issues. In the meantime, I'll call George and ask him to check on a statute of limitations on murder through our legal department. I believe he has some friends there who can answer that," Kiran said.

James was placated by the explanation. He pondered over what she said, and then suddenly asked, "Are SHIV the Destruction saga and the Washington incident related?"

"Yes, it was all over the news, this device SHIV the Destruction caused the Crystal City Shops incident, the Trafalgar Square incident in London, and Delhi Gate in India. Therefore, you know how serious it is. The terrorists stole the devices from the GEETA lab in Delhi. The one we are talking about is the last of the batch. Destiny is probably involving you in something that you wish, you wouldn't to be involved."

James got the hint and his head began to spin. "Wow, you guys are something, the international conspiracy, three continents, and a series of murders. I don't believe this. It's like a spy story from fiction."

"Well, it's a spy story, only it is not a fiction, it's real." Anthony commented with a grin.

James let the information sink in, then asked a question, "If you know it is with Robert, then why are you not arresting him? That could resolve both problems. You get SHIV the Destruction device from Robert and he becomes the traitor, and show the video clips to force the Governor to withdraw his nomination."

Kiran smiled, "I wish it was that simple. We do not know for sure what is inside the package. No one opened the package. It could be a decoy. The device already could be at the BAT Company or some other facility. Robert could very well refuse the search and no judge will issue a search warrant like that without probable cause on the grounds of suspicion. That will alert the culprits and we'll utterly fail in our mission and never see the device. Let me also add one more thing, the video clip is no longer an issue. It won't change public opinion. Elena is still in a coma. In spite of Governor's indiscretion, he did love Elena; his state had observed that over the last two terms. A little indiscretion on the side like this has proven to be acceptable in American society. It happens. The important issue is the murder of Rebecca because of the video clip that is the key factor."

"No wonder they call you the brain in the department," Antony exclaimed in adoration.

"You want to see the real brain, go to India, and meet Commander Bhosle, the head of the spy organization ISHWAR of India. I called him and asked about it all. He cautioned not to make haste. It is extremely imperative to find the real culprits behind the conspiracy, not the pawns. As he put it, we want to concentrate on the queen in the game of chess. He also gave me the news about Operation Hind." Kiran explained to them Operation Hind.

In her last call, she found out from Commander Bhosle that Operation Hind was gaining a lot of momentum. He also mentioned vaguely that he would be sending a couple of agents, probably Ramanuj and Malini to Washington, D.C. He did not give the reason and Kiran did not ask, although, she was glad to hear about Malini visiting America. She decided to invite Malini and Ramanuj to her house for a few days. She remembered how much they both helped her during Ruben's rescue.

Kiran looked at the time; it was past midnight, too late to call Virginia to arrange for a safe location. James cut in, "Ruben, sir, if it's okay, you can stay with me tonight. It is probably safer than living in a hotel. No one knows my address and I am not in the directory; my driver's license has the office address that I use for my PI work. You will be safer with me until you can make other arrangements."

Kiran saw the valor of this stout and tough man, the ex-ATF agent, a well-trained person. She also agreed. She asked Anthony about any movement of the package. He was carrying the receiving surveillance instrument (RSI). However, there was no movement; the package was still in the house. He put an alarm on. The slightest movement would trigger the alarm. They all left.

Chapter 58

Delivery

The next day, newspapers in Chicago printed in bold letters:

Mishap Struck Again To Foreign Correspondent

The newspapers described the near-fatal attack on Ruben Joshi. It became national news because of Ruben's reputation and popularity. The news caught the attention of the higher echelon, not because of Ruben's reputation, but because of the deaths of two henchmen and their link to the Mafia family. The Mancini family was under police radar. This was not acceptable to Gustav and he needed to be isolated from the Mancini family.

Logan received a call from Gustav. He gave him instructions to stay put and to request Robert to deliver the package. Logan called Robert and told him to take the package to the presidential suite of the Hotel Savoy in downtown Chicago.

Robert left immediately with the package. It was around 10 a.m. The Receiving Surveillance Instrument (RSI) came to life. Both Ruben and James entered Kiran's room. Kiran told Anthony and Ruben to stay behind because Robert knew Anthony. She and James followed the RSI signal. Anthony had already arranged the miniature camera with a fisheye lens and audio for recording. He attached the camera to Kiran and James's clothing just before leaving their hotel so they both could record the entire operation from different angles. Kiran was also carrying a compact digital video camera.

Robert first went to the downtown store and parked the car. Then he went to a couple of stores and picked a Ralph Lauren Black Label poly-oxford vest, a crushable Jaxon Ford Fedora, and a pair of glasses with a thick-rimmed frame. His appearance changed considerably with the new attire. Unless one looked closely, it would be difficult to recognize him. He didn't see any reporter following him. He was carrying the package in his hand. He just wanted to get rid of it by delivering it to the address. He went to the front gate of the shopping center. The Savoy Hotel was not far from there so he walked. Kiran and James were following him with the help of the RSI; the implant was working. Robert did not know.

The front desk clerk called the suite and told him to take the elevator to the top floor. Robert thanked her and went upstairs. Kiran entered the hotel, showed her badge to the clerk, and requested her full cooperation. The clerk was an attractive brunet and the assistant hotel manager. The Muslim guy who came in a few minutes earlier tried to flirt with her. She hated that. Kiran asked her about Robert who just came in. Realizing her status and work nature, the clerk voluntarily rendered information to help Kiran. She told her that he went to the presidential suite just a minute ago. She also added that the presidential suite occupants just ordered whiskey and soda. Kiran requested her permission to place her partner James Montenegro in housekeeper dress to deliver the whiskey. She accommodated her request immediately.

Robert knocked on the door. Gustav opened the door and invited him in. There was another Muslim guest in the room. Gustav just ordered a bottle of whiskey for him. Muslim motto is - do not drink in the Middle East, get drunk somewhere else. James, in the hotel porter dress, carried a tray with a bottle of whiskey to the presidential suite. Gustav invited Robert to join in. Robert sat down and delivered the package to Mr. Gustav then excused himself because of the heavy campaign workload. James recorded the scene of the delivery of the package from Robert to Gustav. Gustav ordered another glass, cheese, and biscuits. He was expecting another guest.

Kiran saw a familiar figure entering the lobby carrying a small bag that she recognized. She captured that mechanism during the Crystal City pursuit and gave it to Mr. Austin for safekeeping. She was shocked. She filmed the guest entering the hotel lobby. Then, she called James, told him to follow the new guest arriving in the room and film everything. James was at the door of the presidential suite when the new guest arrived. He held the door open with one hand, and then followed inside. The new arrival sat down, opened the pack- age, removed the mechanism, and handed it over to Gustav, "Take this to the BAT Company and start working as soon as possible."

James was pouring the whiskey for the new arrival while his fisheye camera was recording the scene with conversation. He kept the glass on the table and stepped aside for orders. Gustav looked at him and handed him a handsome tip. James left.

Kiran and James were downstairs keeping close surveillance on the hotel entrance.

An hour later, Kiran heard a beep on the RSI. They recorded Gustav exiting the hotel, carrying the SHIV the Destruction device and the triggering mechanism straight to the BAT Company, then Kiran deactivated the RSI device so no one could suspect.

Gustav opened the packages in his office. He did not notice the microchip attached to the package and threw away the packaging material. The mechanism and the device both seemed okay. The flash drive was also inside. He put the flash drive in the computer but it did not indicate any information. He put everything in a safe and then immediately called the secret number.

"I received both items and they seem to be intact. The flash drive may have some protected password to open it though. I'll ask my experts to come prepared to work until they come up with answers to re-engineer the device. They'll start working on it tomorrow. The engineers will analyze the information, review the data and the formula, and outline the steps to do the reverse engineering to produce them. I do not want to give them the flash drive today, just to ensure secrecy, so they don't go home and blabber mouth about it. Once they retrieve the formula and information, I'll make sure my trusted engineering manager can handle and complete the work himself. Then I'll kill my experts to shut their mouths for good."

The person on the other side listened intently, approved it, and then disconnected the phone line.

Chapter 59

Fortuity

A fter recording the events at the Hotel Savoy, Kiran and James
returned to the hotel. Anthony was guarding Ruben. It was
only 2 p.m. Kiran transferred everything recorded including the telephone clip to the computer and made four copies on a
flash drive. She gave one to Anthony, one for her, one for the office,
and gave the extra one to Ruben, just in case he needed it. It was a
precaution.

James left after a few minutes. He wanted to call Sudarshan to find
out about the test and then meet Tania for a dinner date. Kiran
described the whole event to Anthony. He was not only surprised,
but also shocked. He never expected such an elaborate conspiracy.
Now that Kiran knew the mole in the CIA organization, she
realized the danger. That was how they accessed the processed
paperwork and information. She also remembered the death of the
captured terror- ist found hanging in the cell.

Kiran was planning to talk about her plan to Lisa and Veronica
and confront them with the rescue issue, satellite image issue, the
information that she copied on her flash drive among other
concerns. However, after what she saw today, she did not know
whom to trust. It could be anyone now. She wanted to confirm this.
With Anthony's help, she edited the film to hide salient details, and
then she devised a plan.

Kiran knew that Ruben could expose the Governor. Someone
wanted badly for the Governor to win the election. Therefore, that
person wanted Ruben out of the way. Senator Fitzroy was also dead.
Who would be the next puppet master? Now both of the Mancini

family killers were dead. Kiran wanted to find out whom they would send next to kill Ruben.

Kiran called Lisa, told her about the murder attempt of Ruben Joshi. She gave her the limited account of various sequences of events, including the meeting in the Savoy Hotel and Robert Lange delivering a secret package, each time hiding a few details.

"Anthony and I will raid the BAT Company tomorrow."

She added, "The murder of Senator Fitzroy, attempted murder of Elena, and attempted murder of Ruben Joshi are all connected. Ruben needs protective custody because of the whole mess. I also want authorization to keep Ruben in a safe house in a Chicago suburb in collaboration with FBI."

Under the WPD (Witness Protection Department) program, the FBI has safe houses all over United States.

"I am sorry to hear. This is awful. Are you okay?" Lisa asked.

"I am all right. Please make sure I get the authorization."

"I don't see any problem for getting approval, let me talk to Veronica. I'll call you in an hour."

Lisa narrated all the details that she heard from Kiran to her boss, Veronica, and requested her approval for the arrangement of the safe house. Veronica approved.

"Are you going to call Kiran?" She asked Lisa.

"Yes, I told her I would call her with the approval."

"Let me talk to her. I want to discuss this raid with her."

Lisa dialed Kiran's number, "Hello, Kiran, you got the approval for the safe house, go ahead, and contact FBI. The safe house is secure with an alarm and immediate notification to police in case of emergency. It is in the safest neighborhood with all the necessary security of the subdivision."

"That is great," said Kiran.

"Do you need any more protection?"

"I don't think so, it may arouse suspicion," Kiran said.

"Will you or Anthony stay with him? I can arrange for an extra bed."

"As I told you, Anthony and I will raid the BAT Company tomorrow. So we'll rest in the hotel. Thanks for asking. I'll check with James and call you if I need an extra bed in the safe house," Kiran said.

Lisa gave her the approval number for accounting purposes. "Wait, Veronica wants to talk to you," Lisa handed the phone to Veronica.

"Hello Kiran how is the progress?"

"We are proceeding as planned. It is a major breakthrough and we are doing everything to keep it absolutely secret," Kiran informed.

"How did you find out about the meeting?" Veronica questioned.

Kiran was expecting that question and responded, "Last week when I went to Islamabad, my CI told me about this meeting. I asked him about his source, but he would not tell me. I did not believe his information, but since I was here, I decided to check. During the investigation, I met James Montenegro who saved Ruben's life. He was an ex-ATF agent. James knew someone in the Savoy Hotel. He disguised as a hotel staff porter and filmed it. I was outside. I recognized Robert Lange, although, I was surprised to see him entering the lobby. When I checked the recording done by James, it did show Robert handing the package to the BAT Company owner, and I realized the information I received from my CI in Islamabad was correct. Later, we followed the BAT Company CEO, Gustav, to the factory with the packages. I now believe this is the stolen device from the GEETA lab in India that caused the havoc near the Crystal City Shops."

"Did you see anyone else?" Veronica questioned.

"No, I didn't see anyone. I checked with James Montenegro and he didn't see anyone either. After Robert left, we decided to take turn. While I went to a restaurant to eat, James was outside watching for Gustav to come out of the hotel."

"Can you e-mail the video?"

"Sure, Veronica, I was about to do that because I believe the SHIV the Destruction device is inside the BAT Company premises. I want your authorization to raid the premises tomorrow. Under the provision of the amended law after the World Trade Center (WTC) incident, we can always raid the place if we suspect any terror-related activities. We have the recorded information to support our case."

"Is the recorded information authentic?" Veronica inquired.

"James Montenegro is a trained agent and he recorded. He also saved Ruben's life. Yes, I trust him. The recording is authentic," Kiran answered.

Veronica reviewed the footage after receiving it. The footage clearly indicated Robert Lange handing the package to Gustav and Gustav carrying the package to BAT premises. Kiran also sent her a copy of the video clip that Rebecca took. Veronica saw the footage and discussed it with her boss.

Later, Veronica called Kiran, she sounded serious. She understood the gravity of the situation and expressed her concern.

"I am worried about the safety of the employees working there. I suggest if necessary to take help from the local police."

Kiran told her, "I have help from James Montenegro. I want to keep the whole operation covert. Just attacking the facility will not help. It is dangerous for everyone working there in case the device is deliberately exploded. All will die in the vicinity. Therefore, we will have to handle the whole operation carefully. However, I'll keep your suggestion in mind and discuss that with Anthony. Thanks, boss."

Veronica asked her, "Does anyone know about this footage?"

Kiran assured her, "Except Anthony and James, no one knows about the footage. I kept it secret because of the covert operation required to secure the SHIV the Destruction device before anyone gets hurt."

Veronica asked, "Didn't you mention an Indian name Sudar ..., yes, Sudarshan, the test engineer with James Montenegro, does he know anything about it?"

Kiran was shocked to hear that question. How did Veronica know that the test engineer's name is Sudershan? She never mentioned his name to her. Is Veronica a part of this conspiracy?

Kiran decided to play dumb, "I don't know Sudarshan well enough."

Now she also suspected Veronica. James called later to inform Kiran that Sudarshan Pillai would be conducting the test tomorrow.

Chapter 60

Neelum Valley

The word Neelum means "Blue." The name certainly holds true for the bluish-green Neelum River. The area surrounding the Neelum River is Neelum Valley. It lies on both sides of the river Neelum. The long bow-shaped deeply forested picturesque Neelum Valley is situated in the North and Northeast of Muzaffarabad in Azad Kashmir. Excellent scenic beauty, panoramic views, towering hills on both sides of the noisy Neelum River, lush green forests, enchanting streams, and attractive surroundings make the valley a dream come true. It is a valley of fountains, springs, waterfalls, flowering trees, and plants. It is an isolated area and lacks the infrastructure. The 200-km long valley boasts of lush green mountains, beautiful glacial streams, a roaring blue river, and fruit trees. The local wooden huts built traditionally along terraced fields, fresh and crisp mountain air and complete lack of urban lifestyle enhance the beauty of Neelum Valley. The valley is known to few people, and due to its isolation, it is free of mass tourism and pollution and hence sometimes called "Virgin" beauty. No one would have guessed that death lay behind this virgin beauty.

India was already haggard by Chinese incursion. On top of that, the chatter of Operation Hind was most annoying. The information received suggested that Pakistan started massing strike formations along the LOC. The Times of Bharat published the report about Pakistani troops killing three Indian soldiers and mutilating their bodies in the disputed territory of Kashmir, a flash point between the two nations since their creation.

The news reported that Pakistani troops took advantage of thick fog in a Neelum Valley area to cross over to LOC. It is the de-facto border between the two nations in Kashmir near the villages of Nakara and Shahcot. The Indian military on its routine patrol spotted the Pakistani troops in the Nakara sector of Neelum Valley. During the firefight, Pakistani soldiers killed three Indian soldiers.

India and Pakistan exchanged bitter accusations over it. Pakistan, as usual, reiterated its denial of the accusations. They added that India was trying to distract attention from a weekend clash in the Himalayan territory that left a Pakistani soldier dead. The Indian government accused Pakistani troops of subjecting the three soldiers' bodies to "barbaric and inhuman mutilation," calling the alleged actions "highly provocative." The cross allegations were increasing the strain on ties between the two nuclear-armed neighbors. The question of the hour was, could the countries again be close to a full-blown war?

"Hello Atul, what can I do for you?" Commander Sitaram Bhosle answered the phone. His assistant, Sarika Wadhwani, left today a little bit early to go to a birthday party for her close friend's 1-year-old daughter.

"Come immediately to the Prime Minister's (PM) office. Commanders from all three branches will be coming soon. The acting Defence Minister Naidu from the Ministry of External Affairs will be there, too. You know he is also the Defence Minister for the time being until our Defence Minister recovers from his car accident."

The Commander already knew the reason for this call. In fact, based on his intelligence received, he already cautioned ADI (Army Division of Intelligence) agents that Operation Hind could take into effect immediately. He requested them to inform all chiefs of this intelligence immediately. He also added that due to the Chinese incursion, some battalions should be ready for action on that front as well. He informed the PM of this. Only three days prior, The Times of Bharat predicted the likelihood of the full-blown war. Therefore, the PM decided to have a joint meeting.

At the PM's office, the door of the conference room closed. Atul Chowdhary was outside the door guarding it so no one can enter.

The PM requested Commander Bhosle to share the entire intelligence report with all present.

The Commander began, "This is an Al Taquia philosophy. This is the Islamic doctrine, which mandates Muslims to use subterfuge - deceptive practices, chicanery, and trickery to lie and cheat infidels (Hindus, Christians, Jews, etc.). In reality, they are wolves in sheep's clothing.

We are facing a major calamity on all fronts. Our country has no idea of the calamity that can swallow them. History is repeating itself. In the past, foreigners had attacked and conquered us whenever we were busy enjoying and entertaining ourselves. I do not intend to give you lessons in Indian history, but look at the news," he stopped looked around for the reaction, discerned anger on Minister Naidu's face, all others were listening intently.

"The Pakistan army has gathered massively on the Western front. Chinese are also concentrating on the Eastern front. They both are denying it, but intelligence tells us a different story. Our soft negotiations are not working while they are gathering strength." The Commander continued like this for 10 minutes, describing the war situation and Operation Hind, and inferred the involvement of Indian masses and media toward Bollywood-related activities so the masses would ignore the real danger. He ended his narration repeat- ing the prediction by The Times of Bharat about the eventuality of war. Commander Bhosle's main purpose behind this narration was to get the word "Al Taquia" impregnated in Minister Naidu's brain. After the Commander had finished his narration, the PM asked for opinions.

"That is bullshit," interjected Minister Naidu, expressing his concern. "There is nothing new in this intelligence. It is the same old story."

All chiefs, including the Commander, disagreed.

Commander Bhosle suggested that, "We could get our military ready for action near all frontier posts. We should have the army ready on the Western front to face the Pakistani Army. We should also keep the army ready on the Northeastern boundary to discour-age the Chinese army from any further advance in case war between India and Pakistan erupt. We'll call this mission Operation Kali."

Naidu was angry, "The military operation will cost thousands of crores of rupees and will unnecessarily increase the burden on taxpayers."

The PM appeased him by saying, "Let us keep our military in ready condition as suggested by Commander Bhosle. In case war erupts, Naidu will give the command to execute Operation Kali." Naidu seemed to calm down.

Minister Naidu wanted to get out of the meeting fast. He knew if he could get a lot of money for this information if he could contact *Mia* Zafar Ansari, the Deputy Chief of IBP, and convey him that he is the puppet master of the Operation Kali. He excused himself and left the office as soon as the meeting was over.

Minister Naidu went back to his office, closed the door, and told his secretary to hold all calls. Then on a secure line, he called *Mia* Zafar Ansari of IBP. This time he demanded $50 million from *Mia* Zafar. At first, *Mia* Zafar did not understand what could be so valuable. Mr. Naidu told him about Operation Kali.

He narrated the discussions that took place in the PM's office. The Minister added that he is the puppet master to give orders to the Indian military to attack. Naidu knew that the device, SHIV the Destruction, had already reached US soil and at any moment, the Pakistani army would get the shipment. *Mia* Zafar got the message. He realized that to countermand Operation Hind, the Indian army is putting Operation Kali in place. He agreed to pay that amount.

"You don't have to worry about the Indian Army. As soon as you get your weapons, you attack. They are all near the boundary and would be an easy target for your soldiers. Thanks to Commander Bhosle, he made our job easier. I'll hold them, until you get your soldiers way inside Indian borders, and then I'll give them the command to attack. However, by that time, your forces will have already neu- tralized them. Don't forget to put $50 million in my account before you attack."

Ansari assured him and then Naidu disconnected the line. The EIW Wing recorded his conversation. Minister Naidu did not know that they had taped his secure phone line.

The Commander requested that all three chiefs accompany him to ISHWAR to discuss details of Operation Kali. The PM did not discuss the details and Minister Naidu left in a hurry. Time was of the essence in such an operation. They have already begun preparation based on intelligence received from the Commander a few days earlier. However, now it was official; the PM had given the go ahead.

The Commander explained the gravity of the situation to them. His SSIW and ASIIW Wings and the RIAW officers provided the intelligence and data. He formed his inference from the information received from the intelligence and chatter. The double agents were already in place behind enemy lines. The TIW Wing with the help of ASIIW prepared the map of Operation Kali for counterattack.

During the middle of the discussion, he received the message about the conversation that took place between Minister Naidu and IBP Chief Ansari but he didn't discuss with them the treachery of Minister Naidu. It would have been a big official scandal. The fiasco would have distracted the military and the country from focusing on the main issue. However, once the Ministry issued the orders, he wanted the military to aggressively attack. It would be the destructive attack on Pakistan's forces while keeping Chinese forces occupied and away from Indian borders.

"Remember, we are not at war with China, we only want to deter them from advancing. We want to make sure that they don't take advantage of the situation and march ahead to help Pakistan. We just want to keep them occupied until we clear the mess on the Western front. I do not trust Minister Naidu. However, once the war broke, he doesn't have too much of a choice." They all shook hands and left.

Chapter 61

Exposed

Suddenly, at 2 a.m., the fluorescent-orange reflection glowed around the Glenview neighborhood in a suburb of Chicago. The house at 183 Ebony Road erupted in violent flames, enveloping floors and walls. The peppery flames attacked viciously and devoured the house. The fire protruded from the windows that had already cracked from the heat and pressure. The flames intensified, which created smoke. The house had reached its breaking point as the roof and its crest buckled, creating a massive burning fire. The fire screamed with the crackling of the paint chipping.

The pandemonium of flames woke up the neighborhood. The smoke filled their vision with a bright glimmer of orange. Someone called the fire department and a fire truck arrived within five minutes. A gush of water soaked voracious flames, squeezing out the fire. Finally, the outline of what was the house before the flash of fire had vanished, and what was left was a disturbing sight of charred wood, falling debris of ash, burned draperies, and furniture with an apparition of red sparks still dancing in smoldering remains. It was a horrible site. Kiran and Anthony recorded the whole scene from the beginning. Both could not believe their eyes.

Earlier before calling her boss, Kiran devised a plan to confirm her suspicion and expose the conspirators involved. She knew that whoever was involved undoubtedly wanted Ruben dead and would certainly try again. She explained her plan to Anthony.

"We need a dead body to prop as Ruben for this.

When Anthony heard the plan, he burst into laughter, "Wow, Kiran, you are downright devious. That's a brilliant idea. James is a local guy, he probably can help us."

James helped them to find the body. He called an old friend working in the city morgue and found the body of similar height and weight. No one claimed the corpse. It was on the list for cremation by the city. They arranged to get that body transferred to the safe house, and propped him as Ruben. The police found the remains of that corpse.

The next day, newspapers in Chicago printed the news in bold letters:

Fire Erupts in Glenview Neighborhood

The house at 183 Ebony Road in the Glenview neighborhood in the suburb of Chicago burned to the ground. Police found a burned body inside. They took the body to the morgue for autopsy and identification. The fire department is investigating the cause of the fire. The house was for sale by the G. Brown Realty Company. Police are trying to find the identity of the corpse found in the fire.

Sudarshan Pillai went to the office early. The day before, in the late afternoon, his boss called and gave him the message to come in early. Gustav was waiting for him with his engineering manager. He gave him the incomplete formula with the description. The terrorist who stole the device from the GEETA lab in India captured the part of the formula with a description on the computer screen by camera and used the flash drive to download the data and the files from the computer, which started burning during the download process due to the explosion.

Sudarshan began analyzing the formula and mixed the ingredients as mentioned. It did not work. He tried a few more combinations but they all failed. His engineering manager was standing next to him. He suggested a few hints. Unfortunately, nothing worked.

The engineering manager went back to Gustav and told him, "Our effort to reconstruct the formula is not working. The crucial portion of the formula and the description are missing."

Gustav handed the engineering manager the flash drive, which he took to a software specialist and asked Sudarshan to join him. The software specialist told him there was no information on the flash drive. Zip.

Finally, Gustav opened the safe and took the device and the mechanism out. He handed both items to the manager and told him to replicate them.

"See if your specialists can reverse engineer these two items. Don't worry about funding. Use whatever manpower you need, just do it."

Sudarshan and the technician began working on the mechanism first. The design engineer took the measurements and began preparing the engineering sketch.

Sudarshan began wondering where he read about the egg-shaped device. He thought it looked similar to what he heard about on the news. He expressed his concern and suspicion to the design engineer and the mechanic standing next to him. Gustav was passing by to check on the progress. He heard the conversation, intercepted, and explained to them that this was from their German counterpart. Sudarshan was aware of the company practice and did not approve but there was no proof to act. He needed the job until he found other suitable employment. Gustav told the three of them and the manager to work on the mechanism, took the device away, and headed back to his cabin.

Outside the factory, Kiran was standing with a team from the Anti-Terrorist Squad (ATS) ready to attack if necessary. She did not tell that to Veronica. She also requested the head of the ATS to keep it secret for the next four hours. With the taped information and help from the ATS, Kiran procured the necessary search warrant.

When they arrived at the BAT Company, Kiran noticed a few sharpshooters on the building roof. She immediately cautioned her team. The entire time, Anthony was recording everything on his video camera. The sharpshooters were clearly visible. They were not so careful. Their boss told them only a few would be entering. As soon as Gustav left with the device, Sudarshan called James.

Last night, James told Sudarshan that something fishy was going on in his company and that if he found anything suspicious, he should call James immediately. Sudarshan was not aware of anything that was happening outside. He told James about the formula with part of it missing and the broken mechanism that the design engineer was trying to re-create.

He also added, "There is a safe in Gustav's cabin where he keeps all his work."

The moment they heard about the safe, they were ready to enter the premises.

One of the employees was late because of her dentist appointment. Just when James got the call, she was trying to enter the building. The sharpshooters noticed the woman entering. Their boss told them that a woman would be leading the assault team. One of the sharpshooters aimed and fired the bullet. The woman dropped to the ground, blood oozing from her chest. She was a 25-year-old young woman. Everyone outside heard the shot and so did Sudarshan and the other employees inside the building.

Kiran's team was about to attack the building. James called Sudarshan and told him to get out of the building as fast as possible and warn other employees to do the same. He added that the building would be under attack soon by the ATS. Sudarshan ran out while warning others. There was a pandemonium of commotion. All the office staff got out. The sharpshooters didn't know what to do; they were confused with chaos and the people running out from the building. Some were shouting words like 'bomb' and others were cursing terrorists while the ATS soldiers were entering the premises. Their number was high. All of them were wearing masks with a suit in the event of chemical weapons, just in case they released the device. The sharpshooters didn't expect this, something had gone terribly wrong. They came down.

Gustav ran out of the cabin and saw the employee running out. The mechanism was on the table. He collected the mechanism and went back to the cabin. He also heard the shot. He first thought that the shooters had done the job. However, when he saw the shooters coming down and entering his cabin, he asked them what happened.

The shooters told him that ATS soldiers had surrounded the building and were entering. He looked outside the cabin and saw a few approaching his office. To save himself, he armed the capsule and fired. The firing mechanism was broken and the capsule broke open. Everyone including their bodyguards and sharpshooters, died on the spot. By 10 a.m., the operation was complete.

Veronica received the news of the corpse in the house. She did not hear from Kiran, it did not surprise her. Kiran probably would be busy raiding the BAT Company. In the morning, Veronica received the call. Gustav assured her that all the necessary plans are in place.

It was past 11 a.m., Veronica Ivanov and Nigel Bartlett gathered the staff members in the conference room in the Virginia facility to talk about the death of two traitors in their group. She and Nigel were not aware of the attack on Gustav's factory. Veronica gave the news of treachery of their agents, Miss Kiran Hopkins and Anthony Hurtz, attributing the unexpected stolen device smuggled into the country by them.

"The two agents, Miss Kiran Hopkins and Mr. Anthony Hurtz, are traitors. They were helping terrorists in the Middle East to smuggle the stolen device that is responsible for the attack in front of the Crystal City shopping mall. Both are either successfully captured or dead by now."

She did not express grief or sorrow. There was sheer contempt in her voice. Behind her, the giant screen flickered. The picture on the screen was on with muted sound. While Veronica and Bartlett were talking about the death and explaining treachery facing the audience, the picture on the screen was showing a different story. The giant screen was showing the taped scenes of Bartlett handing the device, Veronica arranging the fire to burn the safe house, military jets at the airport ready to take off, and Veronica boarding a jet in the middle of the night. It was dark, but a beam light from the airport hanger provided enough illumination to record. The display ended with a 10-second flash of the video clip of the Governor's amorous encounter.

The door opened. George entered with Lisa and the chief of the CIA along with a federal judge, a federal prosecutor, and the couple of law enforcement officers. Mr. Bartlett and Veronica saw them and were confused. The audience was watching the screen. Mr. Bartlett and Veronica turned their necks and saw the TV. The vigor disappeared from their face.

Lisa announced, "Ms. Veronica Ivanhoe and Major Bartlett, this is the warrant for your arrest. You will be tried under Military Court under Federal Jurisdiction." The law enforcement officers handcuffed them.

Chapter 62

Operation Kali

I t was past midnight when all of a sudden there was a big explosion on Pakistan's side of LOC near Neelum Valley. No one knew exactly what happened. The Indian Border Patrol heard the noise and saw an ocean of soldiers hiding on the other side of LOC on a sloped tableland on the plateau of the valley near Dudunyal, Shahkot, and Nauseri. They immediately sent the signal to Delhi.

Minister Naidu returned home from a late night party around 1 a.m. He checked his Swiss bank account for the deposit on his computer. It was still not there. He was upset and decided to call *Mia* Zafar in the morning. He poured a glass of Chivas Regal, added ice cubes, and went to his bedroom.

A 14-year-old virgin wench was waiting for him in the bedroom arranged by his faithful servant Kalu alias Kalia Mutku. The girl was standing in the corner. Naidu was enjoying his whiskey while relishing the thought of savoring the virgin flower. The whiskey was having its effect; he was getting lewd. He put his hand around her; she begged him not to touch her. She was shivering and didn't know what to expect. She could not even scream or open her mouth out of fear. Her rejection made him lustier. One by one, he started removing her clothes when the phone rang. It was just 30 minutes past 1 a.m. It was the red phone; the secured line between his office, home, and the PM. He cursed the phone and picked it up. He was already mad for disturbing his lewd act.

"Hello, why are you bothering me now?" He was rude.

The PA told him about the explosion and firing across the border. He cursed Zafar Ansari, "That son of a bitch wants to cheat me out of my money,"

With the thoughts of deceit and sex under the influence of whiskey, he was feeling sleepy and didn't think straight. All he could think of the word "Al Taquia." He was angry and blurted the word "attack," probably not meaning it but his PA noted it down, typed the words, and sent it to ISHWAR headquarters.

The official notification was in the Commander's hand. He immediately issued orders of full-fledged attack. No more telephone silence, the orders to entire frontier battalions were to attack viciously. The Chinese forces on the border also heard the word because there was no telephone silence. They advanced and abruptly halted with surprise to see more than 100,000 Indian soldiers spread across the northeastern borders from Arunachal Pradesh all the way to Chip Chap River and the Ladakh Region.

The Indian Air Force was already behind them. The Commander also asked the Russian Prime Minister for help. The MIGs equipped with long-range ballistic missiles were already in the air to support Indian Air Force if needed. More than 250,000 Indian soldiers were ready all the way across the LOC. It was the plan of Operation Kali. SHIV opened its third eye to destroy the wicked. The Indian Air Force attacked the regions of Karakorum and Hindu Kush with long-range missiles. The death valley of Hindu laborers became the death valley of Pakistani soldiers.

Commander Bhosle knew about Operation Hind from the chatter, the analysis of signals, the information received from his double agents, and the discussion that took place between Minister Naidu and IBP Chief Zafar Ansari. He realized that $50 million is a large sum of money and it would take some time for the IBP Chief to arrange. He also knew that IBP Chief would wait until they are ready to attack before depositing the money into Minister Naidu's Swiss bank account.

He ordered his double agents to join behind enemy lines that night and to arrange for a few explosions to create confusion after hearing the conversation between Minister Naidu and IBP Chief Ansari. It was not that difficult. Because of the slope and cold weather, the security was slack around the ordnance. Farooq and a few other double agents put in fuses to blow up the ordnance. The explosions created chaos.

The well-planned attack from the Indian sides caught them off guard. The fear spread fast. By morning, the Indian army reached up to Islamabad and Lahore. They destroyed the terrorist camps and ran them down to the dust. This time, there was no mercy. It was not fun for them to kill. They didn't like it. They put stones on their hearts.

In the past, the Indian administration, under political pressure, restrained them from attacking while Muslim soldiers tortured and mutilated the bodies of their brothers. It was too much to take. For the first time in the history of an independent India, the Army and the Air Force accepted the word collateral damage. Russian MIGs and Indian Air Force met the Chinese Air Force. They turned back without incident.

The US embassy in Islamabad sent the report of the attack to US. The CIA facility was already going through the turmoil with the scandal of Ms. Veronica Ivanhoe and Major Bartlett. On top of that, news started pouring from the Eastern Hemisphere about the war between India and Pakistan. First reaction was that it would stop like previous wars. They opened the normal channels of negotiations between the heads of state. American jets were ready and they were waiting for orders from the commander in chief.

The acting Defence Minister of India gave the order at 1:31 a.m. The PM had agreed to this earlier in a meeting with him. Because of the emergency, no one could consult with the cabinet. The orders went straight to ISHWAR headquarters and from there to the battleground. The Commander gave the news to the PA of the Prime Minister in the morning. By that time, most of the operation was over.

The intelligence officers, Ramanuj and Malini from India, were already in Washington, D.C. The Indian Consulate office contacted the

US President's office at 6 p.m. US time and showed the intelligence report of the Pakistani activities with photos of their nuclear facilities. No one wanted war. The call from the American Embassy came around 10 a.m., Indian time. The American President requested that the Indian Prime Minister ask the Indian army to retreat. The Prime Minister had no problem. In fact, he was equally surprised.

Commander Bhosle was standing next to the Prime Minister with a note in his hand. The Prime Minister read the note. He looked with a surprise at Commander Bhosle, but in his wisdom, the PM decided to relay the message to the US President. The area between the Afghan border and the imaginary Durand Line was the most difficult mountainous terrain and an epicenter for terrorists. In the interest of avoiding further confrontation and terrorist activities, the Indian PM requested Joint Committee of United Nations and the US to seek approval to abolish the imaginary Durand Line Agreement of 1893 that divided the brotherhood of Pakhtoons.

The Indian Army left main Pakistani cities like Islamabad, Lahore at the request of the PM. They kept their army and secured their posts in the occupied territory of Kashmir and Azad Kashmir. Pakistan did not have much of an army left to fight back. They also occupied the 12,000 square miles of area lost to China in previous wars under pink administration.

Next day, the entire world woke up to the dreadful news. The Indian philanthropic NGOs came forward to help Pakistan. The common Muslim population from Pakistan had no problem accepting their help; half of them were converted Muslims by force anyway. They knew the wrong doings of their Mullahs and terrorists. Some of them were happy.

Mohabbat-E-Masti was almost empty. All the women ran away along with Madam Malika Husaini Shafi to save their lives. Farooq told Surayya the night before, where to hide in case war broke out. Farooq already got the passport for Surayya as Surayya Kaif. He waited for a couple of days.

When flight service resumed, he took Surayya with him and disappeared to Istanbul. From Istanbul, he used the Indian passport under the name of Narayan Swami and Kunjali Swami and they took the plane to Bangalore with the Indian passports. He had no wish to go back. He was sure that his cover was blown. Ramanuj did tell him before taking the assignment that whatever money he got was his to keep. He had enough money with the funds received from the ex-Don, Red Scorpion. He bought a small farm in the village near Bangalore to start a new life with new names, Narayan and Kunjali Swami.

Dalai Lama was in Dharma Shala, India. He heard the news and traveled to Tibet. His followers responded to the call of Buddhism. The Tibet revolution began, brought by youngsters with the help of Nepali Gurkha regiment. The call of Buddhism went all the way to Beijing. The people of China were not happy with the atrocities, persecution, and harassment by the Chinese communist party. The dissatisfaction was mounting up. The revival of Buddhism began in China and Tibet. With Indian victory, they saw the new light and fresh vision. It is the birth of a new era and beginning of the new dawn on the horizon.

New Horizon (Epilogue)

With the help of Federal Agent Kiran Hopkins arrested Robert Lange, Noah, and Logan Mancini. The Federal Court would prosecute them for their crimes.

A couple of days later, Elena came out of her coma. She was depressed when she heard the news of her father's death. The first thing she asked for was a meeting with a divorce lawyer and filed for di- vorce. Governor Giarrusso's empire crumbled. He withdrew from the race. Adam Baker replaced him and became the presidential can- didate for the Republican Party.

James Montenegro was exonerated and he got his job back. He was very happy man and proposed to Tania.

Commander Bhosle sent two of his officers and the CP (Commissioner of Police) of New Delhi to arrest Minister Naidu and his servant, Kalia Mutku. The Prime Minister of India got the report of Naidu's treachery along with the report from the double agent Dabu Kadgul, alias Farooq Khalid, from Pakistan. For secrecy, the reports did not include any names.

During surveillance, the Commander collected enough information to arrest Dr. Bhujang Iftekhar and Professor Haji Ulfatkhan. He arrested both of them. During interrogation, Bhujang spilled most of the secrets and his role in the murder of Nikhil Chaudhary and stealing the capsules.

They reprimanded the PA of the Oil Minister and the Oil Minister resigned from his post.

A week later, Commander Bhosle received an encrypted message from Jahangir from the South of France. He told the Commander that his cover was intact and he would continue as a double agent. He didn't know whether Farooq survived or died. He also told the Commander that someone from the Pakistan army spotted Farooq during the blowing up of the ordnance. Jahangir presumed Farooq died during the war with other double agents.

The Indian election changed the face of the government. With the help from Commander Bhosle, the new government administration established a separate department to scrutinize the activities of the various Muslim organizations in India to wipe out the threat of terrorism. The new administration also set up another department to check the Swiss Bank account of the treacherous Indian Ministers and entrepreneurs to bring the black money back.

The wave of a new thought process emerged. The pressure was mounting to change the constitution of India to make the secular country Bharat, to a democratic Hindu nation Bharat, Hindustan. However, political turmoil was not over yet. It would take some time to overcome the greed and corruption. The democratic Hindu nation Bharat's future is in the hands of the younger generation.

Characters from India

Raw Agency	Administration
Akabar khan alias Ajit Deshpande	Atul Chowdhary
Cmdr. Sitaram Bhosle – NSDI	Balu Naidu Minister External
Dabu Kadgul alias Farooq Khalid	Affairs
Kewal Ahluwalia alias Rasool	Khoja Bahubal
Ahamad	Khoja Suvarna
Malini Soumya alias Farah Akram	Kuldip Singh PM
CBI/RAW	
Manish Gupta of SSIW	**Terrorists**
Manubhai Singhania alias Jahangir	
Pranav Chaturvedi from TIW wing	Bahadur Khan,
Ramanuj Parmeswaran alias	Fahayat Khan
Rajaram	Jayraman Chauhan alias Rangeela
Ramesh Bhakhtiar CBI	Pundu
Sarika Wadhwani secretary of	Latif Ahamadi
Commander Bhosle	Professor Haji Ulfatkhan
Suhasini Gupta of EIW wing	Salamat Khan
Surendra Varma alias Liyaqat	
Habib	**Others**
	Akhtar Fatima and Salman
GEETA	Bhudev Lohana transporter of flesh
	Fayida Lodi and Hamid her son
Dr. Bhujang Iftekhar	Joshi Santosh and Kusum aunty
Dr. Frank Muller – American	Kalia Mutku
Scientist	Mohini - friend of Elena Patil
Dr. Iyer Chief scientists from	Nirmala and Satish with chil-
GEETA	dren Prasad and Rohini
Dr. Nikhil Chowdhary	Surayya Kaif alias Sunayana
Dr. Patnaik	Moodguli
	Urmila, Pralhad's sister

Characters from Pakistan and Middle East

Ansari Zafar, Deputy Chief of Intelligence Bureau of Pakistan (IBP)	Karim Abdul terrorist cell
	Madam Malika Husaini Shafi - courtesan, "Mohabbat-E-Masti"
Ansari Habib his brother and head of Defense Supply Corps	Jahanara Hakim
Asif Basher the cameraman	Mia Ebrahim Quasim
Barkat Niazi	Mia Mamood Massood
Begum Jamia Kazi	Murad Hamid
Hadith Abu	Shabnam Mallika
Imran Quadree Peon in Indian Consulate	Suleiman Quasim
	Usman
	Zillat Pathania Bhai from Karachi

Characters from US

Political Team

Denise Wilson Campaign Manager
Elena Fitzroy Giarrusso: Governor
   Henry Giarrusso
James Spears, campaign team
Jessica Patel
John Haskin, campaign team
Josh Desai
Louise Colvin
Malcolm O'Connor
Dave Patterson - Democrat
President Andrew Zoloft
Ricky Benton, campaign team
Robert Dennison, campaign team
Robert Lange
Sandy Hoover
Senator Adam Baker
Senator Frank Fitzroy: Teddy
   Millican

Mafia

Mendoza Bartoli known as Super
   Fixer
Carlos Garcia known as Point
   Blank
Mancini Logan
Mancini Noah
Fredrik Gustov

CIA

Anthony Hurtz alias Emran Khalid
George Austin
Kiran Hopkins alias Ayesha
   Basheer
Lisa Hargrove
Nigel Bartlett
Veronica Ivanovo

Clans of the Wolf

Alano Aragon
Alexander Ferrari
Joshua Hamilton
Josiah Baron of California
Major John Bartlett 1899
Major John Hamilton 1899
Petrovsky Nikolaevna
Richard Dalhousie
Rothman Chevalier
Sultan Akhmad from Saudi

Others

Adolph Newton TV Producer
Elizabeth Penelope
Anastasia Petrov
Edward Jenkins Sr., the Manager
Hopkins Priyanka
Hopkins, Prof. Lawrence
James Montenegro - ATF
Joshi Olivia
Joshi Pralhad Ph.D. Professor
Joshi, Ruben (Ravindra)
Mancini Cynthia
Mancini Sophia
Matthew and Ava Esposito
Mr. Craig Thomson Managing
   editor
Mr. John Edward - Reporter.
Padington, the State Department
Pillai Sudarshan, BAT Company

Author's Bio

Vijay S. Shertukde is a native of Mumbai, India. At an early age, he read many mystery novels, which fostered his love for mystery. Ian Fleming (James Bond Series), Agatha Christie, Arnalkar brothers from India, and other spy novel writers were a huge inspiration and their books opened a world of intrigue and mystery. The childhood stories of mythological lore added religion to his interest.

After graduating with a degree in Engineering, Vijay moved to the United Kingdom and then to the United States. He completed graduate studies in Electrical Engineering from the Brooklyn Polytechnic Institute of New York.

Although engineering was his career, writing remained his passion that led to the publication of two nonfiction books titled *I Am Hindu* and *Seed* relating to Hindu philosophy. He continues writing on cultural, traditional, and political issues stemming from Hindu philosophy, History, and Human Exploitation.

Vijay S. Shertukde lives in Zachary, Louisiana, with his beloved wife.

Website: www.vbooksite.com

Facebook: www.facebook.com/vshertukde

Twitter: www.twitter.com/vshertukde

GoodReads: www.goodreads.com/vshertukde

Amazon Author Page: www.amazon.com/-/e/B00LXE81CG

www.ingramcontent.com/pod-product-compliance
Lightning Source LLC
Chambersburg PA
CBHW030929020726
47498CB00001B/178